APOCALYPSE NOW NOW

Also available from Charlie Human and Titan Books

KILL BAXTER

APOCALYPSE NOW NOW

CHARLIE HUMAN

TITAN BOOKS

Apocalypse Now Now
Print edition ISBN: 9781783294732
E-book edition ISBN: 9781783294756

Published by Titan Books
A division of Titan Publishing Group Ltd
144 Southwark Street, London SE1 0UP

First edition: April 2015
2 4 6 8 10 9 7 5 3

A CIP catalogue record for this title is available from the British Library.

Printed and bound in the United States.

To Nikita. I promised I'd write you a book.

Now now *(adv.) A common South Africanism relating to the amount of time to elapse before an event occurs. In the near future; not happening presently but to happen shortly.*

'There are questions that run through your head when you find out that you're a serial killer. "Am I more evil than Ted Bundy?" is one. "I wonder whether I'll be on the Crime & Investigation Network?" is another. But on the whole, it's the who, what, when and why of it that really takes up the mental bandwidth. So, here goes:

'My name is Baxter Zevcenko. I am sixteen years old. I go to Westridge High School in Cape Town and I have no friends. I've killed people. Lots of people. Brutally. At least I hear they were people. They looked more like monsters to me. Anyway, I won't bore you with the details. If you're interested, look on the Internet.

'People are saying that I'm satanic, but this is not true. I have seen things. I saw the great Mantis God of Africa fighting a creature from the primordial depths, a billion-year war until finally the Mantis threw the writhing creature from the heavenly sky into the deepest pit. I've seen the past through the lens of the Eye and it wasn't in tasteful sepia. It was etched in blood and death and filtered through a veil of tears. I've seen the sweating, grunting, cawing, scratching, bleeding, yelping feathered, scaled and clawed abyss beneath the city and, believe me when I tell you this, it's not pretty –'

'Baxter,' my psychiatrist interrupts, 'I thought we'd agreed that these delusions were counterproductive?'

I take a breath and force the images from my mind. 'None of that matters. There is no Mantis and there is no dark, primordial creature. There is no weapons chemist, no bounty hunter and no girlfriend to rescue. There is just me and I am sick. In the end, we're all just victims of our own perceptions, sparky. I hope you can see that.'

'Good,' my psychiatrist says as he turns off the camera. 'I believe you're making progress.'

RAINCOATS AND SKULLDUGGERY

'Charlie, Delta, Niner, that's a big ten-four,' Rafe growls into his CB radio. I have ten minutes before I need to make the walk to school. My parents force me to walk to school even when it rains. It's raining. The CB hisses, crackles and squelches like the soundtrack to a horror movie about a demonically possessed computer that considers humanity a lower form of intelligence that must be eliminated.

I'm lying in our living room on the shaggy burnt-orange rug that's so old it's been retro twice. Rafe, my older brother by two years, has his portable CB radio positioned strategically on the small circular glass table next to the TV. Strategic, because he's the Sun Tzu of irritation and the CB radio rattles on the glass creating a perfect frequency of brain death. I push my long fringe away from my glasses and glare at the back of his skull.

'Turn it down,' I say. He turns his shaggy red-haired, knob-shaped head and stares at me with the knowing-eye. I feel the rage build like a dark wave inside of me.

The knowing-eye is a weapon passed down from generation to generation in my family. My grandfather on my father's side has it. I suspect it's what drove my grandmother to alcoholism and sex addiction before reforming, divorcing Grandad and joining a racist commune in the Northern Cape. That and the fact that my grandfather thinks that there are giant shape-shifting crows out to get him.

The eye skipped a generation and now Rafe, the oldest son, has it. In a single glance it can see right through you like an x-ray, revealing your most vulnerable spots, your most sensitive secrets.

Rafe ignores me and flips open one of his stupid South African history books. Apparently most people chilling out on the lower end of the autistic spectrum obsess about things. For Rafe it's South African history. He has a whole library of books, which he peers at constantly, as if trying to find patterns in the sprawling, blood-soaked tapestry of our colonial heritage. He's really weird. It's not enough that his warped mind encroaches on my waking life, but now his weird obsession with ox-wagons and Boers is infiltrating my dreams too.

He turns to me, opens the book to a double-page spread on some long-forgotten Boer battle against the English and jabs his finger insistently at it, like he's trying to teach a monkey to read. It's like dangling a baby in front of a pit bull. I can't help it. The dark wave crashes over me. Snarling with rage, I push myself up from the floor and jump onto Rafe's back, grabbing his neck in a sleeper hold and dragging him to the floor.

From experience I know I only have seconds to inflict as much damage as possible before my mother comes to break us up. I snarl and hiss with rage as I jackhammer my fists into his kidneys and he struggles violently. It's not enough, but at least it's something. My mother's footsteps pound down the stairs. We break apart and I pat Rafe good-naturedly on the back.

'We've just been play fighting, Mum,' I say as she walks through into the living room.

'Baxter, what the hell is wrong with you?' she asks, peeling back the layers of my face with her straight-razor gaze. Clearly she isn't fooled by the old play-fighting ruse.

'The eye –' I start.

'You're sixteen, for God's sake,' she says. 'Do you think picking on Rafe is something a good brother does?'

It's rhetorical, but I can't help but point out her false assumption that I actually want to be a good brother. That goes down like playing Iron Maiden's 'Number of the Beast' at Sunday school.

The crux of the problem is that Rafe has learning difficulties and goes to a special school and, as such, is excused from mundane chores such as reason and responsibility for his actions.

'I wasn't picking –' I begin.

'He can't help it,' she whispers tersely.

This is a losing hand and I know when to fold. My mother and I are just going to have to agree to disagree about Rafe's cognitive capabilities. While she thinks he's some kind of supertard who is totally oblivious to the irritation he directs at me like a laser beam, I disagree. He can help it all right. It's just that his sole purpose on Earth is to drive me clinically insane.

'Apologise,' my mother says, arching a thin eyebrow.

'Sorry,' we both mumble and limply shake hands. I turn, grab my bag and walk out the front door into the rain, ignoring my mother's offer of an umbrella.

I trudge through the downpour. It's unfair. Rafe is the bane of my existence. He barely speaks, and when he does it's all Boer generals, English concentration camps and San mythology. (As far as I can tell, their mythology seems to hold with the golden rule of religious practice in that it's entirely insane. The shape-shifting Mantis God fell in love with an antelope and then created the moon and a whole bunch of weird monsters, because, hey, I'm a shape-shifting god, why not? Seems totally legit.) I wish my parents would just medicate him. But life is unfair; it's like a kids birthday party where the mom rigs the pass-the-parcel so that a kid she likes gets the prize.

I remember how it works. The little blonde kids with cherub faces and dial-up Internet minds (zzrrgggkkkk eeeeee zrgggkkkk) win pass-the-parcel. When I was a kid I went to hundreds of parties and I never won pass-the-parcel. That's statistically improbable and can only point to the fact that none of the moms liked me.

It's because I was one of those kids that made other kids cry, a natural talent that I couldn't help exercising. If there are two things that moms like it's Josh Groban and kids not crying, and since Josh only puts out a new album every couple of years, they tend to focus on the kids-not-crying bit.

The sky is almost the exact grey of the diseased lung of a two-packs-a-day smoker. It makes me want a cigarette. I turn off the busy main road and make my way into the subway next to the train station, the skanky sacred secret grotto where my girlfriend Esmé and I meet to exchange smoke and saliva before school starts.

The subway curves beneath the train line like a dirty catacomb, the chaotic graffiti like the multihued bones of dragons buried in the walls. I cup my hands to light a cigarette and then lean back against the wall and watch the smoke twist and curl like two giant creatures fighting. My eyes wander across the opposite wall and take in the scrawls and tags left by the school-going population that passes through this tunnel daily.

I recognise the Inhalant Kid's tag, a stylised spray can with 'IK' scrawled next to it in radiant blue. Some of his pieces along the train tracks are quite beautiful, in a warped, hallucinatory sort of way. He only really hangs out with the graf kids because they offer a steady supply of aerosol, but he's not actually bad at it.

'Tammy Laubscher gives terrible head' is scrawled in thick black marker next to a drawing of a dick with a cross through it. By all accounts this is a completely factual statement; something about her snaggletooth interfering with her progress as a fellatrice. Next to that is 'Call Ms Jones for a good time. 076 924 8724' in red paint. Our geography teacher clearly got on the wrong side of one of the graf kids. Her real number, I can confirm.

A small, bright piece draws my attention. It's a swollen red eye that seems to drip yellow paint like pus. Beneath it are scrawled five chilling words: 'Baxter Zevcenko is a murderer.' A cold feeling slides from the top of my head right down through my body. Fuck. Kyle must have told someone about my dreams. Guess best-friend confidentiality isn't a 'thing' any more.

I can still remember last night's foray into my chaotic, nonsensical dream world clearly. The smell of the dark, dank moss in the forest was so strong, pines swaying in the wind like the priests of some ancient, lost religion. The moon was a vicious silver-bright sickle overhead and everything was still.

I was on my BMX, easing the wheels forward and listening to their rubber tread making a crunching sound on the pine needles. Then I saw it in front of me: the huge emerald-backed Mantis swaying elegantly, drunkenly in the breeze like it was performing t'ai chi. It dipped its huge inverted-pyramid head, its diaphanous, shimmering wings spread wide as it started to dance, somehow both comical and terrifying at the same time. It turned its head and looked at me with the knowing-eye, but it was terrible, like Sauron with an eye infection, dripping blood and fire into my brain. I tried to scramble away, but it burned its way through my forehead.

After that all I could see were ox-wagons burning in the night and people being massacred. These dreams always end with people being massacred. It's like my sleeping brain is constantly set to the History Channel. If all the re-enactments were directed by Quentin Tarantino.

'Hey.' The familiar jazz-singer voice jars me from my dream recollection. Esmé saunters through the subway and slouches against the wall next to me. Her short dark hair is mussed up and a long strand hangs down across an angular cheekbone of her pixie-like face. Her green eyes are framed with dark kohl, which they'll make her take off the minute she walks into school. She smells of smoke and jasmine perfume.

She pulls a cigarette from the pack in my hand and leans over for me to light it. Her hair falls into her face and I resist the urge to push it back. Something about the combination of the light in the subway, her smell and her closeness does something to me. Time compresses into this single point. My chest feels strange and I can't think.

'Jody Fuller was murdered,' she says matter-of-factly. 'On the mountain.'

'Fuck,' I say. The coldness returns, sliding down my throat like a bad oyster. Jody Fuller was a year older than me but I had kissed her once. I remember she'd tasted faintly of milk and mint.

'It's funny,' Esmé says. 'I hated the bitch and now I kind of miss her.'

'Yeah,' I say.

We smoke in silence and then she flicks her butt into the gutter, pushes herself off the wall and leans across to smear a moist kiss across my lips.

'Find me online later,' she says, and then saunters away, her figure framed like a religious icon by the light pouring in through the entrance. I stay for a moment in the quiet subway. That kiss cleared the cache of an already bad day. I suck down the last of my cigarette and then push myself off the wall and head back into the rain. The rest of the walk is miserable. By the time I get to the old iron gates at the entrance of the school, even my socks are wet.

Thankfully I had the foresight to wrap the contents of my backpack in a plastic bag. Along with my lunch and my school books is a four-page manifesto that could change everything. If all hell doesn't break loose first. I face the gates of Westridge High and wipe the rain off my glasses.

Westridge is an imposing granite structure that has spat generations of suburban Capetonians from its iron jaws. Like all prominent high schools in the leafy Southern Suburbs, we have lush school grounds, sophisticated computer labs that were out of date as soon as they were installed, a debating team, a competitive rugby team, and gangs, drugs, bulimia, depression and bullying.

It's an ecosystem; a microcosm of the political, economic and military forces that shape the world. Some high-school kids worry about being popular or about getting good marks. I worry about maintaining a fragile gang treaty that holds Westridge together. Horses for courses, as my dad says.

I walk fast through the gates, but then slow down again when I see Mikey Markowitz up ahead; a small banana-coloured beacon of dorkiness in his bright yellow rain jacket.

Mikey was my best friend in junior school. He was thoughtful, kind and concerned for my wellbeing. By the time high school rolled around I was rethinking our friendship. It became apparent that high-school kids, or at least the ones who looked like their parents injected them with human growth hormone and then beat the joy out of them with a leather strap, could smell the weakness that Mikey secreted into the air. He's a chubby, pink, blond-haired vortex of neediness that's like shit to the big, violent flies with dyslexia that circle the school. So I made a business decision.

If you're climbing a mountain and the guy below you falls and starts dragging you down into a gaping, icy abyss, what do you do? You cut him loose. Well, high school *is* a gaping, icy abyss and I had to cut the cord that connected Mikey to me. Still, I feel a guilty twinge whenever I see him sitting alone at lunch break staring morosely at his cheese sandwich. I slow down to let Mikey gain distance. There's no sense in dredging up the past.

Mikey disappears into the rain and I quickly scan the groups of blue-blazered juveniles that skulk in the corners. Cold, beady eyes regard me from across the Sprawl – our name for the strip of tar playground that runs from behind the red-brick school hall to the janitor's hut at the edge of the lowest sports field.

The Sprawl is where everything important in the political life of Westridge happens. And important things are happening on this Monday morning. It's a wonder the adults cannot feel it; the lines of power stretched tight across the playground crackling with energy. It's almost pathetic to see the parentbots smile and drop their kids off into the seething ocean of chaos and fury, blissfully unaware and slightly high on expensive Italian espresso.

I stroll across to where the other members of the Spider are huddled in our usual corner and slip in with my clique, my protective bubble in the wilderness of high-school life.

'What's up, Bax?' Zikhona growls, shoving me affectionately with her shoulder and almost knocking me over.

'The demand for our product hopefully,' I say with a grin.

'Amen, brother,' the Inhalant Kid wheezes.

'Anything new?' I ask.

'The gangs are still at each other's throats,' Kyle says.

'They haven't seen my plan yet,' I say with a smug smile. That's what it's all about. My plan. An intricate blueprint for the future of Westridge.

The Spider is different to most schoolyard organisations. In school, like in prison, if you don't affiliate yourself you're easy prey. Although you run a low risk of getting ass-raped (unless you go on rugby camp), it's inadvisable to go without a crew to watch your back. The Spider evolved out of the primordial pit of the Sprawl. We're a new form of life that survives not through strength but through agility.

We're a small operation, but a successful one. We found one another by the kind of freak radar that draws together kids that don't really fit in. There's me with my congenital eye condition and weird glasses. There's Kyle, the freakishly clever kid. Ty the Inhalant Kid, who has found his life's purpose at the bottom of a paint tin, and Zikhona, who is big in a sumo wrestler kinda way. When we found each other it was like pieces of a puzzle fitting neatly together.

'Do you think it'll work?' the Inhalant Kid asks nervously.

'It better,' Kyle says. 'Or we're seriously screwed.'

'We could always kill Anwar,' Zikhona says with a scowl. 'And blame it on the Mountain Killer.' I resist telling her the dreams I have where Anwar is just one of the many unfortunate souls that die screaming.

'You cut the head off the Hydra and another one will grow to take its place,' Kyle says.

'We're not a gang,' I say. 'We're a corporation.'

The truth is that our success hinges on the fact that we remain neutral among the axes of power – the two gangs that control Westridge High. The juggernaut that runs the school is the Nice Time Kids, led by self-styled warlord Anwar Davids. They're dangerous, organised and the prime suppliers of drugs. Their management style is kind of like the Third Reich – big, cruel and requiring absolute loyalty of their members.

The other dog in the pit is the Form, led by Denton de Jaager. They run a business of fake doctors' certificates, parental permission slips and leaked exam papers. They're more like al-

Qaeda – a networked, guerrilla-style militia that blends into the general school populace.

The problem is that the Sprawl isn't big enough for both of them. Over the past year the tension has escalated and now they are snapping at each other's throats, with nothing but the Spider standing between them. Because knives are so cheap and easily available, both gangs carry them. I know Anwar has access to guns too and I wonder how long it will be before Westridge has its debut drive-by shooting. Kyle calls high school a zero-sum game. It's like *Highlander*, there can be only one (in this case gangs, rather than sword-wielding immortals with mullets).

It's not the gutting of students that worries me though. We have a unique selling proposition, a great democratic product that, along with soccer, is the world's favourite spectator sport. Yes, I'm talking about porn.

You'd think that in the digital age a pornography vendor would be as out of date as a crusty old guy in tie-dye selling LPs at a flea market. But like that old hippy, there is a method to our madness. We don't sell a product. We sell an experience.

You're looking for Ron 'The Hedgehog' Jeremy's first skin flick? The original *Debbie Does Dallas*? You've come to the right place; we can get them to you by the end of the day. We're the Cinema Nouveau of the porn world. We deal in the Altman of anal and the Coen Brothers of the cumshot. In a better world we'd be part of Westridge's cultural committee.

One student getting stabbed would be inconvenient. A gang war could be the death knell for our business. Lockers would be searched, pupils would be questioned, parents would be summoned, and there are just too many trails leading to us. So I have no choice but to intervene.

The school bell rings and we shuffle into the school hall for our first assembly of the term.

'Did you tell anyone?' I whisper to Kyle as we troop into the hall, kids around us jostling and yapping like dogs reacquainting themselves with the pack.

'About your necrophilia?' he replies. 'Never, the secret will go with me to the grave. After which you can do with me what you will.'

'My dreams, you tool. Did you tell anyone about my dreams?'

'Oh captain, my captain. Do you question my loyalty?'

'Cut the crap. Did you tell anyone or not?'

'I am your faithful confidant. I would never reveal your sweaty, intimate secrets. They could use thumbscrews, they could use hair shirts, they could –'

'OK, asshole, I get the point,' I snap.

'Are they still ... you know?' He taps his temple.

I nod. 'They're getting worse I think. Pretty much every night now.'

'What does the headshrinker say?'

Dr Basson is the psychiatrist my parents send me to to help me 'work out issues'. He's a weird old guy who's done all kinds of tests on me; intelligence tests, empathy tests, are-you-a-psycho? tests, even crackpot tests that seem like he's checking for ESP. As far as I can tell, my parents are wasting a fortune on the society-sanctioned witchcraft that is the psychology profession.

'He says that they're my psyche's way of dealing with stress.'

'Maybe you should take it easy,' Kyle says.

'Sure, I'll take it easy. How does being expelled, with no source of income except the money your parents give you, sound?'

'Fucking terrible,' he says with a grimace.

'Then don't tell me to take it easy,' I reply.

We slump into our seats in the hall and watch as the Form walk in and take their places at the back left. The Form is like the personification of inherited privilege. They carry themselves like wealthy Bond villains and think along the same lines. They're not interested in money in the way the Nice Time Kids are. They're interested in keeping themselves entertained by beating up everything and everyone that has the audacity to challenge them.

The Nice Time Kids, or the NTK as they're more commonly known, take their places at the back right. If you distilled all the cruelty, all the hormonal surges, all the bad ideas and warrantless arrogance of adolescence into a single obscene organism, it'd be the NTK. They're messy to a point way past the simple apathetic neglect of the rest of us. They wear their messiness like a badge; missing buttons, torn collars and cuffs, shoes scuffed and filled with holes, all ham-handedly proclaiming their affiliation. The rest of us are in between trying to figure out what the situation between the gangs is. Has there been a truce? Will sanity prevail? Will peace, goodwill and huge porn profit margins smile upon the Spider?

Anwar Davids, his uneven crew cut showing patches of his scalp in the artificial light, turns his head and smiles. The school holds its breath. Slowly he brings his hand up, widens his smile and draws his thumb across his throat, and then points straight at the solid figure of Denton de Jaager.

Denton extends his large, chubby hand to look uninterestedly at his nails and then leans back and yawns. A shiver of acknowledgement runs through the masses. At least everybody knows what's happening.

The tension is broken as our headmaster, the Bearded One, ascends to the lectern. He raises his hand for silence even though nobody is talking. He rubs his mousy brown beard and begins to speak.

'Welcome back from, ahhh, what I, umm, hope was a stimulating weekend.' There are titters. Judging from some of the glassy eyes staring blankly forward it's more likely that it was a stimulant weekend courtesy of the NTK.

'Ahh, it's unfortunate to start like this but, umm, the police inform me that another body has been found on the mountain.' There's a collective intake of breath. 'We have, ermmm, asked a representative of the police force to, umm, speak to you this morning.'

A small, balding man sporting both an impressive handlebar moustache and an ugly burgundy suit strides onto the stage and pushes his John Lennon sunglasses onto his forehead.

'Good morning, I'm Mr Beeld, a criminologist working on the Mountain Killer case. I know this is rather traumatic for everybody, but it's important to remember that, worldwide, more people are killed by falling coconuts and defective toasters than by knife-wielding serial killers.' He gives us a smile that's meant to be reassuring. 'Of course, we must take the necessary precautions and awareness is the number-one weapon in the fight against crime.

'What we know is that either the victim knew the killer or the killer is very good at what he does. He used some kind of serrated blade to cut her throat and then carve the bloody likeness of an eye into her forehead. As you may already know, the eye is the calling card of the so-called Mountain Killer, a serial killer already responsible for the deaths of twelve people in the Cape Town area.

'The all-seeing eye is of particular occult significance,' Beeld continues. 'It represents spiritual sight and transcendental vision. The fact that it is used as a calling card means that this could be the work of a cult, or of an individual with an interest in occult lore. Serial killers generally show a lack of empathy and a superiority complex, often with delusions of grandeur. There is a pathological need for control. And murder, of course, is the ultimate form of control.

'If you have seen anything suspicious, please report it to your local police station immediately.'

'I heard that it was Jody Fuller,' Kyle whispers.

'Yeah, Esmé told me,' I reply under my breath.

'Good thing you never actually got together with her.'

'Guess so.' The thought of Jody dead makes me feel cold all over again. My forehead begins to throb and I have to force myself not to think about the goddamn dreams again. I swear I'm going find that fucker who decided to put my name on his little piece of wall art and make him pay.

'She was stuck-up,' I whisper.

Kyle gives me a strange look. 'Yeah, but she didn't deserve to die.'

I shrug. Life is unfair.

The assembly ends and we push our way out of the school hall and into the granite quad that is the heart of the school's 150 years of colonial history. Westridge has been expanded with multiple layers of concrete and fibreglass, but it's this granite centre that contains its ancestral DNA. Rah, rah and tally-ho, boys.

'Hey, Baxter,' Courtney Adams says with a coquettish smile.

I ignore her. She's an NPC, a non-playing character, a pawn who is preoccupied with mindless social programming and is distant from the power centres of the Sprawl. People like her can be used to run interference, used and manipulated, but should never be trusted or considered seriously when planning strategically.

I pass Ricket Hendries and slip a flash drive filled with Asian girl-on-girl action into his hand. He grins and gives me the thumbs up. I grin back and breathe in the sweet smell of sweat, whiteboard marker and fear. The smells of high school.

It's like chess. Jocks, Ricket and his gang of cheap deodorant-scented Cro-Magnons, are knights. You can't directly manipulate them because they believe that their superior muscle density means they're in control. But they can always be moved sideways, obtusely angled so that they believe they are the ones doing the moving.

Rooks are the big violent loner kids like Josh Southfield. His dad is in jail for a white-collar crime, he has gruesome acne and he does badly at school and, as such, has very little to lose. Moving him is as easy as telekinesis.

And me? Well, I don't aspire to be king. That's just like being a highly paid pawn. I'm a bishop, a vizier. I'm always behind the scenes pulling the strings. If I use my full potential, I'm the most powerful piece on the board.

We shoulder our way past the NPCs into metalwork class. Mr Olly, our moustachioed metalwork teacher, looks like a former member of the security police who has been granted amnesty by the Truth and Reconciliation Commission for apartheid atrocities. Most of the classherd comply with the instructions Olly puts on the board, their tongues lolling out of their mouths like they have just been shot through the head with a bolt gun in an abattoir and haven't yet begun to realise that something is wrong. I wait until Olly is distracted and then saunter over to a bench at the back of the class.

'General,' I say to the youth whose oversized head is the result of a childhood case of elephantiasis. He looks up to reveal cool, grey eyes. Toby September; taunted ceaselessly since birth, he channelled his rage into climbing the social hierarchy and is now general of the Nice Time Kids, second only to Anwar himself.

'Zevcenko,' he says, taking his time over my name.

'I need an audience with the Warlord,' I say. The oversized head nods thoughtfully, but when he speaks his voice is acidic.

'Lunchtime at Central,' he says. 'But I would advise against doing anything that will upset him.'

I smile. It is a veiled threat, of course, but I was born for this kind of manoeuvring. I bow my head in thanks and return to my desk. First objective achieved.

Case File: Baxter Ivan Zevcenko
Dr Kobus Basson

Baxter Zevcenko is a sixteen-year-old white male residing in Cape Town, South Africa. At our first consultation Baxter arrived looking slightly unkempt, wearing a hooded sweatshirt and jeans.

He was confrontational at first but our subsequent sessions have allowed him to relax somewhat, giving him the opportunity to speak about his life.

I am able to discern two distinct parts of his personality, although it doesn't seem as if Baxter himself is aware of them yet. One part shows strong correlations with the Dark Triad group of personality traits, showing elements of narcissism, Machiavellianism and psychopathy.

He delights in describing his own manipulative behaviour, taking pride in his ability to lie, failing to respond to normal emotional stimuli and aggrandising his own social roles.

Some of his stories revolve around being the leader of a special group, 'the Spider'. An interesting choice of name considering the implications of a 'web' that Baxter himself is creating. His descriptions of his friends seem to cast them as mere walk-on parts in the grand story of his life, further showing his need for grandiosity and dominance. I wouldn't be surprised to learn that these 'friends' either don't exist, or play very different roles to those that Baxter has described.

The other, weaker part, shows the potential for caring. The descriptions of his grandfather, for instance, show a love and respect that seem absent in his other relationships.

These two parts often seem to be at odds with each other, battling for control of his psyche, and the result is disturbed dreams, a pattern of maladaptive thinking and manipulative behaviour, which I believe is impacting on Baxter's health and relationships.

He has an undercurrent of rage that he has described as a 'dark wave', and his hostility toward his brother is incredibly troubling. Besides fights with his brother he has shown no signs of violence, but his ability to deceive and mask his true personality cannot be underestimated.

SKULL PRESSURE

'Jump, jump, jump.' The low chant from the class grows louder. Miss Hunter, our maths teacher, stands at the window quivering, her dishevelled blonde hair whipping in the breeze.

Encouraging a sweet and fragile teacher – distraught at the thought that we don't care about her class, and driven to hysteria by consistent and vicious undermining of her authority – to throw herself from the second storey is wrong. But it's also fun. Miss Hunter is the kind of teacher who will never last. She believes in our inherent goodness. That's her first mistake.

Control. Teachers know that they now have less of it. They know things have become more complicated and more dangerous, that the student populace is now a networked entity, a hive mind, a multi-cellular organism intent on destroying them. Teachers seek individuals within the crowd to blame for bad behaviour, but we are a faceless mass, absorbing punishment and spreading it among us.

Two teachers have already had nervous breakdowns this year. Mr Henri ran from the classroom screaming, finally cracking after seeing messages about his wife scratched onto his desk. Miss

Franks had just never returned after *that* picture of her landed on the Internet. Gross, even by the Spider's standards. If she had given me better marks perhaps she could have avoided that.

Miss Hunter turns to the class. 'I'm doing this for you,' she says and it seems like she's looking straight at me. Sure, Miss Hunter. You're doing this for us and not because you've watched *Dead Poets Society* and *Dangerous Minds* a few too many times. Give me broadband and YouTube and I'll have the maths curriculum down in a week. The truth is, Miss Hunter, that you're obsolete and your inability to see that is pathetic.

Still, maths is the first class of the day where the whole of the Spider are together and it's time to get some real work done. Miss Hunter gives me a meaningful look and then flees the class tearfully.

'She's definitely got a thing for you, Bax,' Kyle says in his mumbling murmur.

I ignore him. 'Let's get some feedback before we discuss strategy,' I say.

'Stats say there is a trend toward creature porn,' Kyle says, putting his phone in the middle of the desk. We lean over the screen displaying graphs of the previous month's sales. 'We're going to have to make more copies of *Tokoloshe Money Shot*.'

Creature porn is a strange new addition to the porn canon. Guys and girls dressed in supernatural fancy dress and going at it have captured the warped imaginations of the student body, and we're planning to exploit the trend to its full potential. Sales are fuelled by conspiracy theories circulated on Internet forums that the werewolves, zombies and other humanoid beasts getting it on with humans are real. Proof that people will believe anything if it helps them get their rocks off.

'Make more copies but keep an eye on it. It may just be a fad like the Swedish sauna orgies,' I say.

Kyle nods to Zikhona. She's our security liaison officer, our enforcer, a mountain of Xhosa sturdiness in the gold bomber jacket that she wears over her school uniform.

Strictly speaking, we didn't choose Zikhona, she chose us. I remember the day a convoy of black BMW SUVs had pulled up outside the school. Two men who looked like they fought in cages stepped out of the front car and put their hands inside their jacket pockets. A huge black girl squeezed herself out of the door of the centre BMW and stood at the gate, trying to extract a wedgie from her tights.

A teacher walked over to welcome her and perhaps gently remind her that school had started twenty minutes earlier and that the gold bomber jacket she was wearing had to come off. One of the bodyguards stepped forward and shook his head sternly. The teacher backed off. The girl gave up on the wedgie and sauntered through the gates, surveying the groups of assembled students before walking over to where we were and shoving a kid in front of us out of the way.

'What's up, fuckers?' she said by way of introduction. That's how we became friends.

'Increased low-level attacks on the Form by the NTK,' she says in her purring baritone, her large hoop earrings jangling as she speaks. 'Word is that Denton is organising a big retaliation.'

'Shit, we need to get in there before a full-blown war starts,' Kyle says.

'I have a meeting with Anwar at lunch break,' I reply. 'If I can get him to commit to a temporary truce maybe I can bring the Form around.'

'I don't know, Bax,' Zikhona says, raising a carefully manicured eyebrow. 'Denton is acting pretty tough and Anwar isn't taking it well.'

'Idiots,' I hiss and my forehead begins to throb again. 'Can't they see that starting a war is going to take us all down?' I feel light-headed and sweat prickles on my skin. 'They're all in it for themselves, they can't see the bigger picture.' My forehead is pulsing now and I can't think of anything else but the forces encroaching on us.

Suddenly it's as if there's a visual overlay on reality. Spectral shapes move across my vision, women and children being marched into camps. 'They take our land, they rape our women, they kill our children. *Fokken Engelse duiwels! Ek is 'n Siener.*' I slam my palm down on the desk. After a moment the pulsing in my forehead subsides and I see the Spider peering strangely at me.

'Um, are you OK, Bax?' Kyle says. 'You're not having a stroke, are you? Can you smell burning rubber? Is one side of your face numb?'

'No,' I say quickly. 'C'mon, it was a joke. I was joking. They're always banging on about South African history, I'm just sick of it, that's all.'

'Uh-huh,' Zikhona says and waves her hand in front of my face. 'Just promise me you'll never give up porn for stand-up comedy.'

'OK, I promise,' I say with a half-hearted laugh. Jesus, Zevcenko, try to keep your shit together. Whatever the hell is going on in your head it's going to have to wait until this thing with the gangs is over.

'IK, how are new markets looking?' I say, quickly changing the subject.

The Inhalant Kid cups his hands and huffs from a bottle of Tipp-Ex. It doesn't take much to make him nervous and it's clear my little freak-out has jangled his nerves. The Kid is our sales and PR person. He's short for his age, which is unsurprising considering his hobby, with a mop of curly brown hair and large elven ears that make him look like he's always listening to something in the distance.

He's what you might call a connoisseur of chemical contaminants, or perhaps a sommelier of spray cans. Despite the gaps in his memory and a solvent-induced stammer, he is an amazing salesperson. He has the ability to simultaneously make people feel sorry for and scornful of him. It's the perfect sales stimulant. 'The partnership with Dirkie Venter is on,' he says softly. 'If everything goes to plan, we'll double our sales by August.'

I nod approvingly. Dirkie Venter is a possible new distribution partner at Mulderberg Technical High School in the Northern Suburbs. So far we'd kept our operation within the boundaries of Westridge, but we're big fish in a small pond and we need to diversify. Dirkie is our link to the predominantly Afrikaans Northern Suburbs. His hatred of English-speakers has destroyed any previous attempts to pursue this avenue, but he is slowly coming round. He has the greed hook in his mouth and all I need to do is reel him in.

Everyone looks at me. They're awaiting some inspirational words from their leader and now, more than ever, I need to show them that I've got my shit covered.

'This is not going to be an easy week,' I start. 'I don't need to tell you the threat we face. If war happens and we're caught in the fallout, expulsion is almost certain.'

The Inhalant Kid switches to wood glue and sniffs viciously to calm his nerves.

'I'm not forcing anybody to continue on our current course of action. If anybody wants out, say so.' My voice becomes more resonant. 'We have the opportunity to do something great here.' I look at the faces of my team. Not one of them flinches from my bespectacled gaze. I've never been prouder.

When lunch break rolls around, I walk with the Spider down to our corner on the Sprawl.

'I should come with you,' Zikhona says with a snarl. 'I don't trust those wankers.'

I shake my head. 'I'm not going to let them think I'm scared of them.'

'Well, you're a lot braver than me,' the Kid says as he rubs his sleeve across his nose. 'Anwar terrifies me.'

There are bigger, stronger and more violent kids at Westridge, but Anwar is by far the scariest. There is something about his unpredictability and his enjoyment of others' suffering that strikes a chord of fear in everyone, even me if I'm honest about it. Which I never am.

'He's OK,' I say. 'Besides, aren't all bullies supposed to be cowards inside?'

'Only on TV,' Zikhona says, smacking her meaty fist into her palm.

I leave Zikhona and the Inhalant Kid discussing Anwar and walk slowly with Kyle toward the edge of the Sprawl.

'What the hell was that in class?' he whispers as we cross the tar. 'English devils? Sieners? You practising to impress Dirkie?' He pulls his phone from his pocket, taps on it quickly and then reads from the screen. 'It says "Siener – an Afrikaner prophet or religious figure. A seer." What the fuck, Bax?'

'I don't know,' I say, rubbing my forehead tiredly. 'It just hasn't been a good day so far.'

'Well, if you ever want to, you know, talk about shit, I'm here,' he says.

'Thanks,' I say with a small smile.

'Good luck with Anwar,' he says as we reach the edge of the tarmac. 'We're the serious underdogs in this, Bax, so be careful.'

'I don't need luck,' I say, turning to face him and forcing a grin onto my face. 'I have a plan.'

A lesson I learnt early on is that it often pays to be the underdog.

I remember watching the school judo championships when I was very young. Seeing a kid who was not only big and stocky for his age, but who had honed his judo skills to perfection. He was a white-pyjama-suited whirling dervish of death, dealing out throws, trips and chokeholds.

By some glitch in the system he had paired up to fight a far smaller kid in the opening round. His opponent was much younger than him, as well as being a tiny, pasty specimen. It was like watching a maggot fighting a rhino beetle.

The bigger kid grinned, but I knew then that he had already lost the fight. There was no winning outcome for the rhino beetle. If he won the match he would be forced to beat up a little kid. If he lost, he'd be the guy that lost to the maggot.

The match started and the maggot proved to be much more capable than one would expect. He wrapped his legs around the rhino beetle's neck and squeezed for all he was worth. The rhino beetle did exactly what he was trained to do in these circumstances. He picked the little kid up and slammed him to the mat.

The booing and jeering from the crowd was instantaneous. After all, the narrative was clear: big bully picks on the weak, nerdy kid. Every high-school TV show, movie and miniseries contained this premise exactly and the crowd responded accordingly.

The rhino beetle had to fight cautiously, defensively, never being too aggressive or too dominant in case the crowd turned on him. The maggot was in his element and piled on the pressure until the rhino beetle simply couldn't take it any more and gave in to what was a fairly weak submission. It was a mind game and the rhino beetle lost. I credit that maggot with teaching me my first lessons about the politics of the playground.

I look up as I walk through the Sprawl and see that the sky's disease has relented to allow patches of albino through the greyness. That would be a good omen. If I believed in omens. Superstition is for the feeble-minded. So are thoughts of fratricide, but as I see Rafe peeking over the wrought-iron school fence, I'm sorely tempted.

'What are you doing here?' I hiss, looking quickly around to make sure nobody can see us. This is not what I need right now.

Rafe goes to the special-needs school two blocks away, but I'd banned him from ever coming to visit me at lunch break. The fact that I have a retard brother is not exactly a secret, but I'd prefer not to be seen hanging out with him at lunch break.

'What are you doing here?' I repeat.

He lifts a thick book and shows me a picture of a tall man with a huge beard leading Boer commandos across a burning plain like he's some kind of khaki-clad Gandalf.

'Great. Today's little bit of history brought to us by my cognitively challenged brother. Seriously, Rafe, what the fuck are you doing? It's your fault I'm having these dreams. You're always shoving this stuff in my face, always trying to make me read this stupid historical bullshit. Well, congratulations, you've infiltrated my subconscious. It's your fault I'm blurting out bits of Afrikaans in class.'

He looks at me like I'm a raving idiot and then turns and walks slowly away.

'Right,' I mutter as I stalk off. '*I'm* the idiot.'

I get to the edge of the lower sports field. In the corner is a spot where the iron fence has been bent to form a doorway to the outside world. I look around quickly and then duck through the hole. I skirt the alley next to the bridge that connects the surrounding residential area to the highway and walk quickly to a series of derelict rooms that used to be a Freemason Lodge. This is Central, the NTK base of operations. I knock and pull a face at the creepy carved Masonic eye that watches me from above the door as I wait. The door opens a crack.

'Wassup, Russ?' I say conversationally, mostly because I know it'll piss him off. He joined the NTK because he wants respect, but he gets none from Anwar and he damn well isn't getting any from me.

'Zevcenko,' he says. I nod, smile and wait. He wants me to ask to come in and thus to acknowledge his role as gatekeeper. I don't because he knows why I'm here and he won't dare keep Anwar waiting. I begin to whistle and tap my foot. He panics and opens the door like the minion that he is. Pawns are so predictable.

The NTK rank and file are sprawled on couches eating takeaways and smoking tik from light bulbs that they've stolen from teachers' cars. They look up as I walk through, following me with their bloodshot and dangerous eyes. Musty Masonic banners hang from the peeling walls to which the NTK have added their own artwork – thousands of scrawled tags, centrefolds from substandard porn mags and two cheap katanas from a Chinese shop which they've hung crossed on the wall. Classy.

Russell leads me through a doorway to the back room. It's large and curved, almost circular, and has a black-and-purple decaying pulpit that commands the centre of the room. The Masons must have used this room to sacrifice babies or something. No wonder Anwar likes it so much. I can't help but notice a small keypad on the far wall, probably a safe where the NTK keep their profits.

Anwar and Toby are seated on a low, dusty couch in the centre of the room watching a younger kid have his shoulder tattooed. The dog tattoos are a sign of initiation into the gang, a mark of achievement for successfully passing the violent rituals of membership, the bare-fist fights with gangs from other schools, the housebreakings and the weird sexual rites of passage.

Anwar is tall and gaunt. He has a missing tooth and a lazy eye, both of which accentuate the rabidness that he emanates.

He is shirtless and the handle of a gun juts from the waistband of his regulation grey school pants. I knew that Anwar's older brother was connected to a notorious Cape Flats gang and the NTK couriered drugs for him into the suburbs. I didn't know that the NTK actually had guns at Central.

I swallow hard and pull my eyes away from the gun, focusing on the tattoo artist, an old guy with prison ink covering most of his body. He works methodically with a school compass and blue ink from a pen to render the crude drawing of a dog on the clavicle of the NTK's newest initiate. The kid doesn't flinch and Anwar nods approvingly. I wait while the old inker does his work. Finally the tattoos are done and the artist grunts and shuffles out the door. Anwar says a few words to his new minion and then waves his hand and the kid leaves too.

Anwar and Toby stare at me like vultures at roadkill. 'Baxter,' Anwar says, gesturing for me to sit on one of the lumpy chairs arranged in front of the couch of power. I sit and force my body to remain relaxed. 'You have two minutes,' Anwar says.

I pull a folder from my bag and offer it to him. This treaty is what I've been working toward since I started the Spider, a subtle and nuanced blueprint for the future political landscape of the school. 'Why are we working against each other?' is the question it asks. Instead, we can use our various competencies for the good of us all. The possible alliance with Dirkie Venter is the beginning. With Dirkie's contacts, the Westridge business community could expand into other schools. We would be the United States of Schoolyard Contraband. Each gang has its place. Working together there is nothing we couldn't achieve. I would inspire the gangs of Westridge to take responsibility for their future. I'm like Oprah. If Oprah had weird glasses and sold porn.

Anwar takes the treaty and motions for Toby to follow him to the NTK war table. Toby gets up slowly and grins at me as he walks over. Anwar opens the folder and spreads the pages across the table. I bite furtively at one of my nails as they look at it, conferring in low voices. Finally Anwar straightens up and turns to look at me with a smile on his face.

'Baxter,' Anwar says. I allow myself a moment of smugness. Apparently even Anwar's warmongering mind can see the logic. 'You know I've always respected the Spider,' he continues quietly. This isn't at all true. In our earlier days, the NTK had threatened and harassed us until we had imposed porn sanctions on its members. 'But this plan is an insult.' He says the words with such venom that my smugness scuttles away like vermin. I struggle to control myself. 'Just take some time to think about it,' I say. 'You might be strong enough to crush the Form, but the resulting fallout will benefit none of us.'

'The NTK are not weak, power-brokering scavengers,' he shouts, grabbing the handle of his gun and pulling it from his waistband. I'm tempted to grab my bag and run, but I know Anwar would enjoy that way too much. Instead I rise slowly. I pull my bag onto my shoulders and meet Anwar's eyes. 'Then I wish you the best of luck, Warlord,' I say with all the coldness I can muster. In a way I actually mean it. Luck is all that's going to save any of us now.

I light a cigarette and lean against the old oak tree in the northeast corner of the Sprawl. It's the sacred, spiritual symbol of Westridge, the symbol on our school blazers and the essence of our school motto, 'From the roots to the sky'. I look up at the clouds and breathe out a long coil of smoke. Things with Anwar hadn't gone well but I still have a chance with Dirkie. If I can get him on board I can use that as leverage with the gangs. If Denton agrees, perhaps Anwar will see the light.

A battered white van coasts down the road next to the school and parks next to the gates. Dirkie gets out and climbs over the iron railing, then walks quickly to where I'm standing.

'My brothers are in the van with crowbars,' Dirkie says in his thick Afrikaans accent that makes him sound like he's speaking with a mouthful of cacti. 'Any trouble and they'll join us.'

'I'm alone,' I say, holding up my hands defensively. 'Besides, I'm a businessman not a fighter.'

'Sometimes you can't be one without the other,' Dirkie says with a scowl.

I light another cigarette and offer him one. He accepts and tucks it behind his ear. Sporting blond hair shaped by a ragged, pudding-bowl haircut, a tight black WWE T-shirt and a single gold hoop earring that dangles from his left lobe, Dirkie looks like he should be flipping burgers at McDonald's. Instead he's running the biggest schoolyard syndicate in the Western Cape.

'Which makes easy business opportunities all the more attractive when they come our way,' I say.

Dirkie grunts and turns to unzip his fly, relieving himself on the big oak tree as he speaks. 'You Englishmen are so full of shit. The South African English are a rootless, bastard race. The Afrikaans have a culture, a tradition; what do the South African English have?'

'Nothing,' I say. 'It's a miracle we've even survived this long.' Dirkie laughs as he zips up his fly. He wipes his hands on his pants and then pulls the cigarette out from behind his ear. I light it for him.

'We'll supply the merchandise, you market and distribute it in the Northern Suburbs and we split the profits,' I say.

Dirkie takes a drag of the cigarette and looks at me. 'What's the split?'

This is the most dangerous part of the negotiation. The

production cost of the porn we'll be giving him is virtually nothing. He shoulders all the risk and the cost of marketing. Of course I don't tell him this.

'Seventy–thirty,' I say.

Dirkie smiles. 'Just like the English, always thinking we're backward, inbred farmers.' His smile fades. 'Fifty–fifty.'

I purse my lips. 'Sixty–forty is really the lowest I can go.'

'You're taking me for a poes, Engelsman.'

I sigh theatrically. 'The rest of the Spider are not going to like this,' I say. 'But OK. Fifty–fifty.' There is a long pause while Dirkie thinks and then finally he nods his head and extends his hand. We shake.

We smoke in silence for a while and I let my thoughts drift back to the events of the day.

'Do you know what a Siener is?' I blurt out and then instantly regret it.

He looks at me suspiciously. 'What the fok do you want to know about that for?'

'It's, um, for a project I'm doing.'

'Fokking use Google like everyone else,' he says with a disgusted shake of his head.

'Sorry,' I say. 'I just thought …' Jesus, why the hell did I open my mouth?

He looks closely at me. 'If you're making fun of me, Engelsman, I swear I'll –'

'I'm not, I swear.'

He nods and we smoke a bit more in silence. 'They were like religious leaders,' he says eventually. 'The only one I know about was Niklaas van Rensburg, who rode with De la Rey's commando. He was able to see things. You know, about what the English were doing. They were like psychic or something.'

I nod. 'OK, cool, thanks.'

He finishes his cigarette and stubs it out against the tree. 'I don't need to be a Siener to know if you screw me over, Engelsman.'

I smile. 'Dirkie, you have the word of this bastard that I won't.' He snorts and gives me a long stare as if to back up his threat. I return it without flinching. He nods, then leaves me and gets into the van. The tyres screech as it speeds away from the Westridge gates.

FAMILY TIES

The dew on the veld sparkles in the sunlight. The man next to me walks slowly, using a tree-branch cane to navigate through the rough crags and hollows. I jump nimbly between the rocks, relishing the chance to be away from the wagons after our relentless, feverish flight – our eyes constantly searching the horizon for a sign of the invaders.

The man, my father, smiles at my exuberance. 'Careful, little klipspringer,' he says in Afrikaans. 'Don't fall.'

'I never fall,' I say proudly and jump between two rocks to prove my prowess.

'Just like your mother,' he says with a laugh.

We reach a rocky outcrop overlooking a vast plain, the browns and greys of the veld meeting the white and blue of the sky in the distance. I look back toward our laager of wagons, but all I can see is the white flag with the red eye of the Sieners flapping in the wind.

'Beautiful, Papa,' I say, clasping his hand. I know he loves mornings like these. He says they put the fire back in his blood.

'Yes, beautiful,' he says softly. 'But I didn't bring you here to admire the land, my dear one, however radiant she is this morning.'

I peer up at him, his face as hard and strong as the hills and crags that surround us.

'How are the dreams?' he asks, placing a large hand on my shoulder and squeezing gently.

'Scary,' I say with a shudder. 'About a strange boy with spectacles, and a huge animal with many arms trying to grab me.'

He nods grimly.

'It's trying to get me,' I whisper.

'It's trying to get all of us,' he says. 'Our enemies have found the Beast and it strains on its leash to get at us.'

He sits down heavily on an uneven rock. I crouch next to him and look at my toes, bare and dirty like little pink worms in the dust. A hot wind whips across the crags, lashing dirt and silt across our bared skin.

'Papa, I'm scared,' I say and grab his arm, clinging to it like a life raft in a raging river.

He looks at me with the Eye. It bores into me, bringing my soul twisting and writhing onto the hot, dusty ground. 'You must find the chariot of Ezekiel,' he says softly. 'If they find it we are lost.'

I bury my face in his arm. 'I can't,' I croak. 'I don't know how.'

He pushes me away roughly. 'You are a Siener, child,' he says, hauling himself to his feet. I stumble backwards, tears stinging my eyes.

'A Siener like your grandmother, like me and your Uncle Niklaas. You must learn to transform your sight into a sword that will turn back the Devil himself.' He reaches into his waistcoat and pulls out a small medicine bottle filled with liquid. What a liquid! It shines and glistens in the morning sun like the tears of angels.

'What is it?' I say, wiping my tears with my sleeve.

'Blood,' he says. 'Some call it the Blood of the Saviour, but that is just superstition. It is the blood of those who would help us find the chariot.' He hands the bottle to me. I take it and turn it so that the shimmering liquid pools at the bottom of the bottle.

'When the time comes you must drink it,' my father says. 'It will allow you to see further than you thought possible. My sight has dwindled and Niklaas is slowly losing his mind. You are our only hope. You must find the chariot or die trying. You are the last.'

'I'm the last,' I mumble. My face is stuck to the pillow like a giant postage stamp. I peel it off groggily and fumble for my clock. It's seven thirty in the evening. I must have fallen asleep on my bed when I got home from meeting Dirkie. My throat is parched and I feel like I'm dying of thirst in a vast, unforgiving veld.

I wander down the stairs, past the embarrassing professional studio family portraits (my dad carrying my mom on his back, Rafe and I dressed in matching shirts with our arms around each other's shoulders), the embroidered Khalil Gibran quotations and the brass ornaments that my mother collects. Rafe is in the living room watching TV. I make a detour around him and into the kitchen for some orange juice.

My mother is leaning her elbows on the kitchen counter and thumbing through a glossy magazine. 'Bax, I want to talk to you about what happened this morning,' she says when she sees me. I scowl and fling open the fridge, grab a carton of orange juice and take a gulp.

'Glass,' she says.

I sigh, grab one from the cupboard and fill it to the brim with juice. 'Do we really have to do this now?' I say between sips. 'I've got homework to do.'

'It's never a good time for you,' she says. 'This is important and I want to talk about it. Now.'

Her tone doesn't exactly leave much room for negotiation. My fight with Rafe is the last thing on my mind, but apparently my mother has had a less eventful day.

I pull up a stool at the counter and slump forward onto my elbows. 'OK,' I say. 'Let's get in touch with our inner spirit guides.'

My mother frowns. 'That was one time, Baxter, and I apologised for that. I had no idea that Barbara's guru would turn out to be so –'

'Flaky,' I finish for her.

'Eccentric,' she says primly. 'Anyway, that's not what I'm talking about. It just worries me that you show no consideration for your brother's special needs.'

'But I do,' I say. 'He needs a weekly beating and I'm happy to take on that burden.'

'Baxter!' my mother says sharply.

'Relax, I'm joking,' I say. 'He just gets on my nerves.'

She sighs and runs a hand through her brown curly hair. It bounces around like a club full of dancing Slinkies. 'It's more than that,' she says. 'You're lashing out more and more at him lately. You've become really antisocial. I worry that you don't seem to be interested in doing anything with your life.' Like running a highly successful retail business for instance? Sometimes I wish the Spider was legit just so I could get her off my back.

She licks her thumb and flips through the pages of the magazine. 'I've been reading this article –'

'No!' I groan. 'Mom, please. Every time you read an article you diagnose me with some kind of syndrome, disorder or disease. Enough already, I'm fine.' With Rafe's autism and my grandfather's insanity my mom has become totally paranoid that I am hiding some kind of deep-seated mental disturbance. Even with my visits to Dr Basson she regularly subjects me to quizzes, tests and games in an attempt to try and diagnose me with whatever syndrome, phobia or disease is the flavour of the month in one of her mags.

'No, it's not like that,' she says pleadingly. 'It's just that so teenagers have emotional problems and diagnosing them can really help to avert any –'

'Oh, for God's sake, Vivian,' my dad says from the kitchen door. 'Give it a rest, will you?' My dad hasn't gotten out of his pyjamas today, which is usually a warning sign that some kind of parental skirmish is about to happen.

'Well, here he is,' my mother says with a sarcastic smirk. 'The great social-media "journalist" has finally decided to come out of his Batcave and see his family?' My father grimaces. Truthfully, that was a bit of a low blow for an opening volley from my mom. Usually they start small and work up to the truly hurtful stuff. My father was retrenched from his job as a senior editor on a local newspaper and has taken to writing a blog from home. The power of social media to bring people together clearly hasn't worked on my parents' marriage.

'Well, I've got homework to do,' I say as I get up. 'So I'll probably just head on up again.'

'No,' my mother says fiercely. 'You're taking the test.'

Another losing hand and I'm getting tired of having to fold. 'Fine,' I say with a theatrical sigh.

'Good,' she says, smiling. 'It'll be fun.'

I suppress a laugh as my dad rolls his eyes at me.

'Right,' my mom says, clearing her throat. 'Question number one. Do you sometimes feel that you're better than everyone else?'

We go through the lame-ass litany of questions; mostly about communication, empathy and the plight of our fellow man. She ticks the boxes as I answer, arching her eyebrows and nodding meaningfully at everything I say. At the end she tallies the score.

'How did I do?' I say chirpily. 'Am I irrevocably sad and broken?'

'Well, there are no wrong answers,' she says carefully.

'That's a total lie,' I say.

e been thinking that it might not be a bad idea if
Basson to give us reports on how you're doing.'

psychiatrist spy on me for you. Gee, that sounds
like a blast, I say.

'Vivian, leave him alone,' my dad says wearily, tightening the belt of his robe like a karate sensei preparing for mortal combat. 'He's allowed to be cynical of your little pop-psychology quizzes. It doesn't make him crazy.'

'Those are not normal sixteen-year-old answers,' my mom says, slamming the magazine down onto the counter.

I leave them to fight, hearing the argument degenerating into their usual relationship routines as I leave. As far as I can tell, daily tasks are marked on an invisible 'who is contributing most to this relationship?' scorecard. My dad unpacked the dishwasher last night but this was nullified by the fact that my mom had to spend most of the day rearranging their bedroom. 'If you don't fucking care about this relationship then maybe we should just forget about it!' is the last thing I hear my mom scream.

My dad's too soft. When they fight my mom will erupt with a string of curses that would make a taxi driver proud. But no matter how much they argue, he never swears. He probably submerges himself in the pool and screams into the blue nothingness when nobody is around.

I slam my door and fall dramatically onto my bed, then feel a bit stupid because there's nobody to see me. I prop myself up against a pillow and stare at the shrine of superhero posters I've built on the far wall – Rasputin, Machiavelli, Gordon Gekko and Robert Greene. 'Bet you guys didn't have to put up with this shit,' I say to them as I turn on my computer.

I'm checking emails when Esmé's avatar pops up in the corner of my screen:

VampireLust: I'm wetter than a housewife's cheeks during *TITANIC*.

Bax74:   Well, I'm harder than a trigonometry exam, baby.

VampireLust: So why don't you, you know, come over?

Bax74:   On my way.

I ninja my way down the stairs, carefully open the garage door and finesse my bike past the cars. My parents are in their room attempting to put a Band-Aid on the third-degree burn that is their marriage. There's no more screaming, which means they'll probably end up having gross middle-aged sex to a song by Toto and won't leave their room for the rest of the night. Bless the rains down in Africa all you want, old people, I'm going to get some real action.

I skirt the edge of the dirty canal that leads behind my house toward the railway tracks. It smells like wet dog and puke. One thing I love about the canal is its honesty; like a sick, swollen artery beneath the Botox of the suburbs. The homeless wash here listening to the sounds of rich people frolicking in their garden Jacuzzis. Through the windows you can see lawyers watching TV or bankers furtively looking at PornTube, while drunks have sex in the long grass that borders the canal. I pull my grey hoodie over my head and pedal faster.

After exactly seven minutes and thirty-seven seconds of fast cycling, during which I picture myself piloting a heavily armed interstellar craft, I steer my bike into the driveway of number 14 Grove Close and tap the door of the garage. There's the aching sigh of steel on steel as the door opens halfway and I slide my bike through the gap, ducking under to where Esmé is standing in the dim light holding a pair of garden shears and pulling a psycho face. 'Nice,' I say.

'I love that you appreciate my theatrical talents,' she says with a bow.

I push my bike in next to Olaf's silver Audi. Esmé stays here during the week with her mom and her stepdad Olaf, but is forced to spend the weekends with her father in Parow. We sneak through the large chrome kitchen and out the backdoor to Esmé's garden apartment.

Despite the chic fittings, Esmé's pad is a little different from your average teenage girl's. Mostly because she's a raging klepto and her room is like a giant shrine to thievery. She steals from everywhere she goes; coffee cups, clocks, jewellery, an 'Esmé Ave' road sign, a bowling pin and a dressage championship trophy. I know all of her talismans and take great pride in my ability to notice when she has stolen something new.

'Thief and thievee have a special bond,' she said the first time I came here. 'I have a connection with the owners of all these objects. It makes me feel less lonely in life.'

'Seriously?' I asked.

'No, stupid,' she said, rolling her eyes. 'I just like to take stuff without paying for it.'

She doesn't turn on any lights except the kitsch purple-and-green lava lamp that she stole from a crusty old weed dealer who had a crush on her. The resultant murky green ambience is like an underwater Chernobyl and she grins and pulls the psycho face again. 'Better,' I say, sliding closer to her. 'I really felt the bloodlust that time.'

Something scuttles across the floor as I wrap my arm around her waist. 'What the hell is that?' I say, jumping backwards.

'Oh, it's probably Hammy. He's gone missing. Got out of his cage.'

'No ways, that looked bigger than a hamster.'

'Oh please, Baxter, stop being paranoid. It's Hammy, I'm telling you.'

'OK, sorry,' I say, rubbing my eyes with the back of my hand. 'I've been a little stressed out lately.'

She grabs a colourful Mexican throw that was artfully stolen from the wall of a Mexican restaurant, takes my hand and we climb up onto the flat roof of her bedroom. The moon is playing kiss-catch with the clouds and bathing the roof in alternating periods of light and darkness.

Esmé spreads the throw on the roof and lies back on it. The moon dodges a cloud and we're bathed in light. I sprawl on the throw next to her and we look up at the stars.

'Twinkly,' Esmé says, stretching out her hands and wiggling her fingers at the stars.

'Hippy,' I say.

'Don't, like, bring any of your bad energy here, brah,' she says with a thick stoner twang.

'Fully sorry, bro,' I reply.

She rolls onto her stomach and looks at me. 'TILF or Die?' she says.

TILF or Die is one of our finest contributions to the world. It's a game with very simple rules: you give the name of a teacher to the other person and they have to decide if, in the event of a nuclear holocaust, they would sleep with that teacher to repopulate the world or if they'd rather let themself and humanity die first. We'd seen enough of each other's teachers at interschool events to get a good idea of their relative repulsiveness.

'Mr Bailey,' I say.

'Die,' she says as a cloud catches the moon and we're plunged into darkness. There's a flash of light in my brain and I see a vision of Esmé with her throat cut. There is an eye carved onto her forehead. I grit my teeth and blink my eyes frantically to make it go away.

'OK, that was easy,' I say quickly to cover my panic. Sweat prickles on my forehead. 'I get to ask another one. How about Mr Roddick?'

'Ew. Die. Actually, I'd gouge out my eyes first so that his face wouldn't be the last thing I saw. My turn. Ms Hunter.'

I breathe in deeply and force myself to be calm and logical. Stress can cause your mind to do weird things. My subconscious is dwelling on the Mountain Killer. That's a normal reaction. I knew Jody Fuller and she's dead. I'm just projecting that onto Esmé.

'TILF obviously,' I say.

'Really?' she asks.

'Absolutely.'

'Ew,' she says again as the moon frees itself from the cloud's sweaty embrace and showers us with silvery light. 'You OK?' She nudges me with her shoulder.

'Totally. Let's play again.' We play another couple of rounds and then settle into silence. I roll onto my stomach and look at her.

'Stop it,' she says, pushing a dark strand of hair out of her face.

'What?'

'Looking at me. With that all-knowing look, like you're looking right into me,' she says with a shudder. 'It's creepy.'

'Sorry.' I give a small shrug. 'It's a genetic thing.'

'Freak,' she says as another cloud hugs the moon. The darkness feels like it's gripping me by the throat.

'Hey.' She pushes herself up onto her elbows. 'I'm kidding.'

'I know,' I say hoarsely. 'I'm just –'

'It's OK,' she says, sliding forward to kiss me softly on the lips.

My heart cracks like a honeycomb splitting and drips thick gooey love into my chest. You know when you're a little kid and you think clouds are soft and smooth and you dream of rolling around in the sky on them? That's what making out with Esmé is like.

* * *

The next day doesn't exactly compete with the previous night in terms of excitement. My dad has fetched me from school at lunch break to take me to visit my grandfather, who lives in a depressing retirement home, which is a fifteen-minute drive from Westridge. The tyres of my dad's car crunch on the stones of the Shady Pines driveway and I look up at the old vine-covered building in despair. I have a thousand things to do and visiting old people is not on the agenda. I'm here because my grandfather is dying and I have been forced to come and pay my respects to the oldest of the Zevcenko lineage.

'Come on, Bax,' my dad says. 'It won't be that bad.'

'Sure,' I say sullenly.

It *will* be that bad, not least because Grandpa Zevcenko is 'different'. Which is a nice way of saying 'totally insane'. I haven't seen him since the Great Family Brawl of 2008, and that I'd really rather forget.

To understand the Great Brawl you need to understand my uncle Roger. My father's brother is a man who wears a wide-brimmed hat and speaks of the Devil as easily as other men speak about sport. Yes, Uncle Roger is a religious fanatic with burning eyes and a homoerotic love for the biggest Bearded One who patrols the clouds and your thoughts.

When Grandpa Zevcenko brought up the giant crows, Roger would stir like a great monitor lizard poked with a sharp stick, and Christmas 2008 was one such time. Grandpa Zev had been enjoying the Johnnie Walker a little too much that day, but nobody had minded at first. Food had been gluttoned, crackers had been cracked, family nostalgia had been indulged in, and everybody was sitting around in the soporific afterglow. An old, drunk grandfather was tolerable. That is until he started talking about the Crows.

Grandpa Zev, a green plastic Christmas hat perched rakishly

on his shaggy white hair, stood up unsteadily and addressed the room. Even at twelve I was the only one who guessed what was about to happen and I began to barricade myself into a corner with Christmas presents.

'The thing about the Crows is that they'll tear out your throat and then delicately drink your blood like they're sipping goddamn martinis,' he said. As a mood-killer it was a winner on all counts. There was a long silence before everybody tried to divert attention to something different at the same time. In all the noise, only Grandpa Zevcenko's voice could be clearly heard ringing out: 'The Crows will gouge out your eyeballs, if you give them half a chance!'

Uncle Roger stood up and faced my grandfather. 'Dad, there are no such things as giant crows,' he said, his voice tense and forced. Grandpa grinned the wild, ravenous grin of a madman. 'The Crows are more real than your imaginary friend in the sky, son.'

At that my uncle had taken an angry step forward. This was a mistake. Roger is a tall and broad-shouldered man, but Grandpa Zevcenko had been a champion boxer in the army and still had a solid right hook for an old guy. He dropped Uncle Roger easily. That's when all hell broke loose. Roger's wife Mariekie tried to intervene, but she caught the oldest Zevcenko in the midst of the fog of war. He grabbed her by the perm and shoved her head into the granadilla trifle and possibly would have held it there until she'd stopped thrashing had he not been restrained by my father and Darryl, the disabled neighbour, who vaulted off his wheelchair, grabbed him around the waist and pulled him to the floor.

As a twelve-year-old I learnt a lot from this experience. 1) If you're gonna drown someone in trifle, it's best to do it with no one else around. 2) My family are a bunch of circus freaks.

'He's not going to be around much longer,' my dad says as I get out of the car. 'Use this as a chance to say goodbye.'

I navigate the lilac-coloured hallways, past care workers carrying bedpans and mumbling, shuffling old people, until I find his room at the end of a corridor lit by a single, bare bulb. I take a deep breath, knock once, and then enter.

Grandpa's room is a sickly custard colour and it smells of urine smothered with fake lavender air-freshener. It's furnished with a single bed, dumpy beige armchairs draped with standard-issue old-person mohair blankets, a circular table and a small wooden cabinet in the corner of the room. A familiar white-haired figure sits on a rattan bench on the balcony and stares out over the lawn. I walk slowly over and clear my throat. 'I'm Baxter,' I say in the voice I usually use for babies and small dogs.

The figure swings around and fixes me with the knowing-eye. I stand still as it scans me, prodding and probing deeply with its intrusive gaze. 'I know who you are,' the old man says. Grandpa Zev has aged a lot. His skin is pale, almost translucent, and he is much frailer than I remember, but his blue eyes still glint with pure, unadulterated craziness.

'How are you, Grandpa?' I ask.

He shakes his head. 'I'm not your grandfather,' he says. 'I need to tell you the hard truth about your birth before I die.' He beckons me over with a withered hand and I sit on the bench next to him.

My grandfather is clearly insane, but why would he make up something like this? He clears his throat with a wet, hacking cough. 'Your father was the baby of a hooker I used to frequent. When she died of syphilis, your grandmother and I took him in and cared for him as our own.' The words hit me like tiny hammers. 'What...' I choke. 'But...'

He looks at me seriously for a second and then breaks into a bout of coughing laughter.

'I'm just fucking with you, Baxter,' he says, wheezing with

delight. 'That'll teach you to talk to me like I'm an invalid.' Well, it turns out he would say something like that because he's an asshole. Strangely that makes me like him more.

I was worried that there'd be nothing to say, but Grandpa Zev and I talk for ages. Something in my chest stirs as I talk to him, a warm sensation that feels a little like indigestion. I ignore it. He tells me about his parents, his dad a Pole and his mother an Afrikaner with strange religious tendencies. He tells me about growing up in Poland and being a lackey for organised crime as a teen. In a wave of spontaneity I tell him about the Spider and the porn business.

He nods thoughtfully. 'Good business to be in. If we'd have had something like that when I was your age, the war would have been a lot more fun.' He laughs. 'Growing up in Poland before the war we had our own Sprawl. Gangs, small-time thugs, political youth groups; everybody was trying to control the neighbourhood. And you know the most important thing I learnt?'

I lean in closer, eager to hear pearls of wisdom from the oldest, weirdest Zevcenko.

'None of it means shit,' he says with a phlegmy laugh. 'The Nazis came in and took it all. And then they got their ass kicked and then it was the Russians. No matter how powerful you think you are there's always a bigger fish in the sea.' He bursts into a riot of coughing and waves a trembling hand at the small wooden cabinet in the corner of the room. 'Black bottle,' he splutters.

I walk over to the cabinet, open it and survey the vast quantities of medical supplies therein. I locate the large black medicinal bottle and carry it over to Grandpa Zev. He takes it with a shaky hand, unstops it and takes a swig. 'Gin,' he says. 'These fascists won't let me have a drop of alcohol so I have to secrete it away.' He hands me the bottle and I take a swig. The liquid burns brightly in my throat like a welding iron.

'What about women?' he says. 'Are you going steady with anyone?'

'There is a girl,' I say.

'Do you love her?' I want to say no. I want to tell him that a large part of me thinks that love is an unnecessary complication. That no matter what combination of dopamine and serotonin floods my brain when I see Esmé, she's just a piece of the board like everybody else. But I can't.

'Maybe,' I whisper.

He nods. 'We Zevcenkos are strange creatures. We don't find love easily. But when we do we imprint for life and nothing can keep us away from the object of our affections.' He grimaces and takes another swig of the gin. 'Well, almost nothing.'

'You and Grandma?' I say.

He chuckles. 'I'm afraid not, my boy. Oh, your grandmother and I had our moments, but I had already found and lost the love of my life by the time she came around. Nothing she could have done would have changed that.'

'What happened?' I ask.

'Crows happened,' he spits out viciously, gripping the neck of the bottle like it's the hilt of a sword. 'And when Crows happen, there's not much you can do to stop it.'

That cold, uneasy feeling slides down my neck again but I try to shake it off. My grandfather's delusions are the result of a decaying brain. Nothing to get worked up about.

The old man squeezes my hand absently. 'Before I met your grandmother I was in love with another woman. A girl, really, with pale white skin, slanted green eyes and the strangest ears you've ever seen.' He smiles wistfully at the memory. 'She was beautiful, like a strange animal, and just as skittish. She said she was the last of her kind, the last of a lineage of royalty that had been hunted down. We fell in love.'

'You're not screwing with me again, are you, Grandpa?' I say.

'I know it sounds ridiculous,' he says. 'Like a fairytale. Sometimes I do think I just made the whole thing up.'

'So what happened. To you and the … princess?'

'*They* came for her.' He looks at me and his eyes are wide, almost hysterical. 'Terrible, Baxter, like nothing you've ever seen before.' He fumbles for the edge of his shirt and pulls it up to show me his wrinkled, hairy old torso. 'I tried to fight them,' he says pleadingly. 'But there were too many of them. I couldn't have stopped them, I couldn't have saved her.' His finger absently traces a thick, jagged scar that runs from his left nipple down to his belly button. 'Promise me, Baxter,' he says, wheezing now and clutching at my hand.

'Promise you what, Grandpa?' I say softly.

'Promise me that if you love someone like I loved her, you'll fight for them. Promise me.'

'I promise, Grandpa,' I say.

He nods. 'I regret what's happened with my family, but I can't pretend I didn't see what I saw.' He sighs and the weight of the world seems to slip from his shoulders. 'You ever get caught by Crows, kid, this is what you do …'

IndieFilm Magazine
Is Monster Porn the Next Big Thing?
By Joni Stewart

Stilted dialogue, bedroom eyes and werewolves, goblins and vampires; when you start watching a Glamorex film you may be forgiven for thinking you're watching the latest teenage supernatural romance.

It's only when the hot and heavy action begins that you realise this is no chaste foray into the paranormal. Hollywood has been doing big business with franchises involving wizards, angels and vampires, and the porn industry has been quick to follow suit.

With titles such as *Tokoloshe Money Shot*, *Anansi Zombie Chamber* and *Dwarven Ass Patrol*, Glamorex Films has shot to the forefront of this eldritch porn revolution, combining cutting-edge special effects and high production values with the top names in pornography to create films that go way beyond the average pool boy and bored housewife routines.

'There definitely is a trend toward the supernatural,' says Toni McBain, Head of Marketing at Glamorex Films. 'Glamorex was the first to realise that people wanted to see vampires and werewolves swapping more than just smouldering looks.' This realisation has led to Glamorex transforming from a backyard porn outfit into a multi-million-dollar business – all in the space of three years. This rise has partly been fuelled by conspiracy websites claiming that the weird and wonderful monsters in Glamorex's cinematic orgies are the real deal.

McBain laughs at the suggestion. 'Sure they're real. We've got real dwarves, fairies and goblins going at it 24/7. It's a real circus.'

They may not be hiding a menagerie of supernatural porn stars, but Glamorex's business is notoriously secretive. Their performers may not be real monsters, but the company trades on the aura of authenticity, never revealing the true identities of the porn stars beneath the elaborate costumes. The whereabouts of the Flesh Palace, the location where most of their movies are shot, is known only to a select few, those lucky enough to be invited when the establishment opens its doors to offer the city's elite a taste of its delights.

The mysterious Flesh Palace has become the Playboy mansion of the Cape, and the parties thrown for Cape Town's VIPs are rumoured to include strange and forbidden pleasures.

McBain says all the secrecy is just a precaution. 'We've had to keep everything secret to protect our performers. If it's not obsessed fans, it's religious protesters; they're prime targets for crazies.'

However, not everybody is enamoured by this new wave of pornography. The Cape Feminist League is vehement in their criticism of Glamorex's business. 'Creature porn represents a new step in the systematic dehumanisation of those involved in the sex industry,' says Claire Fulton, media liaison officer for the League. 'How can "creatures" be afforded any kind of respect?'

Glamorex's reputation is not helped by the involvement of an alleged member of an organised crime syndicate. Yuri 'the Russian' Belkin is a part-owner of Glamorex and is currently under investigation over allegations that he has kidnapped underage girls to appear in his movies.

Sexual revolutionaries or sickos, whatever your take on Glamorex's business, one thing is for certain: supernatural romance has never been this NSFW.

THE UNBEARABLE INCONVENIENCE
OF HAVING A HEART

My dad drops me back at school later that afternoon and tries to give me an awkward hug which I manage to dodge. I don't know what it is about school gates that brings out the emotional sides of parents. It's like the gates elicit some kind of Pavlovian response for inappropriate emotional gestures. Thankfully, he didn't want to know much about my conversation with Grandpa Zev. Because I wouldn't even know where to begin to explain the crazy stuff the old man was talking about.

Back in class we're learning about the reproductive system of the earthworm for a third straight week. Mr Roddick relishes each detail, almost pleading with us to see the beauty, the complexity and the elegance of Nature's most unappreciated dirt-dweller. It's like a guitar enthusiast trying to share his passion for Steve Vai with a group of deaf people.

There's an air of chaos in the class, as if the NPCs can smell the trouble that's brewing at the top of the food chain. Denton de Jaager sits at the back of the class and confers with some of his lieutenants. He glances over in my direction every now and again, as if to remind me that I'm not forgotten. That's a good thing. I'm just about to casually move over to his desk when the Bearded One appears in the classroom doorway and stands fidgeting while Mr Roddick finishes a particularly dull anecdote about how his enthusiasm for earthworms was first ignited.

The story concludes and the Bearded One leans over to whisper in Mr Roddick's ear. Roddick turns to look directly at me and my heart doesn't just skip a beat, it hurdles over it. Roddick listens carefully to the Bearded One for a few seconds and then nods.

'Baxter Zevcenko,' he says grimly. 'The headmaster wishes to speak to you privately.'

The entire class turns as a single entity to look at me. I stand and make my way to the front of the class. I feel strangely calm, as if I'm in a car crash and I'm watching the glass and metal explode around me. They've linked porn back to me. My mind immediately goes to the worst-case scenario: Dennis Brown, the school's only Jehovah's Witness, plagued by a fit of guilt at the *Big Latino Mamma's Compilation* I sold him, told his real mamma about the porn and where he got it from. Mrs Brown's religious zeal is terrifying and when she decides that something is the work of the Devil she'll destroy it completely. I have no doubt that Mrs Brown thinks I'm the spawn of Satan. I'm going to be expelled. Maybe Mrs Brown will force the school to call the cops. Maybe they'll comply. Maybe they won't. Whatever happens, it's out of my hands now.

'Baxter,' the Bearded One says in the corridor outside the class, 'I'm afraid I have some very bad news. Esmé van der Westhuizen has been missing since last night.' The car crash pauses in midair and I blink furiously trying to make sense of it.

'Esmé?' I say. 'She's probably at her dad's. Or at a friend's.'

The Bearded One shakes his head. 'She's not, Baxter. I don't mean to alarm you, but the police believe she may have been taken by the Mountain Killer.'

The car crash unpauses and turns in a nuclear conflagration. Things explode in my head. Whole cities vanish.

'But I saw her two nights ago,' I say dumbly.

'I'm sorry, Baxter,' the Bearded One says, putting a hand on my shoulder. 'The police are doing everything they can.'

I stumble back into class. The class-herd tries to elicit information from me but I barely register their presence.

'What's up?' Kyle whispers. 'Bax?'

I ignore him. All I can see is the image of Esmé with her throat cut and an eye carved on her forehead.

I walk the hallways in a daze. It seems everybody now knows about Esmé's disappearance and I have to dodge well-wishers and gloaters in equal amounts. I lean against the cool granite wall in the quad and take a few deep breaths. I have a searing headache and my breathing is shallow and ragged. I feel like I can't draw in enough oxygen to survive.

Then something bizarre happens. I can't exactly explain it so I'm going to try to express it in an equation. If I were to mathematically express what is going on in my head it would look a little like: (d)reams + (g)eneral weirdness + (k)idnapped girlfriend = (m)ultiple personalities. I'm not exactly Jekyll and Hyde, but two distinct voices emerge within my head, battling it out for ultimate supremacy of my cranium.

First there's the logical, clinical, businessman me. This is the me that creates plans, devises schemes and shifts pawns around like Kasparov. This me would drink neat vodka while stealing candy from babies and life savings from old people. This Donald Trump of the cerebellum I immediately dub BizBax.

The other is a personality I didn't even know I had. This is the me that feels. Gross, I know. This me probably attends crystal-healing sessions in my cerebral cortex, believes people are important and almost certainly likes piña colada and getting caught in the rain.

He is a flaming metrosexual. I call him MetroBax.

Perhaps these two parts of me have always been there, their chatter a subtle murmur beneath my conscious mind, but since hearing about Esmé's disappearance, they've become seriously talkative:

BizBax: It sucks, but the truth is that Esmé is just a pawn like anyone else. A valuable pawn, one that comes with unique intimacies and affections; a pawn with benefits. But a pawn nonetheless.

MetroBax: This is Esmé we're talking about. Esmé. She introduced us to Nerdcore rap and banana, peanut butter and honey sandwiches.

BizBax: And that information was gratefully assimilated but we can't get nostalgic about it. Besides, what can we do?

MetroBax: We need to help find her. I believe that working together we can achieve anything. After all, it's not our darkness we're afraid of. It's our light…

BizBax: You know what's dark? Geriatric amputee bestiality.

MetroBax: That's disgusting. Why would you even say that?

BizBax: Because I am who I am. I'm the real Baxter, you're just an afterbirth of the psyche.

Insanity; it always seemed like so much more fun on TV. I clutch my head and try to make the voices stop. The businessman part of me is right. I can't let this distract me. A calm comes over me as I ruthlessly shove the emotions back down.

Love? You're an idiot, Zevcenko. Think of all the pathetic love songs ever sung. Think about all that wasted time and effort for something that is now evolutionarily irrelevant. You're programmed to love so that you can secure the perpetuation of your genes. You know what else will secure the perpetuation of your genes? A sperm bank.

The real legacy that I should be thinking about is the Spider.

We have the opportunity to create something great and your brain splattering oxytocin around is just getting in the way. Forget your adolescent dreams. Forget Esmé.

The next morning, it's Whitney Houston that does it. Not content with ruining her life with crack she's taken to ruining mine with the emotional knuckleduster that is 'I Will Always Love You'. The radio switches on at 7.13 a.m. and sends Whitney's high-pitched wailing to kick my ass.

There's a sharp pain in my chest and I feel short of breath. The walls of the room lurch and spin like I'm on an out-of-control fairground ride. I gasp for air. 'Mom,' I shout. 'MOM!' There's a thud of footsteps coming up the steps and then my mother sticks her curl-framed face into my room.

'What's the matter?' she says with a worried look.

'I think I'm having a heart attack,' I gasp, clutching my chest. She sits on my bed and puts her hand on my chest, checks my pulse, feels my head and then smiles at me.

'Baxter,' she says, 'you never were a very emotional boy. You're like your father that way.'

'What's wrong with me?' I say, clutching my chest again. 'It hurts so much.'

My mom smiles her infuriating smile again. 'I think you're worried about Esmé,' she says. 'You're having a panic attack.' The idea is so ludicrous, so transparently, pop-psychologically vapid that, well, it might just be true. My mind becomes unhinged again, split down the centre with logical, clinical businessman Baxter on one side and feely, emotional, metrosexual Baxter on the other.

BizBax: We've obviously been ingesting too much oestrogen from the plastic in our food. It's affecting our judgement.

MetroBax: It's our girlfriend. If we're cut, do we not bleed?

BizBax: Cry me a river. Let me tell you a little story. When Thomas Farnsworth tried to scale the north face of Everest in 1976, his expedition got stuck in an avalanche. His entire climbing crew was lost and he had to cut up their corpses with a shard of glass and eat them to survive. He lost all his fingers and toes from frostbite. While gnawing on the gall bladder of a friend do you think he stopped and cried like a little bitch?

MetroBax: You made that up, didn't you?

BizBax: The factual inaccuracy does not affect the sentiment, which, in case you missed it, is stop being such a goddamn pussy.

MetroBax: That night when you were first with Esmé. You remember that? If you can honestly and truly tell me what you felt I'll leave you alone, you emotionless cyborg. Just tell me.

'Love,' I say.

My mother leans forward from her perch on the end of my bed and looks at me quizzically. 'Baxter?'

'Love,' I say again. 'That's what I felt when I first met Esmé.' My mother beams with all the benevolence of a medieval Christian mystic. 'I knew you were in there somewhere,' she says, softly tapping my chest.

It's time to undergo a fundamental recalibration. A shifting of paradigms brought about by the introduction of new data into what I had previously thought was a closed feedback loop. I thought love was a ridiculous kids' story that only stupid adults believed in. Like politicians' promises and Scientology. But it's real. The shifting of paradigms is finished. The information is assimilated. Old directive: Prevent gang war at Westridge. New directive: Save Esmé from whoever has taken her and rip out their heart. Just try to stop me.

* * *

The Van der Westhuizen house is a riot of activity. I weave my bike through the cops and reporters that have congealed at the front door. 'Nobody but family and friends,' a large cop says, putting a restraining hand on my handlebars.

'I'm Esmé's boyfriend,' I say. 'I've come to see the family.'

'I've got a kid here who says he's the kidnapped girl's boyfriend,' he barks into his radio.

'Let him in,' a voice squelches from the radio. The cop jerks a thumb toward the door. I lean my bike up against the wall and turn the ornate brass handle of the front door to step inside.

Inside, relatives are standing around and patting one another consolingly like great apes. Several policemen are wandering aimlessly around the living room as if expecting Esmé to pop out from behind one of the giant pastel-pink couches. Esmé's mother is perfectly made up and is playing host, as if this were a party she'd thrown. 'Oh, we're trying to be strong, but Esmé is our babbbbieee,' she says, steadying herself against the large ceramic sculpture of a Dalmatian that squats at the entrance to the lounge.

From what I can glean, the disappearance of Esmé went down like this: her mother and Olaf, her stepdad, had gone out to a function and left her watching TV. They'd come back to find an Esmé-less garden apartment. They had phoned her friends, phoned me too, apparently, but my phone had been off. No Esmé.

Sandra van der Westhuizen is a chiselled Aryan specimen who looks like she could headbutt a rhino into submission. Which, in a sense, is what she'd done. Olaf was said rhinoceros, an Incredible Hulk of a man, which only made his matrimonial humiliation all the more poignant. There was no question of who wore the beige chinos in the Van der Westhuizen house.

'Baxter,' Sandra says with pretend enthusiasm, batting her false eyelashes and touching her freckly, gold-cross-adorned chest. She hates me, of course. She told Esmé that it's because she thinks

I'm a bad influence, but I suspect that my eye condition strikes a deep chord of distrust in her ovaries. I'm just a bad genetic choice for her daughter. Sorry, darling, evolutionary psychology is just not that into you.

'I know you must feel awful, just awful, but there was really no reason to come,' Sandra says. She fake-kisses me on both cheeks and leads me away from her relatives. 'We'll let you know as soon as we hear anything, but in the meantime perhaps you can speak to Sergeant Schoeman about Esmé's disappearance. Maybe you know something that might help.' She ushers me into the kitchen.

'Sergeant,' Sandra says to the man sitting at the kitchen table, 'this is Baxter. Esmé's … friend. Perhaps he can help.' She pats me once on the shoulder and then returns to *the* grieving event of the season.

Sergeant Schoeman is a big man. No, let's not euphemise. He is fat. Hugely fat. Obese, in fact. To clarify, Sergeant Schoeman is the Michelin man of the South African police force, a giant cream doughnut of a man stuffed into a worn leather jacket. A dark goatee wraps around his lips like he's been huffing on an exhaust pipe. He nods to me and points to the chair across the table from his.

'So you're the boyfriend, sugar?' he drawls as I sit down.

'What did you call me?' I say.

'Um, nothing,' he says, his large face drawing inward into a deep scowl. 'I'm asking the questions around here. Name?'

'Baxter Zevcenko,' I say.

'Zevcenko, Zevcenko,' he says, tapping his pen against his chin. 'Not one of the Zevcenkos that used to live in Bergvliet?'

'No,' I say.

'Oh, wait, that wasn't Zevcenko, that was Zarkowitz. First question. Did you make the double-backed beast with your disappeared lover?' he asks.

'I'm sorry?'

'Coitus, sexual intercourse, the horizontal mambo on the dance floor of love, the –'

'ok cop, pig, orificer, I get the idea. How's that relevant?' I say.

He curls his mouth into a smile. 'Just trying to ascertain whether it's a crime of passion,' he says, scribbling something in his notebook. His hand is huge but he writes delicately, as if writing in a fluffy pink diary instead of a police notebook.

'You think I had something to do with this?' I say.

'Just answer the question,' he says.

'Yes,' I say. 'I had sex with her.'

'Nice!' he says, holding his hand up for a high five.

I stare at him. He chuckles. 'The thing that interests me is that you also knew Jody Fuller.'

'I barely knew Jody,' I stutter. 'And why do you think Esmé was taken by the Mountain Killer? From what I've read in the papers this isn't exactly his mo.'

'I'd agree with you,' he says. 'If it wasn't for the large eye carved into her wall.'

He opens an envelope and slides a photograph across the table. It's a picture of Esmé's room and, indeed, a large jagged eye has been carved into the wallpaper.

'What do you know about the Eye of the Sieners?' Schoeman asks, tapping the photograph with a thick, sausage-like finger. The word 'Sieners' reverberates through my mind. 'That's what it's called,' he continues. 'The eye. It's some Afrikaans mystical bullshit.'

'I've never heard of it,' I say, averting my eyes from the photograph.

'Like you say, this is something that the killer has never done before. So maybe this is a special case. Maybe he has a special relationship with Esmé.'

'Stop beating around the bush,' I say, sliding the photograph back across the table. 'Just spit it out.'

Schoeman smiles, baring his canines and causing his jowls to wobble. 'Full of yourself, aren't you?' he says. 'But OK, I'll say it. I think you have something to do with Esmé's disappearance.'

'This is ridiculous,' I say, standing up. He leans across the table, surprisingly quickly for a fat guy, and grabs my hand. With a jerk he twists it back so that pain shoots up my arm, forcing me to sit back down.

'What the hell are you doing?' I hiss through the pain. 'That fucking hurts.'

'Don't make the mistake of thinking you're dealing with your average dull-witted cop, Baxter,' he says, leaning in close to my face. 'I'm going to catch the killer and I'm not messing around.' He lets go of my hand and leans back in his seat. 'So I'm only going to ask you this once: anything you feel like getting off your chest?'

'No,' I say, rubbing my hand. 'I didn't kidnap Esmé. So why don't you do your job and find out who did?'

'Baxter?' he says as I get up to leave.

'Yes?'

'If you're the Mountain Killer, I'm going to find out.'

I slip out of a side door and walk around the back to Esmé's apartment. Judging by the grey powder on the doorframe the place has already been fingerprinted. I look around for cops but the media circus out front is keeping them busy. I nudge the door open with my elbow and step inside. There's a pang in my heart as I look through her collection of curios. Everything is pretty much the way it was when I'd last been here.

I look carefully through her stuff, but nothing is out of place. I'm about to leave when I see something sticking out from underneath her dresser. I get down on my knees to look at it. It's a small skeleton. Hammy. He looks like he's been gnawed on by some kind of animal. Jesus. I push the skeleton away with my foot and notice something else as I stand up. A strangely shaped grey tooth is poking out from beneath the rug next to the dresser. I pick it up. The one side is serrated and it's warm to the touch. There's something really odd about it. Out of the corner of my eye it looks like it's glowing.

It's not something Esmé's stolen. I know that because she would have told me the story of the thievery, deftly weaving the tale of the sleight of hand and misdirection that had allowed her to make off with her prize. I slip it into my pocket and then climb over the back wall of her garden and into the alleyway behind her house. I slink round the front, grab my bike and push it slowly along the canal.

I put my hand in my pocket and feel the tooth as I walk home. It's possible that she intentionally left it there to tell me something. But what? Alternatively it's some kind of new calling card for the Mountain Killer, but I can't even begin to process that. This emotionally vulnerable thing is completely new to me and, to be honest, I can't really see the point of it. What's the point of an internal state that makes it impossible for you to think about things rationally? Surely the opposite should apply. Surely I should be rational, clinical and lucid enough to evaluate all of the evidence objectively. But the dull ache in my chest, and the spiralling cacophony of worry that wraps itself around my head, just won't listen to reason.

I squeeze my hand tightly around the tooth and wheel my bike back through the mud, grass and litter next to the canal.

It's one o'clock in the morning before I admit that the insomnia has won. I wait until I can hear the familiar hiss of my parents' white-noise machine and then take my bike out of the garage and pedal slowly through the suburbs. A thin dog slides through the shadows in front of me like an eel. I aim my bike at it and it disappears into the night.

I freewheel down a hill toward the canal and the smell of kids smoking joints in the corners curls around me like a cloak, reaching the old oak tree that looms over the canal. I lean against the gnarled oak and run my fingers over the scarred bark. This is where I kissed Jody Fuller.

Jody Fuller is dead. I try to imagine her empty body and can't. All I can think of is the milky taste of her mouth and the aloof look in her eyes. I wonder how many other people kissed her. Am I alone or part of an exclusive club that know what her lips tasted like? 'Please don't let Esmé be dead,' I whisper to the tree.

'Jy,' a whisper comes from inside the canal like the sound of a bicycle tyre deflating. I stare down into the dark concrete channel and see a man slumped against the wall of the canal. 'Give me an entjie,' he says, putting his fingers to his mouth in the universal gesture for 'cigarette'.

I move a little closer and see that he is sitting on an old paint tin, grinning up at me toothlessly. His face is covered in the grey-green ink of prison tattoos, an esoteric infographic of rank, affiliation and brutal misdeed that I'm glad I can't decipher.

One of his eyes is milky white. He hoists a battered three-stringed guitar onto his lap and widens his gummy grin. I pull my cigarettes from my pocket and toss one down to him, keeping one foot on the pedal and ready just in case he is meaning to continue this conversation with a knife.

He takes the cigarette and I throw him down the lighter. He cups over the cigarette and his face glows orange as he lights it. 'Who don't you want to be dead, laaitie?' he murmurs around the cig.

'Nobody,' I say. 'Can I have my lighter back?'

'You remind me of a girl I once met. On a battlefield long ago. Who are you praying to?'

'I wasn't praying,' I say.

He takes a drag of the cigarette and plucks one of the strings on the guitar. It sends a discordant note jangling into the night. 'You see down there?' He waves the cigarette in a circle to indicate an area further downriver. The light from the coal burns a chaotic pattern on my retina. 'That's where two young men were stripped naked and executed by gangsters as part of an initiation.' He takes another drag. 'And further down, a Congolese refugee hanged himself from a tree because he couldn't get a passport. Strange fruit for motorists to gawk at on their morning commute. And the world forgets, but this black river remembers and carries the memories. This is where the lost spirits of the dead come to cross. I am the Singer of Souls. I lay to rest the spirits of the dead and make sure their memories remain alive,' he says softly, his milky eye rolling back in his head as if examining a part of his brain.

'Sure,' I say. 'Does that pay well?'

He ignores me and begins to sing a wordless song, his voice low and guttural like the gurgling of one of the sewage pipes that empties into the dark water of the canal. The tone rises and falls and then he begins to chant:

'At the beginning of time two brothers, the Mantis and the Octopus, travelled the depths of space searching for a place to call their own. They came upon a planet, untouched and virgin and they each claimed it for themselves. In order to settle the dispute they had a contest. Whoever could give birth to the best creations would claim the world for their own.'

He strums another chord as if to punctuate his words; a jangling, rattling exclamation mark hung behind the image of two ancient space gods having a turf war over Earth. I sit on my bike unable to move, his words painting a vivid picture in the dank air.

'*The Mantis went first and birthed the Watu Makule – the oldest tribe – consisting of the little men, the shining ones, the pointed ears, the horned horses and all the wondrous creatures. The Octopus, looking upon the magnificent Watu Makule, knew he could not beat his brother. The Mantis took pity on him and offered a compromise. They would share the Earth and together they would create a new species, humans, to live together with them. They called them the Strange Ones because of their dual natures.*

'*But the Mantis was tired after his works of creation and fell asleep. He slept for millennia and while he slept the Octopus conspired against him. He was still jealous of the Watu Makule and so alone he created the Feared Ones, black of feather and black of heart, born with the sole purpose of hunting the Watu Makule and killing them. And while the Mantis slept, the Watu Makule were hunted, slaughtered, until they were forced to hide in the shadows. And they became known as the Hidden Ones, forever cowering in fear.*

'*When the Mantis awoke he was so enraged at the genocide inflicted upon his creations that he attacked his brother and for millennia the gods fought so fiercely that their fighting began to threaten the very Earth they so coveted. To save themselves, the Watu Makule and the Strange Ones united to trap their own Creators in living cages to stop them destroying the Earth.*

'*But the Feared Ones missed their Creator, and so the story continues, with the Feared Ones forever hunting down the Watu Makule and seeking a way to release their Creator.'*

Abruptly he stops playing. 'One day the gods will fight again and the world will be destroyed,' he whispers. 'You know this, because the Eye remembers.'

The mention of the Eye hits my nervous system like a well-aimed bullet. Abject fear opens the adrenalin gates and before

I know what's happening I've pushed off from the kerb and am pedalling hard away from the canal. I'm breathing raggedly and my forehead is throbbing with a now familiar pulse. The Eye. I pull hard on the brakes and skid on a patch of gravel, the bike sliding out from under me. I hit the ground hard and feel the sharp fiery pain of my hands sliding across the ground.

I get up and cycle back to the canal. This half-blind asshole is going to tell me what's going on. 'Hey!' I shout into the canal. I stop my bike and throw it down onto the grass. 'I've had enough, OK?' I peer down into the darkness of the canal. There is no one there. No blind singer. No guitar. Just an empty paint can. I look up and down the canal. 'What the fuck is going on?' I say to the night, and at that moment I realise that my life is stretched like a rope tight across a gaping chasm and I can see the fibres beginning to fray and snap. I need help and I need it soon.

Dr Basson's office is a twenty-minute ride from my house. I cycle through the morning traffic, through the taxi rank and up onto the main road, pumping the pedals of my bike ruthlessly. Sweat pours down my face and into my eyes and my forehead is throbbing. I'm on the verge of a migraine but I keep on pedalling. Skipping school and leaving the gangs to their own devices is bad for the Spider. But I have to. For the first time I feel like I'm starting to lose my handle on things.

I pull up outside the office block – all steel, glass and red face brick. I chain my bike to a lamppost and enter through the glass sliding doors. The security guard, sinewy with a mullet and bad skin, looks me up and down as I comb my sweaty hair to one side and wipe my glasses with my sleeve.

'Sign in,' the guard grunts. I sign the book and take the lift up to the third floor. I walk quickly until I find the door – an opaque glass door with 'Dr Kobus Basson – Psychiatrist' written on it in white type. I press the buzzer.

'Yes?' Basson says.

'It's Baxter,' I answer.

There's a short silence and then the door clicks open.

'Welcome,' Dr Basson says in his thin, eager voice. He is tall and emaciated, his nose narrow and hawk-like, his cheekbones jutting sharply from his face. His watery blue eyes look surprised, but he smiles and runs a scarred hand through his greasy, thinning hair, which is tied with a rainbow scrunchie at the back of his head to form a little rattail.

He gestures for me to follow him into his consulting rooms. 'Well, this is unexpected. Your next appointment isn't until Wednesday.'

'I think something's wrong with me,' I say.

He gives me a concerned look. 'Well, then I'm glad you came,' he says. 'You're in luck. I don't have any appointments this morning. Would you like to talk?'

I nod quickly.

'Coffee?' he asks, limping over to an urn in the corner of the room.

'Please,' I say as I sit on the long leather couch next to his desk.

I sit and stare at the two photographs on the wall, something I always do when I come here. One is of Table Mountain, and the other of an old sea captain, grizzled and bad-tempered, a long red beard cascading down his chin.

On his desk there are two photo frames; one holding a picture of two men in military uniform, one turned so I can't see what's in it.

I bounce my feet irritably on the ground. There's a stack of magazines next to me and I flick listlessly through a few of them while Basson meticulously makes two cups of coffee. He has a painfully slow coffee-making ritual and the waiting is making me doubt my reasons for coming here.

I've recently realised that my view of myself – that of the Machiavellian mastermind, unhindered by emotional ties and attachments – is flawed. That's bound to cause me anxiety, right?

My hypnagogic visions, the dreams about Boers and mantises, are merely a biological reaction to stress; a kind of mental defragging process that has understandably been influenced by the historical stuff Rafe unrelentingly tries to shove down my throat.

And my experience with the old homeless guy last night? Well, that was confirmation bias. I'm looking for answers and I made his ravings fit my need for a narrative.

Basson shuffles over to give me my mug and then moves back to his desk where he lowers himself carefully into his chair.

'I'm glad you came,' he says. 'But you've never really shown any enthusiasm for our sessions, so I admit I'm a little surprised.'

'Esmé's been kidnapped,' I blurt out.

Basson raises his eyebrows. 'My God. When?'

'Two nights ago,' I say. 'The police think it might be the Mountain Killer.'

'Oh, Baxter,' Basson says. 'I'm so sorry. Are you OK?'

'I don't know,' I say. 'No, I don't think so. I'm … hearing things; voices.'

A pen materialises in his hand and he begins writing furiously, as if he's possessed by some kind of creative spirit. 'And what are these voices saying?' he says.

'They're arguing,' I reply. 'It's like two parts of me are fighting each other.'

His writing becomes more furious, like he's trying to capture the very essence of my problem in words. 'Stress can have a very powerful effect on the mind. Having someone that you love put in harm's way can be very stressful. You do love her, don't you, Baxter?'

Crunch time. A direct question that I can't avoid. Love.

Thousands of songs, poems, books have been written about the disturbing quivering of internal organs in response to neurochemical stimuli. Is that what this feeling is? Inside I say yes.

Outside I say, 'No. Yes. Maybe.'

He opens a desk drawer and pulls a brown folder from it. 'I have some of your school reports here. They suggest you have a very high verbal and conceptual intelligence far beyond that of your peers. Like many intelligent people, however, your empathetic skills lag behind. And yet here you are expressing your love for a girl. Sometimes when you love someone you can accidentally hurt them. You didn't hurt Esmé accidentally, did you?'

'Fuck you,' is my immediate response. Then, 'You think I hurt Esmé too? Jesus Christ, what is wrong with you people?'

'Do you ever have violent thoughts or dreams?' he counters.

'No,' I say.

He shakes his head. 'Baxter, if we're going to work together you can't lie to me.'

Since when are psychiatrists mind readers? 'OK, yes,' I say. 'I have strange dreams about Afrikaners and ox-wagons. Yes, I have violent dreams and thoughts. That doesn't make me a goddamn serial killer.'

Basson nods. 'Of course not. Tell me about these dreams,' he continues. 'I think they're the key to the way you're feeling.'

I THINK YOU'RE PHONEY AND
I LIKE YOU A LOT

'I've done a complete cost-benefit analysis,' Kyle says. He's wearing mirrored wrap-around sunglasses and a bright Hawaiian shirt, and together they make him look like an extra in the sci-fi remake of *Cocktail*. The rain of the past couple of days has transformed into stifling heat and we're sitting slumped in lounge chairs next to my green, algae-infested pool.

Weeks ago we stole a garden gnome from the next-door neighbour's garden, and today Kyle has set it up on the old, decaying diving board to throw stones at it. Kyle is a big fan of the small things in life.

'Take a look, Bax,' he says. 'I think I've made a good case.' He picks up a large shard of rock with one hand and gives me a page of writing with the other. He lobs the rock at the gnome but it misses by light years.

Kyle has terrible aim but does make a pretty good case for just leaving Esmé kidnapped:

'Point 1: A steady girlfriend at sixteen increases your chances of ending up as one of those people who marry their high-school sweethearts and then realise in middle age that they've lived a miserable, stunted half-life.' All too true. Have you seen some of those people? Missionary city.

'Point 2: You could ride the sympathy wave indefinitely for maximum personal and organisational benefit.' One thing I can say for Kyle: he speaks my language. A kidnapped girlfriend is right up there with cancer and autism as far as getting away with stuff goes. I could probably be dealing porn openly in religious studies class by the end of the month.

'Both sound points,' I say. And it's true. Unfortunately they don't take into account the alien love foetus that's clawing inside my chest. So I decide to come out of the closet. If I can't reveal my true nature to my best friend then I can't reveal it to anyone. 'Maybe some things can't be decided by a cost-benefit analysis,' I say. 'Like love.'

Kyle stares at me. Then a big dumb grin spreads across his face. 'I guess this is what you'd call a defining moment,' he says.

'I guess it is.'

'I'm sorry about that.' He nods at the pages in my hand. 'I thought it was what you wanted.'

I sigh. 'I thought so too. But what can I say? I love her.'

'You're a real boy, Pinocchio,' he says in a high-pitched voice.

'Piss off.'

'Well, now we've established that you love her, what are we going to do?'

I reach into my pocket and hand him the tooth from Esmé's room. He pushes his wrap-arounds up onto his head. 'What in the name of Haile Selassie is that?' he asks.

'I found it in Esmé's room. I think the kidnapper may have left it.'

'It's glowing,' he murmurs as he turns it around between his fingers.

'I know. How weird is that?'

'What kind of tooth glows?'

I shrug helplessly. 'I've been trying to figure that out.'

'It might be some kind of UV spray,' he says thoughtfully.

'Why would a kidnapper do that?' I say as I pick up a smooth stone and balance it on my hand to test the weight.

'Maybe he's into rave?' he says. 'I'll do some research, see if there's any kind of tech that can do that. Oh, and I got into Esmé's bank account online.'

'How the hell did you do that?'

He pushes his sunglasses back down onto his nose. 'Her PIN is her birth date. You might want to tell her to change that when we find her. There are no charges on her debit card since she's gone missing, but I'll change the contact details so that I get a text if she uses it.'

I flick the stone at the gnome. It clips his little red hat and causes him to teeter on the edge of the diving board. I'm about to take another shot when I look up to see my least favourite retard standing at the other end of the pool. Despite the heat he's dressed in camo cargo pants and a thick orange jersey that brings out the redness of his mussed-up hair and makes him look like his head is on fire. He's clutching a magazine to his chest and staring at us.

'What?' I say.

He holds up the magazine.

'Great, so you can read. My hearty congratulations,' I say acidly.

He walks slowly around the edge of the pool and comes to stand in front of the lounge chair I'm lying on. Carefully he places the magazine on the edge of the chair, opens it to a page and then stands back, as if presenting gold to the baby Jesus. I feel the rage rising. 'I don't want to read your dumbass magazine,' I hiss.

'Bax,' Kyle says. He's leaning over the magazine and sucking his teeth like he does when he's thinking hard about something.

'You may want to take a look at this.'

I scowl and lean forward. It's a film magazine from three months ago. Kyle puts his finger onto the page and I read the line he's pointing to: 'Glamorex is owned by alleged member of the Russian mafia, Yuri "the Russian" Belkin, who is currently under investigation over allegations that he has kidnapped underage girls to appear in his movies.'

'They mention *Tokoloshe Money Shot* and *Dwarven Ass Patrol*!' Kyle says. These are two of Kyle's favourite creature-porn offerings. I can understand his enthusiasm.

'It makes sense,' I say. 'He makes creature-porn. Maybe the tooth is from one of the costumes!'

'I don't know, Bax,' Kyle says doubtfully.

'It's right there,' I say. 'He kidnaps young girls and forces them into porn. We need to find out where he's got her.'

Kyle sighs. 'We're going to do something stupid, aren't we?'

'More stupid than kidnapping and torturing a senior member of the Russian mafia?' I say. 'No, not more stupid than that.' I pick up a sharp rock and take aim. 'If he's done anything to her ...' My throw is dead on and the gnome explodes like a suicide bomber.

'Cheerio, chaps,' Douglas says, clutching the two bottles of wine from Kyle's dad's collection that we'd paid him with. 'Thanks awfully for the tipple.' Douglas has just helped us put into action the first phase of what we're calling 'Operation From Russia with Love'.

So far it's been surprisingly easy. The funny thing about the mafia is that they're required to act as if they're legitimate businessmen. Yuri's repeated assertions that he is merely an honest businessman victimised in xenophobic South Africa because of his Russian heritage requires a lot of backing up.

Particularly in light of the current human- trafficking allegations.

So when we phoned him and asked him to be a keynote speaker at the 'South African Business and Technology Forum' he jumped at the chance. Well, when I say 'we' phoned him, I, of course, mean Douglas, the homeless guy with the toffish accent that makes him sound like he's a British Conservative MP, phoned him. Douglas was a denizen of the canal near my house and we sometimes hired him to buy booze for us. He was pleased to be promoted to CEO of the SABTF and gave a solid, if slightly too theatrical, performance.

We'd set up a meeting for the following day to 'discuss the presentation', by which of course we meant 'tase him, put a bag over his head and torture him until he tells us where Esmé is'. Riding the wave of sympathy, I ask my parents if Kyle can stay over on a school night. My mother agrees and we retire to my room, which has become the command post for this little adventure. Kyle shows us a map of the unfinished business park where we've agreed to meet Yuri.

'Target will arrive at sixteen-hundred hours tomorrow, so we'll go straight from school to the rendezvous point,' Kyle says. 'My only issue is the efficacy of the tasers.' He looks down at the small plastic device in his hand dubiously. 'I mean, they were pretty cheap.'

He has a point. Fong Kong rip-offs are great for some things. But when you're attacking a high-level mobster with a reputation for violence, you want to make sure your weapons actually work.

I look at Kyle and smile.

'Uh-uh, no ways,' he says, 'you're not testing them on me.'

Rafe backs away from both of us and looks ready to run.

'OK, relax,' I say to them, 'we'll find someone else to test it on.'

Tuesday night in Claremont is like a jock convention. Drinks specials designed to get people out during the week run in all the clubs. We dodge two girls in short skirts throwing up onto their high heels as we walk down the main road.

Guys with popped collars and pseudo-mohawks hug each other and shout at passing cars. Kyle, Rafe and I wander the streets looking for suitable subjects. We only have two tasers between the three of us and antagonising too big a group would result in a beating. We still need to be able to run in case the tasers don't work properly.

After ten minutes of trawling, we isolate the perfect targets: three huge jocks standing in an alley initiating mating behaviour with a group of girls. They puff out their chests and find a reason to point to their crotches every few seconds. The girls laugh, lick their lips, flick their hair and thrust their hips forward.

Kyle, Rafe and I walk down the alley toward them. 'Hey, it's time for bed, kiddies,' one of the jocks says as he sees us approach. I smile. 'That's what we were thinking,' I say, 'so why don't you and your boyfriends go and touch each other inappropriately and we'll show these girls a good time?'

Time stands still. The jocks are taking a little time processing this. Eventually a 'What the fuck did you say?' comes from the jock in a pastel-pink golf shirt. Confrontation initiated, time to ratchet it up a notch.

'Oh, but then your mother might get jealous,' Kyle says, 'so why don't you go and service her first and then carry on with your rugby-buddy orgy?' Gay, gay, your mother, your mother. It's a time-honoured fight starter.

The three gorillas peel themselves off the wall and walk toward us. The look on their faces says that they can hardly believe their luck. The opportunity to beat up people smaller than them in front of women doesn't come along every day. Providence has smiled upon the jock kingdom tonight.

The resulting conflict is short and brutal. Kyle and I drop two of them almost instantly, the tasers working like a charm. The third stands bewildered, wondering exactly what is happening. Kyle does a spinning jump and tasers him in the neck, like he's an anorexic Jet Li. Rafe, obviously disappointed that he hasn't had any action, walks over and kicks one of the jocks in the groin.

'Rafe, what the fuck?' I say. He grins at me and shrugs.

'I think they work,' I say as we stand over the groaning bodies. 'Indeed,' Kyle replies.

The bevy of future Botox victims look at us with horror. 'Enjoy your evening further, ladies,' Kyle says. Their wide eyes watch us disappear into the night like fearsome avenging angels of geeks and freaks everywhere.

Yuri hadn't brought anybody with him. The prospect of being accepted by the legitimate business community made him ignore his native Russian cautiousness, which was unlucky for him because he's now tied up in Kyle's garden shed with a jump rope.

So far our plan to kidnap a member of the Russian mafia has gone surprisingly smoothly. We'd given him directions to an unfinished office park in Obs and then tasered him as he wandered around looking for the non-existent 'Clayton Enterprises'.

I'd driven his Audi A5 back to the house and between the three of us we had managed to drag the semiconscious gangster down to the garden shed. Kyle's parents are academics and they're out at a conference, and won't be back until they've either solved issues of gender and ethnicity or are too drunk to stand.

'First, we just want to say that we're big fans of your work,' Kyle says. '*Tokoloshe Money Shot* is one of the finest works of pornography –'

'I will feed you to my dogs,' Yuri shouts, veins popping out of his sweaty, shaved head and saliva dripping down onto his maroon suit. He rocks back and forth, struggling futilely against his bonds.

After a couple of minutes he calms down a little and looks at us, eyes wild like a wolf with rabies. To be fair we must look a little strange. Our strategy for avoiding Russian mob retribution consists mostly of wearing the masks of former South African statesmen that Kyle's parents had bought as a joke for Halloween. I'm F W de Klerk, Kyle is P W Botha and Rafe is Hendrik Verwoerd.

'No need to be rude,' P W says, waggling his finger in Yuri's face. 'We're crossing the Rubicon now.'

'I will rip your eyeballs out,' Yuri growls, resuming his struggling.

Hendrik calmly picks up a half-brick from the floor of the shed and smacks Yuri in the knee with it. 'Arhggggeeeee,' Yuri screams.

'What the hell, Rafe?' I say.

'Do you know who I am?' Yuri shouts. 'I will have you all killed.'

'Scalpel,' I say and Kyle hands me a rusty pair of garden shears. I open them and place them gently on Yuri's thick neck. 'We know exactly who you are,' I say.

The Russian stops struggling and breathes in and out forcefully. 'What do you want?' he croaks. I pull my wallet from my pocket with one hand, balancing the garden shears against his neck with the other. The rusty metal bites into the folds of flesh beneath his chin and a thin line of blood trickles down onto his shirt.

I flick through my wallet and pull a picture of Esmé from it.

'Dude,' P W says, 'you've got a picture of her in your wallet? That's soooo romantic.'

'Fuck off,' I say. I hold the picture in front of Yuri's face. 'We know you've taken her to be in one of your movies,' I say.

Yuri looks at the picture and then bursts into an unpleasant bout of laughter. 'You think I took her to work on a movie?' He laughs then winces at the pain from his knee. Hendrik lifts the brick again, but I hold up my hand. 'Did you?'

He leans forward. 'If I want white girls I find them in Eastern Europe. It's easier. Besides, your bitch – she's not pretty enough.'

I look at the photo of Esmé. She is pretty, but I know what Yuri means. The girls in *Tokoloshe Money Shot* are six-foot blonde-haired nymphs. Esmé doesn't really fit the profile. I stuff the picture back into my pocket and pull out the tooth. 'What about this?'

His eyes widen and then his mouth curls in a sneer. 'You don't want to know what that is.'

I grab both handles of the shears tightly and close them so that the rusty blades are tight against his neck. 'That's where you're wrong,' I say.

Yuri pushes his head back to try and get away from the blades. 'If I tell you, you let me go?' he says.

I nod.

He breathes out deeply. 'You don't know what you're getting yourselves into. My business caters to a very specific market. Sometimes when I need to find actors I require a little help.'

'Who helps you?' I say.

'There's only one person in Cape Town who deals with finding the weird,' he says. 'You need to see Jackie Ronin.'

The wagon stops with a jolt and I awake with a start, feeling like I haven't slept at all. The boy in my dreams is intent on finding something, but he doesn't see the huge dark creature bearing down on him, or the terrible man giggling like Tessie and Mari playing with their dolls. I'm scared for him.

I poke my head through the flap and feel the cold dread slide down my back when I see the men talking, their hands busy loading rifles as their eyes look toward the horizon. I follow their gaze and see dust spiralling upward in the distance.

My father, a rifle in one hand and a Bible in the other, strides over to me. 'They've found us,' he says, causing the dread to dig its claws into my spine.

My father lays his rifle on the ground and holds my shoulders in his large hands. 'You cannot be scared, little klipspringer,' he says, putting his face close to mine. I look into his craggy face; the long grey beard falling downwards, the hard blue eyes locked on mine. 'If you survive you must find the vehicle.'

It's that 'if' that gets to me. If I survive. We have been running from the English forever, their threat constant. But I never thought they'd catch us. I look into my father's eyes and feel him looking into me. He is angry, but not afraid. He squeezes my shoulders painfully. 'You have to find it.' He reaches down and grabs my hand, placing it on the Bible. It looks so small against the large cross worked into the leather.

'Promise me, child.'

I want to cry, want to plead with him, want to tell him that I can't, that I don't know what he expects me to do. But I know that would disappoint him more than anything I've ever done. 'I promise,' I choke out.

He nods and pulls me into a rough hug. 'Stay under the wagon,' he says.

I clamber beneath the wagon and lean my back against the sturdy wooden wheel, pulling my knees to my chest and tucking my feet beneath my dress. I'm in a safe place where I've been a thousand times before, running here when my father or Uncle Niklaas has been angry with me. Nobody can reach me here.

I hear the men talking softly and the soft sobs of children, probably little Theuns and Mari. I close my eyes and after a while the sounds begin to blend into the sounds of the veld.

I'm lulled by the waiting so my heart leaps in my chest when the first gunshots crack. There are shouts, then screams, a horrific mess of noise so different to the usual camp sounds. From beneath the wagon I can see legs swarm through the laager, like the legs of huge ants.

I see my aunt on her knees, screaming as she is speared with a bayonet like an animal. I watch her, unable to believe it. Surely this is some game that is being played, like when she would mimic Uncle Niklaas, her face severe and frowning, as she strode about pointing her finger at us. We would all collapse with laughter at her portrayal, so comical but strangely accurate. I see Dirk, the boy I've liked since I was little, braining a soldier with a hammer. He swings around to find another, but is brought down by a gunshot that takes off half his face. I press my eyes closed again.

When I open them I see a black man sitting in the middle of the laager crooning over a body. The red soldiers move around him but none seem to see him. I look down to the head cradled in his arms and see the long grey beard. 'Papa!' I shout.

Before I know what's happening I realise I'm running toward him. A hand tries to grab me but I dodge it, running frantically, the harsh smell of gunpowder in my nostrils, tears, saliva and snot streaming down my face. 'Papa!' I shout again. The black man looks up, one of his eyes completely white. I stop in front of him and his expression doesn't waver as I let out a sharp scream.

'He has been sung to the other side,' he says softly in Afrikaans. I kneel down next to him and take my father's face in my hands. 'He was right,' the man says. 'You have to find it.'

Hands grab me and pull me to my feet. The man is undisturbed by the soldiers and begins to sing again. I focus on his low, crooning song as the soldiers drag me away.

* * *

I feel good the next morning despite the genocidal dreams and the intense throbbing in my forehead. It feels like a spider has lain eggs between my eyes and the babies are trying to burrow into my brain. I go through to the bathroom to take a piss and then wake Kyle up and together we look again at the card Yuri had grudgingly given us before we'd tasered him again and left him in his car next to the Liesbeeck River.

Dr Jackson Ronin – Herbalist and Supernatural Bounty Hunter, the card reads, with *Dr Ronin will help you get rid of a goblin infestation, mix you a love potion or get rid of your bad juju* emblazoned on the back.

'Excuse me for stating the bleeding obvious,' Kyle says, 'but this guy doesn't exactly seem legit.'

'It doesn't matter,' I say. 'Yuri said he could help us.'

'Yeah, to save his head from being lopped off,' Kyle says, snapping his hands together like he's using shears.

'Got any better ideas?'

Kyle thinks for a moment and I can almost see the microprocessors doing their work. But the neural Google search comes up empty and he shakes his head.

'I'm going,' I say.

'*We're* going,' he replies firmly. 'Bax, I know you think you've got to be the leader in all this, that you've got to be tough and ruthless. But you've admitted to me that you love someone. That's something I thought I'd never hear you say, you've always been way too cynical for that. So maybe you should let other people help for a change. Let me help you find Esmé.'

This is the first kind of emotional exchange I've ever had with Kyle. Our friendship is tight, but it's built on late-night gaming sessions, shared business goals, weird philosophical debates, a mutual love of Mexican food and the ability to make each other laugh insanely. We don't do feelings. Well, until now. I nod once.

It's a bit cold, I know, but I've only just discovered my ability to empathise with other human beings. Give me a break.

We sneak slowly down the stairs, but Rafe appears at the bottom and looks up at us with his head tilted to the side quizzically. He stares at me and taps his forehead once. Kyle turns to me. 'He has a headache?'

'Who the hell knows?' I say quickly. I jump the last few steps and push past Rafe. 'You're not coming,' I say to him. We walk quickly to the door, but Rafe follows us like a stray dog that has been given food.

'Rafe, not now!' I say.

'Baxter,' my mother's voice calls from upstairs. 'What's going on down there?'

'Keep him here,' I hiss to Kyle. I open the door and Rafe tries to follow but Kyle steps in front of him. 'I want to come with,' he hisses back.

'You said you want to help,' I say, giving him an imploring look. 'Please, just keep him here.'

'Will you be OK?' he says.

'I'll be fine. Just keep him here. The last thing I need is him hanging around.'

'What should I say to your folks?' he asks, turning quickly and grabbing Rafe in a headlock. Rafe fixes me with the knowing-eye from under Kyle's armpit.

'Play the sympathy card,' I whisper. 'Say I've gone for a walk, say I'm at church praying. Say anything, just keep him here.'

I walk quickly down to Claremont station. I wait briefly for the clattering yellow-and-grey train to appear, and then climb on and find a seat next to a large woman who smells of incense, her grey dreadlocks held back by huge headphones that emit thumping trance music.

I close my eyes and only open them again when I hear the blind buskers shuffle down the aisle singing gospel, the same song they always sing about flowers and bright mornings and Jesus. I pull a coin from my pocket and drop it self-consciously into the cup. The train rattles through stations in quick succession until it rattles into Cape Town station. I look out to my left and see the dark walls of Good Hope Castle, which splay open like the points of a giant granite starfish.

I've always hated that place, but now it causes an undefined paranoia in my gut, a feeling that runs up to my forehead causing it to itch and throb even more. I have to force myself not to scratch flesh from my face.

The decrepit old office block is a short walk from the station. It's called the Flamingo, except that the 'a' and the 'm' in the sign have long since fallen off and thus renamed it the Flingo.

A group of guys in tracksuits huddle at the door, whispering offers of weed, coke, acid and mushrooms out the sides of their mouths, their eyes never ceasing their relentless roaming up and down the street.

I mumble vague apologies and push the dirty revolving door, forced to shove it hard to move it the few inches required to gain entry into the dull grey, ammonia-scented lobby. I find the elevator and press the button several times. Nothing. Nothing. I give up and take the stairs, stepping over a black cat that's either dead or incredibly lazy.

The fifth floor is deserted except for a shifty-eyed cleaning lady playing solitaire in the stairwell. She scowls as I step over her cards. I walk past several doors until I get to number 56. 'Jackie Ronin – Herbalist and Supernatural Bounty Hunter' is stencilled on the wooden door. Beneath the stencilling, graffiti kids have scrawled 'Who you gonna call?' and a bad reproduction of the

Ghostbusters logo in permanent marker. I knock twice.

'I said I'd have your rent next Tuesday, you Lebanese bloodsucker,' a gravelly voice calls from inside.

'I'm looking for Jackie Ronin,' I shout.

'Do you work for the Revenue Service?' the voice says.

'No.'

'Did I sleep with your wife or sister?'

'No.'

There's a long pause. 'Then it's open.'

Inside, a guy, forty-something and rough-looking, is seated on a grubby mould-coloured couch in the middle of the room with a cigarette hanging out of his mouth. He's leaning over a Monopoly board and placing a little red hotel carefully on one of the blocks.

'Are you Dr Jackson Ronin?' I say.

'Last time I checked,' he replies, not looking up. He gestures irritably for me to sit down on a dirty beige recliner opposite him. I gingerly remove a sandwich and the broken-off head of a ceramic Buddha from the recliner before lowering myself into it.

The guy throws the dice and gets two ones.

'Snake eyes,' he hisses and then moves the little silver dog two blocks forward. This looks like it might take a while.

I look around. The office is really more like an apartment. The kitchen to my left is lit by a single bare light bulb, which illuminates the fact that it's really small and dirty. There's a bedroom to the right and what looks like an office straight ahead.

The living room itself is a dump; old papers and magazines are stacked in teetering piles in the corners. There's an old wooden TV set with a smashed screen, above which a badly preserved moose head rots. It stares menacingly at me.

I'm pretty sure there are crack dens with better interior design than this place. Ronin looks like he has grown organically from within this apartment like fungus, a human-sized version of something you'd find growing under the sink.

His face has the texture of an old loofah. His large Roman nose looks like it has been broken several times and never reset, a crag-like protrusion that gives his face a wizardly cast. His long reddish hair is streaked with grey and held out of his face by a white tennis sweatband with the words 'Sport Activ' printed on it in neon green. A long brown-and-black feather hangs from his left earlobe and his impressive red beard has a single long braid extending from it.

He throws the dice again and gets a five and a three. He picks up the little silver top hat and moves it eight spaces forward. The top hat lands on a space that is infested with hotels. Ronin curses and upends the board, sending dice, counters and cards scattering everywhere. He suddenly seems to notice me and looks at me, his red caterpillar eyebrows meeting in the centre of his forehead in a frown.

'Trying to sell me something?' he says warily.

'No, I need –'

'What I need is some fresh air,' he growls, and he gets up and strides to the window. He yanks it open and climbs out onto the rusty fire escape that clings precariously to the side of the building.

'I need to talk to you,' I shout after him.

'You have some kind of medical condition that prevents you from going outside?' he says, peering back through the window.

'No, I just would prefer that we –'

'You're not one of those bubble boys, are you? I saw one of them on TV. He could only live in a bubble because all the germs and shit would kill him.'

'No, I'm not a bubble boy.'

'Then if you want to talk to me I'll be on the roof.'

Shit. I'm quickly starting to feel like this isn't going to be as easy as I'd hoped. I put my hands on the windowsill and lift myself through, easing my feet onto the old metal platform.

The metal shrieks under our weight.

I walk carefully up the stairs, wincing with every whining step, forcing myself not to look down into the alley below. I finally hit the last rust-covered step and clamber onto the rooftop with a real sense of relief.

The roof is covered with plants. There are dozens of orchids underneath a shade cloth and I notice the familiar six-pronged marijuana leaf rising up behind them. In the corner, a chicken-wire aviary holds a selection of pigeons sitting and preening themselves in the sun.

'You've got two minutes. If you try to sell me a cellphone contract or enlighten me in the way of the Harry Krishna, they'll never find your body,' Ronin says matter-of-factly.

'Ha ha,' I say without enthusiasm.

He looks at me quizzically. 'Something funny?'

He takes off his trench coat to reveal a dirty wifebeater and old-fashioned braces that clip onto his pinstripe suit pants. He is heavily tattooed; some kind of military heraldry with a shield and crossed swords decorates his left forearm, writing in a jagged, arcane script shows over the neck of his vest and a naked woman smiles salaciously from his right bicep. 'Wait till you see what she does when I flex,' he says with a grin.

Only now do I notice the sawn-off shotgun that hangs in a long holster at his side. He pulls the shotgun out and lays it reverently on the rooftop. The handle is made of a polished dark wood and the twin chrome barrels are engraved with pictures of mermaids, dwarves and some kind of weird monster, woven together in an intricate pattern. 'Pretty, isn't she?' he purrs as he strokes the weapon. 'Her name's Warchild. Touch her and I'll rip your pancreas out.'

'Whatever,' I say. I don't touch the gun.

'What can I do for you, sparky?' Ronin says, stretching his arms above him and looking out at the smog-shrouded CBD.

'I'm Baxter Zevcenko,' I say. 'I'm looking for my girlfriend.'

He lights another cigarette and drops into a martial-arts stance, the cigarette jutting from the corner of his mouth like he's the Keith Richards of kung fu. 'Is she Bulgarian and fond of latex?' he asks.

'No,' I say.

'Then I haven't seen her.'

He extends his front hand forward like a claw and executes a series of strikes that would definitely cause some serious oesophageal damage if used on a human being. He stretches down into the splits and takes a long drag of his cigarette.

'Pocket of my coat,' he says, taking the cigarette from his mouth and using it to point toward his trench coat.

I walk over and dig my hand into the pocket, hitting something solid and pulling it out. It's a steel hipflask in a leather pouch. I walk over to where Ronin is sitting contentedly in the splits and hand it to him. He grabs it from me, unstops it and takes a long sip.

'It's nine o'clock in the morning,' I say.

'Are you one of those talking alarm clocks?' he barks, wiping his mouth with the back of his hand.

'What are you doing anyway?' I say. 'I really need to talk to you.'

'Relentless Drunk Immortal Fist,' he says, taking a deep drag of his cigarette and then pushing his hands out in front of him and breathing out the smoke. 'Created at the Jade Stem Temple in China. Lemme tell you, those little bastards created some of the most vicious fighting styles in the world.'

'They'll probably be ruling the world in a couple of years,' I say. 'You might want to try to be a bit more PC.'

'Not the Chinese, asshole,' Ronin says. 'Dwarves. Jade Stem

Temple was a Dwarven monastery in the 1300s.'

'Dwarves?' I echo.

'Listen, sparky,' Ronin says, pushing himself up out of the splits and onto one leg, an arm sweeping up above his head and whipping from side to side like it's a venomous scorpion tail, 'get to the point or get the hell off my rooftop.'

'My girlfriend has been kidnapped,' I say.

He nods. 'It happens, kid.'

'You deal with strange occurrences, right?' I say.

'Not to burst your safe little suburban bubble, but kidnapping isn't that strange in this town.'

'This is different,' I say.

He rolls his eyes and then twists his body and holds his hands in front of him like dragon claws, an effect which is made more impressive by the cloud of cigarette smoke he exhales forcefully from his nostrils. 'Gimme a break,' he says. 'Your girlfriend has probably run away or, worst case, been kidnapped by organ harvesters who want to sell her kidneys on the black market. Either way, it's not my problem.'

'I found this,' I say, taking the glowing tooth from my pocket.

He wobbles unsteadily in his kung-fu stance and almost topples over. He grabs my wrist and pulls the tooth from it, holding it up to the light as if he's appraising an antique. 'Now this changes everything.'

Ten minutes later we're in his office. Ronin is sitting in the swivel chair with his boots up on the old desk. His ragged red head is barely visible above piles of folders that spill yellowed dog-eared paper onto the floor. I can't help but notice that some of the papers on the floor have the words 'final notice' and 'unpaid' stamped across them in red. A variety of old scientific equipment – beakers, vials, brass tubing – is haphazardly arranged behind him on a shelf.

'So you can help me?' I say. My head is throbbing viciously and a headache is relentlessly punching its way into my brain. 'I mean, you're a doctor of this kind of stuff, right?'

He pulls a face. 'Well, I'm not exactly a doctor, per se,' he says. 'More like I've got a PhD in the school of life with a specialisation from the school of hard knocks.'

'Sure,' I say. 'With an honorary degree from the school of bad drugs.'

He frowns. 'How do you know about that?'

I move a stack of dusty magazines from a low chair and sit down. 'I don't know anything. Listen, I don't care if you're a real doctor or not. What I care about is if you can help me find my girlfriend.'

The headache rings in my ears and I put my hands to my temples. Nausea sloshes around fitfully in my stomach and I'm forced to steady myself on the chair.

'Headache?' he says.

I nod.

'Gets all of us sometimes,' he commiserates. He gestures at the hipflask on his desk. 'Although some more than others.'

He yanks open a desk drawer and deposits a black cloth bag on a stack of papers. It's about the size of a bowling ball, with angular silver lettering woven into it. 'Don't feel like playing Dungeons & Dragons,' I say.

He snorts and shoves his thick hand into the bag and rummages through it. He pulls a curled black root from it. 'Chew on it,' he says.

'No thanks,' I say. 'I could do with some codeine though.'

'Chew it,' he says again, shoving the root toward my face.

'Sure, and then I pass out and wake up in a cellar smeared in my own blood. I've seen this movie.'

'So what you're saying is that you don't trust me?' Ronin says.

'Well, if you don't trust me to help you with your headache, how the fuck are you going to trust me to find your little lovie boo-boo?'

'You're not going to help me unless I chew on your root?' I say.

'Precisely,' he says.

I sigh and reach across the table, grab the root and give it an exploratory sniff. It smells musty. I nibble the end. It tastes like old socks smell. 'There,' I say.

He grins and sits back in his chair. 'Your headache will be gone in no time.' He rummages again in the bag and pulls out a small leather pouch, which holds a syringe and three vials filled with liquid.

'Whoa,' I say. 'Can't that wait till I'm gone?'

He lifts up his wifebeater and slides the needle into his stomach. 'It's for diabetes, dickwad,' he says. 'Try having a little fucking respect for the chronically ill.'

'Oh,' I say. The tension in my head has begun to recede.

Ronin winces as he spikes himself in the abdomen. 'Never get used to this,' he says. He replaces his diabetic paraphernalia in the bag and then grabs the tooth from his desk. He places it carefully on an old brass microscope on the shelf behind him. He adjusts a series of small dials and knobs. 'Yep, yep, yep. We've got ourselves a genuine Obambo tooth,' he says, his eyebrows bouncing up and down on his forehead in amazement. 'Goddamn, that is something interesting. And connected to a kidnapping.' He shakes his head in disbelief.

'Sorry,' I say, 'but what is an Obambo?'

'A perfectly rational question,' he says. 'With what you might find is an entirely irrational answer.'

'Try me,' I respond.

'Just remember you asked,' he says. 'Obambo. The Glowing Ones. Called ghosts, spirits or apparitions in most parts of Africa. Well, they *were* called that. They were hunted down and slaughtered. Some missionaries said that the locals had begun to worship them as idols and they needed to be eradicated. Some said they were children of Lucifer, light bringers and fallen angels. And the ones villagers and missionaries didn't get, the Strange Ones did.'

'Ghosts?' I say. 'You're joking, right?' He raises an eyebrow and looks across the desk at me. 'You came to a supernatural bounty hunter, what did you expect?'

'But ghosts have my girlfriend? C'mon …'

'They're not really ghosts. If they were you'd be shit outta luck.'

'If they're not ghosts, what are they? And why do they have my girlfriend? You're fucking with me, right? This is some kind of prank?'

Ronin sighs. 'It always happens. They come to someone that has "supernatural bounty hunter" on the door. I tell them that a supernatural creature is their problem and they look at me like *I'm* the crazy one.'

'I'm just trying to understand what you're saying,' I say.

Ronin raises his hands palm up like he's imploring the gods for patience. 'What I was trying to say, if you'd stop running your mouth for one goddamn second, is that this is clearly an Obambo tooth. The faint glowing around the edges of the tooth is characteristic of the species.'

'So you mean these things glow?' I say. 'Like as in emit light?'

'Well, aren't you an intellectual of surprising depth,' Ronin says. 'Yes, Obambo glow. As in emit twenty-four-hour neon ambience.' He strokes his long beard braid. 'My major concern is that it's common knowledge they're all extinct.'

'So now you're saying an extinct glowing ghost has my girlfriend?' I say.

'I'm not saying anything, sparky,' he says. 'You're saying you found this tooth, I'm telling you what it is.'

'Well, if one of these glowing things has Esmé, then I need your help,' I say.

He frowns and reaches over to rummage in his black bag yet again. He pulls a domino, a bone and an old key from the bag and holds them cupped in both hands. 'I need to consult the ancestors before I decide to help you,' he says.

'Oh, c'mon!' I say, standing up and leaning my hands on his desk. 'You've plied me with this shit since I got here and even you admit you're not even a real doctor. I'd walk out of here, but you're the only person who has given me any clue as to what this glowing tooth is. Please, just cut the crap and help me.'

Ronin raises an eyebrow. 'You don't believe in your ancestors? You don't believe that those in the past have an effect on those in the present?'

'No,' I say, 'I don't.'

He shrugs. 'It doesn't matter. The ancestors are there, whether you believe in them or not.'

'OK, fine,' I say. 'Do your hoodoo-voodoo. Then can you help me find Esmé?'

He smiles benevolently. 'If the ancestors will it.'

He shakes the three objects in his cupped hands and then throws them into the air. They cartwheel upwards and then drop, all three spinning like kites caught in a crosswind. The key hits the desk with a metallic *ching* and lands pointing toward me. The bone bounces off a stack of papers and lands on top of the key. The domino skitters across the desk and then flips up and balances perfectly on its side.

Ronin has gone into some kind of trance. His eyelids are flickering wildly and his tongue lolls back between parted lips. I lean forward and try to see if he's faking. 'The chariots are found and they will be unlocked,' he says, and then with a gasp he falls forward, knocking a pile of papers onto the floor.

'Bravo,' I say, giving him a slow clap. 'That was some theatrical bullshit.' If nothing else he's proven that I'm no longer the craziest person in the room. Ronin rearranges his sweatband and looks at me with his blowtorch blue eyes.

'Now, are you going to help me or not?' I say.

'Sparky,' he says, leaning across the table, 'I think I'm the only one who can help you.'

Internal Martial Arts Journal
The Roots of Dwarf Gong Fu
By Dr Earl Francis

'He who hesitates, meditates in the horizontal position'
Monk Han Wukong

This is the first in a series of articles exploring the mythical framework of the Chinese internal martial arts. We start with an esoteric discipline that is now little known outside of a few practitioners but was once a feared martial art, which renowned martial scholar Sun Lutang commented made 'gods and demons quiver in fear'.

Zhuruquan (Dwarf Fist) is a subset of the Northern school of Chinese gong fu and shares some characteristics with traditional Shaolin forms such as *Xiao Hong Chuan* (Small Flood Fist) and *Taizu Changquan* (Great Ancestral Longfist). Adding a simple brutality to the more elegant forms of the Northern style, Dwarf Fist has been called the 'art of overkill' by martial-arts historians due to the proliferation of eye gouges, neck cranks, foot stomps and other 'dirty' street-fighting techniques within the system.

Dwarf Fist has also been called Relentless Drunk Immortal Fist, a term that refers to its unsteady, swaying posture that hides an ability to generate an immense force in striking. Not much is known about the actual history of *Zhuruquan* but, as with so many of the Chinese martial arts, myths and legends abound.

According to legend, the story begins with the Buddhist monk Han Wukong at the Shaolin temple in China's Henan province. Han Wukong was a formidable Shaolin fighter and had achieved great mastery of the traditional Shaolin forms of meditation, qigong and gong fu, but was notoriously rebellious and contemptuous of the temple's strict monastic code.

The legend says that Han Wukong was a superlative fighter but a horrible monk, drinking ferociously, sleeping with many men and women, and going out of his way to taunt and embarrass the abbot of the temple.

After Wukong embarrassed him in front of visiting dignitaries, the abbot expelled him from the temple and a still drunk Wukong stormed out, famously responding that 'pious white-arsed virgin monks can never reach Nirvana'.

For many years after his expulsion he wandered the countryside fighting, teaching meditation, drinking and sleeping with farmers' daughters. He also produced a voluminous amount of poetry, many poems being regarded by contemporary Buddhists as important works within the Buddhist canon. Perhaps most famous of these is his 'Drunk Vagrant on a White Lotus' verse in which he gives a lucid account of his philosophy:

Outwardly I'm a ragged, wandering fool
but inwardly I live with a diamond mind
Outwardly, I enjoy drinking wine, penetrating women with my
jade stem, and singing lecherous songs
but inwardly I work for the enlightenment of all beings
Who is crazy, and who is wise?
Only time will tell.

The next account of Han Wukong sees him travelling to the

Himalayas where he encounters a village of 'dwarves' while seeking a cave to drink wine and meditate in. Although no records exist of such a village, these 'dwarves' may well have been an isolated tribe of smaller people, possibly of Tibetan or Nepalese descent.

Han Wukong stayed in the village to teach meditation, brew wine and sleep his way through the local female population. To the villagers he became known as the 'Divine Dragon Madman' and was gradually adopted as their resident holy man.

During this time his teachings deviated from the traditional Buddhist training of his youth and became a mix of Buddhism, Hinduism and the Tibetan shamanistic Bon religion. Primary in his teachings was the worship of the praying mantis as a theriomorphic form of the Buddha Amitaba.

He began building a following, and soon people from all over China, Nepal and Tibet came to listen to his teachings.

He instructed his new followers to build a temple near to the village, a large but simple stone structure that became known as the Jade Stem Temple. At the centre of the temple was a mandala of the Great Cosmic Battle that showed the eternal struggle between the mantis and the many-armed demon, an image that was said to represent the battle between humankind's higher and lower selves.

Raids by mountain bandits may have resulted in Han Wukong teaching his disciples the forms of Shaolin gong fu, forms that gradually changed and shifted due to the need for a self-defence system that was practical, particularly for the smaller villagers.

Legend says that the influence of Tibetan shamanism resulted in the formation of an elite group of fighting monks called 'Battle Shamans' who were said to have supernatural fighting abilities. Esoteric magical practices involving sex, drugs and music were certainly part of Han Wukong's system, but no record of the specifics of the Battle Shaman system remains.

The Jade Stem Temple became famous for the vicious fighting

style of *Zhuruquan,* but raised the ire of the Chinese Emperor. The temple was reportedly destroyed by giant crows, commonly thought by historians to be a reference to the Tengu, the mythical Crow demon that is associated with the Japanese ninja. How or why ninja came to attack the Jade Stem Temple is a matter of historical conjecture, but some say the Chinese Emperor was suspicious of the warrior-training at the temple and sent foreign agents to make sure the threat was neutralised.

Legend says that a few Battle Shamans escaped, carrying the secrets of the Relentless Drunk Immortal Fist and the practices of the Jade Stem Temple to India, Japan, Vietnam and perhaps even further afield.

Whatever the true roots of *Zhuruquan*, the legendary history – a heady mix of myth, religion and tall tales – remains a unique and compelling narrative within the broader framework of the Chinese martial arts.

ELEMENTAL, MY DEAR BAXTER

Ronin has jammed an old cassette tape labelled 'Cruising Tunz' into the car's tape player and is manically tapping the steering wheel to a compilation of surf rock. His powder-blue Ford Cortina is as messy as his office and smells of alcohol and cigarettes.

We screech to a halt at a set of traffic lights. 'I'm not cheap, kid,' Ronin says, leaning back in the seat and playing an intricate air-guitar riff.

'Great, I'm not poor,' I say, and I mean it. Spider profits make me twenty times what my folks give me as an allowance.

'Have you got your parents' permission to be hiring a bounty hunter?'

'What does it matter to you? The rent isn't going to pay itself and you look like you have more than a few debts to cover.'

He snorts. 'I bet you're a real little bastard at school.'

'You have no idea.'

'A thousand up front and five hundred a day after that.'

He puts his fist out and I bump it with mine. It's like punching a slab of knobbly iron.

'As good as signed in blood,' he says. 'I just need to finish one last job and then I'm on your case like a Chihuahua in heat.'

There's a hoot from behind us as the lights turn green. I look in the mirror and see a guy in an SUV gesticulating wildly for us to move.

'Excuse me for a second,' Ronin says and opens the car door. He walks over to the driver's side of the SUV, sweeps Warchild from underneath his coat and slides it through the open window.

I walk up alongside the car and see the weapon's twin barrels pressing into a balding suburban dad's throat. Ronin reaches in with his free hand and pulls a cigarette from a pack on the dashboard, pops it into his mouth and then lights it with the guy's Zippo.

'You see those lights up ahead?' Ronin says, holding the cigarette between his teeth. The guy nods weakly. 'You would have gained about two seconds. What would you have done with those extra two seconds?' The guy gulps and the gun pushes into his Adam's apple. 'I'll tell you what you would have done,' Ronin says. 'You'd have used them to get pissed off about some other insignificant thing in your life. You'd have complained about your fucking Internet speed or your garden service. All the while a little more of life would have passed you by. Your arrogance is so heavy you need this SUV to pull it.' He blows smoke into the suburbanite's face and then slides Warchild back under his coat. 'If I hear anything more behind me, I'm coming back and performing a buckshot amputation, comprende?'

'Part of my suburban re-education programme,' Ronin says as he gets back into the car.

We pass through Observatory and are heading onto the N2 when there's a *whoop* and a flash of lights behind us.

'Great,' I say. 'Your little suburban re-education programme is going to get us arrested.'

Ronin pulls over and adjusts the rear-view mirror and watches as a large form walks slowly toward us. I turn my head around and see the large form of Sergeant Schoeman blotting out the sun behind us.

'Fuck,' I say.

'Something you want to tell me, sparky?' Ronin says, arching an eyebrow.

Schoeman lurches up next to the passenger-side window and taps on it with his large, meaty paw. I roll it down slowly.

'Impressive little display back there,' Schoeman says with a smile that makes his jowls dance the cancan. 'Although I admit I was waiting for you to help your buddy out by cutting his throat and carving an eye onto his forehead.'

'I told you I'm not the Mountain Killer,' I hiss.

Schoeman snaps his fingers like he's just had a eureka moment. 'Gee, well, in that case I'll leave. Thanks for sorting that out for us.'

Ronin leans across me. 'Don't you have a sumo match to get to, Detective? Either arrest us, eat us or let us go.'

Schoeman chuckles. 'Jackson Ronin. Codename Blackblood. Former MK6 operative and member of an apartheid security-forces biological-weapons unit. You're certainly no stranger to killing. Are you giving our little buddy here a few pointers?'

'You're strangely well informed for a pig,' Ronin says with a smile. They stare at each other for a long moment before Schoeman gives a nonchalant shrug.

'I'll let you be on your way,' Schoeman says. He looks at me. 'Try not to kill anyone.'

Ronin starts the car and pulls back onto the freeway. 'You could have told me that there was a cop on your ass,' he says as the surf rock gurgles back to life.

'And you could have told me that you're some kind of agent and apartheid spy.'

'*Was* an agent. Things changed.'

'What happened?'

'None of your fucking business. It has no bearing on this case. What does, however, is that there are cops on our tail apparently trying to prove that you killed your girlfriend.'

'I didn't fucking kill her,' I say.

'You're weird, sparky, but it's a bit obtuse, even for a punk like you, to hire me to find someone you've cut up and are storing in your refrigerator.'

'Thank you,' I say.

He reaches across and grabs me by the T-shirt. 'And if you did kill her I'm going to pistol-whip you, drag you into the cop shop and claim a reward. Are we clear?'

'Crystal,' I say. 'Just help me find Esmé.'

He releases my shirt. 'First we have to get rid of this tail.'

We coast between the buildings until Ronin finds an alley next to a Chinese import–export warehouse. There is a mountain of refuse in the middle of the alley, fed by two battered and overflowing dumpsters. Wind caught in the alley whips the refuse into little junk devils that leap and spin through the air.

We climb out of the car and are immediately assailed by the stench of grime and dead animals.

'This place stinks,' I say, holding my sleeve up to my nose. Ronin shrugs as he produces his mojo bag from beneath his coat and pulls a vial of fine white powder from it.

He kneels on the ground and sprinkles the powder in the shape of three intersecting triangles.

'What's that?' I say. 'Some kind of hoodoo powder?'

'No,' he says, replacing the vial in the bag. He retrieves the domino from the bag and places it in the centre of the middle triangle. 'It's cocaine. Make sure it doesn't blow away.'

I huddle over the lines, trying to shield them from the wind with my body. Ronin pulls a thin, black-bladed knife from his boot and stalks into the mountain of rubbish. 'Here little buddies,' he calls softly. 'Don't worry, I just want to talk.' There's a skittering of claws on tar as a large grey rat bolts from the refuse toward a dumpster. Ronin leaps forward and scoops the rat up in his hand, holding it tight as it writhes and squeaks frantically.

He carries it over to the triangles on the ground.

'This is the part where you tell me what the hell you're doing,' I say.

'Guess,' Ronin says as he quickly draws the black blade across the rodent's throat. The blood drips down onto the triangles, slick and bright.

Cocaine and blood mix, forming a grimy design on the tar. Ronin hawks and spits into the centre and makes an elaborate gesture, mumbling a jumbled string of words that sound like a record being played backwards. He drops the rat corpse and then reaches down and retrieves the domino, placing it back into his mojo bag.

The whole process has stunned me into a bewildered stupor. Ronin is insane, and I'm insane for hiring him. Ronin turns to me with a grin and wipes his bloody hand on his trench coat. 'Cheer up, sparky,' he says, clapping me on the shoulder with a still bloody hand. 'This is just a minor evocation. Wait until you see the higher-grade stuff.'

We drive around backstreets until Ronin is sure we've lost our tail. Whether the 'spell' worked or whether Schoeman just got tired of following us is up for debate, but Ronin can't get rid of the smug grin on his face.

We get back onto the freeway and drive, the houses flanking the N2 becoming increasingly dilapidated the further we go. Emaciated cows graze on weeds on the sides of the road watched by kids balanced on plastic milk crates. We take a turnoff to the left and follow the road round into the township.

The road takes us through a neighbourhood of shacks made with corrugated iron, cardboard and old wood. We get to a T-junction and Ronin stops the car and leans out of the window to hail an old man sitting on a bright yellow chair next to rows of broken appliances.

'Sorry, tata,' Ronin says. 'We're looking for the First Baptist Church.' The old man stares at us with watery eyes. 'First Baptist?' Ronin repeats.

The old man raises a finger and points toward a spaza shop on the corner. We turn the corner at the shop and pull up alongside a red face-brick church. 'First Baptist Congregation' a sign says in bright colours.

Ronin gets out of the car and pops the trunk, motioning for me to follow. I climb out and watch as he hauls a mess of equipment out of the back. First a long plastic square that looks like a remote control. He flicks a switch on it and it begins to emit a low keening noise. Next, a long electrical cord that he loops around his shoulder. Finally, a rusty, bent metallic implement that looks like a cross between an old TV antenna and a trident.

If the 'spell casting' eroded any faith I had in Ronin, then this smorgasbord of junkshop trinkets dissolves it like hydrochloric acid. All he needs now is a tinfoil hat and a book by David Icke. My only ride home is going to be wandering through the townships hunting goblins with a TV antenna. Brilliant plan, Baxter.

Ronin shoves the TV antenna trident into my hands. It's not very heavy but it's unwieldy and I struggle to get a good grip on it, accidentally slamming it into the Cortina.

'You're paying for that scratch,' Ronin growls as he hefts an old car battery onto his shoulder and slams the trunk closed.

I sigh and follow Ronin as he walks through the shacks, holding the beeping remote in front of him with one hand and balancing the car battery on his shoulder with the other. The houses here look deserted and I start to feel more than a little paranoid.

What if Ronin really is a psycho? Only Kyle knows that I went to his offices, but he has no idea where I am now, and he's still back at home, babysitting Rafe. Ronin could kill me and bury me in the townships and nobody would worry until later tonight.

I hold the TV antenna in front of me like a weapon. If he tries anything I'll fucking stick him with it. We turn a corner and slam into the back of someone crouching against a shack. The TV antenna jams into Ronin's back and he turns around and gives me a scathing glare.

'Jesus,' Ronin says.

'No,' the man we walked into replies, 'just one of his humble disciples.'

The guy is probably in his late forties and has well-coiffed dark hair that is liberally peppered with grey. He's wearing a purple shirt and stands with a stoop, his small eyes flicking back and forth between us. A large silver cross hangs from a chain around his neck.

'You are the one I called?' he asks.

Ronin's mouth curls into a wolfish smile. 'The one and only.'

'Praises,' the man says, holding his hands out to us with his palms up. 'I fear the Lord is testing us with this foul demon in our midst.'

Ronin snorts and rubs the back of his hand across his nose. 'If we're dealing with an elemental, which I suspect we are, your Lord is probably sitting back with some popcorn to watch the light show.'

The priest frowns. 'Our community is being terrorised by a demon sent by Lucifer himself.'

Ronin gives a quick shake of his head, which causes his red beard braid to wobble back and forth like a fishing line that's snagged a big one. 'Not a demon, padre. If it was, all your cross waving might actually have some kind of effect. From your description I'll bet my last pair of underpants that it's an elemental, and if that's the case, well, the quicker we deal with it the better for all of us.'

'A knight of Jesus sent to save us,' the priest says, leaning in and kissing Ronin on the cheek.

'Yeah, something like that,' Ronin replies, wiping his cheek with the sleeve of his trench coat.

The priest guides us through a narrow alleyway at the side of the church toward a large open plot of land. I can see sweat stains forming on the back of his shirt.

'Thanks, padre,' Ronin says as we reach the plot. 'Why don't you go and count out my money for me?'.

The priest doesn't leave.

'What is it?' Ronin says. 'Spit it out.'

'I'm afraid some of the community have committed a sin and hired a sangoma to rid them of this devil.'

Ronin swears. 'You could have told me about this and saved me a drive. Do you know what this sangoma's name is?'

The priest shakes his head.

Ronin pulls out his phone. 'Still got signal. The elemental can't be that close.' He dials a number and then waits as it rings. 'Protocol 4,' he whispers into the phone and then waits again. 'Tone,' he says. 'I know … Yes, I goddamn know. Are you going to lecture me or answer my question? Do you have any of your people tracking an elemental? … OK … Yes, thank you so much, your goddamn highness. Fuck you too.' He hangs up.

'Your little bone-throwing buddy is a charlatan. Which leads to the unfortunate conclusion that she's going to become a sangoma smoothie unless someone steps in.' The bounty hunter claps the priest on the shoulder and pushes past him. 'But have no fear, my Bible-thumping friend. Ronin's here.'

Ronin waves the priest back to the dubious safety of the alleyway. The keening sound from the remote has begun to increase in frequency – yipping and squeaking like a little digital dachshund. My hands begin to tremble slightly and I watch as the hairs on my arms spring to attention.

'Definitely an elemental,' Ronin says. 'And it's getting closer. We should get a visual soon.' He drops the car battery and holds his hand out for the antenna.

'What exactly are we looking for?' I say as I hand it to him.

'That,' he says. I follow his gaze to where something is moving slowly from behind a shack on the other side of the plot of land.

'Holy shit,' I say. I feel like I've been hit by one of the tasers we used on Yuri. My mind jumps the diving board of reality and does a bellyflop in the messy waters of consciousness below.

BizBax: Not to be Captain Fucking Obvious, but there's a giant electricity beast meandering toward us.

MetroBax: Let's just get the hell out of here. I don't want to be here, I don't want to see that thing.

BizBax: We could be suffering a stress-induced psychosis.

MetroBax: It looks pretty real to me. Oh my God, is that its tongue?

If my mind is creating the creature that shuffles toward us, then it's being pretty damn creative. The hulking mass of blue flame that stumbles closer is an electricity troll with a massive crackling energy furnace body. Its face is distorted, eyes yellow swirling vortices, framed by a beard of spitting sparks. Its long simian arms are topped with lightning-bolt talons that drag on the ground creating a scorched trail behind it. It is the most terrifying fucking thing I have ever seen in my life.

It looks at us and grins, a tongue like an electric eel whipping back and forth in its gaping maw.

'Pure electricity mixed with equal parts bloodlust and hatred. Nasty bastards, and this one's a biggie,' Ronin says calmly.

The thing lumbers slowly forward, tasting the surrounds with its tongue, sending whip-crack bolts of energy into the air. I'm mesmerised by the shifting patterns of current that writhe and twist in its body.

Ronin unwinds the cord he has looped around his shoulder and attaches one end to the bottom of the trident and the other to the car battery. 'Blood,' he says. 'It's the only thing that keeps them on the material plane. That's why they're called township ticks. They're made of pure energy so people make deals with them. Communities feed them goats, sheep, the occasional thief or rapist convicted in a kangaroo court, and the elementals let whole neighbourhoods hook power lines into them.'

He makes an adjustment to the pole and then lifts it up to examine it. 'Sounds like a good deal when you've got no electricity.' He hefts the antenna in his arm like a javelin to test the weight. 'All hunky-dory until some of their kids go to fetch a ball in its sewer and get devoured. And if there's one thing elementals find finger-licking good, it's young life force. Now they can't stop the thing.'

The thing hunches forward onto its arms like a baboon and contemplates us. Its tongue darts in our direction and I feel a shiver of static pass through me. It looks at me with its swirling eyes and grins. With a lurching movement it begins to move in my direction, faster this time.

'Young life force,' Ronin says. 'It can taste you.'

'I'm getting the fuck out of here,' I say.

'Run and it'll hunt you,' Ronin says, 'and unfortunately we can't kill it. Energy can't be created or destroyed and all that jazz.'

'What?' I say. 'So what the fuck are we going to do?'

'We capture it and starve it until it has to leave the physical plane,' Ronin says. 'Oh look, and here comes tonight's light entertainment.'

An old sangoma approaches the elemental with her arms spread wide like she's going to give it a hug. She's dressed in faux-Chinese animal skins and has a flimsy-looking whip, which she's trying unsuccessfully to crack above her head. She chants in a quavering voice.

'That's a love spell, you daft old bat,' Ronin shouts. He breaks into a sprint toward her. The sangoma shrieks as the elemental shrugs its fiery body toward her. Ronin reaches and grabs her around the waist, but she struggles furiously against him. She scratches at his face, breaks his grasp and runs at the elemental. Ronin tries to grab at her, but it's too late. She stops, frozen in her tracks.

Ronin jogs back to me. 'She's in its field,' he says. 'Don't look if you don't want nightmares.' The sangoma tries to back away from the creature, but she looks like she's swimming underwater. Ronin quickly connects the trident to the battery.

I watch as the elemental approaches the sangoma, slowly, almost tenderly. Sparks ripple across the ground and for a moment it illuminates her nervous system like a biological Christmas tree, the patterns of her nerves clearly visible through the skin.

It lifts its claws and grabs her by the shoulders, burning her like blowtorches. She screams, a horrible primal sound like an animal caught in a trap. With delicate precision its tongue darts from its mouth and into one of her eyes, slicing through her eyeball as if it were soft white cheese.

She whimpers and sags, but the thing's claws hold her up. With a horrible fizzing sound it drags the life from her body, digging its tongue deep into her to make sure it gets every last drop, and then discards her corpse like an empty bottle.

It wipes its mouth with its arm and then turns to us. Second course is bounty-hunter tartare with a side order of love-struck teenager. It lopes toward us, clearly invigorated by the sangoma hors d'oeuvre.

Ronin stretches his neck and loosens his shoulders like a runner preparing for a race. 'Ronin,' I say. 'It's coming for us.' He ignores me and hangs forward and touches his toes. The elemental picks up speed, letting out a hissing cackle of glee at the thought of devouring us.

Ronin casually lifts the trident and spins it like a Shaolin monk with a staff, the cord to the battery whirling around him. He drops into a low stance with a palm out in front of him and the trident tucked under his arm. I begin to retreat, scuttling backwards to where the priest is cowering in the alleyway.

'Get ready to run,' I whisper to him.

He gives me a terse nod and begins to mumble a prayer.

The creature reaches Ronin and stops, contemplating him like an epicure in front of a bucket of fast food. The elemental is clearly not impressed with Ronin's gastronomic potential, but is not above a quick greasy snack.

It lurches forward and Ronin spins, fighting the effects of being in the thing's field but still blindingly fast, jabbing the end of the antenna into its large body. There's a fizzle, hiss, crackle and pop as the antenna makes contact and leeches energy from the elemental.

The thing howls as energy whips down the cord and into the battery.

'Olé,' Ronin says.

With a snarl the elemental turns and jumps at Ronin. The bounty hunter coils like a snake and sends the antenna spinning through the air like a javelin. It hits the creature in the centre of its body.

Energy erupts from the creature, sending a blast wave rolling out in all directions. I can feel it coming, my hair whipping around me manically before a concussive blast throws me from my feet like a rag doll, slamming me into the side of the shack.

Black spots drip down my vision like blobs of ink. My forehead feels as if it's imploding and I collapse forward. Spectral images flicker in my vision. I see a panorama view of Cape Town burning as a nuclear blast engulfs it. I see huge creatures, things that make the elemental look like a baby, engaged in a death struggle. I see a flag with a red eye painted on it flapping in the wind. The eye locks onto me and burns into my forehead like a cattle brand. High-pitched manic laughter rings in my ears, an original soundtrack to insanity.

When my vision clears I have my hands around the throat of the priest. He is struggling against me, but I have an insane amount of strength. I could crush his windpipe effortlessly, like crushing a takeaway coffee cup. 'Please,' he hisses.

I drag my hands from his throat. 'I'm sorry,' I say. 'I don't know what got into me.'

I look around and see Ronin desperately holding onto the cord like a deep-sea fisherman that won't let go of a prize catch. Slowly, the creature shrinks, mercilessly sucked down the cord and into the battery. Then, with a sharp crack, it disappears completely.

Ronin gets up and brushes dirt from his trench coat. He looks over to where I've collapsed, gives me a smug grin and bows with a flourish. 'And the crowd goes wild,' he says, holding his arms above him like a gymnast who has nailed a landing.

'Brilliant,' I say, pushing myself to my feet. 'One of the best near-death experiences I've ever had.'

'Oh please,' Ronin says. 'That's a far-death experience, trust me – I'm something of a connoisseur.'

'Right,' I say.

'Don't stress,' he says. 'You get over it after the first few times.'

'I don't intend to do that again,' I say.

'You'd be surprised,' he says. 'You get addicted to it.'

The priest emerges slowly from the alleyway, looking at me

with almost as much fear as he had the elemental.

'What was your little disagreement about?' Ronin says, with a curious look. 'He trying to preach to you?'

'No,' I say, giving the priest a guilty look. 'I don't know what happened.'

'Adrenalin, turns all of us into fucking maniacs. Now, padre,' Ronin says, putting his arm around the priest's shoulders, 'where's my money?'

'Yes, of course,' the priest says and tries diplomatically to extricate himself from under Ronin's arm. He pulls a tattered envelope from his pocket and hands it to the bounty hunter.

'Pleasure doing business with you,' Ronin says, flicking through the blue bills. 'Fancy a drink, sparky? I'm buying. Daddy just got paid.'

He turns to walk back to the car, but something in his peripheral vision catches his eye.

'What the hell?' he grunts and strolls over to a shack that was torn open by the blast from the elemental. I follow him, not eager to be left alone with the priest I almost strangled.

We peer inside through the shattered wall. Several dozen sets of strange shining eyes blink up at us.

'Hell in a handbasket, why can't things just be simple for once?' Ronin says with a sigh. 'Looks like we're going to have to call Dr Pat.'

Seven sprites sit on my lap and peer up at me with saucer eyes, their warm, furry little bodies rising and falling as they breathe together in unison.

When you're faced with too many reality-bending things, your mind goes into a kind of stupor, a weird blank funk that can do nothing but stare dumbly while deeper levels of your consciousness try to process the information and spit out something resembling sense. So far the output is less than satisfactory. Magic bounty hunters, electricity monsters and now sprites.

Sprites, the latest introduction to the alternate reality that I've stepped into. They're grey and squat, like square-headed, chubby little rabbits that stand upright. They have huge black eyes that make them look like they've taken copious amounts of LSD. They stare at me with unwavering eyes. One puts out a little paw that looks more like a tiny, pink human hand and pokes me in the stomach as if trying to figure out what I'm made from.

I'm in the passenger seat of a yellow VW van. The driver, Dr Pat (I'm not sure if she has the same approach to qualifications as Ronin does), turns her curly white-haired head toward me, causing her long crystal earrings to jingle.

'It's a good thing Jackson called,' she says with a smile that crinkles the corners of her almond-shaped eyes. 'These little dears are in need of some good food and rest.' Ronin has taken the rest of the sprites in the Cortina and is meeting us at Pat's house.

I look down at the creatures on my lap. One is chewing on an old car-freshener.

'And how have you come to be in the dubious company of Jackson, dear?' she asks as we turn onto the highway.

'I'm looking for my girlfriend,' I say.

'Ah, well, if she can be found, Jackson will find her.'

'How do you know him?' I ask.

'Oh, we were in the agency together, my dear,' she says. 'Until the incident,' she says, pursing her lips. 'But you should ask Jackson about that, dear,' she says. 'He wouldn't want me talking about it. He's still a little sore about that.'

I try to press her further about Ronin and this agency but she remains tight-lipped. We pull into the driveway of a smallholding in Philippi. The land is wildly overgrown and it takes me a second to pick out a canary-yellow farmhouse peeking out through a blanket of vines and creepers.

'Welcome to the Haven,' Dr Pat says with a smile.

I open the door and the sprites on my lap move as a single unit to hop out of the car. They stand together in formation and continue looking up at me and blinking. 'Stop it,' I say to them. 'You're creeping me out.' They break into a perfectly synchronised smile, which shows the sharp little teeth in their mouths. I take a step backwards.

Ronin pulls up next to us. He gets out and takes his pack of cigarettes from his trench coat, taps one out and lights it. 'Get some of your guys to fetch these little bastards and we'll be on our way,' he says.

Little furry bodies and huge saucer eyes press up against his rear window, their synchronised breath misting up the glass.

'Jackson!' Pat says with a stern look. 'Since when have you been blind to the plight of the Hidden Ones?'

Ronin rolls his eyes, but opens the door and grabs an armful of sprites. 'Come here, you little fuckers,' he says. 'Bite me and I'll kill all of you.'

Two guys come out of the farmhouse with wheelbarrows and help us to unload the sprites from the vehicles. 'What are the Hidden Ones?' I ask Pat as we wheel the sprites toward the farmhouse.

'Jackson Ronin takes you hunting elementals but doesn't explain the supernatural ecosystem?' she asks. I shake my head. 'Disgraceful,' she says and gives him a dirty look as he passes us on his way to grab more sprites from his car.

We hit a bump on the driveway and one of the sprites catapults into the air and lands with a thud on the gravel. The sprites wince in unison. 'I'll get him,' I say and jog over to him before gingerly picking up the furry little creature.

'Let's get these little darlings inside and then I'll explain some of the things that Jackson has obviously neglected to tell you,' Pat says.

'This is a veterinary clinic?' I say as we wheel the sprites around to a barn at the back of the farmhouse. 'In a sense,' Pat says. 'We cater for the needs of a rather different kind of animal.' She keys a password into a keypad and then flings open the barn doors.

We step into a zoo. Animal enclosures line the walls and there are sounds of shrieking, snuffling and gobbling, as well as more unpleasant sounds of ripping, tearing and biting.

'Don't be afraid,' Pat says, seeing my face. 'They're all really lovely in their own unique ways.'

'Lovely' isn't what I'd use to describe the creature sitting on a perch next to the doorway chewing on a piece of raw meat. It's a lynx with a jagged scar across its face. Long white tufts sprout from his ears and large white wings sprout from his back. Just your average flying lynx, then.

'What the fuck?' I whisper.

'Language, dear,' Pat says. 'This is Tony Montana.' She pats the hybrid creature on the head. 'Say hello, Tony.'

The thing bares sharp teeth and hisses at me. I've never really liked cats and one with the ability to swoop down and rip out your eyeballs seems like it'd make a really terrible house pet.

'He's a bit shy,' Pat says. 'Our city has been cruel to its unusual inhabitants, and they're wary of humans.' The flying lynx looks like it wants to bury its teeth in my jugular.

Pat takes my hand in hers and leads me over to a cage where a little goat-like creature paces behind bars. It is small, stands upright on two legs, is covered in coarse brown hair and is very, very ugly. It has slitted pig eyes, horns that rise like two jagged spirals from its head and a huge grey penis, which it drags around on the floor like some kind of deformed python. I recognise it from creature porn, back in the good old days when I thought they were midgets in fancy dress. The reality makes me feel ill.

'That's a tokoloshe,' I say. It glares at us through its slit eyes.

'Quite right, dear!' Pat says. 'Isn't he gorgeous?' I make a non-committal sound. 'There used to be ninety-four different species of tokoloshe,' Pat continues. 'Now there are fewer than seven. Can you believe they have been captured to make pornographic films?'

I make another sound. The creature in the cage snarls and makes lewd gestures and grotesque pelvic thrusts in her direction. 'Fukfukfukfukfuk,' it chants.

I'm glad when she takes my hand again and leads me gently away from the cage. We walk around to the pens and Pat names the creatures they hold. There's the Nevri, a black-and-red, double-headed viper that can repeat words like a parrot, and the Jepsen, a small orange-haired monkey with three eyes and twelve arms.

We stop in front of a cage that holds a naked woman standing in a clay pot. Her breasts jiggle as she moves and she stares at me with bedroom eyes. 'Nymphang,' Pat says matter-of-factly, ignoring the fact that the woman has begun to writhe in ecstasy in front of us. 'Indigenous Hidden Flora distantly related to fynbos, I believe.'

I stare at the woman running her tongue over her lips. 'You mean that's a plant?'

'Oh yes, dear. What you see is an adaptation designed to lure humans.' Pat picks up a thin wooden rod and pokes it through the bars of the cage. The woman's body splits in half like a giant mouth, revealing a row of serrated fangs. The mouth lunges forward and snaps the stick in half. 'You see why we have to keep it in a cage, dear; I've lost more farm workers than I'd care to admit.'

'You keep talking about the Hidden,' I say as we continue through the barn.

'The Hidden Ones,' she says. She walks over to the Nevri cage and gently lifts the double-headed snake from it. The dark viper wraps itself around her neck and contemplates me with lazy eyes. 'Broadly speaking, the term refers to all of the magical races that exist on the fringes of human society. It includes the so-called intelligent Hidden races, as well as our animal friends here. Both have been subjected to torture and genocide at the hands of humans, although the Feared Ones have also helped to destroy them, of course, but one can't really blame them. That's just their nature.'

'The Feared Ones?' I say.

'Also known as the Murder, they're religious assassins, black of feather and of heart,' Pat says. 'Zealots dedicated to their god, with the sole purpose of releasing him from his prison. Or so the story goes. They have inflicted such atrocities upon the Hidden that it beggars belief. But that's who they are.'

'What about an Obambo? Do you have one of those?' I say.

Pat looks at me and for a moment I see more than just a kind old lady. There's a taut readiness to her stance and I feel like she's ready to punch me. 'What do you know about the Obambo, young man?'

I give an awkward shrug, trying to deflect some of her intensity away from me. 'Not much.'

Pat brushes her curly hair delicately from her eyes. 'Obambo are one of the casualties of the Feared Ones,' she says, stroking both heads of the Nevri simultaneously. 'Wiped out completely. Extinct.'

'Feared Ones,' one of the snake's heads whispers in an eerie, guttural voice.

Pat lifts the head up to her face and kisses it on the lips. 'Yes, my precious little darling, but I won't let anything happen to you.' I avert my eyes. I didn't think there was anything worse than cat people. Until I met my first monster person.

'Nevri want a cracker,' one of the snake's heads says. 'No, dear,' Pat says. 'You eat small rodents. I really wish Elias hadn't taught you that.' She unwinds the Nevri from her arm and gently puts it back in its cage. 'Sleepytime,' it hisses as it snuggles down into the sawdust.

We make our way to the back of the barn and watch as the last of the sprites are unloaded into a spacious pen. They stand around blinking at one another.

'They don't really do much, do they?' I observe.

'Well, they don't really need to, dear, they're telepathic,' Pat says.

'They're –' I start, then stop and peer at the furry little beasties.

'Telepathic, dear – they're apparently more intelligent than dolphins. Although you'd hardly know, bless them.' I stare at the blinking saucer eyes. They stare back.

We exit the barn and Pat resets the alarm code. 'Come and have some lemonade,' she says. 'You must be exhausted after the day you've had.'

Exhausted is not exactly the word for it. 'Stunned' is closer, but it also doesn't quite convey the sense of confusion, wonder and abject terror I'm feeling about the world behind the looking glass I've just stepped through. I know I should be freaking out more, but in a way I feel it's a homecoming.

I've been bathed in the warm glow of supernatural fantasies ever since I can remember. The fairytales my parents read me as a kid, TV, video games, it all kinda feels like they've been preparing me for this moment. It feels somehow natural and the other world, the one with taxes, life insurance, twenty leave days a year, cancer, and the realisation that you're never, ever, going to be a celebrity, is the shadow, the fantasy and the delusion. The world is as I always intuited it to be: weird, fractured and full of monsters.

The farmhouse is actually two buildings: the old yellow house that I saw from the driveway and a newer set of apartments that have been built next to it. We're walking down the path between the two buildings when a boy pops his head through an apartment door.

'Shhh, Big Ones,' he says sternly. His hair is long and brown and he wriggles his nose as if sniffing the air.

'Baxter, meet Klipspringer,' Pat says with a smile.

The boy sticks his head around the door again. 'Pleasure-tomeetyouthankyou,' he says.

'A pleasure,' I say. 'He ... works here?'

'Oh God no,' Pat says. 'Trying to get him to tidy his room is trouble enough.'

Klipspringer walks out from behind the door. 'Whoa!' I say, stepping away quickly.

He chuckles with delight. 'Whoa!' he mimics, jumping backwards, his little hoofs clattering on the driveway.

Klipspringer is about twelve years old and has the body of a springbok and the torso and head of a human. His little white tail wags with delight as he trots up and down looking slyly at us, his nose twitching with happiness.

'It's OK,' Pat says to me. 'He won't hurt you.'

'Won't hurt you, Big One,' Klipspringer says. 'Duh, Big One, duh! You smell funny.'

'Now,' Pat says, putting her hands on her hips, 'what did we say about being polite?'

'Alwaysbepolitenevertellpeopletheystink,' the boy recites dutifully.

'That's right,' Pat says as she tries unsuccessfully to comb back his wild hair with her fingers.

Klipspringer tries to wiggle away.

'Hey!' he says brightly. 'Want to see my room, Big One?' He trots up and down on the spot excitedly. 'Want to see my room?'

'No thanks,' I say. 'Ronin probably wants to go and –'

'Baxter,' Pat says, 'do I have to give you the speech about being polite as well?'

I sigh. 'OK,' I say. 'Let's see your room.'

I squeeze in through his door, moving an old, rusty tricycle out of my way. An abstract sculpture made entirely from doorknobs wobbles unsteadily as I pass. I dodge underneath a whole army of plastic action figures that hang from the ceiling on pieces of string, pushing a plastic Skeletor with my finger. He swings back and forth from the noose around his neck.

The room is stacked high with a random assortment of rubbish. Posters of 2 Unlimited, André Agassi and Steven Seagal plaster the wall of Klipspringer's incredibly messy room. Klipspringer flicks a switch and the whole room is illuminated with dozens of strings of brightly coloured Christmas lights.

'Ta-da!' he says with a sweeping gesture. 'Best room in the universe.'

'It's great,' I say.

'Duh,' he says, slapping his forehead. 'Of course it's great.' He grabs my wrist and looks around theatrically. 'You ever seen a nipplestar?' he whispers. 'In the paper book, hey?'

I shake my head. He winks knowingly and holds up a hand for me to wait and then disappears behind a stack of old soft-drink cans. I hear sounds of things being thrown around. He returns with something behind his back. 'You wanna see, huh, huh?' he asks. I nod. 'Now are you sure you wanna see?' he says with a grin.

'Just show me,' I say.

He beams as he pulls out an old eighties nudie magazine from behind his back. 'The nipplestars,' he says reverently. He opens the magazine to the centrefold. Her blonde permed hair, high socks and naturally pendulous breasts seem strange to my refined porn sensibilities. But that isn't what Klipspringer is interested in. His eyes are fixated on the silvery stars that cover the nipples, put there by the conservative apartheid government to protect South Africa's delicate white souls.

'They shine,' Klipspringer says in awe. 'From their chests.'

I laugh. 'Those aren't stars, bok-boy,' I say. I scratch a little with my fingernail on the silvery nipple supernovas to reveal the fleshy areolae beneath.

'They aren't real?' he says.

His nose twitches with disappointment and I feel like I've just told a kid there's no Santa Claus. 'Don't worry,' I say, remembering something, 'the real thing is much better.' I take my phone from my pocket and scroll through the images I've saved on it; big women, small women, women of every racial type.

The bok-boy wrinkles his nose up. 'I like the nipplestars,' he says. I'm about to give up when I scroll to one of the creature-porn images I've saved to show potential customers. She's topless, her arms crossed beneath her breasts, but the lower half of her body is a tangled mess of shaggy brown goat hair. I used to think the photo was fake, but now I'm pretty sure it's not.

Klipspringer grabs the phone and looks with awe at the photo. 'What's her name?' he says softly.

I squint at the small print in the corner of the image. 'Jasmine.'

'Jasmine,' he repeats with reverence. He scampers away again and comes back holding a newish smartphone.

'You have a phone?' I say with a laugh.

'Course,' he says. 'I like to play the gamegames. *Pew-pew-pew.*'

I transfer the image to his phone. 'There,' I say. 'Now Jasmine's in your spank bank.' He looks quizzically at me. 'Never mind. I'll tell you when you're older,' I say.

'Now I give you something,' he says.

'No, it's OK,' I say. 'That was a gift. You don't have to give me anything.'

He trots away and comes back with something in his palm. 'I do. I do,' he says. 'I remember now. Boy with spectacles and lookthrough eyes. The lady told me to give it to you.'

'Dr Pat?' I say.

'No, Big One, duh. Not Dr Pat. The other lady.' He opens his palm and shows me a pendant on a leather cord. It's a little brass mantis with shards of blue semiprecious stones for eyes. 'Take it,' he says pushing it into my hand. 'She told me to give it to you. Take it.'

I take the pendant and pull the cord over my neck, slipping the brass mantis under my shirt. It's warm against my skin.

'Thanks, goat-boy,' I say.

'No problemo, Big One,' he says with a smile. 'But be careful. It has the strongstrong magic.'

RATTLE & HUM

'The problem with madness is that you don't know you're mad until you suddenly realise you're lying on the floor and chewing on your curtains, and wondering why the word "jelly" sounds so strange if you say it more than twenty-four times in a row,' Ronin says as he scoops noodles into his mouth, dribbling soy sauce onto his thick red beard.

We're sitting in his car eating takeaways from Mr Hong's Chinese Takeout at the tail end of Long Street. This part of the CBD is murky and decaying. Girls loiter beneath a brothel smoking and groups of guys hang around looking for customers, victims, or both.

'I took four microdots of acid to help me pretend I was mad to get out of fighting on the Border,' Ronin continues, rubbing his beard with his sleeve. 'Turns out after four microdots you don't really have to pretend. But I was drafted anyway. Apparently psychosis is a desirable trait in a bush war.'

'What is this agency you're involved with anyway?' I say.

He looks at me, the last of the noodles hanging from the chopsticks that are halfway to his mouth. 'How do you know about that?'

'Pat said you were an agent with her. Before "the incident".'

'Nothing,' he says, as he shoves the chopsticks into his mouth. 'What happened at MK6 is none of your goddamn business. Just drop it.' He chucks his empty takeaway box onto the backseat.

'You're right, let's rather focus on all the leads we've found today,' I say sarcastically.

We've been trawling the streets of Cape Town, looking up all Ronin's contacts, and coming up with nothing. A big fat zero. Nobody knows anything about an Obambo with a missing tooth. In fact, nobody knows anything about an Obambo at all, them being completely extinct and all.

If nothing else it's been an insight into Cape Town's sweaty underbelly; we've seen advertising execs who deal in illicit organs on the side, junkie ex-journos who have given up the word habit but not the needle, and a Congolese midget named Frank who directs sci-fi and fantasy porn. I took his number for future reference. They all say the same thing: the Obambo are all dead and hence incapable of kidnapping anybody.

'I hoped it wouldn't come to this, but I'm going to call in a favour,' Ronin says. 'It may take a couple of hours to set up.'

'Fine,' I say. 'I need to go somewhere. Do you think when I get back we might make some actual progress?'

'Sure thing, boss,' Ronin says sarcastically. I'm really starting to dislike this guy.

We drive back to his office and he drops me on the pavement outside. 'Be back here in two hours,' he says. 'Oh, and sparky? You owe me a thousand bucks.'

I walk quickly down to the station. A hyperactive guy selling bootleg Nollywood DVDs and hair products whistles and tries to catch my attention. I ignore him.

The 'somewhere' I have to be is Dr Basson's office. He sent me a text saying he'd like to see me again today and quite frankly

I'm not above a little psychological help at the moment. It's not so much the weird creatures that are getting to me, although my mind is still struggling to come to terms with those too, it's more the headaches and visions that have me worried. I'm starting to suspect that there may be something seriously wrong with me.

I see the train pulling into the station up ahead. I sprint through the crowd and make it through the doors just as they begin to close. As I sit down next to a sweaty lady in a wig reading a bumper compendium of Victorian erotica my phone rings. 'Jesus, Bax,' Kyle says. 'I've been trying to call you all day. What happened? Did you meet the bounty hunter?'

'I met him,' I say.

'And…'

'He's a frikken psycho,' I say.

'I told you so!' he says with relish. 'But, like, you're OK?'

'Yeah, I'm fine. He's a psycho but he knows what he's doing. Kinda.'

'OK, if you say so,' Kyle says doubtfully. 'We've got another problem. Dude, Rafe has gone even more mental than usual. He's drawing all kinds of weird pictures; real bizarre shit with eyes and praying mantises and stuff. I think he's gone off the deep end. There's this insane one of you holding a trident and fighting this fire-creature thing. It's like something out of frikken *Conan the Barbarian* or something. It's actually kinda cool.'

'Holy shit,' I say.

'What?' he says. 'Does that, you know, mean anything to you?'

I don't know what to say. I desperately want to tell Kyle about all the crazy things that have been happening, but also it's not the easiest thing to say over the phone. Especially on the train with about fifty people in earshot.

'Forget it,' I say. 'Take Rafe to your house. Tell my parents that I'm meeting you there and that the three of us are having a sleepover.'

'Er, not to poke holes in your super-spy tactics,' he says, 'but that doesn't exactly sound plausible.' It's true. I've never invited Rafe anywhere with me. Let alone to stay over at a friend's house.

'Just do it,' I say. 'I'll take care of my parents.'

'OK, fine,' Kyle says with a sigh. 'This sucks, man, I should be there with you. Are you sure you're OK? You're sounding really stressed out.'

'I'm fine,' I say with as much conviction as I can muster. But the truth is I'm not really sure that I am.

Dr Basson gives me an appraising look. He leans back in his chair and taps his pen against his chin, quickly scribbles something down in his notebook, and then continues the tapping.

'So, just to clarify,' he says. 'You're talking about supernatural creatures? *Real* creatures, not metaphors or myths?'

'Yes,' I say. 'And I think my brother is psychic.'

This has not gone well. I had come here with the intention of talking about my headaches and visions and had ended up spilling the beans completely.

'And these dreams you've been having,' he says consulting his notebook, 'they're always about the past?'

'Always about this girl,' I say. 'In the middle of some kind of war.'

Basson nods contemplatively. 'And this is all accompanied by an unidentified throbbing in your forehead?'

I nod. 'And these two voices in my head that fight over things.'

'Baxter, I hate to indulge in guesswork, especially with something this serious. We can't rule out the possibility that you have something physically wrong with you.'

'What, like an illness?'

'Well, a tumour for instance –'

'A tumour? Jesus.'

Basson holds up his hand. 'I'm not saying it is a tumour. What I'm saying is that certain organic damage caused by disease could be causing these delusions. There is, of course, a hereditary history of mental illness in your family...'

'Listen,' I say. 'I know it sounds insane.' I bark out a high-pitched laugh. 'But I saw these things. They're real.'

'You saw –' he looks down at his notebook again '–an "elemental", several dozen "sprites" and a boy who was half human and half...'

'Springbok,' I say.

'Half springbok,' he echoes with a small smile. 'Your brain creates your reality, Baxter,' he says. 'When your brain is affected, your perception is affected. What seems ridiculous to others might seem entirely real to you. I think it may be prudent if you come to a facility that is specifically designed to deal with this kind of thing. We can do some tests –'

'No,' I say. 'I'm not going anywhere for tests. I'm finding Esmé.'

He sighs. 'I can't force you, Baxter. And I can't tell your parents without your permission. But I strongly advise you have a physical examination.'

'After I find Esmé,' I reply.

'Well, I hope for your sake that you find her soon.'

'Me too,' I say.

Back on the train next to an old guy in a fez playing Tetris on his phone. I call my mother and tell her that Rafe and I are staying over at Kyle's house. I tell her that I've taken her words to heart and that I want to spend more time getting to know Rafe. We'll bond. We'll hug. We'll run through fields of flowers together. That sort of thing. She's so amazed and happy that she suspends disbelief and buys into it. It's so easy I almost feel bad. Almost.

The thought of a tumour, on the other hand, makes me feel slightly sick. It swirls around in my head along with images of elementals, sprites and a barn full of other beasties. My mind does its little two-sided mambo.

BizBax: It makes a lot of sense.
MetroBax: You think this has all been some kind of delusion?
BizBax: I don't know. It's kind of hard to diagnose when we're one of the symptoms.
MetroBax: True. How are we going to know if this is all real or not?

I rub my forehead experimentally. There's nothing there. 'No kidding, genius,' I whisper to myself. 'You can't feel a tumour with your fingers.' The old guy next to me gives me a scared look and then turns so that his body is angled away from mine. I don't fucking blame him.

I stare out through the window at the mountain as the train jolts to a stop. If a tumour is squeezing my brain and causing me to see elementals and bok-boys then what else is it making me do?

It does make a lot of sense. My sudden discovery of a heart, my delusions. Maybe a tumour is making me believe I love Esmé. Making me dig her little ski-slope nose that I sometimes imagine tiny snowboarders doing backflips off of. Her haughty green eyes (with yellow flecks) that conceal something a little crazy and scared. Making me remember running my fingers along the long scar on her left hand from where she caught it on a barbed-wire fence while climbing into the mountain reservoir to swim.

She hated dolls as a child. She loved broccoli. She sometimes sucks her thumb when she's asleep but I never tell her. The way she dances is a bit dorky, with straight arms and weird pelvic tilts and thrusts, but I think it's kinda sexy too. She has four piercings in her left ear and three in her right. She's designed and redesigned a tattoo about a thousand times but never had it done because she can't stand the thought of that kind of commitment. She looks at me like I actually mean something. I have a mental catalogue like this that stretches into the distance and doesn't seem to end. Maybe it just means I'm creepy and obsessive, but I don't care. I don't care if I have a tumour or if I'm insane. I'm going to find Esmé. I *have* to find Esmé.

There's nobody under the bridge but a pack of feral cats with green, flashing eyes. They dart across the litter-strewn pavement and disappear into the windy night. Ronin parks the car in a deep shadow and puts his feet up on the dashboard. I count out his money on my lap and hand it to him. He counts it again and then shoves it into his coat with a grin.

'And now?' I say.

'And now we wait.'

'For?'

'Tone,' he says.

'Tone? Sounds like an R&B singer.'

'Codename, smartass. He's head of operations for MK6.'

'Somebody has yet to tell me what that is. I mean, besides a shadowy government organisation.'

Ronin interlaces his hands behind his head. 'They're mostly sangomas, witchdoctors, mages, witches, that sort of thing. They keep an eye on the Hidden and make sure that nothing untoward happens.'

'Like what?'

'Like the wrong people seeing them for one. They don't care if the Hidden stay in the shadows. But if anybody tries to tell their story to the media then they step in.'

'They can't be doing a very good job,' I say with a laugh. 'I saw stories about tokoloshes in the tabloids long before I knew they were real.'

'Yeah exactly, genius,' he says. 'And what did you think when you saw those stories?'

'I thought they were tabloid bullshit,' I say.

'Bingo,' he says. 'They seed a lot of those stories. Who's going to believe a story about a tokoloshe or unicorn if they read it in a tabloid?'

'Clever,' I say.

'Goes way deeper than that,' he says. 'The South Africa Sceptics Alliance is an MK6 front. They spend a lot of time and money debunking the stuff that does get leaked.'

It sounds so damn plausible to my pop-culture-attuned mind. Shadowy government organisations, secret agents, mass cover-ups. If I'm not completely insane, that is.

'Do you ever think you're crazy?' I say. 'I mean, crazier than you are normally. That you're ill and you're making all this supernatural stuff up?'

'Every single goddamn day,' he responds with a laugh.

A black van appears under the bridge and moves slowly toward us. Its chromed wheels glint in the dim light. The van has tinted windows and plates that say MK 962. It stops in front of the Cortina and kills its headlights.

The doors open and two guys get out. One is absolutely huge, a professional wrestler with a blond crew cut and a badly fitting suit, his hairy forearms jutting from the cuffs. He has an assault rifle hanging on his shoulder and he leans against the front of the van and points it lazily at our windscreen.

The other one is much smaller, a black guy with grey hair that's pulled back into cornrows. He's dressed in an expensive suit that has grey and white beads crossed over it like bandoliers.

He isn't armed except for a walking-stick, which clacks against the concrete as he approaches.

'Blackblood,' he says in a slow drawl.

'Don't know who you mean, Tone,' Ronin growls.

Tone shrugs. 'You know what they say about leopards and their spots.'

Ronin hawks and spits on the tarmac. 'That they'll fucking bury anybody who brings it up?'

Tone smiles. 'Your belligerence is misplaced, old friend.'

'Well, unfortunately your boss isn't here, so you'll have to do.'

Tone rolls his shoulders in a non-committal shrug. 'Mirth is what he is. Not everybody likes it, but he's the boss now.'

'Everybody loves a Rottweiler until he turns around and rips out your throat.'

'I assume you didn't invite me here to reminisce about old times, Ronin?' He looks at me and then back to Ronin. 'Rent boy?' he says.

'Screw you,' I say.

He purses his lips and emits a sharp squealing whistle. It hits me like a sonic hammer in the solar plexus and my knees buckle involuntarily. Ronin grabs my shoulder to stop me from falling.

'OK,' Ronin says. 'I think he gets what a supremely powerful warlock you are. The very earth trembles at your name and all that shit.'

I steady myself on Ronin's arm. 'Tacky,' I say. 'You must be bummed you only got the cocktail-party powers.'

Tone bursts out laughing. 'Where the hell do you find these clients, Ronin?'

'I have no idea,' Ronin says with a sigh.

Tone waves to the big guy back at the van. He peels himself off the hood and stumps toward us, the assault rifle swinging from its strap.

'Half-breed giant,' Tone says, leaning in to whisper to me. 'His great-grandmother got lonely on the plaas and banged one of the mountain giants in the area.'

'Great,' I say, rubbing my solar plexus. The pain subsided quickly but has left a dull ache. 'What's his codename?' I ask.

'Savage,' Tone says. 'We let him choose his own.'

Up close I see just how big Savage is, like a granite slab with legs. He pulls a rolled-up brown folder from the inside jacket pocket of his suit and hands it to Tone. 'I was kidding with the rent-boy comment. I know all about your problems, Baxter Zevcenko,' he says. 'Fortunately for you, your girlfriend's disappearance intersects with the case we're working on.'

A bright spark of hope ignites in my chest. He hands us photographs of a group of street people being herded into a van by a guy in a lab coat. A close-up of the clipboard he's holding shows an invoice with a red octopus on the letterhead.

'Human-trafficking operation,' Tone says. 'Our intel says it's not for sex, which makes it quite unusual. Our agent inside said he's seen an Obambo, which makes it downright odd, given the fact that they're supposed to be extinct.'

'What's that logo?' Ronin says, pointing to the red octopus.

'Corporate called Octogram. They're into a lot of things; mining, pharmaceuticals, weapons. We've been keeping an eye on them for a while, but this is the first time we've actually found anything tying them to illicit activities.'

'Doesn't sound like your usual beat,' Ronin says.

Tone smiles. 'I'll tell you why we're interested, and you're going to love this; it turns out their base of operations is the Flesh Palace.'

'Goddamn,' Ronin hisses through his teeth.

'The place where the creature-porn stuff is shot?' I say.

'The very same,' Tone replies. 'Which makes it even weirder that the trafficking is not part of the sex trade. We're particularly interested in what part the Queen of the Anansi is playing in this.'

Ronin's face has gone pale and he starts to flex his fingers convulsively. 'I'd like to send that bitch back to hell.'

'I thought that's what you'd say. Our problem is that the Flesh Palace is on the social radar of many of our esteemed politicians and we're reluctant to carry out a raid in case we catch somebody too high up on the food chain. But if an independent operator were to go in there...'

'So what you're saying is that we should go in, do your job for you, and then maybe you'll create some paperwork about it?' Ronin says.

'Isn't that the way it always works?' Tone says with a bright smile.

'We'll do it,' I say.

'Now hang on, sparky,' Ronin says. 'We need to talk about this.'

'What's there to talk about?' I say. 'The Obambo is in the Flesh Palace. We go in, we find him, we make him tell us where Esmé is. That's why I hired you.'

'He's got a point,' Tone says.

'Fuck off,' Ronin says.

Tone lifts his hands in mock defence. 'Don't shoot the messenger, Ronin. Anyway, I'll let you boys discuss it. Savage and I have to rattle someone.' He looks around. 'And this is as good a place as any.'

Tone gestures to Savage and the half-giant opens the backdoor of the van and pulls out a small bald guy wearing a white T-shirt, grey jeans and fashionable glasses.

'You're still doing that medieval bullshit?' Ronin says with disgust.

'C'mon, Ronin,' Tone says. 'You used to enjoy this stuff.'

Savage drags the guy across to Tone and pushes him onto his knees. 'Please,' the guy gasps. 'A free, independent media is vital for a democracy. You can't have government agencies that are not accountable –'

'Actually you can,' Tone says. 'And it's worked for us pretty well so far.' He undoes his jacket and pulls a thin black syringe from a scabbard at his waist.

'What are they doing?' I whisper.

'Rattlebone,' Ronin says softly to me. 'Made with black-mamba poison. Ugly stuff. It attacks the brain and takes out the memory. It would be better if they just killed him.'

'What...' the reporter says, struggling against Savage's iron grip. 'You can't kill me! There'd be an investigation.'

'We're not going to kill you,' Tone says. 'We're just going to press control-alt-delete and restart you.'

'Wha –' the guy starts but Tone slides the needle deftly into his neck. The reporter's eyes widen and his body locks into a grotesque spasm before he collapses onto the floor and begins to shake uncontrollably.

'Urgh,' he says, staring through us with vacant eyes. 'Uhhhhaasppphhft.'

'The stress of reporting,' Tone says, spinning the syringe between his fingers and replacing it in the scabbard like a gunslinger. 'It gets to everybody eventually.'

'You put on that little show to impress us?' Ronin says. 'I'm not impressed.'

'Just showing your friend here what happens to people who run around telling people crazy stories about elementals,' Tone says with a dangerous smile.

The sun is setting behind the mountain as we drive through Epping Industria. We pass over an abandoned train track and through a dingy street filled with tyre merchants and industrial cleaning equipment distributors.

'Charming,' I say.

'It only gets better,' Ronin says. He's been in a bad mood ever since we left the bridge and I'm pretty sure it's because we're headed toward the Flesh Palace. I, on the other hand, am excited. Not only is the Obambo there, but it's also the place where a large percentage of the porn I've been selling is made. I feel like I'm going on some kind of pornographer's pilgrimage.

We pull up next to an ugly grey warehouse and Ronin kills the headlights. An old drunk wanders down the road, stopping near the Cortina to take a leak, before disappearing into the darkness.

We step out into the pools of murky light on the pavement. Ronin nods to the gaudy facade of a club about a hundred metres away on the other side of the road. I can see two large bouncers outside.

'ok, sparky, I'm not going to bullshit you,' he says. 'If we step foot in that club, there's a pretty good chance that we're both dead.' He breathes in deeply through his nose, holds it for a couple of seconds and then lets the air out with a whoosh. 'Either we can go in there and try to find the glowing man and probably get killed. Or we can go home, I'll give you back your money and you forget that your girlfriend ever existed.'

'We go in,' I say decisively.

He looks at me intently. 'I must admit, I wouldn't have pegged you as the knight-in-shining-armour type.'

'I'm not.'

He nods. 'I get ya. Who can understand the cruel commands of the heart, eh?'

'Yeah, something like that.'

He flexes his fists and rolls his neck from side to side. 'I had a girl once. We were going to get married and everything.'

'What happened?'

'I stood her up at the altar and she's been trying to kill me ever since.'

'Brilliant,' I say. 'Now I know who to come to for relationship advice.'

'Stupid thing is, I really loved her.'

'So why'd you stand her up then?' I say.

Ronin stretches his arms above him and in the half-light he looks like some kind of demented Viking praying to Odin. 'It may be difficult to believe, but I've got a lot of baggage,' he says.

'Oh,' I say, 'I think I can believe it.'

He takes another breath, looks up at the sky and lets it out into the night air. He pounds himself a couple of times on the chest, slaps his cheeks, and then hands me his keys. 'Well, if we're going to do this I'm going to need what's in the trunk,' he says. I grab the keys and walk around to open the Cortina's trunk. It's a mess, but I quickly isolate what Ronin wants from the jumble. Although I could be wrong, I'm pretty sure the Hawaiian boardshorts, the copy of *Eat, Pray, Love* and the cheese grater are not what Ronin's after. Which leaves a bandolier of shotgun shells and a short, brutal sword in a red scabbard.

I grab them both, slam the trunk shut and take them back to the bounty hunter. He takes off his coat and straps the bandolier across his chest, then pulls the sword from its scabbard and cuts the air a couple of times.

'This is Hagaz,' Ronin says as if he's introducing me to an old friend.

'Do you name all your weapons?' I say.

'Only the ones that have killed beings with higher-order brain function,' he says. Strangely, that makes me feel better. He slides the weapon back into its scabbard, straps it around his waist and pulls his coat back on. He reaches into his mojo bag and takes out what looks like a weird green root with little black veins beneath the surface.

He breaks a piece off and puts it into his mouth. 'Eat this,' he says, pulling a face as he chews.

I take the green thing in my fingers. 'What is it?' I ask.

'Urfrog,' he says. 'It'll help if the Anansi get too friendly.'

'Frog?' I say. 'No thanks.'

'Trust me,' he says. 'It tastes bad but it's better than the alternative.'

I sniff it and then place it gingerly in my mouth. It tastes dry and old, like some kind of weird fungus. I close my eyes and chew until I can swallow it. Ronin offers me a sip from his hipflask and I take a gulp and wince at the sharp, medicinal taste. He takes a couple of sips, breathes in deeply again, and then he nods to me and starts to walk toward the entrance of the Flesh Palace. As we get closer I can see that the bouncers are well over six foot and immaculately dressed in black tuxedos. Their faces are jagged and uneven, their skin the grey and purple of Table Mountain, and greenish fungi juts from their heads like samurai topknots. One carries a huge, grisly halberd and a katana protrudes from a sheath on the back of the other.

'Golems,' Ronin whispers to me. 'They're new. The Queen must have access to a high-level sangoma to animate these bad boys.'

'What do we do?' I whisper.

'Don't worry, they're mostly for show. You usually have to answer some dumb question and they'll let you in. The punters love it, think it's hilarious.'

The golems loom over us, their eyes black with a rainbow sheen like an oil spill. The Roman numeral I is set in gold into the forehead of the one with the halberd, and II into the forehead of the other.

'What is the name of the Flesh Palace's most popular performer?' II says, his voice like the sound of rocks being crushed.

'John Smith,' Ronin says.

'Incorrect,' II says.

'The *Queen* herself invited us.' Despite the obvious attempt at diplomacy, he says 'Queen' like he's talking about a particularly virulent STD. 'You're not going to stop one of her guests from entering, are you?'

'Answer?' the golem repeats.

'I think we've come to the wrong place,' Ronin says. 'We'll just stop hassling you and leave.'

'Incorrect,' I intones. 'You have one more guess.' II draws the blade from the sheath on his back. 'Answer or die,' I says.

My mind kicks into action. The two most successful Flesh Palace franchises are *Tokoloshe Money Shot* and *Legless Legolas.* It's possible that Legless Legolas, the elven amputee, is the most popular, but I don't think so. His popularity pales in comparison to the manky, grey-haired tokoloshe with the big belly and an even bigger ... well, it can only be him.

'Rumpelforeskin,' I say confidently.

'Correct,' I rumbles. 'You may enter.'

Inside, the place is a frenzy of flesh and fluid. Heavily tattooed waitresses push through the crowd with trays of drinks, one of them with a long, reptilian tail jutting from the back of skin-tight PVC pants.

We walk past the stage where naked women gyrate on poles for squat, bearded men. 'Dwarven Legionnaires,' Ronin murmurs as we pass them. 'Don't stare. They've killed people for less.'

I look down as we pass them, which gives me a good view of the grungy wooden floor. Judging by the dark red stains, beer isn't the only thing that regularly gets spilled in this place. Topless dancers with suspiciously pointy ears proposition us and Ronin grins and winks at them.

'A double Devil's Tail,' Ronin says as he gets to the bar. 'With extra Devil.' The bartender is the most beautiful transsexual I've ever seen. Not that I've seen many. Especially ones with wings.

She has blue-black skin, platinum-blonde hair and large white eyes that have no pupils or irises. A red latex dress sticks to her skin and a long string of pearls hangs between small breasts. Large white angelic wings are folded neatly behind her and they flutter gently as she gives us a jaw-dropping smile.

'Katinka,' Ronin says.

'Jackie boy,' she replies in a husky voice. 'Have you decided to end it all? Death by the Anansi Queen?'

'Is that any kind of greeting for an old friend?'

She smiles and leans over the bar to kiss him on the cheek.

'How's the hormone treatment coming, darlin'?' Ronin says.

She sighs and cups her small breasts in her hands. 'Expensive, Jackie. Dwarven doctors are a bunch of bloodsucking cunts at the best of times. When it comes to cases like mine ... well.'

'Dwarves are not really known for their tolerance of the transgendered,' Ronin says. 'Can't you just, you know ...?'

'Illusion,' Katinka says dismissively. 'I use it when I have to. But it's not just the looks, you know? Beneath it all I still have to look at myself in the mirror in the mornings. So it's the goddamn dwarves, they're the best with hormones. Luckily they'll forget their allegiance to the dogma of the One Mountain God if you flash enough cash in front of their fat little noses,' Katinka says and then spits on the ground. 'A curse on their whole inbred race.' She puts a hand in front of her mouth and breathes in deeply. 'I'm sorry,' she says. 'That was unladylike.'

'Never been fond of dwarves myself,' Ronin says. 'Well, besides Baresh.'

'He was different,' Katinka says softly. She pats Ronin gently on the shoulder and then turns her strange white eyes on me.

'Are you ... an angel?' I blurt out. Smooth, Zevcenko. Really smooth.

Katinka laughs throatily. 'Many of my clients think so, sugar, but technically I'm an Osira.'

'The Osiraii are like African Valkyrie,' Ronin says. 'Tasked with fetching the souls of fallen warriors.'

'Mucho-butch,' Katinka says, looking down at her blood-red nails. 'No task for a lady.'

'The Osiraii are all women,' Ronin explains. 'They keep a few males around for mating purposes, but the rest…' He draws a line across his throat with his finger.

'They kill them?' I say.

Katinka shrugs. 'Why do the religious do anything? Part of the mythology. It has something to do with the female Mantis and her mating habits. The Flock says that the males are blessed and are sung onto the other side.'

'By the Singer of Souls,' I blurt out again. I'm on a roll in the not-thinking-before-you-speak department tonight.

'You *are* a smarty-pants,' Katinka says, raising her eyebrows. 'Osiraii legends say that he was put in place to guard the gateways of space and time, that he is both the spirit of a place and a manifestation of its mythology.' She shrugs. 'Anyways, that shit is way too woo-woo for me. I'm more a sex, drugs and rock 'n' roll kinda girl. My mother and sisters sheltered me and pretended I was a girl to the Flock. First opportunity I got the hell out of Dodge and created a life where I live by my rules.'

'These days Tinks is a body entrepreneur,' Ronin says.

'That's what I love about you, Jackie,' she says, patting his cheek. 'Always tactful. Yes, when I'm not tending bar, I'm a working girl and my warriors are those slain by nine to fives and bitter wives. Although admittedly my methods are a little different.' She takes the cigarette Jackie offers her.

'Methods?' I say.

She smiles and raises her little finger, and my mind explodes with scenes of orgies, bodies writhing together in a rhythmic concerto of flesh, lust and bodily fluids.

In an instant I'm back and gripping the bar with both my hands and shaking my head slowly as the last of the sinful memories drains from my mind.

'What was that?' I say.

'The Osiraii are master illusionists,' Ronin says with a grin. 'Who needs the Internet when you've got Tinks?'

Katinka laughs. 'Well, I'll try to take that as a compliment, Jackie-O,' she says. 'But what about you, candy cane?' She eyes me up and down, her mouth curving in a smile as Jackie lights her cigarette for her. 'What battles are you fighting?'

'My girlfriend,' I say. 'She's missing.'

'Oh, they all are, honey,' she says, tapping her chest. 'Emotionally distant. Empty inside.'

'No, I mean she's really gone. Like as in disappeared, vanished.'

'Well, then you're lucky,' she says. 'All you need to do is find her.'

Ronin is looking around the club uneasily. 'Tinks, we need some intel.'

'Of course, Jackie,' she says. 'Anything for you, sugar.'

'Thing is, we're looking for a glowing man,' he says. 'An Obambo.'

Katinka nods. 'One of the strangest men I've ever had.'

'You had sex with him?' I say.

'Well, let's just say we didn't sit and play Sudoku all night, sweetness,' she says. 'But it might have been better if we had. He was an actor in one of the Flesh Palace films. One night he came to my room to talk. And, well, one thing led to another. But he was distracted and kept talking about his dead wife and kid. It's a bit of a slap in the face for a lady with my considerable skills.'

'Where can we find him?' I say.

'That's where you're out of luck, boys. A while back the Queen took an unnatural interest in him. Haven't seen him since.'

'An unnatural interest,' Ronin says. 'That's the only kind of interest she has. How is Her Majesty?' Ronin says.

Katinka shrugs and blows a delicate smoke ring. 'The usual; cruel, ambitious, horny.'

'Think you can get us an audience?'

'I don't think you need to worry about that,' Katinka says, nodding to something behind us.

We turn to see four guys approaching us. Their skin is slightly grey and mottled, and they smell like an old cat-lady's flat. 'Her Majesty wishes to see you,' one of them says in a slow, drawling monotone.

Ronin nods. 'Lead the way, spiderman.'

It's only when they turn that I see the distended, bulbous arachnid bodies jutting from the backs of their necks, black but coloured with sickly yellows and bright warning reds.

'Stop staring,' Ronin whispers in my ear. 'Nobody ever said they were pretty.' He downs his drink. 'Come on. I'd hate to keep *Her Majesty* waiting.'

Katinka reaches across the bar and grabs Ronin's arm. 'Try not to become a fallen warrior, OK, Jackie boy?'

Jackie laughs. 'She can't still hold a grudge, can she?'

South African Military History Journal
The Nostradamus of the Transvaal
By Neels Marais

The title of Siener is most often associated with Niklaas van Rensburg, adviser to the Boer general Koos de la Rey and mystic, whom many Afrikaners believe had the power of prophecy and far sight. Lesser known is Dawid van Rensburg, Niklaas's younger brother, who was also rumoured to be born with a special sensitivity that some believed was a gift from God to help the Boer nation in their struggle against the English.

In contrast to Niklaas's strict spiritual moralism, Dawid grew into a rather eccentric and antisocial man. He left home at a young age, and travelled widely in and around South Africa, eventually returning to his people many years later with a child in tow. He never told anyone who the mother of his beloved daughter was. The few accounts of her describe her as a pretty, dark-haired child. Niklaas had already established himself as a Siener and welcomed Dawid back with open arms, but it soon became apparent that Dawid had travelled a very different path to his brother.

While Niklaas's prophecies were heavily steeped in biblical language, Dawid developed a form of Afrikaner shamanism that drew heavily on the indigenous cultures and included divination, magic and spiritualism. He had become a smoker of marijuana and a chewer of the Khoisan herb kougoed, believing both to be potent enhancers of his abilities.

He also spoke about the ingesting of the 'glowing blood', which gave him a revelatory experience that would impact heavily on both his life philosophy and prophetical output. This 'glowing blood' may have been a reference to a naturally occurring hallucinogenic, perhaps the seeds of the morning-glory plant.

Niklaas disapproved of his brother's ways but never publicly denounced him, correctly fearing that the super-religious Boer community would cast him out, or worse. But after Dawid began telling his prophecies to all who would listen, Niklaas became convinced that Dawid's abilities were not a gift from God, but the by-product of a demonic possession. It may have been a prophecy Niklaas considered particularly heretical, the so-called 'Great Battle' prophecy, that convinced the older Siener of Dawid's satanic con nection:

> Two brothers arise from the womb,
> Intertwined brethren of creation and destruction
> The Mantis and the Octopus wrestle for supremacy
> Children of Chaos and Children of Light
> balancing on creation's razor blade
> The Glowing ones show the way
> to the vehicles which are the key.

Many believe that the Octopus was a metaphor for the many 'tentacles' of the spreading imperialism of the British Empire, while the 'vehicles' may have been an astrological reference to Ezekiel.

Anthropologists have pointed to the fact these symbols and themes have also been found in an Ndebele funeral song that calls for the dead to be sung across the chasm of space and time into the land of the ancestors. It may well have been that Dawid encountered this oral tradition in his travels.

But it was the substitution of the San Mantis God for the Christian Yahweh that was more than Niklaas could bear, and he swore to exorcise the Devil from Dawid's heart. But he never got the chance. Dawid's commando was attacked by the British and he was killed in the fighting. His daughter was captured, but her ultimate fate is unknown.

It is widely believed that along with Niklaas van Rensburg's daughter Hester, she died in a British concentration camp.

THE ZOMBIE HORROR NINJA SHOW

'The bodies are controlled by venom injected into the spinal cord,' Ronin whispers as we walk down the long staircase that descends into the bowels of the club. The stink of the place is unbearable. The smell you get when a rat dies under a floorboard? Distil that into its purest form. Eau de decay. I gag a couple of times and have to steady myself against the wall. 'They're zombies, essentially,' Ronin continues. 'That is until the creepy little spider assholes wear the body out and have to latch onto a new host.'

The staircase deposits us onto a heaving, phantasmagoric dance floor. A decaying corpse in latex bondage gear grins at me as it shimmies past, yanking a short chain connected to the spiked collar of a large and hairy middle-aged man who crawls after it.

The bass rumbles through my chest and strobe lights pulsate, highlighting naked zombies hanging in cages from the ceiling. They sway back and forth and peel flesh from their bones to throw to human punters watching them from below. 'Take it all off,' a sweaty guy in a suit shouts as we pass by him. His tie is loose about his neck and his face is flushed. The zombie obliges, peeling off muscle and tendon from her face until only bone remains. The guy hoots and slaps his friends on the backs.

Our escorts push their way through the sweaty bodies on the dance floor and lead us through a doorway that's guarded by more zombies. We step into a dim corridor lined with more doorways. A quick glance affirms my suspicion: we're in the studio where creature porn is made. I think I'd be more excited if it didn't smell like death and decay.

A dressing-room door left slightly ajar gives me the opportunity to glimpse a celebrity. Through the slit I see the Flesh Palace's most successful tokoloshe lounging in a chair, chewing on a fat cigar and watching us uninterestedly with his cruel pink piggy eyes. He's wearing a red velvet gown and a fat gold medallion hangs among his matted green chest hair. A naked zombie kneels at his feet scratching his large grey belly and feeding him something that looks suspiciously like a rodent. Rumpelforeskin grins smugly and then raises his hand to give us the middle finger.

Each new doorway offers a glimpse into another nightmarish set. Clearly the type of films I've been distributing were only scratching the surface of the kind of depravity that Zombiewood produces. We see a young guy being held down by two spidered zombies, while a third rips chunks of flesh from his thighs with its teeth. 'Oh, mistress, I've been a bad boy,' the man groans. 'Eat me, eat me.' On film, from a distance and thinking this was make-believe, I would have thought this was groundbreaking. From where I stand now, it makes me gag again.

'Easy, tiger,' Ronin says, putting his hand on my shoulder. I'm forced to swallow sour bile as we continue, grateful when we're led out of the studio to a large ornate set of doors.

I look up at the carved dark wood. It depicts nightmares and atrocities on a level I've never seen before. Hell has been shaped from the wood, spidered humans performing gross acts of torture. Two zombies in military cargo trousers and black muscle vests stand before us, necrotic muscle Marys flexing, and grinning toothlessly when we're presented to them.

One grabs me by the collar and shoves me against the wall to frisk me for weapons. The smell of him is overpowering and I just pray that there is no cavity search. Ronin swears as they remove Warchild and Hagaz from under his coat, but he doesn't have much choice. Satisfied that we're not hiding any other guns, knives or insecticide, they swing open the doors and shove us through.

A quick glance around shows we're in some kind of arachnid-zombie-dominatrix sex dungeon, which, as it turns out, is not nearly as cool as it sounds. The carvings on the door were entirely realistic. We're in Hell.

The walls are decorated with naked people trapped in rancid black spiderwebs that drip viscous fluid. The poor trapped souls are in stages of life/death/decomposition. They moan, scream and call out in pathetic voices, creating a sonic tapestry of despair.

'Ronin,' I whisper, resisting the urge to cling to his sleeve like a little child.

'Steady,' he whispers back. 'Try not to look at them.'

It's like telling someone not to look down when they're on a high wire. I can't help but look at the horror around us. A voice calls from above and I look up to see a man plastered to the ceiling by webs, trying desperately to free an arm from the disgusting black threads. It's useless. Even if he could free himself his legs look like they've been gnawed away. He's half a man stuck to the ceiling by zombie spiders. It's not looking good for him.

In the centre of the room is a dais surrounded by zombie soldiers. They lounge around like spoilt dogs. Spoilt dead dogs. Their eye sockets are hollow and black, and flesh hangs from their decaying bodies in strips. They watch us eagerly with their glassy eyes, like kids pressing their faces up against the window of a candy store.

The thing lounging on a throne on the dais is worst of all the nightmares in this place. Thankfully most of her is covered by a bloodstained Victorian bodice and skirt, but the skin I can see is red and raw, like it's been sliced away with a potato peeler. Her face is bone-white, except for dark and suppurating wounds that look like tears beneath her eyes. She holds a parasol and taps it rhythmically against her knees like a funeral drum.

The facial decay is just foreplay. The real nightmare is her eyes, two dark pools of tar – pools of tar where the bodies of nuns who have been violated and murdered have been dumped. They watch us approach with a mixture of curiosity, lust and I-wanna-suck-out-your-bone-marrow. A huge distended red body bulges from the back of her neck and it seems to pulsate slightly as she moves.

Ronin bows at the foot of the dais, grabbing my shoulder and forcing me to do the same. The Queen shrugs her gruesome body from the throne and saunters down to us. She extends her hand daintily toward him. He takes it and kisses it quickly. She floats her hand gently across to me and I follow his example, the stench thick in my nostrils as I barely touch the back of her cold hand with my lips.

She spins her parasol as she saunters back and forth in front of us, and with a lurch in my stomach I realise that it's made from skin stretched over bone. The Queen of the Anansi is into arts and crafts. Perfect.

'Blackblood,' she says, her voice like the sound of two alley cats fighting, 'I told you if you ever came back I'd kill you.'

Ronin smiles. 'Oh? I thought you were just exaggerating, Sergeant.'

She pushes the parasol under his chin. 'That's Queen to you.'

He shrugs. 'Old habits die hard.'

The Queen smiles cruelly. 'So will you, I hope. I want to enjoy it.'

She turns her eyes to me. 'You've brought a child along with you? A gift of young flesh to buy mercy?'

'I know mercy's not your style,' Ronin says.

He's right. I know the Queen's type. She's just like Anwar; a bully. She isn't going to let us go, she just wants to play with her food for a little bit. 'We've come for the Obambo,' I say and force myself to look up into those terrifying black eyes.

'You're making demands of *me*?' the Queen says. She puts the point of her parasol to my throat, lifting my chin. 'Well, it's refreshing at least. Too many sycophants are not good for one. Yes, I had your glowing man but I traded him for something much, much better.' She smiles, showing her black teeth and bloody gums. She sighs and leans in and sniffs at my neck. I try to suppress the shudder but I can't. 'Urfrog?' she says, sticking her bottom lip out like she's a little girl sulking about not being able to play with a favourite toy. 'You don't play nice, Ronin. Young bodies last so much longer. But no matter, we can still have fun with you.' She waves a hand at her zombie guards. 'Put them in the cage. That's why you walked into certain death, Ronin? Because you're looking for an Obambo? I must admit I'm a little disappointed. I thought you'd have a far better reason than that to die.'

'Tone is coming to shut you down,' Ronin says.

The Queen smiles. 'MK6 is a diverse and changing organisation, Blackbood. You know that better than I. Sometimes the rules can change without warning.'

Ronin stares at her for a moment, as if looking at one of those patterns that make a 3D picture if you stare at it hard enough. 'Mirth,' he says finally, spitting the word out.

'I never understood why you hated the man. He made you what you are,' the Queen says.

Ronin grins and it looks more like a wolf baring its teeth.

'His giggling always pissed me off.'

'Not very becoming, I agree. Thankfully, when you're powerful you can do whatever you want. You probably could have stopped him if you'd stayed,' she says and clicks her fingers. 'But you always were just a sideshow, Ronin.'

Zombies force us through a low concrete passage and into a large room like the one that hosts the zombie strip club. Except instead of throbbing techno this room serenades its patrons with classical music. We're dragged between elegant circular tables adorned with white tablecloths and silver candelabras.

I look around desperately and see some surprisingly familiar faces. Darlene Matthews, the soapie star, sits at one of the tables dabbing her mouth with a napkin. Gert van Zyl, musician, actor and reality game-show presenter, is gingerly scooping brains from a severed human head on a silver platter. 'We're being held hostage,' I shout to them. 'Help. Call the cops.' Gert smiles and raises his glass to us as we're dragged past.

Politicians are delicately sucking the marrow out of dismembered pinkie fingers, and several members of the national cricket team sip congealed blood from martini glasses. The Cape Town elite, it seems, are into zombie-chic gourmet cannibalism. Fucking poseurs.

'MK6 should have closed this down a long time ago,' Ronin whispers.

'But they haven't,' I say as I struggle against the zombie's iron grip. 'Please say you've got a plan.'

'I'm more of a spontaneous kind of guy,' he says with a maniac grin.

We're pushed toward a large cage made out of bones, kitsch even for a zombie queen. I brace my feet against the cage to stop the zombie from hoisting me inside, but he grabs the back of my shirt and lobs me through the cage door. I land hard on the mat and my glasses skitter across the floor. I scramble to my feet to reclaim them.

'You should get one of those straps,' Ronin says casually. 'You know, the ones that hold your glasses in place?'

'Can we talk about my glasses later?' I say.

There is someone else in the cage with us. He's tall and sinewy, leaning back on the cage with a top hat tipped rakishly on his head. His dark suit looks like an undertaker's and is old and tattered. Through the frayed elbows and jagged cuffs I can see his thin, pale limbs. He regards us with narrowed eyes, twirling a long moustache that droops over his restless twitching mouth. Ronin stares at him with a look of disbelief on his face. 'It can't be,' he says. 'She wouldn't.'

'What?' I say.

There's a cheer from the crowd as the Queen enters the arena on a throne carried on the backs of a phalanx of humans in bondage gear. She gives a stately nod as she's carried toward a spot next to the cage.

'I see you've met your opponent,' she says with a smile.

'You've aligned with these insane bastards?' Ronin splutters. 'MK6 will destroy you for this. Get ready for an army of sangomas coming to tear down your evil little kingdom.'

The Queen taps her lips with a long finger. 'Well, gosh, here I am breaking taboos left, right and centre. And where, oh where, is the great and powerful Tone and MK6?'

'You don't know what you're doing,' Ronin says. 'They don't form alliances, they use them and then destroy them.'

'Aww, are you worried for the poor widdle Queen?' she says. 'Well, dry your tears. Dober and I have an understanding. Besides, I thought you'd be happy to face one of the Crows. After what they did to Baresh.' She clicks her fingers. 'Kill them, Crow,' the Queen says. 'And make sure it's a good show.'

Top Hat lazily pushes himself off the cage and Ronin quickly rips off his coat and wraps it around his forearm to create a makeshift shield. Top Hat points a finger at me. 'I can smell your corruption from here, half-breed.'

'Your mother dresses you funny,' I say.

He laughs, a long barking sound, and advances slowly toward us.

'I've always wanted to know what it would be like to kill one of you,' Ronin says.

'Then I'm afraid you will gain no satisfaction here,' Top Hat says, taking off his coat, revealing a dirty white shirt beneath. His skin begins to ripple and twist. There's a cracking of bone and sinew, like the sound of a carcass put through a grinder, and black feathers begin to sprout from his face. His mouth crunches as his jaw dislocates and begins to twist into the shape of a long beak. Large leathery wings erupt from his back and a scorpion's tail rises above his head. Top Hat has ceased to be a shabbily dressed gentleman and has become something from a nightmare. A singular Cyclops eye stares at us from the centre of the Crow's forehead and two claws clench convulsively on the side of its head.

'Grandpa Zev was right, there *are* giant crow demons; Jesus, that thing looks evil,' I whisper.

'Well, let's just say I wouldn't let it babysit,' Ronin says, grabbing me by the sleeve and pulling me behind him. 'Look for an opening in the cage,' he whispers. 'And make it fast.'

The thing shuffles toward us with its wings raised. Ronin circles out of its way and throws an explosive kick at its bloated leg. It barely seems to notice. It spreads its wings and retaliates with the force of a freight train, slamming into us and sending me to the mat with a wing. Ronin ducks the other wing, but is caught by the beak and flung into the centre of the cage, landing with the sound of a sandal slapping a wet sheep carcass.

He drags himself to his knees. A long, ugly gash has opened up on his forehead and is dripping blood. 'Any ideas?' he wheezes.

'Well, I don't want to get in the way of your spontaneity,' I say, 'but I do have an idea.'

Grandpa Zevcenko won't leave me much when he dies. No offshore investments. No money or property. My sole inheritance is advice on how to fight giant crows and I'm cashing it in. 'Fire,' I say to Ronin. 'It's the only thing that'll stop it.'

'And you're now the world's leading expert on Crows?' Ronin says groggily.

'Trust me,' I say.

I look out through the bleached white bones of the cage and into the eyes of a punter enjoying a meal. Human brain by the looks of it; a small congealed pink mess surrounded by squiggles of marinade and topped with an artfully carved cucumber. Even gourmet cannibalism is a rip-off.

I spot a vintage oil lamp providing tasteful ambience for the table. I squeeze my arm through the cage and grab the lamp. The man grabs my hand and for a second we struggle over it. 'Let it go,' I hiss. The guy seems to think this is part of the entertainment and holds on tightly with a dumb grin on his face. With my other hand I scrabble across the table and find a heavy silver fork. With a grunt I jam the fork into his forearm. He screams and releases the lamp, and I wrench it from his grasp and pull it through.

Ronin takes it from my hand just as the Crow launches itself at us. I scramble out of the way and watch as the bounty hunter stands poised, brandishing the oil lamp like it's some kind of superweapon. I really hope Grandpa Zev is not completely insane.

As the Crow jabs its beak forward, Ronin twists to the side and brings the burning lamp down on its head. The hot oil runs down and scalds its single eye and I smell burning flesh. The Crow shrieks in pain and lashes out blindly with its wings, colliding with the cage and ripping a jagged hole in the bones.

We scramble past the flailing Crow and Ronin climbs through the hole and reaches back to help me. I grab his arm and struggle through the opening but am viciously yanked backwards. The floor hits me hard and drives the air from my lungs. There's a lancing pain in my side. I groan. It feels like one of my ribs is broken. I don't have time to check because a claw grabs me by the throat and lifts me into the air.

The blind Crow caws in triumph. Hanging suspended from the muscular appendage of a bird-like monstrosity while the air is choked from you really puts your life into perspective. I see a vision of fair-haired children playing happily on playground swings, while a young mother, radiant in the sunlight, laughs with carefree abandon. I'm slightly disappointed when I realise that it's a scene from a popular washing-powder commercial. The jingle plays in my head as I begin to lose consciousness.

My forehead throbs to the rhythm of my last few breaths and I find myself sliding out of my body with the feeling of a bar of soap slipping from your fingers. My disembodied consciousness looks down and sees my body being slowly choked, my face a hideous shade of magenta, my eyes rolling back in my head.

Something cool takes my hand and I look up and see a girl about my age floating above the cage with me. She gives me a smile and tugs at my hand. I follow her and we float up through the ceiling and to the club above. More of the men in top hats at the entrance of the club are pushing through the throng of patrons and strippers.

She leads me away to the side, to one of the lap-dance booths. It appears my dying brain desires a lap dance from a ghost. Well, OK. But the girl gestures to a door at the back of the booth and we watch as a woman in a hairnet opens it and steps out.

She gestures again to the door and then reaches forward and

places her hand on my forehead. A warm glow fills my head. 'Am I dead?' I whisper. She smiles and an image of the red Eye fills my brain. I smile back at her.

With a start I find myself back in my body. The pressure increases and I get the feeling that the Crow is enjoying watching me die. I let my body go limp. I'm ready to die.

Out of the corner of my blurred vision I see Ronin crawling back through the hole with a steak knife between his teeth like he's a pirate scaling the side of a ship. He climbs up the bones and then turns and launches himself off, hanging in midair for a split second like a hawk in flight before slamming down on the Crow's back, pulling the knife from between his teeth and relentlessly stabbing the Crow in the face.

The Crow drops me and lashes out at empty air. Ronin tumbles from its back and lands on the ground next to me. He pulls me back to the hole and gives me a boost through. I crawl over the sharp bones, gashing my arm on the edge of a humerus.

I crash onto a table and it gives way; I roll off and hit the ground. Ronin hoists me to my feet. The room of diners stare at us, some in the back standing up and craning their necks to get a better look. 'All part of the entertainment, folks,' Ronin says, spreading his arms like a showman.

'Ronin!' a voice behind us screeches. We turn to see the Queen holding her arms out above her like she's blessing a Black Mass. A dark, wet web erupts from her necrotic body and its long cords slither toward us. They leave a trail of gore behind them as they elongate and spread through the diners, covering and wrapping around them.

The crowd begins to scream, overturning tables and climbing over each other to get away from the dark, lecherous strands. Ronin grabs a famous newsreader in a headlock and uses him as a shield as a strand whips forward. 'I know people,' the newsreader screams as the cord wraps around his foot and begins to pull. 'Please, I'll get you anything – money, women, you name it.'

'How about some good news for a change?' Ronin says. 'South Africa's not all about crime, you know.' The cord drags the newsreader from Ronin's hands and twists his head off, sending a fountain of blood arcing through the air.

'Ronin,' I shout and point toward the Queen's throne, where Warchild and Hagaz are hung on steel spikes like trophies. Ronin leaps over a writhing cord and sprints toward the throne. He dodges past two zombie guards and his fingers close around Hagaz's hilt and drag it from the scabbard.

'Kill them,' the Queen screams. Three cords slide toward Ronin like fat black anacondas. He slashes one as it rears up in front of him. It begins to ooze black liquid but continues to attack. More cords slide forward, tangling together to form a huge, wet mass that pushes him back. Ronin hacks at them, the black liquid splashing onto his face as he tries to beat them back.

More cords pour from the Queen's zombie body, which begins to dissolve, leaving nothing but the large hideous spider that rises up the black cords like it's surfing a black wave.

One of her cords wraps around Ronin's leg and drags him to his knees. He hacks viciously at it, but another grabs his hand and begins to drag him into the roiling wet mass. Ronin stretches the sword behind him as far as his arm can reach and then with a grunt hurls it.

The blade slices through the air and buries itself hilt-deep in the Queen's fat red spider body. She shrieks hysterically and the cords whip frantically about like high-pressure hoses.

Ronin extricates himself from the mass of cords and limps over to the throne to retrieve Warchild.

The Queen's many legs scrabble on the ground, but Hagaz is buried deep in her abdomen and toxic black ooze is pouring from the wound. Ronin walks over to her and prods her with the shotgun's barrels.

'Convince me not to kill you,' he says conversationally. 'What's that? You can't speak without a host body? Well then, I guess you're out of luck.'

The spider scrabbles frantically, but Ronin pushes Warchild into her abdomen and then fires both barrels into the fat body. Fetid black liquid sprays everywhere. Ronin wipes his arm across his face.

A guy stumbles past me and I notice an Octogram lanyard peeking out through his jacket. Instinctively I stick my leg out and the guy trips, hitting the ground hard. Ronin raises an eyebrow.

'Octogram,' I say, pointing to the lanyard.

Ronin drags Hagaz from the Queen's body and holds it against the guy's throat and then reaches down to look at the lanyard. 'Looks like you're coming with us ... Dave.'

'We've got to go to the lap-dance booths,' I say.

'Let's save the celebrations until we get out of here, sparky.'

'There are more Crows coming,' I say. 'They're in the club. One of the booths has hidden stairs. Unless there's some other way to bypass the Crows, that's our only way out.'

Ronin grabs Dave by the throat. 'Is that true?'

'Chop shop,' Dave gurgles. 'I've heard there's an exit into the sewers there.'

Ronin looks at me appraisingly. 'Well, you're really getting into the supernatural swing of things, aren't you?'

We plough through the disorientated zombies. Without the Queen they seem to be content to tear random diners apart. We take the stairs that lead to the upper level and move quickly through the corridors to the line of lap-dance booths. 'That one,' I say, pointing to the one on the end.

Ronin opens Warchild and slides in two new shells and then

drags back the curtain. A zombie in a thong is gyrating on the lap of a young guy with square glasses and a chequered shirt. 'Out,' Ronin says. The guy scrambles to his feet and disappears through the curtain, but the zombie hisses and scratches at Dave's face with her bony fingers. Ronin raises Warchild and pulls the trigger. Her head explodes, spraying flesh and bone onto the velvet cushions. The body collapses sideways but continues to claw manically at the ground. We step carefully over it and head to the stairs.

Ronin shoves Dave first and presses Warchild to the back of his head. We head down a long flight of stairs. I look back up, but there doesn't seem to be anyone in pursuit. Yet. The stairs end in a large smoky room filled with industrial equipment. A group of women are sitting next to a conveyor belt, chatting and smoking as they dissect human corpses and shove internal organs into packets.

'And then her sister says, "Your husband was all too happy to watch me undress",' the hairnet woman I saw in my vision says. The other women shake their heads. 'Disgusting,' says a pretty younger woman with a scar down the side of her face. She pulls the intestines from a corpse and begins to feed them into a surgical bag marked with the distinctive red octopus.

I clear my throat and ten pairs of eyes turn to look at us. 'The dead hookers are upstairs, you perverts,' hairnet woman says.

'We're looking for a tunnel,' I say.

The woman takes a drag of a cigarette and squashes a bloody heart into a packet. 'The Queen know you're here?'

'The Queen is dead,' Ronin says with satisfaction.

'Yeah, no shit, genius,' the younger woman says. 'She's a zombie.'

'Dead dead,' Ronin says. 'The spider part too.'

'So you don't have to work here any more,' I say. 'You're free.'

A large woman with a red cloth tied around her head takes a drag of her cigarette. 'Are you going to pay me twenty-five rand an hour, as well as overtime?'

'Ja, you think we want to go back to working at Chicken Ranch with a manager that tries to grope our titties every two seconds?' hairnet woman says. 'No thanks. We may work for zombies, but at least the pay is good and they leave us alone.'

'We have a TV,' the younger woman adds. 'We can watch *Generations* every day while we work.'

'There's a bus that takes us home,' the large woman adds. 'And we always go to a fancy restaurant for our Christmas party.'

'But –' I say.

'The tunnel is in the back, perverts,' hairnet woman says and blows smoke out through her nostrils.

The women shake their heads in collective disgust and ignore us as we make our way quickly past the production line.

The passageway opens out into a dank tunnel. Ronin drags Dave through, kicks him against the wall and jams Warchild into his mouth. 'We have questions. Only truthful answers will ensure longevity here today, understood?' Dave gives a short, terrified nod.

'We don't have time for this,' I hiss. 'The Crows.'

'He'll slow us down if we take him.' Ronin looks at Dave. 'Quick answers. Let's start with the human body parts; why does Octogram need them?'

'I don't know,' Dave says.

Ronin cocks both of Warchild's hammers. 'I'm not sure you understand the gravity of your situation, Dave.'

'OK,' Dave whimpers. 'Please.' He takes a deep breath. 'The Queen supplies us with biological material that we use for research purposes.'

'Researching what?'

'Weapons mostly,' Dave says.

'And what do you give her in return?' Ronin asks. 'Last time I checked the Queen didn't do much pro bono work.' He pushes Warchild against Dave's forehead.

'Oh God,' Dave says, his eyes squinting as they look up at the twin barrels of the shotgun that pins his head to the wall. 'Freedom. She gets to do what she wants. MK6 doesn't interfere. Actually they help. I don't know any more than that, really I don't. I'm just a junior executive.' Ronin looks at him for a second and then nods. 'I understand. Corporate hierarchy, right? You work and you work and what do you get? Nothing. They keep you in the dark, make you do all the work while they're off running up huge expense accounts?'

Dave nods.

'I believe you,' Ronin says.

Dave sighs with relief. Ronin smiles benevolently. And then viciously slams the butt of the shotgun into his temple. Dave slumps into the dirty grey water.

'That's what you get for being a yes-man,' Ronin says with a smirk.

We make our way through the long pipe and into some kind of tunnel system, which runs under the club. The tunnel smells like a portable toilet at a rock festival. All things considered, the smell of faeces is preferable to the smell of death. Still, I can't keep from vomiting into the grey water which is ankle-deep in the pipe.

The sun is injecting daylight into the veins of the city as Ronin and I finally scramble out of a manhole several blocks away from the Flesh Palace. We make our way through the streets and back toward the Cortina. We get close and peer around the corner. Several black vans are parked outside the entrance.

'MK6,' Ronin whispers.

'Let's go ask Tone if he's found Esmé or the Obambo,' I say, moving forward. Ronin shoots out his arm and pushes me against the wall. 'Tone's not there,' he says. 'It's Mirth. With Sabian Dober, the head of the Murder.'

Dr Kobus Basson
32 Riker Place Business Park
Cape Town

Dear Mr and Mrs Zevcenko

Over the past few months I have attempted to gently shepherd Baxter toward a more healthy worldview, one where he is able to consider the impact of his actions on himself and others. Unfortunately at this stage I believe a more direct approach is needed.

Baxter's delusions are such that I believe he may be becoming a danger to himself and others. A discussion about voluntary commitment into a mental health facility was immediately dismissed and has merely resulted in Baxter fabricating further about himself. I believe that the potential for violence, either to himself or to others, is acute. I hope we are able to frame this in a way that is consistent with this journey Baxter believes he is on.

Mental illness is nothing to be ashamed of and I know that during this time you will be tempted to look for things that you could have done to prevent this. There is nothing you could have done. Brain chemistry is as unique as a fingerprint and some of us are more vulnerable to mental illness than others.

I would like to schedule a meeting with you to speak about the possibility of involuntary commitment for Baxter. Although I don't take this step lightly, I believe that it is the best thing for your son.

Please contact me at any time, night or day, should you have any questions. You have my sincere promise that I will do everything necessary to make Baxter well again.

Kind regards,
Dr Kobus Basson

OBAMBONATION

*L*arge windows let in the sun, for which I'm grateful. I stop my work for a moment and lift my head to the rays and enjoy the feel of them on my face. But I quickly return to plunging my cloth into the bucket and then pulling it out and scrubbing the floor vigorously.

My new life is one of solitude and hard work. I scrub the floors of the house until they shine, but it never seems to be enough. The housekeeper is a small woman with a ruddy complexion, a thick neck and oval face, and a sharp tongue. She punishes my 'laziness' by pulling my ears viciously. More than once I have thought about strangling her. But I don't want to go back to the soldiers. I'm not sure whether I could avoid their advances this time.

My father and everyone in the commando are dead. I know this, but it is difficult to come to terms with. Sometimes I hear children outside and think, just for a moment, that it is Mari or Tessie. Or I hear a male voice in the distance and expect the craggy, bearded face of my father to appear. But it never does. Most often it's the magistrate. He's a tall man with a gaunt face, but he's kind. He seems to take an interest in me, asking me many questions about when I was first brought here. What do I dream? What do I know about my father and my uncle Niklaas's gift? I don't tell him about the boy with the spectacles. I don't tell him anything. I am a Boer and he is an English dog.

I finish scrubbing the floor and haul the heavy bucket into the kitchen. The cooks are laughing and one cuffs me playfully on the ear. At least they speak Afrikaans. I empty the bucket outside. A girl covered in bandages stands outside. Even her face is covered, but her eyes are black and shiny and she looks directly at me.

'Lepers,' the housekeeper hisses and crosses herself. 'Lord help us all.' She turns to me. 'What are you doing staring like you're lovesick? Would you like to join the lepers outside?'

'No, mistress,' I say, bowing my head and looking at the floor. I've learnt that this is the proper response to anything she has to say to me.

'Yes, well, you're lucky,' she says with a cruel tug of my ear. 'The master seems to have taken a liking to you. If it were up to me you'd be out onto the street with the rest of those scum.'

She sends me to fetch more water from the well and I lift the bucket and carry it outside. The leper girl follows me as I walk. I imagine myself with my face wrapped in bandages and a chord of fear strikes in my heart. The girl follows me to the well and then stands a distance away watching.

'Who are you?' I turn to say to her in Afrikaans. I'm allowed to speak Afrikaans in the kitchen, but never in the rest of the house. I refuse to speak English when I'm not forced to.

'Luamita,' she replies in Afrikaans.

'I'm Ester,' I say.

'Ester,' she says as if tasting the name in her mouth. 'You're a Siener.' I turn around sharply.

'Don't worry,' she says soothingly. 'I am a friend.'

'You're a leper,' I say, more harshly than I mean to.

'No,' she says matter-of-factly. She looks around quickly and then unwraps one of the bandages that covers her face. Beneath are not the grotesque sores I'm expecting, but a patch of bright, shining skin.

I drop the bucket and the water spills onto my shoes. I stare at her. 'I'm an Obambo,' she says softly, quickly wrapping the bandage back. 'We are friends to your people.'

My hand shoots to the little bottle around my neck. Luckily none of the soldiers thought it valuable enough to take it from me and they allowed me to keep it.

'That was a gift from my people to yours,' Luamita says, nodding to the bottle. 'And the time has come to use some of it.'

'No,' I say, clutching the bottle protectively in my hand. 'My father said to use it only to find the vehicle.'

She smiles and steps forward until she's standing right in front of me. 'There is more to the finding of the vehicle than you understand. It is a journey that will take a long time. And even then the outcome is uncertain.' She takes my hand in hers. Her grasp is soft and warm. 'The boy with the spectacles,' she says simply. 'He is sixteen years old and a Siener like you.'

'I am sixteen years old,' I say dumbly.

'The time when a Siener's powers are awakened,' she says gently. She lifts a hand and removes the necklace from around my neck. 'You and he are connected,' she says. 'And he needs your help.'

I hold the little bottle in the palm of my hand and look at the luminous liquid that shifts around inside. 'The blood of my people,' Luamita says. 'Intended to help you to save us all.'

I unstop the bottle and then look at her. She nods.

I take a sip and the world explodes around me. Lights shoot past my eyes like fireflies racing each other in the wind. I feel like I'm picking up speed, going faster and faster like I'm in a carriage that is careening down a mountain pass. It's terrifying but also

*exhilarating. My forehead expands as if water is erupting from it,
and I can see everything around me. Everything. The tiny ladybird
on the plant down the road. The perspiration on the forehead of a
worker grunting as he lifts bags of flour onto a wagon. Everything,
together, in the blink of an eye.*

*My mind roars like the Cape Doctor whipping the branches of
trees back and forth during a storm. I can see Cape Town down
below me; people like ants in the dirt. The masts of the ships in the
docks and beneath them the sailors laughing and cursing on deck.
And then Cape Town changes and becomes monstrous. It seems to
grow thick and grey, taking over the surrounding landscape like a
plague of locusts.*

*Tall, grey glass monoliths rise up from the ground like savage,
pagan monuments. I gasp and clutch at my head. This is horrible,
this is all wrong. My mind sweeps down like the wind and I can
barely make out the grotesque and terrible shapes that loom up in
front of me. I'm in a house and see a man. A man like Luamita,
a man who glows. He is tall and strong and his body shines like a
lantern. He is stroking a mountain lynx that sits on a perch like a
bird. A mountain lynx with wings.*

I wake up with a jolt. My face is stuck to the leather of the couch
in Ronin's lounge. We'd come straight back to his place and
I'd collapsed like a drunkard and fallen asleep instantly. Light
streams in through the bamboo blinds and painfully needles my
vision. I lift my hand to shield my eyes and wince. It hurts when
I breathe and I have a nasty headache.

I lift my T-shirt and pull a face at the dark purple bruise that
stretches from my left nipple right down the left side of my body.
I sit up and make my way gingerly through to the kitchen and
take a long drink of water from the tap.

I open the freezer and grab a handful of ice, roll it up in a dirty dishtowel and press it against my ribs. The bounty hunter strides into the kitchen wearing nothing but silk boxers with Taz, the Tasmanian devil, on them.

'Trendy,' I say softly.

He shrugs. 'Chicks dig 'em.'

He grabs a beer from the fridge. 'Ibuprofen?' he asks, offering me several pills in the palm of his hand. I nod gratefully and pop two into my mouth and wash them down with more water from the tap. Ronin slugs the rest back with his beer.

Seagulls wheel and pitch above us like TIE fighters as we climb out onto the roof to drink beer and eat cereal. Every spoonful of Rice Krispies is unpleasant because my ribs are so bruised that lifting the spoon hurts. Plus, I can't get the smell of the Flesh Palace out of my nostrils.

Last night's events are a haze of fear, blood and death. I sip my beer and try to gain some sense of perspective.

'Tone would never have allowed that shit to happen,' Ronin says through a mouthful of bran. 'Which means he's probably dead by now.'

'This Mirth guy was involved in the incident Pat was talking about?' I say.

Ronin laughs and chases his mouthful of bran with a gulp of beer. 'You could say that. When I was drafted into the army in '84 my talent for fucking shit up didn't go unnoticed. I was put into this new experimental weapons unit. Thought it was pretty standard until I saw what the weapons were.'

'Missiles and stuff?'

'I wish. No, it was some real Frankenstein shit, splicing together biological material to create an army. The National Party, going all out in their bid to perpetuate apartheid, were preparing for a civil war and Mirth was their supernatural golden boy. They made him the head of the unit and threw money at him. They didn't care that he was twisted. The fucker giggled like a little girl when he experimented on living things. That's how he got his codename.'

'So what happened?'

'Apartheid ended. Everybody thought they were going to see him jailed for life. But the Occult Truth Commission was a sham. He knew too much about the Hidden and was too powerful and too useful for the government to get rid of. So they hired him.'

'Jeez,' I say. 'Talk about not holding any grudges.'

'Yeah, well, it's all about the money and power. As I soon found out. They made him the head of MK6, and he requested that I join him – either that or he'd have made me a scapegoat for the things our unit did on the Border.'

'Like what exactly?'

'Bad shit and lots of it. I can't really remember that much, because Mirth had me on a whole lot of experimental drugs to increase strength and endurance.' He tries to smile but it comes out more like a grimace. 'I was pretty screwed up,' he says softly. 'Well, *more* screwed up than I am now. Baresh helped me. Stopped me from going crazy and stopped me from being the monster that Mirth tried to make me into.'

I watch him as he lights a cigarette and gets up to stretch. I feel sorry for Ronin. He's like a dog with rabies; unpleasant and aggressive with a sense of doom surrounding him.

'We all do bad things,' I say, a little lamely. I tell him about Mikey Markowitz, how we spent a whole holiday programming a game in BASIC together. There was this sense of camaraderie that we'd had. I still remember the feeling. Two months later I had to cut him loose.

'Why?' Ronin says.

'Politics. Mikey was not a good person to be around. He

attracted scorn and ridicule and I couldn't have that while I was building the Spider. So I ignored him and pretended not to watch him become a sad loner. I guess I'm not really a good person either,' I say to Ronin.

I end up telling him about how I've pretty much manipulated everyone I've ever known. I can remember them all, each little betrayal, false flag and fake emotion I've used. Surprisingly, Ronin doesn't laugh. He looks at me the whole time with his weird blue eyes, smoking his cigarette right down to the filter as I talk. When I've finished, he strokes his beard. 'You're a pretty weird kid,' he says.

'I know,' I say, and wonder whether I'm genuinely just realising this now or whether I've always known it.

He shrugs. 'Guess we've all got our problems.'

'Yeah,' I say.

We sit for a while in silence. 'So what happened to Baresh?' I eventually say to break it.

'Baresh was powerful and Mirth resented him for it. When the Crows killed him, I wanted to go after them but Mirth wouldn't let me. We had a falling-out and I resigned. I thought I would be nailed for sure, but Pat stood up for me. She quit too. I don't know what I would have done without her.

I think about last night's weird dream. 'Do you trust her?' I say. 'Pat, I mean.'

'Completely,' he says. 'Why?'

I tell him about the dream. Well, the part about the glowing man stroking Tony Montana.

He looks at me. 'This dream. It felt like finding that door in the club?'

'Kinda,' I say. 'I don't even know what that was.'

I'm about to continue when my phone rings. It's Kyle and he's panicking. He says that Rafe is pretty much bouncing off the walls and that I have to get there. Now. The tone of his voice doesn't leave much room for manoeuvring. Kyle is a pretty laidback guy, but when he gets freaked out it's like trying to reason with a Chihuahua on crystal meth.

'I've got to go sort this out,' I tell Ronin with a sigh. He nods but he's stroking his beard braid thoughtfully. 'Obambo are more than rare – they're extinct. If she thinks she can stop him from being killed ...' He looks up at me. 'I'll give Pat a call,' he says.

I don't have time to wait for a train so I phone for a cab. It comes quickly, a sputtering grey Mazda with a skew 'Taxi' sign on top of it. The driver is a sullen Senegalese guy wearing a muscle top and a beret. It doesn't take long to get to Kyle's house and I pay him and get out.

'What's up, hombre?' I say when Kyle opens the door. He looks tired. His hair is mussed up and he has dark rings around his eyes. 'This is up,' he says, holding up several pages of computer paper. 'Fifteen hours of this.'

Rafe has been drawing. A lot. Nonstop, in fact. Kyle has had to play nursemaid and try to keep my parents from figuring out that I'm not there.

'Your mom phoned like four times,' he says. 'I'm out of excuses for why you can't come to the phone.'

'I'll phone her,' I say. 'I'll tell her that we're having a great time and that we want to stay another night.'

'What?' he says. 'Bax, I don't know whether –'

'What the hell are these?' I say.

Rafe's crayon drawings are scattered around Kyle's room like some kind of postmodern art installation. Hundreds of them.

There's one of me next to a guy with fiery red hair and a sword. There are several where we're walking with grey men with weird colourful bulges on their necks. There's one of a big black creature with wings looming above me. 'This is what I've been trying to tell you,' Kyle says tiredly. 'He hasn't stopped.'

Rafe is lying on the floor of Kyle's room and scribbling furiously with his crayons on a sheet of paper. 'Rafe,' I say. 'Rafe!' He looks up. 'What is this? How do you know to draw this?'

He shrugs and lifts the drawing he's been working on. It's a picture of what looks like me with a knife in my hand and a red eye on my forehead.

'That's why I've been freaking out,' Kyle says. 'He's been drawing stuff with the Mountain Killer eye on it.'

'Jesus, Rafe,' I whisper and sit down next to him on the floor.

He takes the crayon in his fist and writes a single word on top of the picture: 'Siener'.

'Bax, seriously,' Kyle says. 'You need to tell me what's going on.'

So I do. I tell him about what's been happening. About *everything* that's been happening. He looks at me sceptically when I tell him about the elemental; his eyebrows raise so high when I tell him about the Flesh Palace and the Anansi that I swear he's going to burst a blood vessel in his eye.

'Seriously,' I say, 'I know it sounds totally ridiculous, but it's true.'

The painkillers are wearing off and my ribs begin to throb again. I shift uncomfortably.

'Bax, are you sure you're OK? I mean, I don't think you're lying. It's just that maybe something's going on in your head.' He makes a swirling motion above his head.

'I don't know what's going on,' I say. 'But we're going to find the guy that the tooth belongs to. He must know where Esmé is and after that, well, it doesn't matter.'

'I'm coming with you,' Kyle says, folding his arms. 'I'm sick of being left out of this.'

'No, please,' I say, 'I'm begging you. I need you to run interference with my folks and keep Rafe away from all this. If my parents find out that I've hired a supernatural bounty hunter they'll probably have me committed.' Kyle doesn't unfold his arms. 'I didn't want to do this,' I say. 'But I'm invoking the Angela Dimbleton favour.'

Invoking the name of Angela Dimbleton is not something I'd do lightly. But I don't have a choice. The Angela Dimbleton favour is an oath that I swore to Kyle and it happened like this: Kyle's first attempt at sex wasn't, well, very successful. It was with a girl named Angela Dimbleton, the biggest, most loud-mouthed gossip at Westridge. YouTube videos went viral slower than Angela Dimbleton spread gossip. When she and Kyle got it on the results were less than spectacular. They were dismal in fact. Kyle was a little quick off the mark. Like hadn't-even-gotten-his-pants-off quick.

Having anything embarrassing happen in the presence of Angela Dimbleton was bad news, but suffering from premature ejaculation while getting it on with her was pretty much like posting it on your Facebook wall.

Kyle called me, mortified, and asked for my help. Luckily for him I'd been preparing a dossier on Angela Dimbleton. I'd hoped to use the dirt to force Dimbleton to help us sell porn, but Kyle begged me. So I'd phoned Angela and had a little talk about her, her super-religious family and the abortion clinic she'd been seen coming out of. She'd folded, and the story about Lightning-Quick Kyle had been quashed. Kyle had been so grateful that he'd promised he'd do anything should I call in the favour. ANYTHING.

'Angela Dimbleton?' he says morosely. 'Really?'

I nod. 'Sorry, but I really need this.'

'OK,' he says. 'But then the debt is paid.'

I smile. 'In full, Flash.'

'Screw you,' Kyle says with a rueful smile.

* * *

Kyle's mom is heading out and offers me a lift. I decide it would be a good idea to accept. If my mom phones her she can say she's seen me. 'Yoga class?' she says enthusiastically as she steers the car onto the highway. 'I've always wanted to do yoga.'

'Very good for the spine,' I say with a smile. 'Helps with all kinds of lifestyle diseases.'

'Modern life is so dangerous,' she says sadly.

I get her to drop me a block away from Ronin's. 'This is where you do yoga?' she says, looking doubtfully at the decrepit industrial buildings. 'My teacher is very authentic,' I say. 'She doesn't believe in materialism.'

'Oh, of course,' Kyle's mom says with a smile of acknowledgement. 'You must give me her number.'

'I will. Namaste,' I say, putting my hands into prayer position.

'Namaste,' she says solemnly.

I wait until she drives away and then take a side road that leads toward Ronin's building. I'm walking past a large rusty metal gate covered in a graffiti mural of an angel when a car pulls up in front of me. A large familiar shape struggles out of the car and lumbers toward me.

'Well, if it isn't my favourite serial killer,' Schoeman says.

'This is harassment,' I say, trying to walk faster and then exhaling in pain as my ribs start to hurt again.

'No, this is police work,' he says, coming to stand in front of me, his huge frame blocking my way. 'A new victim means new evidence.'

'Esmé?' I say, a sick feeling in my stomach.

'No,' he says. 'But maybe you can tell me why the time of death of this new unfortunate was found to be during the exact time that you evaded our surveillance?'

'Incompetence?' I suggest. His thick arm darts forward like a python and slams me against the rusty metal gate.

'We get a call from people inside a club known for making pornography. One that you and your crazy bounty-hunter friend were seen entering. They say it's total chaos, they need help. We get there, but it's already surrounded by black vans and guys waving government- agency badges. We're told to step down.'

'I've seen this movie,' I say. His fist tightens on my T-shirt.

'A reporter who was working on some kind of story involving a supernatural dog-fighting ring shows up at home blubbing uselessly. And you, well, you spontaneously decide to hire some kind of supernatural bounty hunter. Would you like to guess what the common thread is here?'

I widen my eyes. 'That you have no idea what's going on?'

He leans his chubby face in toward mine. 'You're testing my patience.'

'You're subjecting me to police brutality.'

He points a chubby finger at me. 'I'm putting you away, Zevcenko. You're not going to juvenile detention. You're going to Pollsmoor. You know what they do in –'

'Spare me your prison fantasies,' I say.

He slams me into the metal gate once more for good measure and then releases my T-shirt. 'I know it's you,' he says. 'I just have to prove it.'

He waddles away and I wait until he's gone before I make my way to Ronin's.

I meet Ronin outside his office and tell him about Schoeman. He looks down the road and waves. 'Yep, there's an undercover car sticking out like a teenage zit,' he says. 'We're going to have to lose them again.'

'Where are we going?' I say.

'Pat's,' he says. 'I spoke to her. She's definitely hiding something.'

Ronin repeats the ritual with the cocaine and the rat and we spend almost an hour losing the cop car. While we drive Ronin explains to me about magic.

Apparently it's connected to genetics. While anybody can theoretically do any kind of magic, every genetic pool has a specific connection to their heritage, a Wyrrd, which gives them a predilection for a specific kind of hoodoo. The Xhosa are apparently good with air and sound magic. That's why Tone is able to do what he does.

'I probably have some Dwarven ancestors,' Ronin says. 'I'm bringing this up because the stuff you saw at the Flesh Palace might be connected to your Wyrrd,' he says. 'If you don't get some training it can fuck you up.'

'The Sieners,' I say.

'You're Afrikaans?' he says.

'Polish and Afrikaans on my dad's side,' I tell him.

He nods. 'It's possible. Although very few people have those genes. The English made a point of trying to wipe them out. Enemies with genuine far sight are a pain in the ass when you're trying to build an empire. The English have a long tradition of sending warlocks into South Africa, an essential part of their efforts here. That's where Mirth's specialities come from, mostly spirit work, which translates to demonology or necromancy if you're an asshole, which Mirth most certainly is, exacerbated by the fact that he's half Crow.'

'The head of MK6 is one of *those* things?' I say.

Ronin nods. 'Half-breed. It's one of the reasons the government wanted to keep him around. He's one of the few existing Crow half-breeds, because not many humans can survive the mating process.' I shudder and try not to think of one of those things having sex. 'He can't transform like they can,' Ronin says. 'But it makes him powerful and difficult to kill.'

Ronin speeds through a red light and cuts in front of a taxi.

'Crows,' he says as we exit the highway and head toward Philippi. 'I'd happily kill them all.'

We pull into the driveway slowly. The Haven is peaceful. I can hear birds chirping softly as we get out of the car and head toward the door. At least I think they're birds. I'm not sure after seeing what Pat keeps in her barn.

'So lovely to see you again so soon,' Pat says, opening the door. 'Come in, come in.' She ushers us into the kitchen and starts filling an old battered kettle with water. 'You two look like you've been pulled through the briar patch backwards,' she says over her shoulder.

'It's been a weird couple of days,' I say.

'It always is with Jackson,' Pat replies.

'We're not here to have tea, Pat,' Ronin says.

'I hope you're not endangering this boy or taking him to unsavoury places,' she says quickly, ignoring him and bustling over to put the kettle on the gas stove. I think of the Flesh Palace and wonder if there is a more unsavoury place in Cape Town.

'Pat,' Ronin says.

'If you want Baxter to learn more about the Hidden, I'd be happy to teach –'

'That Obambo kidnapped Baxter's girlfriend,' Ronin says. 'For all we know he could have killed her.'

'Tomas? Never!' Pat says, shocked, and then slaps her hand to her mouth.

'Pat, please,' I say. 'We have no idea where Esmé is. That glowing man is the only link to her.'

'Where is he?' Ronin says firmly.

Pat's kindly old face crumples in defeat. 'He's in the attic.'

I follow as Ronin bounds up the stairs.

'Don't you hurt him. Don't you dare hurt that poor man!' she says.

Ronin pulls Warchild from beneath his coat and slams open the hatch that leads into the attic. I follow as he vaults up the rickety wooden ladder.

The Obambo is tall but thin, has the facial features of a West African, and glows with the light of a small sun. He sits quietly on an old cast-iron bed in the corner of the room, with his hands on his lap as if he has been expecting us.

'Have you come to kill me?' he says in a deep voice.

Ronin levels Warchild at his chest. 'Depends.'

'It doesn't matter,' the Obambo says, getting off the bed and kneeling on the hard wooden floor.

Ronin's fingers don't leave Warchild's twin triggers as he pulls a vinyl tie from his coat. He walks over to wrench the glowing man's hands behind his back. Pat grips my shoulder and a small sob escapes her lips. 'I'm so sorry, Tomas.'

He smiles sadly. 'It is not your fault, Patricia.'

'Open your mouth,' Ronin says. 'Now.'

Tomas looks at us with calm, sad eyes and then opens his mouth wide. The bounty hunter grabs him roughly by the jaw. 'Missing incisor. This is our guy.'

'Where is she?' I ask.

Tomas frowns.

I pull Esmé's picture from my wallet. 'Her. Esmé. Where is she?'

He studies the picture intently. 'I am sorry. I have never seen her.'

Ronin grabs him by the throat. 'Listen, disco ball, we're not playing good-cop bad-cop with you.'

Tomas looks up at Ronin. 'You can't hurt me any more than I've been hurt already.'

'You'd be surprised,' Ronin says, viciously pushing his head back.

'Jackson!' Pat screams.

Ronin pushes Warchild against Tomas's forehead. His eyes are pinpoints and he's bared his teeth a little.

The Obambo looks up at the gun. 'Do it,' he says calmly.

'Ronin,' I say nervously, 'c'mon, we need to find out where Esmé is.'

The bounty hunter pushes Tomas's head back with the gun. 'You better start talking,' Ronin says.

'Please,' Tomas says, 'may I sit?'

'Sure, would you like a cup of tea and a scone too?' Ronin says, but gestures for Tomas to sit. The Obambo shifts his knees out from under his body and awkwardly sits on the wooden floor.

I pull the tooth from my pocket and hold it in front of the Obambo's face.

'I found this in her room after she was kidnapped. It's yours.'

He nods. 'Yes, it is mine.' He shifts slightly and Ronin points Warchild menacingly at him. 'I worked at the Flesh Palace,' he says. 'I was an actor in one of the porn series called *Light Fantastique*.'

I nod. I've heard of it but it was never one of the Spider's products.

'I married one of the actresses, another Obambo,' he says.

'There are more of you?' Pat says. 'Tomas, that's wonderful!'

'No,' he says bitterly. 'Not wonderful. We had a baby; a beautiful, healthy, glowing boy. We were happy. The three of us, I think, were the last of our kind. Then the Queen formed a new partnership and the partner became very interested in my family. The demon birds came and forced us to go with him, to be tested. At first he just asked us questions. Where had I been born, when and where my son Adam had been conceived.'

'Oh, Tomas,' Pat says softly.

'I watched as he prodded and poked my wife and son. He cut

flesh from them and put it into jars. He drained the blood from them and videotaped as they writhed and screamed, all the time laughing, laughing like he was having fun.'

'Mirth,' Ronin hisses.

Tomas looks up at him. 'Adam died quickly, thank God. But Lila was always strong. It took days, but I watched as she faded in front of me until eventually her light went out.'

A small, thin wail escapes Pat's lips. Tomas glances up at me and his eyes are like black coals in the furnace of his body. 'I don't know why he pulled out that tooth.' He drops his head and little golden droplets stream down his face and spatter the floor. Pat rushes over and puts her hand on Tomas's radiant neck. Tears stream down her face too. 'You escaped,' Pat sobs, grasping his hands. 'Thank God, you escaped and found me.'

My phone begins to vibrate in my pocket. I pull it out and look at the number. It's Kyle.

'You're not going to believe this,' he says. 'I've think I've found her.'

'Esmé?' I say. 'Where?'

'I got a text a couple of minutes ago saying she used an ATM,' he says. 'At a caravan park in Parow. I'll send you the details as soon as I hang up.'

'I think I might kiss you when I see you,' I say.

'I'm going to take that little nugget of homoeroticism as thanks,' Kyle says.

I hang up and look at Ronin as my phone buzzes with the details from Kyle. 'I think we've found her,' I say.

Sceptics Alliance Newsletter
Charlatan of the Week: Dale Sheldrake

Isn't it enough to see that a garden is beautiful without having to believe that there are fairies at the bottom of it too?
Douglas Adams

Dale Sheldrake is not your average conspiracy theorist. His books, talks and multimedia products earn him millions of dollars every year, and he even has a range of herbal supplements that he says can help you to become aware of the supernatural creatures in our midst.

Yes, supernatural creatures. Sheldrake's entire business is based around the bizarre belief that these creatures – dwarves, gnomes, tokoloshes, and a staggering variety of other hobgoblins and spooks – roam the streets right beneath our noses, neatly filling the gap left by the end date of the Mayan calendar and the murder of David Icke (which Sheldrake now claims was a collaborative assassination by group of covert governmental organisations from several different countries).

Sheldrake, once a respected anthropologist at the University of Cape Town, claims that experience with psychedelic psilocybin mushrooms 'opened the gateway' to allow him to become aware of the supernatural eco-system that exists alongside our own.

His body of work is astounding in its outlandish claims, claustrophobic paranoia and delusional beliefs. His first book, *The Hidden Ones*, is a drug-fuelled paranoid rant about first impressions of this other world, which has become something of a counter-culture classic. His second book, *Spider Cult*, claims the British royal family are being controlled by parasitic arachnids attached to their brainstems and that several 'wizards' were mysteriously killed just days before they were due to take the Randi test.

His latest book, *Trapped Gods*, claims that there is a plot by government organisations to cover up the existence of interdimensional craft that were created by ancient alchemists to imprison gods. An excerpt from the book shows his typically disordered and rambling stream-of-consciousness prose:

The night falls softly, silently, my alert inner storyteller making connections between the seen and the unseen. Dirty, fallen angels litter the sky, broken glass, candy-coloured collections of CREATURES. Here half-breeds make themselves useful to pilot the vehicles. Interlocking circles spin in the cockpit, written in the ancient angelic script of the *Chayot*, a language of transcendental fire. Piloting the vehicles requires the sight of the Siener and the strength of a caged Crow.

Of course, extraordinary claims require extraordinary evidence, but of this there seems to be no sign. Are these ramblings the work of a madman or the sales tactics of a very savvy businessman? Whatever the case, Dale Sheldrake continues to cynically make money off the easily led and feeble-minded, making him our Charlatan of the Week.

Next edition:
'From the Mundane to the Bizarre:
Debunking the 9/11 Controlled Demolition Conspiracy'.
From holographically projected aircraft to the 'Dwarven Mercenaries' hired by the CIA to destroy the Twin Towers, we take a look at the crazy beliefs of 9/11 conspiracy theorists.

PREDATORS

'Keep Tomas here,' Ronin says to Pat through the window of his car. Her face is tear-streaked, her white hair frazzled and her hands trembling.

'You're not going to go after Mirth, Jackson,' Pat says softly. 'He'll kill you this time.'

'He killed Baresh,' Ronin says. 'He's working with the Murder and I need to know why.'

'I know what you're talking about is important,' I say, 'but can we go and find Esmé?'

'Good luck,' Pat says.

The roads are mostly empty and we make it to the Klein Varkie Caravan Park & Predator Zoo in Parow quickly. We pull into a dirt road that winds through rows of decrepit caravans and a man in dungarees waves us down. He's red, pudgy and balding; as we stop I see that he's missing part of his ear and has a large hole in his nose.

'Here to visit the Predator Zoo?' he says in a pleasant but slurry voice as he leans down to the car window.

'No,' I say, 'we're looking for –'

'We have new eagles,' the man says. 'Vicious bastards.'

'No, we just –' I try again.

'You like scorpions?' the man says.

'Not really,' I say.

'Pythons get fed at one,' the man says, 'you can still make –'

He is cut short by Ronin reaching through the window, hand clamping on his throat. 'Listen, boet. We appreciate the offer, but we're not here for that.' The man's eyes bulge and he breathes heavily through the hole in the side of his nose. I hold Esmé's picture in front of his face. 'Have you seen her?'

The man nods slowly and Ronin lets go of his throat. 'She's in the Honeymoon Caravan,' the man says, rubbing his neck. He reaches into his dungarees and hands us a map of the park, jabbing a dirty finger to a spot in the corner.

'Thank you,' I say.

'You can still make the python feeding if you hurry,' the man mumbles as we drive off.

We follow the winding dirt road through the rows of grungy caravans. The Honeymoon Caravan is easy to find, given the fact that it's a garish pink with a large heart sloppily painted on the side.

Nice. Weeds jut out from beneath it, and pastel-coloured deckchairs are set out on the lawn next to a platoon of plastic flamingos.

Ronin pushes open the car door and signals for me to wait. I watch as he slides his hand into his trench coat and carefully approaches the caravan. I fling open the car door and jog toward him. Ronin hears my footsteps and turns to me with a scowl. 'Never listen, do you?'

There's a low creak, the caravan door opens and Esmé appears in the doorway like an angelic vision. Well, an angelic vision wearing a polo neck.

'Who the hell are you?' Esmé says to Ronin. Her voice is slightly flat and mechanical and I wonder whether she's been drugged.

'It's OK,' I say hoarsely. 'We're here to rescue you.'

She laughs and flicks her hair back. 'Do I look like I need rescuing, Baxter?'

A blond guy with a mullet and wearing a stonewashed denim jacket over a polo neck comes from inside and stands next to her. Together they look like a double-page spread in an eighties fashion mag. Ronin points Warchild at the guy's chest.

'On your knees,' the bounty hunter says.

'Tell this idiot to put the gun away,' Esmé says acidly.

'Lovely lady,' Ronin says. 'I see why you like her. Now down on your knees, boy. Don't make me fire a warning shot into your gut.'

Esmé descends the steel steps that lead down from the caravan door and stands in front of me. I want to touch her, but her eyes look through me. 'Tell him to put the gun away,' she says, spitting out each word.

'Just put it away,' I say to Ronin.

Ronin looks at Esmé and then at mullet boy and then slides Warchild back into her scabbard. 'No sudden moves,' he says, pointing a thick finger at Esmé's companion.

'You're safe now,' I say gently, reaching out to take Esmé's hand. She jerks her hand back like I've burnt her with a cigarette.

'What happened to you?' I say. 'Where have you been?'

'I've been here,' she says. 'With Niels.'

'Why didn't you tell me?' I say. My forehead is throbbing unpleasantly again. 'Let's just get out of here,' I say. 'I'll take you back to your family and we can talk about this. It's been so crazy. You won't believe the shit I've –'

'I'm staying here,' she says firmly. She reaches over and kisses Niels, wrapping her fingers into his mullet and mashing her lips against his for several seconds before pulling away. 'I'm staying here,' she repeats. 'With Niels.'

Wait just a goddamn second. Of all the possible scenarios I imagined, being ousted from a relationship by a guy with a mullet wasn't one of them. My brain refuses to accept what's just happened. It gets stuck in a loop replaying the kiss I've just witnessed.

'Why?' I say dumbly.

Her lip curls with contempt. 'Because of you, you fucking cretin.' She pushes me on the chest. 'You're not a good person, Baxter.' She pushes me again. 'You're self-involved and manipulative and oh-so interested in your little porn business. It's pathetic.'

'I thought you liked that I'm entrepreneurial,' I whisper. Don't you fucking cry, Zevcenko. Not here, not in front of Esmé and mullet boy.

'You hurt people, Baxter. If I mention you to somebody, anybody, they've got a story about how you sold them out or how you got them to do something they didn't want to do. How long before you hurt me?'

'It's part of the business,' I croak, tears welling up in my eyes.

'You sell porn, for Christ's sake,' she says.

'Is it the porn?' I say. 'The Spider is a small start-up. We're flexible, we can branch into other industries.' Jesus, what am I saying? Someone stop me before I commit the Spider to selling Amway.

'You're not going to change,' Esmé says. 'You're a horrible excuse for a human being, Baxter. Just accept it.'

Tears squeeze out of the corners of my eyes and roll down my face. I'm not sure whether they're because I'm heartbroken or because I'm furious at myself for being stupid enough to think I was 'in love'.

I put my hand into my pocket and pull out Tomas's tooth. 'What about this?' I shout to her. 'What about the fucking eye carved onto your wall?'

'What eye?' she says with a laugh. 'Are you feeling OK, Baxter? Are you sure the stress isn't getting to you? I always thought you'd fucking crack and go postal. Has it finally happened?'

I feel that dark wave of rage and anger rising. My brain pounds against my forehead like a kick drum. 'Fuck you,' I whisper.

'Sorry?' Esmé says with a laugh. 'I didn't quite catch that.'

'Fuck you!' I shout, walking toward them.

'What are you going to do, Baxter?' Esmé says gleefully. 'Beat us up? Kill us?'

I'm about to launch myself at them and their smug little smiles when a hand grabs my shoulder.

'Come on, sparky,' Ronin says. 'Let's get the fuck out of here.'

'Go with your little hobo crackhead friend,' Esmé says.

Ronin leads me back to the car and I slide in and slam the door.

'Sorry, sparky,' he says as he gets into the driver's seat. 'That was rough.'

'It doesn't make sense,' I say, trying to wipe away the tears that are pouring from my eyes. 'What about the tooth?' I repeat as he starts the car. 'Tomas said that Mirth pulled it.'

'If there's anything I've learnt about the Hidden it's that they're oily, untrustworthy bastards. Our glowing friend would probably say anything to try to help himself.'

Esmé puts her arm around her new lover and gives me a sarcastic little wave as we reverse. Mullet boy gives me the middle finger. I'm too tired to return it.

'Doesn't fucking make sense,' I say.

'Want to go and see the pythons?' Ronin says as we drive through the park.

I shrug. 'Whatever.'

Ronin pulls the car in next to a bamboo enclosure that has a sign saying 'Snakes' in neon-yellow spray paint. Ronin gets out and then walks around to tap on my window. 'Get out,' he says.

'We're talking about this now. Leave it to linger and it'll fester like a dirty sore.'

'I don't want to talk about it,' I say. 'I just want to go home.'

'Get out,' Ronin says.

Lacking the ability to do anything but blindly obey, I open the door and walk into the enclosure with him.

The guy in the dungarees is there with a bucket of dead vermin. There is a glass-fronted cage on one side of the enclosure. I can vaguely make out the shapes of snakes in one corner. 'So you decided to come?' the guy says, rubbing his throat.

'You sold it so well we felt we couldn't miss out,' Ronin says.

The guy grunts and walks to the back of the enclosure. Ronin fumbles around in his trench coat for a while and pulls out his wallet. He opens it, delicately slides a picture out with his fingertips and hands it to me. 'Sue Severance,' he says. 'Smuggler, pirate and the love of my life.' I look down at the picture. The woman in it is black with long dreadlocks tied back with a bright scarf. She is about forty years old, beautiful, but with a jagged scar that crosses her face. Her nose is slightly misshapen, like it has been broken more than once. She's wearing a white low-cut vest and has a large tattoo of an anchor on her chest.

'She's pretty,' I say.

'Pretty fucking dangerous,' he says with a laugh.

'Do you still love her?' I say. 'Even though she tried to kill you?'

He sighs. 'Probably love her more because of it. I was a coward. I was terrified I would suck her down into the black hole with me.'

'At least I don't have to worry about that any more,' I say bitterly.

The dungaree guy appears in the cage. I peer through the glass and watch as he throws mice to the immobile snakes in the corner. They begin to move, slowly unwinding their bodies and sliding sluggishly toward the food.

'You'll bounce back,' Ronin says.

'Did you?' I say.

'No,' he says. 'Not really. But you're young.'

I shake my head. 'I just don't get it.'

'Relationships don't make sense,' he says, punching me on the arm. 'They're like electronic goods with the instructions translated from Chinese.'

'You're going to give me the relationship talk?' I say.

'Well, somebody clearly needs to,' he says. 'Didn't your dad talk to you about this kinda shit?'

'He tried,' I say. 'I resisted and he just gave up.'

'Well, then he's letting you play hopscotch in a minefield,' Ronin says. 'Relationships are about as easy to understand as particle physics – are they waves, are they particles? Hell, they're both, and trying to wrap your head around it will get you nowhere.'

'Helpful,' I say.

'What I'm trying to say, smartass, is that you're not exactly the first asshole in history to have his heart broken. This won't be the last time either, although this one will always hurt a little, like a small bruise that never goes away.'

'Right now it feels like a gaping wound from a nail gun.'

'That passes eventually. What you need to do is get drunk. I know a place that'll give you a hangover worse than any heartbreak.'

'Can we stop at the Haven first?' I say. 'I want to ask Tomas why he lied. He seemed so genuine.'

Ronin snorts. 'That shiny hustler was just trying to save his own skin. But it's not a bad idea. I can even provide the motivation for him to talk, if you want.'

I barely notice us driving back to the Haven farm. All I can think of is Esmé sticking her tongue down another guy's throat. If Niels is what I got dumped for, I clearly need to re-evaluate my self-image.

'There's something wrong,' Ronin says as we pull into the

Haven's driveway. He points to where a thin trail of translucent blood glimmers on the cobblestones. 'You're not going to listen if I say "stay here", are you?'

I shake my head.

'Well then, stay behind me,' he says.

The farmhouse door is a ruin of glass and wood splinters. Ronin keeps the shotgun in front of him as we step carefully into the house. The old battered kettle is upturned and chairs have been smashed. A long jagged rip is slashed into the wall, and there's blood, red blood; a small pool on the floor and a smear across the pink wallpaper. 'Fuck,' Ronin says.

Tomas's room is untouched. Perhaps he was downstairs with Pat or perhaps he just didn't offer the attackers any resistance. We walk downstairs and out to the barn. The doors have been ripped apart and are standing open like a gaping mouth.

Inside, Pat's menagerie has been destroyed. Toni Montana is lying on the floor with his head twisted at an unnatural angle. The Nevri, one of its heads ripped from its body, is wriggling limply in the corner. 'Sleepytime,' the remaining head hisses. The tokoloshe runs from underneath the table and latches onto my leg. It begins to hump it manically. 'Fukfukfuk,' it shouts, pumping its hips into my jeans. I shake my leg, but that only seems to make it grip onto me harder. I have to resort to kicking the little horned maniac across the room. It hits a wall hard and then gets up and begins to hump a chair leg.

'Shit,' Ronin says, kicking one of the cages. 'I'm a goddamn idiot. I shouldn't have left them here alone.'

'Klipspringer,' I say, suddenly remembering the bok-boy. I run out the barn and into the alley between the buildings. Klipspringer's door is open.

'Bok-boy!' I call. 'Hey, Klipspringer!' There's no answer.

Dread crawls over my stomach like a thick grey leech. Surely they wouldn't have killed that little punk? I look into his room. It's dark and I can't see anybody through the mass of junk.

'Hey, bok-boy!' I call.

'Wherethoseuglythingsgo?' Klipspringer says, peeking his head out from behind a castle made of ice-cream sticks.

'You dumbass,' I say, clutching my heart. 'You almost gave me a goddamn heart attack.'

'Ha,' Klipspringer says, jumping up. 'Those ugly birdbirds are too dumb to catch Klipspringer.'

'Yeah,' I say, grabbing him and putting an arm around his shoulders, 'they are.'

'Let go, Big One,' Klipspringer says, unconvincingly trying to shrug my arm off. He's shivering and there's a wild, terrified look in his eyes. 'You going to find the nice PatPat and the glowing man?' he asks plaintively.

'Yeah,' I say. 'Yeah, we are.'

'You're not,' Ronin says from the doorway. 'You've found your girlfriend. Go home and forget all this shit exists. That's what I would do if I could.'

He's right. My mission is complete. I found Esmé and she hates me. More than that, she's right about me. I'm not a good person. I realise that now. I manipulate people. I use people and I hurt people. Like Mikey Markowitz and NPCs like Courtney Adams. Like Esmé.

MetroBax: It's true. We only do things if they benefit us.

BizBax: And the problem with that is ... ?

MetroBax: Pat doesn't deserve this.

BizBax: Let's face it, nobody really deserves to be Crow meat. That's just how it happens sometimes. Seriously, there are easier ways to assuage your middle-class guilt. Like stopping pirating music. Or recycling.

MetroBax: We feel things now. There's no going back. We're going to help Ronin find Pat.

BizBax: All I wanted was to be the adolescent porn king of South Africa. Was that really too much to ask?

'Please get her back, Big One,' Klipspringer says to me. 'You have to.'

'You need help, Ronin. You don't even know where they are,' I say.

He grimaces. He knows I'm right. With Tone gone he doesn't have anyone he can call. He could go tearing through the supernatural under-world but it probably wouldn't do much good. He's on his own and I'm all he has. I'm going to do the right thing, whatever that's worth.

'Can you help?' he says finally. 'Do what you did at the Flesh Palace?'

It's a good question. That thing I did back at the Palace was only because a giant Crow was choking the life out of me. I'm not really sure I can repeat it.

'Can you control it?' Ronin says.

I shake my head. 'I don't even know what *it* is.'

Ronin walks into Klipspringer's room and clears a bunch of action figures from an old wooden chest and sits on it. 'OK, let me tell you about magic,' he says. 'It's none of this New Age bullshit. No positive thinking and create your own reality and Law of Vibration or whatever.'

He holds two fingers out like he's holding a gun. 'If you want to alter the stubborn, belligerent fucking bastard of physics, you have to punch it in the face, put its nipples in a clamp and then twist until it agrees to your demands.' He arches an eyebrow and a flame curls from his outstretched fingers. 'Magic is S&M without a safeword,' he says. 'All that Kabbalah, mysticism, Daoism, mantra, tantra, yantra are all just elaborate ways of forcing the world to conform to your motherfucking badass intentions.' He looks at me intently. 'Try.'

I nod and close my eyes. It's my intention to see where Pat is. How would I focus on that? I picture typing it into the search bar in the browser of my mind. My forehead begins to throb. OK, that's something. But I need to focus more. I picture myself floating up and out of my body like I did in the Flesh Palace. I slowly begin to feel myself sliding out. Not easily this time, more like I'm trying to squeeze the last bit of toothpaste out of the tube.

I begin to rise and see Ronin and Klipspringer looking at my stationary form. OK, good. It all seems to be going OK. I look around but there's no girl to guide me. I try to focus my attention on Pat. I picture her old, kindly face framed by her jangling earrings. My forehead begins to throb harder. I hold the image in my mind and let the rest of my attention drift. There's a quick flash, an image of something, but I'm not sure what.

I refocus my attention. There's another flash. It's the attic in the Haven. I see Pat talking to Tomas. She touches his shoulder and then bends down to affix a bracelet around his ankle. She lifts a small GPS unit from the bed and turns it on and then smiles at Tomas. The vision fractures and light pours in from all directions. I try to open my eyes but they're stuck together. I scream and clutch at my forehead as something begins to gnaw hungrily through my brain.

The magistrate and I are going to have a baby. He is a kind man, not handsome, but kind to me. I understand that we can't be married. In this world I'm a servant and he is the master. I hope that my father would understand. It has been two years since I've come here and the magistrate's affections have been difficult to ignore. He gives me presents and makes sure I'm treated well.

'You are a pretty girl,' he says to me. He runs a scarred hand through his grey hair. 'Have you had any more dreams?' he says with a smile. I shake my head. 'Ah, what a pity,' he says touching my face. 'I'm something of a student of dreams and yours seem so interesting.' I've never told him any of my dreams, but he seems insistent that I have them.

'You're going to have my child,' he says with a smile and touches my growing belly. 'A child that will have the blood of a Siener in it. I hope to learn more about your people and their gifts.'

I smile and try to look dumb. 'I can't do what my uncle and father could do,' I say.

'Oh, come, child,' he says. 'You're being modest. Perhaps if I tell you my secret, you'll tell me yours? Come.'

He turns to walk down the long corridor that runs down the middle of the house. I follow him. We enter his study and he turns to lock the door behind us. The room is sparse and simple. I have never been in here, but I expected it to be more impressive; something that befits an important man like the magistrate. It doesn't look like he spends much time here.

He doesn't sit down, but rather bends over to pull open a cellar door that is set into the floor. He smiles at me. 'After you,' he says, gesturing toward the stone steps that descend into the darkness.

'Where are we going?' I say.

'To my secret,' he says.

I step forward and he hands me a candle – the flame sputtering and flickering like my heart. I step down into the darkness, holding the candle in front of me like a charm against evil. I can feel the magistrate close behind me.

We reach the bottom of the stairs where another corridor extends into the darkness.

'Continue,' he whispers into my neck. I continue walking, feeling the coldness of the walls around me and their dank, mildew smell. I force my breath to remain steady and even.

The corridor eventually opens up into a large room. The magistrate takes the candle from my hands and lights several torches that have been set into the walls. The room erupts with light and I scream as a large shape seems to rear up in front of me. It is the creature from my dreams; many arms reaching out to grab me. It is a thing of evil. I scrabble backwards, away from it.

'Be still, child,' the magistrate says in a soothing voice. 'You are witnessing a thing of great power, the prison of one of our Creators.' I press my back against the wall. My breathing is too fast and I feel like I am going to faint at any second.

The magistrate walks over to the thing and strokes it. Again I force my breathing to return to normal. I look up and see that the many-armed thing is actually like a statue. It is made from metal; bronze, copper and gold. Its large octopus head is like a carriage and it has a chair inside where a man can sit. The eyes are made from thick panes of dark glass and the tentacles are made from scaled metal.

'Beautiful, isn't it?' the magistrate says, running his fingers over its shiny surface. I don't say anything. It is many things, but it is not beautiful. A deep sense of unease and illness runs through me when I look at it. It is an occult thing, a thing of corrupt power. I can feel it tingling in my body like a disease.

The magistrate walks over to me and puts his hand on my belly. 'In your body you carry one who is part Siener and part Feared One. A creature destined for greatness.'

'I don't understand,' I say, pulling back from him.

'You don't need to, my dear,' he says. 'You just need to make sure it survives.'

* * *

'Sparky!' a voice calls from far away. I groan and open my eyes. My cheek is pressed into the cold floor. Ronin is kneeling at my side and shaking me gently. 'Are you OK?' he says.

'Boyboy,' Klipspringer says, trotting up and down. His face is screwed up with worry. 'Don't die!'

'I won't, bok-boy,' I say, pushing myself up onto my elbows.

'Anything?' Ronin says, helping me up.

'There's a tracking device. Pat put it on Tomas when we left.'

Ronin chuckles. 'That old gal is a lot craftier than I give her credit for.'

We search the house and find the GPS unit in a drawer in the kitchen. Ronin switches it on and a small dot blinks on in the middle of the screen. 'That's on the mountain,' he says with a frown.

'Why would the Crows take them there?' I say.

'There's an old military base there that our unit used. Mirth might have resurrected it.'

'So you're letting me come?' I say.

He shrugs. 'Your call, sparky.'

I turn to Klipspringer. 'You going to be OK?'

'Course,' he says. 'Just bring back the lady PatPat.'

'I will,' I say and give him a quick hug.

'Gross,' he whispers, but doesn't pull away.

We fill the Cortina's trunk with as many cans of petrol, solvents and flammable agents as we can find at the Haven. As I slide into the passenger seat, Ronin reaches into the glove compartment and pulls out a long-barrelled revolver. 'Well, if you're coming, at least make yourself useful,' he says, giving me the gun. I take the heavy revolver in my hand. Yes, it's true I am a terrible person. Yes, my girlfriend has dumped me for a life of trailer-park inbreeding. Yes, I am voluntarily attacking a nest of giant Crows. Without Esmé, I'm not going to be getting lucky, punk. But, on the bright side, hopefully I'll get to shoot something in the face.

RIP OFF MY FACE AND TELL ME
THAT YOU LOVE ME

The orange dirt track curls up through the pine forest and past the ranger station with its helipad and fat red helicopter that's used to fight forest fires. We strap heavy bags, filled with all the flammable liquids we could find at Pat's house, to our backs.

Trekking in silence through the cool forest, past a couple of dreadlocked hippies with drums and several intense-looking joggers, we ascend through the foliage and onto a steep mountain track. I start to sweat, the sunlight like thick warm liquid that I'm swimming through. My heart is aching like a fresh bruise, but at least I have something other than my existential crisis to focus on. Like the little red dot on the GPS screen.

'We've got to get up above the blockhouse,' Ronin says, pointing to the squat building we can see on the hill above us. 'There's a series of caves a couple of hundred metres above it. They lead deeper into the mountain to the lab.'

'Sounds easy enough,' I say.

He wipes sweat from his face. 'Easy in theory, but it's going to be tough to get into them without being seen.'

'You can't do any ...' I say and then wave my hands around in the air a bit. 'You know ...'

'Is that hand-waving you're doing meant to mean magic? I might be able to work a few charms to get us past the guards, but Mirth is going to have other measures in place. He's no slouch.'

'So what are we going to do?'

He shrugs. 'Improvise.'

'Yeah, because that turned out so well the last time.'

'Ye of little faith,' he says.

'And little common fucking sense too, apparently,' I say.

We slog up the path for at least an hour. By the time we stop at a fork in the dusty orange track my T-shirt is soaked with sweat and my breath is coming in small, whooping gasps. I stop to take a long sip of water.

'You OK?' Ronin calls back to me. 'I don't want you to die of a heart attack.'

'And I don't want to be the first of your clients to shoot you for being an asshole,' I say, pulling up my shirt to reveal the revolver that Ronin gave me at Pat's. I've shoved it into my waistband like a total gangster, although it's not very comfortable and it keeps threatening to fall out.

He pulls down the neck of his vest, revealing a large angry mess of scar tissue on his chest. 'You wouldn't be.'

The path stops climbing and levels out to form a large rocky plateau that stretches like a ledge along the side of the mountain. Ronin steps out onto the ledge and edges his way around.

'Are you sure this is safe?' I say.

'Just get on the ledge.'

I step onto it and follow him, flattening myself against the rock face and trying not to look down at the city stretched out below. We shuffle around until we come to a cave.

'OK,' Ronin says, squinting his eyes to peer into the darkness. 'This will take us toward the compound. I'm pretty sure that Mirth will have these tunnels warded so I'm going to try something.'

'Try what?' I say suspiciously.

'Well, I haven't exactly done this before, so I might need to practise it a few times first.'

'Great,' I say.

Ronin pulls out his mojo bag and begins rummaging through it. I take the heavy bag off my shoulders and sit down against the cool rock. I'm sweating like I've been running a marathon, but thankfully it's cooler here. I look up to see Ronin staring at me like I'm some kind of oddity on display in a museum.

'What's your problem?' I say.

'Around your neck,' he says, pointing to me. 'Where did you get it?'

I look down at the little pendant. 'The goat-boy gave it to me,' I say.

He walks over and picks up the little mantis and holds it in his palm.

'What?!' I say.

'That's a talisman,' he says.

'Cool,' I say. 'Maybe I can sell it.'

'The hell you will,' he says. 'That's some potent muti you've got around your neck.'

I look down at it. 'What does it do?' I say suspiciously. 'It's not dangerous, is it?'

'I don't know,' he says. 'But I can do a simple charm to find out.' I pull it quickly from around my neck and hand it to him.

He places it on the cave's sandy floor. Pulling his knife from his boot, he positions the pendant and then draws a circle around it with the point of the knife. He produces a small bundle of herbs from his mojo bag and proceeds to light one end of it with his lighter. The aromatic smoke wafts through the cave and he begins to trace shapes in the air above the pendant with his hand, while mumbling in a harsh guttural language. Eventually he takes a deep breath and then stubs out the burning bundle of herbs in the sand. 'That, my young friend,' he says with a satisfied smile, 'is a shape-shifter's charm.'

'So it shape-shifts?' I say.

'No,' he says impatiently, 'it helps the user to shape-shift.'

'Shape-shift...' I say.

'Sometimes I think you're just acting stupid to piss me off,' Ronin says. 'Transform, magically transmute into another form.' He puts his thumbs together to make a bird shape. 'If we use this we can fly into the compound, change back into our human forms, find Pat and then get the hell out of there.'

'Brilliant,' I say. 'Let's do this.'

'Hmm,' Ronin says, rubbing his beard.

'Problem?'

'Well, these kinds of things are a little bit finicky. Talismanic lore suggests that certain talismans are usable only by those they're given to.'

'I'm not fucking doing any magic after what happened last time.'

'A few visions. I goddamn set myself on fire the first bit of magic I tried to do.'

'Yeah, but that's you,' I say.

'C'mon, all you need to do is to tap into it,' he says. 'And hold the form you want us to transform into in your mind.'

'And you're sure it's that easy?'

'Only one way to find out,' he says, handing me the pendant. 'But we're going to have to strip down first.'

I grudgingly take off my clothes and avert my eyes from the naked form of the hairy, ginger bounty hunter like its a gym changing room. I follow Ronin's lead and stuff my clothes into my bag.

I take the pendant and feel its comforting warmth. I breathe deeply and try to clear my mind. I feel a little tug from it in my palm. That's a good sign.

'Just clear your mind completely,' Ronin says. 'And remember to focus on the transformation for both of us. It's going to be useless if you transform into a bird and leave me standing here without wings.'

I nod and fix both of us in my mind's eye. Ronin with his red beard and wild hair. Me with my dark hair and glasses. This is easier than I thought. The pendant gives another little tug of confirmation.

'An eagle,' Ronin says. 'An eagle or maybe a hawk. Something airborne, quick and that won't be prey.'

I'm concentrating hard when I hear scuttling near my legs, and something runs over my foot. God, was that a ...?

'You're an idiot,' Ronin, the little grey vermin, chirrups. 'What part of "eagle" didn't you understand?'

'You look good,' I chitter to Ronin as I rub my face with my brown paws. Being a rat isn't so bad. You can get into small places, you have sharp little teeth and there's none of the abstract anxiety of the human world. You're small, you're dirty and you don't care. The problem is that being a rodent isn't exactly suitable for our purposes. Klipspringer's strongstrong magic turned out to be a little unstable; instead of flying into the base we're going to have to scuttle.

'Come on, it worked pretty well,' I say. 'I even managed to transform our stuff.' The little bags strapped to our rodent backs have our miniaturised clothes, weapons and flammables that we brought with us.

'This is going to end badly,' Ronin says with a little rodent scowl.

'C'mon, lighten up,' I say. 'At least we're not going to get executed on sight.'

'Just don't eat any suspicious-looking cheese,' Ronin chitters as we scamper through the network of dark caves.

We reach a large, cathedral-like cavern that's littered with large chunks of shiny quartz and edge past a vast pool of stagnant grey water, finding ourselves in front of an electrified fence that blocks access to a concrete bunker built into the walls of the cave.

'This is where those wings would have come in handy,' Ronin says, baring his little incisors. He's right. The fence throbs with electricity and the gaps between are way too small for us to get through. We scuttle around it looking for an entry point. Nothing. I see a small patch of fence that runs across a part of the floor that's dirt, not rock, so we can dig under it.

'Over here,' I chitter excitedly.

'Um, sparky,' Ronin says.

'We can dig under it.'

'No, just –' His rat eyes have become unfeasibly large.

'What? I know you're the badass "supernatural bounty hunter",' I say, making little air quotes with my paws. 'Sometimes I have good ideas too.'

'Yeah, you're great,' Ronin says. 'It's just that there's a huge snake behind you.'

I spin around just in time to see the bullet-shaped head of a cobra darting toward me. My rat reflexes get me out of the way just as the fangs extend and snap through the empty air.

I scramble backwards as the sleek, shiny body flies forward, just missing me again. The snake contemplates us with little black eyes. 'Aren't they more scared of us than we are of them?' I gasp.

'That's when we're humans, asshole. Right now we're food,' Ronin chitters as the bullet-shaped head lashes forward again.

My little rat legs plough into the ground and I make a break for it back through the tunnel. The snake whips its long body around and lunges after me, sliding easily over rocks and branches, and gaining on me as I run for my little rat life.

The menacing hiss from behind me spurs me on to feats of super-rodent effort. I rush past bushes that jut from the cave, wincing as sharp little thorns dig into my fur, and make a wide circle through the cave. It's then that I see it. There in the electrified fencing is a hole. It's a small hole, sure, but then again I am a rat.

I scamper toward it as the snake rises up to lock onto me like a heat-seeking missile. I know I'm not going to make it. Those huge, poisonous fangs are going to dig into my little rat torso and I'm going to die instantly of shock. It somehow seems fitting that I die as a rat. I'm sure Esmé would approve.

Then the grey rat attacks. In a normal Darwinian universe the cobra would win a fight with a rat every time. But in this case it is fighting a transmogrified psychotic bounty hunter so I'm guessing the same rules don't apply.

With a screech of fury, the little grey bundle of terror lands on the snake and begins ripping at it with its mouth. Little teeth tear at the snake's head and eyes. It reels around and snaps its jaws millimetres away from Ronin's furry flesh. With a shriek Ronin drops down and latches onto the throat of the angry cobra.

The snake whips about, but Ronin hangs on like some kind of rodent rodeo cowboy. The cobra slithers down to the ground and tries to move, but it can't. It lies on the ground, its lithe body jerking about with its final death spasm.

The grey rat trots toward me, its face blackened with snake blood. It grins, revealing its bloody little teeth. 'Maybe being a rat isn't so bad after all,' he says.

'Thanks,' I say, still watching the cobra.

'Come on,' he says. 'I don't know how long this transmogrification will last.'

We scuttle through the hole and onto the cold concrete. The bunker leads into a long, illuminated tunnel and we stay close to the walls as we move forward, keeping a furtive lookout for more snakes. The tunnel opens out into another huge cavern, which holds a cluster of square, grey buildings. The concrete is wet with some kind of rancid-smelling liquid. I can't help but think of the human polony that has been shuttled into the lab from the Flesh Palace and I sincerely hope we're not wriggling through organ juice.

As we get close enough to the buildings for my rat eyes to focus properly, my heart base-jumps into my stomach. Two monsters stare blankly out from a guard post at the entrance to the buildings.

They're bipedal, but hunch forward like chimpanzees, their heads fat and warped with large white eyes. Short black hair juts unevenly from their faces and bodies. They are, in short, disgusting. 'Gogs,' Ronin whispers. 'I fucking hate Gogs. One of Mirth's little inventions.'

We make a large circle around them and get into one of the buildings through an air duct. Ronin leads, his bushy tail in my face as we patter through the long, metallic chute. The air is humid and the further we get into the maze of the ventilation system, the more it begins to stink of flesh and death.

'We need to find somewhere to change back or we're going to get trapped in these ducts,' Ronin says. The smell has become stronger and things begin to get hazy as noxious fumes pour in from the laboratory. I spot an opening up ahead. I have no idea where it leads but we need to get out of here, and fast. 'There,' I say.

Ronin scrambles toward the vent and jumps through. I follow his grey tail as we hurtle down the metallic chute toward a light. Then we're in the air and tumbling through open space. Ronin hits a metal table with a clang and bounces off onto the floor. I slam into a cabinet and claw frantically for a foothold as I ricochet from shelf to shelf. My paw catches on something and there's a blinding white flash of pain as the nail is ripped out.

It's while I'm lying dazed on the floor that I begin to change back. I feel my body turning to liquid and pooling on the tiled floor like a spilled soda. I can feel my hands ooze together and regain feeling as my body sucks itself out of the ooze and reshapes itself. Finally I'm able to flex my fingers. I feel whole again. I feel human. I look down at my hands and see that the nail of my left index finger has been ripped off completely. It hurts like hell and is bleeding all over the white tiled floor.

Ronin has finished his transformation too and is crouched on the floor, naked except for his backpack. I push myself to my feet and take my backpack off my shoulders and pull my clothes out. My forehead is still throbbing and the pain from my left hand is making me feel faint.

Ronin dresses and slides Warchild home into her scabbard. 'How's the hand?'

'Hurts.'

'Well, suck it up,' he says. 'Being a rodent was the easy part of this little adventure.'

I pull the rest of my clothes on and jam my finger in my mouth to try to stop the bleeding. The metallic taste of blood fills my mouth. 'Here,' Ronin says, handing me a dirty cloth from one of the shelves. I wrap the cloth around my hand. The bounty hunter walks over to the door and looks through the glass panel into the corridor. 'OK, we're not here to fight,' he says. 'We find Pat, free her and get the hell out of here, got it?'

'What about Tomas?'

He shrugs. 'If the disco ball isn't dead he can come too.'

'And if we meet any of the Murder?' I say.

Ronin takes off his backpack and hauls out a canister of petrol. 'Then we torch them.'

We slide out into the empty corridor and walk quickly toward a door at the bottom of it. He peers through the glass panel. 'Gog,' he mouths. I shake my head and point back to the way we came. He smiles, draws a finger across his throat and opens the door. Great, so much for not being here to fight.

Ronin is a blur of movement as he buries his blade in the Gog's thick, bulbous neck. With a bellow it lashes out and grabs him by the coat. Ronin smashes his elbow into its head and a fountain of blood sprays from its face. It screams and spins him around, slamming him into a wall. With a wicked precision it rakes syphilitic claws across his face.

I try to land a kick on the creature's muscular black-haired back, but my foot glances harmlessly off it. Way to go, Bruce Lee. It nonchalantly flings a simian arm backwards and knocks me to the ground.

The Gog returns to Ronin, trying to rip off his face with its jaws. He frantically jams an elbow under its throat and holds its gaping mandibles away from his face. I start to push myself to my feet and my hands come into contact with a metal stand for an IV drip that has been left in the corridor. I haul myself to my feet and wrap my fingers around the stand, wrenching it back and forth until the metal pole comes loose.

Without any kind of fighting skills to rely on, I revert to the age-old tactic of jamming a sharp object as hard as I can into an opponent's head. The metal pole enters the Gog's head at an odd angle beneath the left ear and skewers its brain like a kebab. It slumps spasmodically and I grab the pole as the thing tries to regain its feet. I pull the pole free from its head and then stab it furiously into its body like I'm skiing on a slick red slope. Gog blood sprays onto my clothes and face. I keep stabbing until the thing stops writhing and then I sink to my knees breathing hard. Baxter Zevcenko, monster killer!

'No time to rest,' Ronin says, pulling me to my feet.

'You OK?' I gasp.

'I'll live,' he says, touching his lacerated face gingerly.

'Suck it up,' I say with a grin.

We peek through a door that opens up to a large laboratory, which houses huge vats of dark liquid that gurgle and spit smoke into the air like fat, diseased smokers. I recoil and cover my face with my arm. The place reeks of fat and flesh and oil like a huge cannibal takeout grillroom.

Guys in lab coats are attending to Gogs that are in various stages of existence. Several of the creatures' heads are floating in a vat, tendrils trailing beneath them like jellyfish. There are Siamese Gogs, joined at the spine, which are having needles and probes stuck into them. Another, similar to the one we just killed, is being cut and probed – its agonised reactions being recorded by the dispassionate men of science that scuttle around the lab.

As we turn back into the corridor I'm flung off my feet. I hit the ground hard. My glasses are thrown from my face and I try to get up, but the world spins around me. I scrabble for my glasses and put them back on. I see a Crow lifting Ronin into the air. I see a Gog lumbering toward me.

'Go,' Ronin says as he struggles.

I scramble to my knees and pull the revolver out from my waistband.

Ronin hangs from the Crow's claw, his feet swinging like a dead man hanging from the gallows. He still manages to wrench Warchild from beneath his coat and turns, sights and then fires. Warchild roars and the Gog's head disappears in a magenta shower.

The Crow responds by carelessly knocking Warchild from Ronin's hand and slamming him onto the ground. I fumble with the revolver and squeeze off a shot. 'Urgh,' Ronin shouts as the round clips him on the shoulder. 'Jesus, sparky,' he shouts. 'Try shooting at the bad guys.'

I aim the barrel of the gun more carefully this time, making sure it is dead centre with the dark shape before squeezing. The kick jerks my hand back, but the blast hits the Crow in the chest. Bull's-eye. The bird shrugs it off as if it were a paintball. I don't see or hear the other Gog until it's right on top of me, its arm slashing down. My head bounces off the concrete floor and there's a high-pitched ringing in my ears. Darkness pools over my eyes like an oil slick.

I want to scrub my skin with the brushes that the scullery maid uses. I suspect even then I couldn't get rid of the smell of him from my body. His kindness has given way to corruption. I've stopped thinking of him lurching on top of me like an animal in heat laughing, that terrible, childlike giggling.

I can feel the growth in my belly. No, not the growth. The daughter. I know it is a girl. Klara, I decide to name her. A daughter to be born of the union of a Siener and whoever the magistrate, and the monster he worships, really is.

I think of killing him. That's what my father would want me to do, to kill the enemy, to creep into his study with a knife from the kitchen and stab him until he stops moving. But even now I can't.

I'm in the kitchen wringing the dirty water from the cloths. A movement in the corner of my eye catches my attention. I look out of the window and see Luamita crouched in the road. She beckons to me. I shake my head desperately. To go outside without permission would mean punishment. Punishment that I'm not sure I could stand.

She beckons again and touches her hand to her neck and mimics drinking. I clutch at the small bottle of luminescent blood around my neck. Luamita beckons again, insistently. I know I shouldn't, but I go anyway, slipping through the kitchen door and out into the road.

Luamita takes my hands in hers. I can feel the sunlight from her skin. 'It is time to leave this place,' she says in an excited whisper.

'How?' I say. 'They'd know immediately. They'd alert the soldiers and I'd be found before I could even find a way to leave Cape Town.'

She smiles and removes something from around her neck and presses it into my hand. It is a small pendant made of brass that has been forged in the shape of a praying mantis. 'This connects you to the Creator's vehicle,' she whispers. 'With it you can draw on some of that power and change your shape. You can be anybody or anything, but only for a short time.'

I hold the mantis in my fingers. It's warm to the touch. 'But where must I go?' I whisper. 'I could try to get passage on a ship, but once I change back I'd be named a stowaway.'

'You'll come with me to the mountain,' she says. 'My family is there. We'll hide you.' Her eyes shine with purpose and I can't look away. In them I see my father and his father and his father before that, stretching back into history. I see myself and Klara. I see the boy with the spectacles and then his son and his son's son and daughter. We are connected. We are a family.

'Seee, see, seeee.'

I open my eyes and see a dull concrete ceiling. I try to sit up and then stop as pain lances through my skull. I touch my temple and feel a huge lump.

'See, see, see,' the voice screeches again.

I force myself to sit up. I'm on a steel bed and a guy is crouching on the end of it like a bird. He's thin and pale, is dressed in a dirty medical gown, and has the look of pure crazy in his eyes. He scratches at the few strands of grey hair sprouting from his head, grabs one and yanks it. Blood dribbles from his scalp as he hands me the strand.

'No thanks,' I croak. 'I'm trying to cut down.'

He looks at me, looks at the strand of hair and then shoves it into his mouth, chewing happily and then swallowing.

I hold my head and get up groggily. Clearly I'm in a cell of some kind. There's a basin in the corner and there's another steel bed directly across from me. A large door, presumably locked, is the only exit.

The man hops off the bed and looks at me quizzically. 'Monkey?' he says, turning his head from side to side. 'Monkey, monkey see, monkey, monkey do.' Then he wets himself. The urine pools on the floor. 'Monkey, monkey see, see, see,' he says again. From my vantage point I can see scars from incisions that have been made in his head.

There is the sound of keys in a lock and the steel door swings open. A stout orderly with a chubby, kindly face opens the door.

'Nigel,' he says to the monkey man. 'Time for your meds.'

'Monkey, see, see, see,' the monkey man says excitedly as he downs the pills that the orderly hands to him.

'And now you, Baxter,' the orderly says.

'No thanks,' I say. 'I'd rather get away from you and the giant Crows.'

'Now, now,' the orderly says. 'What did Dr Basson say about those delusions?'

He comes to stand in front of me with his hands on his hips. 'Are you going to take your meds or are we going to have to do this the hard way?' he says like a testy parent talking to his uncooperative four-year-old.

'How about we do it the get-me-the-hell-out-of-here way?' I say.

'OK, tough guy,' he says. His hand snakes out and grabs my arm. He's surprisingly strong and I can't resist as he slides a needle into my flesh. The walls begin to melt pleasantly away.

'Monkey, seee,' Nigel says.

Case File: Baxter Ivan Zevcenko
Dr Kobus Basson

My attempts to facilitate a smooth transition into a psychiatric facility have proven somewhat naive. Police brought him to Stikland after finding him trespassing in an old military installation. He was covered in blood and police investigation found the body of a caretaker with multiple stab wounds nearby. Baxter admitted killing him.

The resident psychiatrist contacted me and I was present at Stikland when Baxter was brought in. Upon admission, Baxter was in a state of severe confusion. His glasses were damaged and he had a minor wound on the index finger of his left hand. He seemed to be talking to somebody who wasn't there.

He became agitated and violent, mimicking using a gun to shoot one of the orderlies. His agitation became so severe that I was forced to sedate him.

MENTAL-STATE EVALUATION
Baxter experiences extremely vivid auditory, visual and kinesthetic hallucinations, which he is unable to distinguish from reality.

He describes talking to people and fantastical creatures, which form part of a supernatural world that he has created. He is an avid reader of science-fiction and fantasy novels, which may have informed some of the content of his hallucinations.

'Jackie Ronin', Baxter's primary hallucination, is an amalgam of several influences. This laconic detective is part father figure, part animalistic totem, fulfilling the role of guide and protector in Baxter's hostile universe.

In addition to these hallucinations, Baxter suffers from grandiose delusions of being a kind of mystical prophet with the power of 'seeing'. His embarrassment about his eye condition seems to be connected to his delusions about this mystical act of 'seeing'. The eye carved into the foreheads of the victims of the Mountain Killer seems to have a particular resonance with him.

His obsession with the San Mantis God may be part of a much broader social syndrome affecting white suburban youths. These youths tend to view themselves as being part of a rootless culture and harbour a deep-seated guilt for the atrocities of apartheid. Much like young white Americans becoming superficially interested in Native American cultures, these young white South Africans resort to a heavily romanticised obsession with the mythology of the indigenous cultures of South Africa.

Baxter has developed a rich mythology in order to cope with the world. He is the wise-cracking antihero, the Machiavellian kingpin and the mystical saviour of a cruel and unforgiving world; exactly the sort of delusions that would appeal to a lonely isolated boy.

MEDICAL HISTORY

On physical examination, Baxter had a BMI of 16. His pulse was 58bpm. His BP was 110/60 and his temperature was 36.5°C. His records show treatment for a minor eye condition, which forces him to wear prescription spectacles. His records also show a brief childhood episode of asthma.

During our sessions he reported severe headaches and a throbbing in his forehead. An MRI scan has been scheduled to occlude an organic defect from the diagnosis.

SOCIAL HISTORY

Baxter immediately displays features of a paranoid personality. He describes his world as one where survival of the fittest reigns and where people are judged according to his harsh and exacting standards. He shows no guilt or remorse for the way he treats people, believing that they are deserving of nothing but scorn and condemnation.

He describes his autistic brother as a 'retard', and most of the people around him are 'NPCs', non-playing characters, a term borrowed from gaming culture for the incidental characters in a game world played by the computer.

Baxter's school life is viewed through the lens of this gaming metaphor. In his world, people are merely game pieces. This is consistent with reports from Baxter's parents that he has no real friends, and lives an isolated existence.

During our consultations, he revealed that he had been having repetitive dreams about an Afrikaans girl during the Boer War. He expressed a belief that Afrikaner culture has a deeper sense of heritage than his own globalised sense of self, which is largely drawn from pop culture, including television and computer games.

RECOMMENDATIONS

During admission to the Stikland Medical Facility, Baxter confessed to being the Mountain Killer, the notorious serial killer. The investigating officer, Detective Schoeman, has been notified and has asked for a full report of my work with him. Further investigation is necessary; we cannot be sure whether Baxter committed these crimes or whether he is merely a copycat. His delusional beliefs and hallucinations represent a profound break with reality. It is my evaluation that his discomfort with feelings of guilt and remorse make him a prime candidate for violent, and possibly homicidal, behaviour.

INSANITY PLEA

'**Y**ou're ill, Baxter,' Dr Basson says, his smile splitting his bearded face like a gaping wound in the body of a quivering rabbit. My hands are shackled together uncomfortably and I'm wearing a hospital gown that exposes my bare ass cheeks to the cold steel chair I'm sitting on. My body feels loose and rubbery; my lips are stuck together. I lick them tentatively.

'Have some water,' Basson says, passing me a plastic cup. I awkwardly reach out both handcuffed hands and take it.

'How do you feel?' he asks as I sip.

'Like I've been captured by a fucking lunatic,' I shout. 'Let me out of here. Where the hell is Mirth? Are you working for him?'

'Baxter,' Basson says, 'these delusions are hindering your chances of coming to terms with what you've done.'

'What delusions?' I ask croakily. 'That I've been captured by an alchemist who's creating an army of mutants. That you're working with him?'

He crosses and uncrosses his legs. 'Hmm. Yes, exactly. Those delusions,' he says. 'How much of the past few days do you remember?'

'Oh, cut the crap,' I say. 'You seriously think I'm going to fall for this whole "Baxter, you're insane" spiel?'

'How much?' he says.

'Everything, you head-shrinking asshole,' I say. 'I remember everything. Elementals, zombies, Gogs. Everything.'

'And …' he consults his notepad, 'Jackie Ronin?'

'Yes, Ronin,' I say. 'What have you done to him?'

'Tell me about him,' Basson says.

'He'll fucking shoot you in the face,' I shout. 'How's that?'

'So you would consider him something of a hero, a protector?' he asks.

I laugh. 'An insane one, sure.'

Basson nods meaningfully. 'So Ronin is the one who's insane, not you?'

'Oh fuck off,' I say. 'Is this your idea of bad-guy torture? You're going to question me to death?'

'You think we're torturing you?' Basson asks. 'Why?'

'Because Mirth is insane.'

'So Ronin is insane and this Mirth is insane, but you're acting rationally? Tell me, why did you go to that military installation?'

'To rescue Pat,' I say. 'And Tomas.'

'And did anybody get in the way of this rescue mission?'

'A Gog,' I say.

'And what happened to this "Gog"?'

'Ronin and I killed him.'

'You killed him, Baxter,' Basson says. 'It's an important distinction to make.'

He reaches down to pick up an envelope. From it he pulls a photograph and slides it across the table. I look at it and then look away quickly.

'Look at it, Baxter,' Basson says.

I try to stop myself but I can't. I look at the picture. It shows a man's body, in bloody overalls. His face is mutilated beyond recognition except for the eye that is carved into his forehead.

'Henry Mqulo,' Basson says. 'Henry was a caretaker at an old military facility on Table Mountain. Did Ronin do this?'

'No. No, that's not right. That was one of the mutants,' I croak.

He slides another photograph across the table. The body in this one is wearing a Victorian bodice and the head is dark-haired and pretty, with an eye carved into the forehead. 'Casey Icon, owner of the Flesh Palace,' Basson says. 'You went into the club, into her office, and killed her. Why her Baxter?'

'She's not ... it's because ... dammit, it's because she's the Queen of the Anansi,' I say.

'And these Anansi are ... ?'

'Zombie-creating spiders,' I say. 'The Queen tried to kill us, but Ronin killed her first.'

'Ah, Ronin again,' Basson says, snapping his fingers. 'He always seems to pop up when you're having difficulty taking responsibility for your actions.'

I tug at my handcuffs. 'Let me the hell out of here. I want to go home. There is a supernatural underworld. This is a secret experimental lab that creates monsters.'

Basson shakes his head. 'No, Baxter. We're at Stikland Medical Facility. In a ward for the criminally insane.'

'No,' I say. 'This is bullshit.'

'Zombies, mutants; I hope you can hear how ridiculous this all sounds. You've been led down a very dark path.'

'Why?' I say. 'Why would I make all this up?'

Basson raises his eyebrows and spreads his hands as if offering a variety of options. 'A feeling of inferiority perhaps. The specifics of your delusions are ultimately unimportant. They've all clearly been concocted on the spot.'

He points to a small pile of magazines on the floor next to

him. 'I noticed you looking at them when you came to my office and I made an effort to read through them. Imagine my surprise when I could piece together your story verbatim. An article in a film magazine about creature porn, which gave detail to your supernatural fantasies; significantly it also mentions the Flesh Palace, which was to be the scene of your next crime. Next, there is a martial-arts article that mentions Crows, then an article about South African history...' He holds two magazines up in front of me. 'I hope you see where I'm going with this.'

'I didn't make Ronin up,' I say fiercely.

'Tell me about your bounty hunter,' he says. 'What does he look like?'

'Red hair, beard,' I say.

'And is there anything from my office that you remember fitting that description?' he says.

'The painting on your wall,' I say. 'The sea captain.'

He nods. 'The painting on my wall. It actually belonged to my parents. A bit kitsch I always felt.'

'No,' I say. 'No, this is all wrong. I hired him to help me find Esmé.'

'Ah, Esmé,' he says. 'Another one of your fantasies. Describe her to me.'

'She's medium height with dark hair. She has a little ski-jump nose,' I say.

He reaches into his pocket as I speak and pulls out his wallet. 'My daughter Anne,' he says, opening his wallet to show me a photo inside, 'I have a picture of her on my desk.'

'No,' I say.

'Believe me, I don't want to show you this,' he says. 'The idea of a serial killer creating this kind of delusion about my daughter is, quite frankly, terrifying. But, Baxter, I'm asking you, pleading with you, to look.'

I look. In his wallet is a picture of Esmé.

* * *

I've lost track of time. I sit and watch Nigel rip strands of hair from his head and chew them. There are not many follicles left to feed his habit. I absently wonder what he'll start eating when all the hair is gone. Toenails? Skin? Whole appendages?

'See,' Nigel says.

My mind feels fuzzy. Is that a tumour pressing against my brain? 'The thing about madness is that you don't know it's happened,' Ronin said. Which is ironic considering Ronin doesn't exist. Split personalities ENTER STAGE LEFT.

MetroBax: I'm confused.

BizBax: Now there's a surprise. Let me clear this up for you. The fact that the two of us are talking seems to give credence to the idea that we are, as a whole, insane.

MetroBax: How can you be like this? We've killed people.

BizBax: It was going to happen at some stage.

MetroBax: You knew?

BizBax: No. But c'mon. The violent video games, the family issues, the antisocial behaviour. Textbook psychopath. I just wish I could remember it, even just a few mental snapshots. If we're going to be put away for murder at least we should enjoy it.

MetroBax: You're sick.

BizBax: Duh. 'criminal psychiatric facility'. They didn't put us in here for the food and entertainment.

We've been playing word-association games. I've been trying not to say things that sound psychokiller-ish. It's been hard.

'Holiday,' Basson says.

'Friends,' I say. He nods and jots something down.

'Let's explore that theme for a while. Your parents say your

231

lack of friendships has always worried them.'

'You've spoken to my parents?'

'They're not in good shape, Baxter. I think your mother in particular feels that she should have picked up on something.'

'Pity "How to know if someone is a psycho" is only the *Cosmo* quiz next month,' I say.

'You don't feel remorse that you've hurt them?'

Oh, I feel. I feel like I'm teetering over a deep, endless pit. I have no sense of myself. Whatever I thought I was is being slowly eaten away by the growing certainty that I am what they say I am. There is no supernatural underworld. I am the monster.

Basson thinks I should make a video diary. Something that will help me take responsibility for what I've done. What I've done. Which is killed people. I feel bile rise in my throat. I always thought I was a bad person. But not *this* bad.

I feel like I need to do this, to get rid of this stupid facade, this mask, this myth. I am not Baxter Zevcenko, mastermind. I'm Baxter Zevcenko, serial killer.

Basson positions a small camcorder on a tripod and fiddles with it for a few seconds. I compose myself. If I'm going to speak about what's happened, I have to have clarity. That, unfortunately, is in short supply at the moment. All I have is an overabundance of fuzz. I need to focus on the sessions we've had and try to drag sense and reason from them.

Basson finishes fumbling with the camcorder and gives me the thumbs up. I stare at the little black-and-silver Cyclops eye. Here I go.

'There are questions that run through your head when you find out you're a serial killer. "Am I more evil than Ted Bundy?" is one. "I wonder whether I'll be on the Crime & Investigation Network?" is another. But on the whole, it's the who, what, when and why of it that really takes up the mental bandwidth. So, here goes:

'My name is Baxter Zevcenko. I am sixteen years old. I go to Westridge High School in Cape Town and I have no friends. I've killed people. Lots of people. Brutally.

'People are saying that I'm satanic, but this is not true. I have seen things. I saw the great Mantis God of Africa fighting a creature from the primordial depths. For billions of years they fought until the Mantis threw the writhing, many-armed creature from the heavenly sky into the deepest pit –'

'Baxter,' my psychiatrist interrupts, 'I thought we'd agreed that these delusions were counterproductive to your healing?'

I take a breath, force the images from my mind and continue. 'But none of that matters. There is no Mantis and there is no dark, primordial creature. There is no weapons chemist, no bounty hunter and no girlfriend to rescue. There is just me and I am sick. In the end, we're all just victims of our own perceptions, sparky. I hope you can see that.'

'Good,' he says as he turns off the camera. 'Very good.' He puts a hand on my shoulder. 'Baxter, why did you say "sparky"?'

'That was what Ronin called me,' I say softly.

'So, you've realised something about Ronin?' he says. I nod. 'And what have you realised?'

I look back up at him with tears in my eyes. 'That he's me.'

I wake up with someone's hand over my mouth. At first I think that it's Nigel, hairless and ravenous and coming for my eyeballs. But it's not. It's Ronin.

He puts a finger to his lips and then lifts the hand from my mouth. 'Ready to blow this joint?' he says. There's an awkward silence. I'm not sure what to say to a full-blown hallucination.

'What's up with you?' Ronin says.

'It's just…' I say. 'It's just that you're not real.'

He takes a little time to process this. His facial expression undulates like the surface of a tidal pool. 'What's that supposed to mean?' he says eventually.

'You're a hallucination,' I say. 'A surrogate created to express the parts of myself I couldn't.'

Ronin's mouth twists into a smile. Stutters of laughter begin to throb in his throat. He clamps his hand across his mouth to stop himself from making a noise. Having a part of myself laughing at me is a little unsettling. He looks so real, full-on flesh and blood, not at all the product of a diseased mind. Well, except for the shaggy red eyebrows – those are a little over the top.

'Have you been taking anything? Any drugs, medication?' Ronin asks.

'Just my meds,' I say defensively.

'They're probably messing with your head. Are you finding it difficult to think clearly?'

The grey fuzz in my brain shifts and lurches. 'No,' I say.

'Listen,' Ronin says, 'Mirth used some of the same shit on the Border.'

'Dr Basson is helping me,' I say.

'Dr Basson?' he says. 'Describe him.'

'Tall, spindly, grey ponytail,' I say uncertainly.

Ronin slaps the side of my head. 'That's Mirth, moron.'

'Basson is Mirth?' I say.

The delusion sighs. 'I don't have time for this now, I need to find Pat. When I find her, I'm going to try to come back for you. You better be ready to leave.' He stands up and sidles over to the door. 'Sometimes the truth is stranger than delusion, sparky.'

MetroBax: Ronin is convincing but he lacks a certain something, which makes me want to go with Basson.

BizBax: This is not *X Factor*, asshole. We're talking about a fundamental break with reality. Either we're fighting a crazed weapons chemist, or we're a psychopathic murderer and this very conversation is indicative of a deep-seated chemical flaw in the brain.

MetroBax: Occam's razor. Right? Isn't that what Kyle always talks about? The simplest solution is usually the best.

BizBax: Good thinking, but there are two fundamental problems with that line of logic. 1. Kyle may not exist. 2. Which, in this scenario, is the simplest solution?

'See?' Nigel whispers from his bed.

'Go back to sleep, Nigel,' I whisper. 'I was just having a nightmare.'

The next morning – at least I think it's the morning – I'm taken to an interview room. It's cold and sterile like everything else in this place. The orderly makes me sit at a steel table and is about to chain my hands behind my back when Basson enters with a cup of coffee in one hand and his briefcase under his other arm.

'No, there's no need for that.' He looks at me. 'Is there, Baxter?'

'No,' I croak.

He smiles and sits down across the table from me before producing a newspaper from his briefcase. He pushes it, a *Sunday Times*, across the table to me. 'THE FACE OF A TEENAGE SERIAL KILLER' the headline reads and beneath it there's a picture of me. I scan the article. It's not very complimentary. 'We tried to delay this,' he says. 'But it was inevitable. I'm going to testify in your defence,' he continues. 'But you need to cooperate with me as much as possible.'

I nod.

'Have you seen Ronin again?' Basson asks.

I nod again.

'And what was it that he said to you?'

'That you've got me on drugs that are messing with my head. That you used the same on him on the Border. That you're Mirth, the head of MK6,' I say, slightly embarrassed.

Basson holds his hands up and twiddles his fingers like he's a stage magician doing a trick. He chuckles. 'I apologise, Baxter, I don't mean to make fun of you. But it just sounds so ludicrous.'

I'll be honest, it does sound insane. Baxter Zevcenko, the teenage Machiavelli who went trawling through Cape Town's supernatural underworld in a search for his girlfriend. How adventurous, how noble, how lame.

'My daughter says this supernatural stuff is very in vogue at the moment,' Basson says. 'Vampires, werewolves and wizards. It's unsurprising that it was incorporated into your personal mythology. If Blackblood visits you again, you must tell me right away,' Basson's face locks into a rigor-mortis smile. 'Ronin,' he corrects quickly. 'If Ronin visits you again.'

My mouth is dry. I roll my tongue along the inside of my lips. 'What did you call him the first time?' I say.

'It's just psychiatry-speak,' Basson says carefully.

Blackblood. Somehow I doubt I'd find that in any psychiatry manual.

Basson's eyes search mine. I maintain a blank look. The doctor's eyes crinkle at the edges with a look of understanding. He knows that I know that he knows that ... well.

BizBax: Are we in agreement that something is gravely amiss?
MetroBax: Agreed.

'Let's cut the crap,' I say.

'So, are we going to let go of these delusions?' he says.

'Yes,' I say. 'As soon as you tell me where Ronin is.'

Basson smiles ruefully. 'One small mistake. Still, I'm impressed that you picked up on it. I've seen soldiers completely insensible on the amount of Dimurasane I'm giving you.'

'What does it do?' I say, struggling with the fog around my head.

'It reduces resistance, increases compliance, makes everything seem unreal.'

'Sounds about right,' I say, blinking my eyes. 'Why not just kill me?'

He smiles again. The kindly doctor routine has been dropped. Basson is gone completely and only Mirth remains.

'You're my great-great-grandson,' he says. 'You know that, perhaps? I'm not quite sure what level your gifts are now at, but I intend to find out.'

The dream about the girl becomes sharp and clear in my mind. My great-great-grandmother. 'How did you do that?' I say. 'And why?'

He lets out a long shrill giggle and holds up two fingers. 'Two vehicles, two prisons. Individually more powerful than any technology. But together – oh, together.' He wraps those two fingers around each other. 'You cannot even imagine the power. Time and space melt away into insignificance.' He smiles at me. 'I'm no dictator, Baxter. That would be beneath me. I could be that with just the power of one of the vehicles, the one that my heritage and talents allow me to control.'

He scoots his chair forward until he's sitting right in front of me. 'I'm an explorer, a navigator. With the power of both together I could touch the edge of the known universe.'

He shakes his head and gives a little giggle. 'No, no, I'm being modest. I could go beyond the known universe. I could go to *any* universe.'

'And you thought, "Hey, let's screw a young girl while I'm at it"?'

'Oh, yes, your great-great-grandmother. I took no pleasure

other than the thrill of scientific achievement from that,' he says.

'Sure,' I say. 'And you read *Playboy* for the articles.'

'I need the perception of the Sieners and the hardiness of the Murder in one body,' he says. 'Your body, I'm afraid.'

He looks at me like a child looking at a new puppy. 'I waited,' he said. 'Looking for the signs that someone in your bloodline would awaken to the gift of the Sieners. I made a pact with the Crows to keep your genetic line unsullied –'

'That's why you had Grandpa Zev's princess murdered,' I say.

'Ah, yes. She was of elven stock,' he says. 'Thoroughly unsuited to my purposes. We steered your grandmother toward him. Your father made an acceptable choice and so no intervention was necessary. Then you and your brother appeared and I saw the gift begin to blossom in both of you. I've watched you for a long time,' he says. 'And I've become more and more excited that you might be the one.'

'And here I am,' I say.

'Yes,' he says. 'Here you are, with your powers growing, but not yet fully realised.' He giggles and raises a hand lazily. The chubby orderly appears. 'I must admit I'm glad this charade has come to an end.' The orderly hands him a syringe. I yank at my handcuffs but they just bite deeper into my wrists, causing a thin trickle of blood to drip down onto the floor.

'Psychosis is a terrible thing,' Mirth says.

'You would know,' I spit out.

He holds a syringe in front of my face. It is filled with a radiant liquid. 'Your Obambo friend was very generous with his donation,' he says.

'You killed him?' I say. The orderly wraps a thick arm around my neck and holds me in place.

'He's not dead,' Mirth says with a little laugh. 'Yet.' He slides the needle into my arm and pushes the plunger.

Deep fault lines of pain open up in my skull and dark, blotchy spots begin to swirl in front of my eyes. A worm pushes through my brain and begins gnawing at the space between my eyes, trying to get out. The brainworm begins to chew through my grey matter and I scream as it erupts in my skull. It's not a worm at all; it's an eye on a thick cartilaginous stalk. Awareness cleaves through existence. I can see. Everywhere. With my eye I travel the facility. I see rooms filled with horror; people being experimented on, things in various stages of transformation.

The walls of this facility can't contain me. My mind roars into the night sky like a dragon searching for prey. It curls around the mountain, stalking, swirling, whipping in a never-ending frenzy of perception. The blanket of lights spreads out below me. In its streets, businesses, shops, brothels, restaurants, flats, houses, churches, mosques, yoga studios, crack dens, student digs, old-age homes, taverns, spaza shops and shebeens.

I can see the throbbing pulse of beliefs, ideologies, secrets, desires, memories and ambitions like halos around the ant-like people. They flow together like some giant four-year-old has poured food colouring onto an ant farm and is watching the colours mingle.

My mind races up toward Devil's Peak and blasts through the cloud-covering. All around it's misty and silent; a dense fogbank that has rolled in from the sea. Gradually the mist begins to part like theatre curtains to reveal a man quietly packing his pipe on a flat circular disc that is floating in a black sea of nothingness. He's huge and gangly. An old wide-brimmed hat perches on top of his thick green creeper-like hair, which winds and curls its way down to the floor. A mushroom grows from his forehead like a bulbous third eye and his shaggy, decomposing hands are covered in moss and lichen.

He looks up at me and his eyes are serene and terrible. 'Radial foguzzy serenth,' he says, his voice warbling as he speaks, slow as erosion and warm and loamy as decaying plant matter, and it feels like a radio is being tuned in my cerebral cortex. He shakes his ancient head and dirt falls to the floor. 'I haven't spoken in a hundred and fifty years,' he says finally, revealing a black tongue that's covered with toadstools.

'Are you the Devil?' I say in awe.

At that he laughs, a deep rumbling boom that shakes my bones. 'I am Van Hunks who still smokes with the Devil. I am Hoerikwaggo, the mountain in the sea. I am Adamastor and I am the spirit of the Mother City. I am the Singer of Souls. I believe we have met before, although perhaps not in this form.' He smiles and lights his pipe.

'You?' I say, remembering the one-eyed guitar player at the canal.

'Two Sieners climb the mountain of time to meet me. They cannot see each other, but I speak to them both.'

'You?' I say. Luamita's necklace had allowed me to escape the magistrate's house easily. I'd simply concentrated, let my mind become still and then focused on a form that would help me to get away. I became a sailor; a thick-necked, hairy man with dark hair and a beard. It had been so very, very strange to be a man that I had just stood there for a moment marvelling at the dense, sturdy and sweaty form I had assumed.

Luamita had urged me to go, saying that the magic worked only for a short time. We had walked quickly through the streets together, people ignoring my rough appearance and shrinking away from Luamita's. We'd made our way onto the mountain, struggling up the haphazard path until we'd found a copse where I could return to my own shape.

Back in my smaller, more frail form the going was even harder, but I was used to walking for hours in the veld and I didn't mind. Because I was free. Free from that terrible man and his evil plans. Luamita led, showing me the way through the thick underbrush until we reached a cave. 'We can rest here,' she said and led me into the darkness.

'Big Ones!' came a joyful squeal in Afrikaans from inside the cave and I was startled to be confronted by a boy, or, rather, half a boy. The other half of him consisted of the hindquarters of a springbok. He cantered up and down excitedly and gave Luamita an enthusiastic hug. 'This is the boy,' Luamita said with a smile.

'You don't have a name?' I said, shaking his small hand. He shook his head and looked very forlorn.

'I'll call you Klipspringer,' I said, smiling. 'That's what my father called me and you look like you're very good at climbing.'

'Exceptionallygoodthankyou,' he said proudly, jutting out his chest. 'CanIhavemypendantback?'

'Thank you,' I said, returning it to him. 'You have helped me more than you can know.'

'I always help Sieners,' he said with a grin. I thought of the boy with spectacles from my dreams. So alone and afraid sometimes. 'If you ever meet a Siener boy with spectacles will you help him?'

He nodded. 'Yesladyyes.'

Luamita had urged us to continue and, saying our goodbyes to Klipspringer, we'd carried on up through the mountains, eventually reaching a cave where her family stayed. Seeing four of the glowing people without any of the concealment that Luamita was forced to use was astounding. It was like being a planet caught between numerous suns. After introducing ourselves we'd decided that there was no time to waste. I'd consumed the last of the liquid in my bottle and, once again, the world had ignited.

* * *

'I am the gateway between worlds. It is to me you come to speak to those that are distant from you in space or time.' Van Hunks folds his large hands into gestures that look like rock 'n' roll horns and I feel something like a swirling vortex in my forehead. It spins faster and faster like a star imploding. My vision blurs and when I open my eyes I am staring at a beautiful girl. The girl of my dreams. Literally.

We're standing on the disc, but the Singer of Souls is nowhere in sight.

'Hello,' I say awkwardly. Damn, she is very, very pretty. For a great-great-grandmother, I mean.

'Hello,' she says with a thick Afrikaans accent.

'Um, I think you're my great-great-grandmother,' I say. Direct and straight to the point, there's no other way to do this.

'Oh,' she says shyly.

'So ...' I say. That awkward moment when you don't know what to say to your hot great-great-grandmother when you're standing on a cosmic disc that transcends time and space.

'Yes ...' she says.

'I'm sorry about what happened to you,' I say. 'I'm sorry about what he did to you.' Although I'm not sure that I am. If Mirth hadn't done what he had done then I wouldn't exist, would I? Or would I exist, just in another form? Or would I exist in another version of this universe? I don't really know. This time-travel stuff has always confused me.

She holds her stomach protectively. 'I'll have Klara,' she says. 'I'm not sorry about that.'

I think of Grandpa Zev and the picture in his room. Klara, his mother. 'Yes,' I say. 'You will.'

'You need to destroy the vehicles,' she says. 'It is beyond me now.'

'I'm not sure I can either,' I say.

'You can,' she says. 'You must.'

* * *

I look at the boy in front of me and I want to cry. I can see my father in him, the shape of his face, the brow, and in those eyes behind the spectacles. They are confused eyes, but kind. Good eyes.

'You are a good person,' I say. 'I can see that.'

He laughs unpleasantly and looks at his feet. 'You're probably the only person who thinks so.'

'I am proud of you,' I say. 'I am proud that I am connected to you.' He looks up at me. 'I promised my father I would destroy the vehicles,' I say. 'But I have failed. I need you to promise me, your great-great-grandmother, that you will destroy them.'

His face is pained and his eyes confused, but he gives a short nod. 'I promise,' he says.

Just like that she is gone and the Singer of Souls coalesces in the smoke once more. He waves his hand and the smoke from his pipe begins to rise and dance in the air. The smoke is everywhere, weaving itself together like the threads of a huge tapestry. Whole worlds form in the air; cityscapes of huge buildings with spires and minarets dissolve into volcanoes erupting on islands to destroy ancient civilisations. I see intelligent life destroyed by robot uprisings in distant worlds.

I see. I see dimensions collapsing in upon themselves. My sight rips into matter. I'm on the top of Table Mountain and then I'm soaring. I am the South East wind, the Cape Doctor, whipping mercilessly through the city. Every tree, every blade of grass, every molecule in existence is an extension of my awareness. I swirl above the city screaming with the agony and the ecstasy of it all. I scatter myself into a million different pieces and blow through the minds of the tiny ant-like people walking on the streets. I feel firsthand their coarse desires, their bright thoughts, their sticky emotions, their incredible beauty, their infinite shame. I draw myself together into a singular thought and scream. Hear that in your third eye, Cape Town.

ANCESTORS

'**W**elcome to the Jungle,' a familiar voice says as I open my eyes. My head feels like it's been kicked repeatedly. I touch my fingers to my forehead. Nothing there, thank God. I'm not exactly sure what I would have done if I had encountered an eye on a stalk.

We're in a cell like the one I was in with Nigel, the monkey man. Ronin is slumped in the corner, his face a mess of dried blood, but humming the Guns N' Roses tune while strumming listlessly on an air guitar.

Tomas lies in the centre of the room covered by Ronin's trench coat, but shivering, groaning as Tone kneels next to him, trying to rouse him. The sangoma is hurt too; his suit is burnt, with some of the material stuck to seeping wounds on his chest and shoulders.

'Well, here we all are,' Tone says.

'What happened to you?' I ask. 'Where's Savage?'

'He's how Mirth knew we were on to him. Didn't think he was smart enough, but Savage was working with him all along. Never trust a half-breed,' Tone says and then gives me a small smile. 'No offence.'

'So you … know about me?' I say.

'We know you're part Crow and part Siener,' he says. 'That you're a science project Mirth has taken on.'

'You've known all along that Mirth was after me?' I say, standing up unsteadily.

Tone looks at me. 'You're not going to like this,' he says, 'but I suppose you have a right to know.'

'Know what?' I say, feeling dizzy and leaning my hands on my knees.

Tone looks across at Ronin and Ronin makes a 'go ahead' gesture with his hand. 'Ronin never really left мк6,' Tone says. 'He and Pat have both been working as part of a shadow team to prove that Mirth had gone rogue.'

'Fucking great,' I say.

'Sorry, sparky,' Ronin says. 'We needed to pantomime a bit to keep you out of the loop.'

'Well, everybody seems to know who, what and why I am,' I say. 'Except me.'

'We'll tell you what we know,' Ronin says, 'but it's not a whole lot. Mirth has been interested in you for a long time. We have surveillance records going back years; besides his little weapons project here you seem to be his number-one priority.'

'And Esmé?' I say.

'Nothing to do with us,' Ronin says. 'She seems to have run off of her own accord. We just used her situation to bring you closer into our sphere of influence.'

'Motherfucker,' I say. 'You used me.'

'Yeah, well, sorry, sparky,' he says. 'But with Mirth so keenly interested in you we couldn't take the chance that you'd get killed storming through the supernatural underworld on your own.'

'So where's Pat?' I say.

'We don't know,' Ronin replies. 'Combed the whole facility before they caught me.'

'Shit,' I say.

Tomas gives a small groan and his body shudders involuntarily. I give Ronin a dirty look and then kneel beside Tomas and pull the coat down a little so I can see his face. He is almost transparent. Through opaque layers of skin I can see his heart lethargically pumping the last of his translucent blood.

'Hey,' I say.

He tries to smile, but the effort causes another shudder to ripple through his body. 'I'm dying,' he says softly. I want to argue with him but it's undeniable. 'I'm going to meet my family in the land of my ancestors.'

I nod and give him what I hope is a comforting smile. I've never seen anyone die before, let alone the last of an extinct species of glowing people.

'I want you to take my blood,' he says.

'No,' I say. 'It's OK, I don't need it.'

'If you're going to fight *him* you will.' Despite his weakness he invests the word 'him' with so much venom I flinch. 'He needs you, Baxter,' Tomas says. 'He's not going to let you go. The only way you're going to escape is if you're ahead of him, if you can see more than he does. You can't do that alone. I know you have a struggle inside you,' he continues hoarsely. 'My people have always been attuned to the gift of the Sieners. I see how the Crow and the Siener inside you fight each other at every turn.'

'We're not going to kill you,' I say. 'We'll take your blood if you die. Not before.'

Tomas's body is racked with coughing and he has to wait a few moments before he can speak. 'You can't do that. Once I'm gone my blood will be useless to you.' He reaches his hand up and grabs my hand. 'Please, Baxter,' he says. 'You have to do this.' I grip his hand. 'OK,' I whisper.

Ronin produces a small vial of diabetes medication that he hid in his boot. He's sweating profusely and his hand shakes as he pours the liquid out onto the floor. 'Can't use it without a syringe,' he says. 'Take it.'

I grab the vial and take it over to Tomas. 'How are we going to get the blood?' I say to Tone.

'I can make a small sonic drill,' he says. 'It'll be painful for him, but it'll do the job.' I look at Tomas and he nods. Tone whistles shrilly; a harsh piercing sound that seems to ricochet off the walls.

Tomas takes my hand again. 'Kill him,' he whispers to me.

'I will,' I say.

The sound reaches a crescendo and then plunges like an invisible dagger into Tomas's chest. The shining blood begins to bubble out. I hold the vial near the wound to collect the precious liquid. Tears sting at my eyes and for once I don't care. Tomas didn't deserve to die and neither did his family. I push the stopper into the vial. I hear a low, familiar singing. It throbs in my ears for a moment and then Tomas sighs and the last of his light flickers frantically for a moment before it goes out.

'I want Mirth,' I say, wiping my eyes with my sleeve. 'I want to rip off his fucking head and use it as a bowling ball.'

We sit in the cell and wait. Ronin begrudgingly allowed his trench coat to be used as a shroud for Tomas's body, but my eyes keep sliding over to the mound.

'I'm, umm, sorry I lied to you,' Ronin says.

'You could have just told me,' I say. 'It would have made things easier.'

'Not for us,' he says. 'Would you really have hired me if you thought I was working another angle? We thought Mirth had kidnapped Esmé. It seemed like a win–win.'

I look around at the empty walls. 'Didn't exactly turn out well, did it?'

He chuckles. 'No, not really.'

A muffled explosion comes from the east wing of the building. 'I told you she'd come,' Tone says. Ronin pushes himself to his feet and assumes a relaxed fighting stance. I help Tone to stand and we wait as another explosion rocks the building and the sound of fighting echoes down the corridors. 'Sounds like she's brought a small army,' Ronin says with a smile. 'That's my girl.'

Gunshots crack outside our door and there's a shrieking, howling sound. 'Stand away from the door,' a voice calls from the other side. We flatten ourselves against the walls of the cell as bullets rip into the door. Something large smashes into the steel and the door folds inward. A large bulk squeezes in past the shattered door.

'You!' I say.

Schoeman cradles an AK-47 against his large bulk. 'Hey, candy cane,' he says.

'Nice going, darling,' Ronin says and Schoeman leans down to give him a peck on the cheek.

'What the . . .' I say.

'Lovely to see you too, sugar,' Schoeman says. 'Or perhaps you prefer me like this.' His bulk shimmers for a second and then Katinka, the Osiraii barmaid and erotic illusionist from the Flesh Palace, is standing in front of me, her wings folded back against her body and her hand stroking the muzzle of her gun suggestively. 'Or like this.' She shimmers again and Miss Hunter appears. 'Oh, please behave,' she says in a trembling voice. 'Oh, gosh, please.' Another shimmer and Katinka appears again with a grin splitting her voluptuous crimson mouth.

'Did I forget to mention that Osiraii are shape-shifters?' Ronin says with a chuckle.

'You've been my maths teacher all this time?' I say. I feel like I've been living in *The Truman Show*.

Katinka sticks out her bottom lip. 'It's only an illusion, sugar, or I wouldn't still be going to doctors for hormone injections. I'm sorry about the deception, sweetheart, but we had to have someone to keep an eye on you at all times.'

'But Schoeman?' I splutter. 'You almost convinced me I was the Mountain Killer.'

'Oh, come now,' she says, putting a hand on her hip. 'Give yourself more credit than that. We needed a reason to follow you. A fat, incompetent cop who had you pegged as the prime suspect was perfect.' She pulls a disgusted face and brushes imaginary dirt off her shoulders. 'However distasteful the disguise was.'

'We need to get out of here,' Ronin says, gratefully accepting the revolver that Katinka hands him. 'What's happening?'

'Mirth took a chopper out of here,' Katinka says. 'But he left enough Gogs and Crows to make sure it's going to be a bloody fight.'

Ronin spins the chamber of the revolver. 'Good.'

We step over the bullet-riddled body of a Gog and fan out into the corridor. Katinka braces the butt of the AK-47 against her shoulder and stalks down the left-hand branch of the corridor. Ronin follows her, holding the revolver like a gunslinger at his hip.

Katinka turns a corner up ahead and immediately rattles off a burst of gunfire. There's a bellow of pain and she swings back around, pulling the empty magazine from her gun and shoving another one in its place.

'Gog,' she says. 'A big one.' She sticks the gun around the corner and rattles off another volley of gunfire. The Gog bellows again and I can hear the thump of a body hitting the ground.

'You're so pretty when you're killing evil things,' Ronin says to her with a wink.

'Oh, stop, you,' Katinka says, giving her hair a flick.

We step over the huge twitching Gog body – this one has gross, oversized spider fangs. Up ahead, six short figures in grey hooded cloaks turn a corner, bringing handguns to bear on us and then lowering them and throwing back their hoods.

'Gredok,' Katinka says to the lead figure. He is squat and massively muscular with a bushy blond moustache that curls up at the ends. His hair is shaved into a mohawk and his fingers are covered in chunky silver rings. 'Agent,' he says to Katinka. 'Battle Shaman,' he says, inclining his head to Ronin.

'You're going all formal on me?' Ronin says with a grin and grabs the dwarf in a bear hug. 'Where the hell have you been, old man?'

The dwarf shrugs. 'Afghanistan mostly.'

As we continue down the corridor I learn that Gredok is Baresh's little brother. He's also a mercenary, after being dishonourably discharged from the Dwarven Legion for going AWOL after Baresh died. He has recently returned to South Africa with his small crew of soldiers of fortune.

He and the five other members of his crew are carrying handguns and thick blood-covered swords. Three of them are also carrying heavy backpacks full of equipment strapped on over their grey cloaks.

'What's the score?' Ronin says, nodding to the blood on Gredok's sword.

'Personally? Twelve of those Frankenstein bastards.'

'Not bad,' Ronin says.

'We met a Crow, but it took all of us to kill him. Even with Molotov cocktails. If we meet any more of them we're in trouble. Unless...' He gives Ronin a meaningful look.

Ronin shakes his head vigorously. 'I've never commanded a unit myself. And after Baresh...'

'He trusted you,' Gredok says, stopping and facing Ronin.

'What's he talking about?' I whisper, but Katinka puts a finger to her lips.

'Baresh wanted you to succeed him,' Gredok says.

'I'm not a dwarf,' Ronin says.

'Who the fuck cares?' Gredok replies. 'The Dwarven Legion are corrupt. They're propping up dictators throughout Africa, they're helping protect poppy fields in Afghanistan. They've forgotten what the Code is even about.' He puts his fist on Ronin's chest. 'Baresh lived by the Code and he believed you did too. That's why he trained you. You're not going to dishonour him, so you're doing this.'

'OK,' Ronin says.

'Impi formation,' Gredok calls out and his unit forms into a loose diamond pattern in the corridor.

'Dwarven battle trance,' Katinka whispers and gives me a wink. 'This is going to be good.'

Ronin stands behind them and lifts his fist, beginning a slow rhythmic chant in the same thick, guttural language he uses for his charms. The dwarves begin to rock back and forth. Ronin stamps his foot on the floor and a shiver of energy runs through them. 'Let's go,' Katinka says.

We proceed down the corridor, the dwarves in front moving like a single organism. We push through a set of swinging doors and straight into a pack of Gogs who are in a feeding frenzy over the body of a scientist. With Mirth away the Gogs will play, it seems. They stop feeding and look up at us, their jaws stained with blood.

Ronin stamps his foot again and the grey-hooded dwarves move like mercury. It's like watching *Swan Lake* performed to Swedish death metal. Handgun Haiku. Necksnap Nureyev. The dwarves flow between the monsters. I see Gredok take off a Gog's arm with his sword and then spin to fire two bullets into its brain from beneath its chin. Gog blood splatters into the air and the body drops instantly.

I'm so intent on watching them that I only manage to duck

at the last second as a Crow sweeps down from the ceiling. I fall back onto my ass and scramble beneath a surgical table. The Crow's hooked claws land on the ground next to me, but it is knocked away by a blast of shrill sonic power from Tone. The bird stumbles backwards and then arcs its tail forward and pins a dwarf to the wall.

Two of the dwarves drop their swords and reach into their backpacks for Molotov cocktails. The Crow drops the dwarf and shrieks as two cocktails explode on its back. It tries to take off but stumbles and smashes into a vat filled with a dark liquid. The liquid explodes out on the floor.

'Acid!' Tone shouts and we scramble out of the way of the deluge, Katinka spreading her wings and swooping to lift the injured dwarf away from the rapidly spreading pool of caustic liquid. Gredok helps Ronin pull her out of the lab and the rest of the dwarves carry their wounded companion. I grab onto Tone's arm and he shepherds me out of the doors.

'Mom?' I say into the phone. We're sitting around the table in the kitchen of the Haven. Katinka dabs Tone's chest lightly with a cloth while Ronin sits on a chair in the corner and drinks cheap whisky from the bottle. We'd escaped the facility in a blaze of gunfire, fire and death, and now I want nothing more than to tell my mom about it and have her shush me and stroke my hair.

Gredok and his unit are mourning the death of their companion. Watching Crow venom at work had been terrifying. The dwarf's face had gone purple, the veins in his neck sticking out like thick black slugs. Then he had begun to bleed out of the nose. And the mouth. And the ears. And pretty much every other orifice. It had been a long and painful process and had left me with the unwavering determination never to be stung by one of those bastards, the fact that they're distant family notwithstanding.

'Baxter!' my mother says. 'Where the hell are you?' Completely uninformed about my heroic escape, she's doing less gentle shushing and more shouting. 'Lucinda says she's hardly seen you. Rafe is distraught. Come home. Now.'

'I can't, Mom,' I say, my voice all choked up. The truth is I can think of nothing better than going home and having my mom make me hot chocolate and then sitting in the lounge and watching TV, but I know Mirth will come after me. He has to. He needs me.

'You can't?!' my mother storms. 'I've been on the brink of calling the police. You can't just disappear and expect me to accept it. You really need to take some responsibility for the effect that your actions –'

'Mom,' I say, 'listen to me. Over the past few days I've become aware that I haven't exactly been the best person in the world. You're right; I haven't been a good brother to Rafe. I haven't really been much of a good anything to anyone.' She tries to interrupt but I talk right over her. 'I'm not going to lie to you any more. I'm not at yoga class or at photography lessons or volunteering at an organisation that helps dyslexic rural kids. I'm not doing whatever Kyle has told you I'm doing. I can't tell you what I am doing, except to say that it's important. So you're going to have to trust me. You're going to have to realise that I'm almost an adult and that sometimes I need to make my own decisions.'

'I do trust you, Baxter,' my mother says. 'I know Esmé's disappearance has hurt you. I understand.'

'I'll be back soon, Mom,' I say. 'Oh, and I love you.' My mother's stuttering surprise is the last thing I hear before I hang up.

'We can't do anything now,' Katinka says. 'We all better get some sleep.'

Slowly everyone leaves the kitchen until it's just me and Ronin left. He has put Warchild on the table and is polishing her with a soft cloth. 'Don't worry,' he slurs to the gun. 'Daddy's got you, baby.' He picks Warchild up and plants a large wet kiss on one of the barrels. I avert my eyes from this inappropriately intimate scene between man and shotgun.

Ronin takes another gulp of whisky and gives me a drunken smile. 'Heishhparky,' he says.

'Mirth scammed me,' I say.

'Yeah, no sshhhit,' he says.

'You apologised to me so it's my turn. I'm sorry for thinking you were a hallucination.'

He shrugs. 'Youshh figured it out eventually.'

He hands me the bottle and I take a swig.

'I'm part Crow,' I say.

'Yeshh you are,' he confirms.

'The Crows killed Baresh,' I say.

'And you're going to help me kill the Crowsshh,' he says. 'You gonna help me find Pat, right, sshparky?' he says. He smiles and tries to give me a hug. He smells of whisky and blood so I push him away. He flops forward onto the table and begins to snore as I make my way up the stairs.

GUNS, PORN AND STEEL

The huge chicken-blood star is starting to turn black as the blood dries. Tone chants in Xhosa as he walks the perimeter of the star, his bare feet leaving bloody footprints on the wooden floor.

Gredok has lugged a huge rock into the Haven barn and placed it in the centre of the star.

'You can control it,' Tone says. 'You just need practice.'

'It's not that easy,' I say. My sight is not a superpower at all, it's a bad acid trip. 'It's not like playing the guitar. I can't just sit in my room and practise until I can play "Stairway to Heaven".'

'Maybe not,' Tone replies, 'but at least we can help you to direct it.'

Ronin taps me on the shoulder. 'Hair of the dog?' he says, offering me the hipflask. I shake my head. I assume this will be more unpleasant and dangerous if I'm drunk. The sangoma approaches us. His hands and feet are stained with blood but his eyes are bright and intense. 'Magic,' Ronin says. 'It's a drug and sangomas are the biggest junkies.'

I push myself to my feet and Tone leads me to the centre of the star and helps me to stand on the big rock.

'Once it starts you have to see it through,' Tone says. 'There's no pause button, you understand?'

I nod. I understand all right. It's just that I'm not all that enamoured by the idea of going through this again. I'd experimented, I'd explored a little and I'd come back with the knowledge that I'd rather take acid and ketamine in an abattoir than go on another little trip into the ether.

Tone strips off the bright tie-dyed T-shirt he'd taken from Pat's cupboard to replace his burnt suit. Gredok carries a squawking chicken toward him. The little brown bird struggles in his meaty hands. Tone nods once and the dwarf snaps the chicken's neck and hands it to him. The sangoma raises the dead chicken above him and cuts its neck. Blood splashes down his arms and onto his body. I wrinkle my nose. Whatever else magic is, it sure ain't pretty.

Tone starts to chant and I feel the throbbing in my forehead again. It's like the subwoofer of migraines; low, deep and rumbling. Ronin begins to chant too in the thick, guttural Dwarven tongue and the throbbing becomes more intense. I brace myself for the eyestalk to burst through my forehead again. When it does I'm ready for it. But that doesn't help at all.

The eyestalk writhes and whips like a garden hose left on the floor of my head. My brain is flooded with light and I reach my hand out blindly, desperately needing something to grab on to.

Then I feel Tone. The sangoma's power is like a leopard that stalks across the waterfall of light, grabs me by the scruff of the neck and drags me back to lucidity.

I see Cape Town burning in a towering nuclear inferno. I see them. The Mantis and the Octopus, brothers locked in an infinite fight to the death. Our death. Space and time rip apart and the Earth becomes like the depressurised cabin of an aircraft. Whole chunks of matter are torn away, splitting reality into billions of jagged parts.

Then I see a dark warship cresting black waves. A huge, swirling whirlpool next to it seems to suck matter and life into it like a black hole. On the deck is a huge iron cross and on the cross a bird, its wings stretched and impaled. It turns its head weakly toward me.

I pull away from it and my sight spins wildly. I'm heading toward the whirlpool, the blackness replacing the light. Everything is disappearing, draining from me. I scream but the leopard is with me again and pulling me away from the black pit. Its teeth dig into my neck and I begin to feel blood pour down my shoulders. I scream again and this time I don't stop until everything disappears.

'The conquering hero returns,' Ronin says with a grin. He claps me on the shoulder as I sit down. 'How you feeling?'

'Terrible,' I say, accepting the cup of coffee Gredok offers.

'Dwarven coffee,' he says. 'Not any of this insipid human crap.'

I take a sip and the dark liquid jumpstarts my brain. I feel like I'm drinking a Ritalin-and-energy-drink smoothie.

A map of South Africa is spread across the kitchen table, held down in the corners by empty bottles and weapons of various descriptions. Through the window I can see the other dwarves, Fell, Wref, Mike and Tony, going through training drills with knives in the garden. Katinka is lying on a towel on the grass, slices of cucumber delicately positioned over her eyes.

'How long have I been out?' I say, rubbing my eyes.

'About three hours,' Ronin replies.

'Shit,' I say.

'Did you see anything?' Tone asks.

I look down at the map and my eyes trace the meandering line of the east coast of South Africa.

'There,' I say, putting my finger down in the Indian Ocean, close to East London. 'It's around there.'

'On a ship?' Ronin says.

I nod.

'Bingo bango,' he says, clapping his hands together.

Gredok takes a slurp of coffee. 'We need more weapons,' he says. 'My lads only have handguns and we're almost out of ammo. We're going to need a shitload more firepower if we're going to do a marine assault.'

'I may be able to get some,' I say.

They turn to look at me. 'We're also going to need to make fire, household solvents, petrol, things to make Molotov cocktails,' Ronin says.

'It happens I know just the guy,' I say with a smile.

'I can't say that I wasn't a little surprised by your phone call,' Anwar says. He's alone in Central, sprawled on the couch and watching us curiously. 'You're keeping strange company these days, Zevcenko.'

He casts a lazy eye over us. Kyle, Zikhona and the Inhalant Kid had met us at Central, with Rafe in tow. I'd arrived with Ronin, Tone and Katinka. Gredok and the other dwarves had stayed behind to organise our little trip up the coast.

'I know your crew of degenerates,' Anwar says, waving a hand at the Spider, 'but who are these three? That one looks like an escaped mental patient.'

'And you look like you have rabies, kid,' Ronin growls. 'Maybe I should put you down.'

'You better tell your friend to play by my rules,' Anwar says, shifting nervously in his chair. It's the first time I've seen him this uneasy and I won't lie, it's quite gratifying.

'Why are the Spider arming themselves, anyway?' he says. 'I thought you were pacifists.'

'This has nothing to do with Westridge,' I say.

He shrugs. 'You can understand how I might be reluctant to arm a competing faction with my own weapons. So tell me, what's in it for me?'

'A cut of porn profits,' I say. 'Thirty per cent of everything. That's including our new deal with Dirkie Venter.'

Anwar laughs. 'I think you may have mistaken me for one of the actors in your porn, Zevcenko. I have no desire to get fucked in the ass.' He strokes his chin. 'I want it all. You give me the infrastructure and contacts to control the porn at Westridge and convince Dirkie Venter to deal with me. Then you can have as many guns as you can carry.'

'All of it?' I say.

'With a non-compete clause, of course,' Anwar says with a smile. 'If you do this, you're done with porn. The Spider ceases to exist.'

'Fuck you,' Kyle shouts at him.

'Oh, Baxter's little dog barks,' Anwar says.

'I need to discuss it with my people,' I say.

Anwar shrugs. 'Go ahead.'

I retreat into a corner with my friends. Rafe follows us and hangs around on the edge of the circle we've formed. 'Last time I checked, you weren't a member of the Spider,' I say to him.

He stares at me.

'Why the hell did you come along anyway?'

He shrugs once.

'Perfect,' I say.

'You're not going to do this, are you, Bax?' Kyle says. 'We've worked so hard. You've worked so damn hard for this.'

I sigh and look at them. 'The Spider is the best thing that has ever happened to me,' I say. 'And this fucker, this guy we're after, tried to convince me that you guys didn't exist.'

Kyle is peering intently at me, Zikhona is chewing gum loudly and watching me, the Kid is sniffing, his eyes darting from side to side.

'But even with the most powerful drugs he had, he couldn't make me forget you miscreants. He couldn't make me believe. You're right. We've all worked damn hard to make the Spider what it is. Giving it away just like that is not something I would ever want to do. But the thing is, we're not just a corporation, we're best friends, and Anwar can't take that away from us. This guy, Mirth, is going to come for me at some stage. I'd rather go for him first.' I rub my eyes with the backs of my hands. 'I'm going to fucking end this one way or another.'

'Give it to him,' Kyle says without hesitation. Zikhona nods. The Inhalant Kid takes a moment and then nods too.

'Are you sure?' I say.

'You created the Spider,' Kyle says. 'And you gave me a place in it. That was always more important than business for me. Besides, selling porn was ruining the experience of watching it for me.'

The Inhalant Kid nods. 'I'll do whatever you guys do. You're the only people who don't think I'm weird.'

'Ha, you *are* weird,' Zikhona says, punching him on the arm.

'Give him the porn, Baxter,' Kyle says.

I turn, walk back over, and nod to Anwar. He smiles.

'To the end of the Spider,' he says. 'And the growth of the NTK.' He gets up to key in a PIN on the keypad on the wall. There's the sound of a lock clicking. He pulls one of the Masonic banners off the wall to reveal a huge safe.

'Combat shotguns, assault rifles, Glocks,' Anwar says. 'A gun for every occasion.'

If I ever had any doubt about who would win should the

gangs go at it, it was instantly quashed.

'Damn,' I say. 'Where the hell did you get all this?'

'My brother and I have a little deal. I funnel drugs into schools in the area, and he provides me with guns.'

'A flamethrower,' Ronin says gleefully, picking up the pack and strapping it to his back.

'There's enough weaponry for a small army here,' Tone says, his eyes wide with disbelief.

'Welcome to the education system,' Anwar says, spreading his arms. 'And to the death of the Spider and the end of an era at Westridge.'

I sigh. 'At least I'll have time to join the choir.'

'Giant Crows?' Zikhona says through her gum. 'That's some serious sci-fi shit right there.'

'Tell me about it,' I say.

'I can't believe this stuff is actually out there,' Kyle says. 'I mean, it makes you wonder, doesn't it? If that's been kept from us all this time, what other stuff is real? UFOs, the Bermuda Triangle, who built the pyramids...'

'Slaves,' says Tone. 'Slaves built the pyramids.'

'Oh, sure,' Kyle says. 'I bet that's exactly what you government types want us to believe.'

'Trust me,' Ronin growls. 'The less you know about what really goes on the better. That stuff will give you nightmares.'

We've piled our load of weapons and the flammables, courtesy of the Inhalant Kid, into the back of Pat's vw. Gredok and the dwarves are strapping equipment onto fat black motorbikes and checking the weapons from Anwar.

'The sooner we leave the better.' Ronin climbs into the driver's seat. 'So say your goodbyes to your little buddies.'

'I'm coming with you.' Kyle gets into the back and crosses his arms across his chest like a little kid.

'There's no way I'm having the computer-geek club coming to raid a ship with us,' Ronin says.

'Hey, I'm coming too,' Zikhona says.

'Me too,' the Inhalant Kid pipes up.

'Maybe I didn't make myself clear,' Ronin shouts. 'You're not coming with us.'

'Guess you don't want the schematic of the Russian *Titan* destroyer then,' Kyle says, holding up his phone. 'From what Bax described, that's what you're attacking.'

'How about I crush your testicles and take your phone from you?' Ronin replies.

Rafe taps me on the shoulder. I turn around. He scribbles something on a notepad and holds it in front of my face. 'Take me with you or I'll tell Mom where you're going,' it says.

'Oh for fuck's sake, Rafe,' I sigh. 'Do you have to do this every single minute of every single day?'

He nods.

'How about they come with us until we find a boat?' I say. 'They can take the bus back to Cape Town.'

'If they get killed I'm not being held responsible,' Ronin says.

'Deal,' Kyle says.

'But call your folks. The last thing I need is a soccer mom shooting me for kidnapping her darling,' Ronin says.

They make the calls to their parentbots. Rafe texts my mom to tell her that he's OK. She's probably having a nervous breakdown, but there's nothing I can do about that now.

Ronin starts the engine and we reverse out of the Haven. Truth be told, a bright yellow VW van doesn't really make one feel very badass. But the gym bags filled with semi-automatic weapons and incendiaries definitely help. So does the crack platoon of Dwarven mercenaries on custom bikes behind us. I swap places with Tone and squeeze in next to Kyle. Katinka slams the door shut.

'Road trip!' Kyle shouts.

I doze off for a while into blissful dreamless territory. When I wake up it's dark outside. I peek over the seat in front and see the sangoma at the wheel and Ronin smoking in the passenger seat with his boots up on the dash.

'Are we there yet?' I say.

'Go back to sleep,' Tone murmurs.

We're watched uninterestedly by locals with hangovers when we stop off in small towns for food and to stretch our legs. Apparently not even heavily armed dwarves on bikes are noteworthy when you've got a cheap-wine hangover.

Back on the road and I'm suddenly incredibly uncomfortable, shifting positions every couple of minutes, Kyle's head lolling onto my shoulder. 'Dude,' I hiss, pushing him off me as drool begins to soak into my T-shirt.

Ronin takes over driving duty and I convince Tone to swap seats with me. Sucker. I climb into the passenger seat and sigh with relief as I stretch my legs onto the dashboard. I look in the rear-view mirror and see that Tone has created a sonic shield between him and Kyle, and is lying back comfortably. Asshole.

'What's bothering you, sparky?' Ronin says through the cigarette clamped between his teeth.

'Does it ever get easier?' I say. 'Knowing that there are these monsters out there. Actually, scratch that. Knowing that you're one of the monsters.'

'The whole "you're part Crow thing"?' he says. 'Yeah, that's gotta suck.'

'Thanks for all your wisdom, Yoda.'

He shrugs. 'You're part Crow. You're related to Mirth. Your girlfriend dumped you. Not exactly sure how you want me to sweeten that.'

I sigh. 'I don't know.'

'I once saw an agent suck on an assault rifle and pull the trigger,' Ronin says. 'Splat. At the time I thought he was an idiot, but I wonder daily whether he was, in fact, the smart one.' He blows smoke out through his nose. 'The Hidden are a bunch of fucking problem children that the government wants nothing to do with unless it's to exploit them. We're like Nazi concentration-camp guards overseeing the genocide. I find a particular blend of drugs and Jack Daniel's helps.'

'Wow, thanks,' I say.

He sighs. 'You know David Copperfield, the illusionist, right? He did this one trick where he walked through the Great Wall of China. They made a huge thing of it, attached heart-rate monitors to him, in case he got "stuck" inside the stone. He walked through and the wall went all stretchy, but the whole time you know it's all crap, it's just an illusion that you want to believe is real.'

At this stage I have no idea where Ronin is going with this, but I decide just to go with it. I nod.

'Well, that's what becoming an adult is like,' Ronin continues. 'You think there's this great dividing line between child and adult, you're brought up believing that you're gonna do this trick, right, walk through the wall between the two, become an adult. But you get to the other side and you realise it's just an illusion; there was no wall, just some smoke and mirrors. There is no line between old and young; the only things that mark your passing are the things that go wrong – the car accidents, cancers and heart attacks.'

That's Ronin's idea of a motivational speech and strangely, in a way, it works. After all, if I'm going to die, it's good to know that most of what I'm going to be missing out on is mortgages, waiting in traffic and misunderstanding my wife. Sure, hopefully there'd also be threesomes in hot tubs, hoverboards and the Singularity, but weighed against the absolute certainty of the mundane nature of real life, it all somehow looks less attractive.

Plus it stops me from worrying about death and starts me thinking about the practicalities of finding a supernaturally guarded, mutant-infested ship.

I slide into sleep again and when I wake up we're passing through the streets of a small seaside town. The roads are deserted as we coast down the high street and toward the beachfront. Ronin steers the van down a narrow road. There's a lopsided circus tent sprawled on the dry grass that borders the beach. 'Magical delites: You won't beleef your eyes' a sign says.

We park next to the tent, the dwarves pulling their bikes in next to us. Ronin nods toward a shifty-looking tavern. A blinking neon light on its roof shows a picture of a large manta ray. 'Stay here,' Ronin says and then climbs out and strides off toward the tavern.

The rest of the Spider are still sleeping, but Rafe is wide awake. I don't think he slept during the whole drive. He looks at me and gives me a grin. Then he opens the van's sliding door and jogs off after Ronin.

'What the hell is he doing?' Tone hisses.

'Being an idiot,' I say. 'I'll go get him. He won't listen to anybody else.' I doubt he'll listen to me either, but I don't tell the sangoma that.

I climb out of the vw and sprint after Rafe. He saunters through the doors of the tavern like the sheriff in a cheesy Western and I follow. A pall of smoke hangs in the tavern's interior like smog. The place smells like salt and sweat. Small groups of circus people and sailors cluster around jugs of beer and stare up at a TV that flickers in the corner.

Rafe is sitting next to Ronin at the bar.

'Sorry,' I say as I reach them.

Ronin shrugs and takes a sip of his beer. 'Too late now,' he says in a low voice. 'Sailor at four o'clock has a gun under the table.'

I turn to look and Ronin clamps a hand on my shoulder. 'That doesn't mean look at him, Professor Subtle. I just want you to know the situation we're in.'

'This person you're meeting. It's a friend, right?' I say.

'Not exactly,' he says. 'It's an ex-girlfriend.'

'Not –' I start to say, and Ronin nods.

'You've brought us here to meet a woman you left standing at the altar? Are you insane?'

'C'mon, she must have forgiven me by now,' he says. He turns on his barstool to face the rest of the punters. 'We're looking for Captain Sue Severance,' he announces in a loud voice.

'Good for you,' a clown mumbles into his drink.

'Never heard of her,' an old sailor says. 'No captain of that name here.'

'Well, maybe one of you can help us with something else then,' Ronin says. 'We're looking for a ship.'

'Try the marina,' the old sailor says.

'No, this is a military ship,' Ronin says. 'A destroyer, painted all black.'

The sailors laugh and turn back to their drinks. 'That ship doesn't exist,' says a tall, dark-haired sailor in a tight black T-shirt with a broken heart on it. His forearms are criss-crossed with scars and he has a gold tooth that shines dully.

'That's not what we've heard,' Ronin says.

'Well, then, you heard wrong,' he says. 'So why don't you take your little friends and get out of our pub?'

'No need to get aggressive, friend,' Ronin says. 'We were just asking.' The sailor stands up and downs his ale. 'Perhaps you didn't hear me,' he says, approaching us.

'What you gonna do, Popeye?' Ronin says with a contemptuous snort.

What the sailor does is swing a wild haymaker that could crush rock. Ronin ducks the punch, grabs the barstool, turns it and shoves the legs into the sailor's crotch. The sailor grunts and doubles over and Ronin follows up with a vicious knee to his face. He crumples to the floor, blood streaming from a severely broken nose.

Ronin pulls Warchild from under his coat and shoves it into the sailor's neck. 'Now,' he says, 'for the slow and hard of hearing, I repeat: we're looking for Sue Severance.'

'A bit heavily armed for tourists,' a husky voice says.

I turn to see a woman standing at the centre of a group of sailors armed with Uzis. I recognise the woman from the photograph. She's wearing a fedora perched on her dreadlocks and a lacy pirate's shirt, which is unbuttoned to reveal the anchor tattoo on her chest. My eyes are drawn to it and to her breasts, which are visible through the thin lace of the shirt.

'What you looking at, boy?' she rasps. She cups a breast in each hand and jiggles them up and down. 'This one's called Port and this one's called Starboard, where would you like to unload your cargo first?'

I avert my eyes and mumble something incoherent.

She snorts. 'That's the problem with men, all talk and no action.' She turns to her crew.

'Put your guns down, boys,' she says. 'I know these pieces of dickcheese.' She looks at Ronin menacingly. 'Well, one of them at least.' She waves us over into the back room.

Captain Severance sits down at a poker table with a skeletal old sailor. His few curly strands of grey hair hang down the sides of his head like seaweed and he slurps at a huge tankard of beer.

'Jackson Ronin,' Severance says, shaking her head. 'The last time I saw you, you were declaring your undying love for me.'

Ronin smiles. 'Well, I'm not dead, am I?'

Severance returns the smile. 'Not yet.'

'You're looking good,' Ronin says.

'Well, you look like shit,' Severance says.

'Yeah, we've had a little trouble,' Ronin says.

She laughs. 'Knowing you, that's an understatement. Who are your little friends?'

'Baxter Zevcenko,' I say. 'This is my brother Rafe.'

'Kids the only ones that will hang out with you these days?' she says.

'We need your help,' I say.

'That much I know. If it wasn't the case, then Ronin wouldn't be here. In fact, I'd wager you *desperately* need my help.'

'They've got Pat,' Ronin says.

'Jesus,' Severance says and takes a gulp of her ale. 'Who's got her?'

'Mirth.'

'A monster with a ponytail,' Severance says. 'I was hoping I would never hear that name again.'

'I need you, Sue,' Ronin says.

She leans back and puts her boots up on the table. 'And I needed you once, Jackson. Remind me what happened there.'

'I'm sorry,' Ronin says. 'Truly sorry. I shouldn't have come here.'

'Just like you,' Severance says with a shake of her head. 'Quitting at the first sign of resistance. I didn't say I wouldn't help you. I like Pat, but I'm not willing to risk my ship for her. The milk of human kindness does not flow from my teats.'

'What do you want?' I say.

Severance reaches beneath the table and pulls two long-barrelled silver pistols from beneath it and places them on the table.

'Jesus and Judas,' Ronin says.

Severance smiles. 'My salvation and my downfall,' she says breathily. Great, that's all we need, another psycho with a weapons fetish.

'Beautiful pieces,' Ronin says.

'But an incomplete set,' Severance replies. 'They have a larger brother that I would love to get my hands on.'

Ronin grimaces as if the very thought he's having is giving him physical pain. 'Forget it,' he says. 'Baresh gave you Jesus and Judas and he gave Warchild to me.'

She shrugs. 'Your choice.'

'Ronin,' I say, 'you're seriously going to leave Pat to rot for a gun?'

Ronin clasps his hands together like he's praying. He holds them there for a couple of seconds and then nods. 'She's yours,' he says. 'After I've used her to rescue Pat.'

'And anything else we find on that ship,' Severance says.

'Fine,' Ronin says. 'I'm not going to stop you.'

Severance spits on her hand and holds it out. Ronin spits on his and takes it. Looks like we've got a ride.

The sailors grudgingly help us to pile our gear into Severance's boat, a solid-looking fishing trawler called the *Salt Dragon*. Once inside it becomes apparent that the vessel is no fisherman's skiff. Gun turrets are hidden beneath fishing nets on the deck, the hold is reinforced with steel and there are several secret compartments for storing contraband.

With our equipment stashed I return to shore.

'You're going to be OK, right?' Kyle says.

I nod. 'You?'

'Bus leaves at twelve,' he says. I can tell he desperately wants to come with me, that he's on the brink of insisting. I divert him instead. I look around. 'Where's Rafe?'

'Probably back in the van. Don't think he wanted to say goodbye.'

'Typical,' I mutter.

Kyle grabs me in a hug. 'Don't get killed,' he says. I smile and pat him on the back. 'We've got to rebuild a whole empire,' I say. 'Getting killed wouldn't be good business.'

I say my last goodbyes to Kyle, Zikhona and the Kid, and then climb up onto the deck and Ronin and I make our way up to the bridge. The command centre of the boat is decked out with sophisticated radar and tracking equipment, perfect for a smuggler like Sue.

She's lounging against the wheel wearing a white captain's hat with a playing card, the Ace of Hearts, shoved into the brim, and sucking heavily on a cigar. 'She's near the Maelstrom,' Severance says. 'Whatever your boy Mirth is into, it's something big. That whirlpool is huge and dangerous. Couple of fishing vessels have been lost and it's a no-go zone now.'

The *Salt Dragon* gains speed and I make my way down to the deck. I stand with my elbows on the bow, watching as the boat cuts through the dark water. 'Nervous?' Katinka asks. She leans down next to me and pushes me playfully with her shoulder.

'After this week I don't think anything can make me nervous,' I say.

'Sorry to hear about your girlfriend, sugar,' she says. 'I've had my heart broken too. First time for you?'

'I was stupid to care for her. I should have stuck to my plan: no commitments.'

'Sounds like a one-way ticket to depression town, sweetheart,' she says. 'You got to care for somebody sometime.'

'Turns out this time wasn't the time, then,' I say.

'Listen,' she says, 'I'm not going to give you a "dance like nobody's watching" speech, but the fact that someone made you feel like that means you're no robot, sugar. And that's cause for celebration.'

'Hooray,' I say.

She chuckles. 'If we get out of this alive, I'll make you a mixtape for broken hearts. It'll sort you right out.'

'If we get out of this I may even listen to it,' I say.

Later I'm staring at the ceiling of one of the cabins thinking about Esmé when I hear the sound of feet running on the deck above.

'Incoming,' Severance calls from the bridge.

'Get the Molotovs,' Ronin shouts. 'Quickly!'

We scramble below and frantically haul the bags full of Molotovs to the deck. Ronin hastily straps on the flamethrower.

Back on deck the sailors have cleared the nets from the deck guns and are watching the skies nervously. I clutch a Molotov in one hand and a short, heavy handgun in the other.

Heavy machine-gun fire breaks the tense silence. A dark shape wheels in the air and heads toward us; behind it other dark shapes become visible, silhouetted against the night sky. The heavy deck guns strafe the air.

There's a whoosh as a Crow swoops over us and Katinka leaps from the deck to chase it, an Uzi in one hand and a Molotov in the other, her white wings spread like a falcon's as she dives after the bird, outpacing it and bringing it down in a flaming heap with a well-timed throw.

Another Crow lands on top of the bridge. The sailors swing the guns and empty dozens of rounds into it, knocking it from its perch onto the deck. I lob my Molotov and it hits the huge bird dead on, smashing and dousing it in flammable liquid. It's only then that I realise I forgot to light it. I swear and search my pockets for a lighter as the bird claws itself back to its feet.

I aim the gun and fire into its body, but the liquid doesn't ignite. The dark shape looms above me but screams as it bursts into flames. It tries to take off but is brought down by another burst of gunfire. It sprawls to the deck, a sizzling barbecue of feather and flame.

Ronin shouts to me and throws me his lighter. I catch it, stuff my hand in my bag and pull out another Molotov.

A Crow dives across the deck and knocks a sailor off his feet. He spins and manages to catch it with a Molotov as he hits the deck. The flaming bird whirls frantically through the night sky and then plummets into the ocean below.

I look up and see Rafe standing on the deck, a look of relaxed concentration on his face and a Molotov in his hand. Am I hallucinating? Rafe smiles at me and gives me the thumbs up. Nope, the idiot is really here. 'Rafe,' I shout. 'Get the hell out of here.'

I try to run over to him but I slip on something on the deck and land hard on my knees. I look down and see a thick river of blood. A sailor looks at me and then down at the gash in his abdomen before collapsing on the deck.

'Rafe, what the hell are you doing?' I shout out. 'Fight or you're going to get killed.' He looks at me and then takes the Molotov cocktail and lighter out of my hands, lights the cloth and throws it nonchalantly at a bird. It explodes into flames and he gives me a smug smile. Smartass.

A sailor in a yellow anorak runs across the deck, turning and firing into a Crow that's swooping down on him as if he were a rabbit. 'Use fire!' I shout, lighting the cloth of another Molotov. The Crow slams into the sailor and then lifts him from the deck to drive its beak into his head. Blood and bits of yellow anorak spill onto the deck.

I launch my Molotov, but I've misjudged the distance and it sails over the top of the bird, hitting the bow and exploding into flame. My feet get tangled in a net on the deck and I fall over myself. A claw lashes out and, instinctively, I throw a hand up to defend myself. The razor-sharp talon neatly separates the pinkie from my left hand at the knuckle.

I shout in pain as the bird stands over me, its monstrous beak dripping with blood. It dips its head to peck at me, but is driven off by Severance who is hacking manically at it with a chainsaw that has been doused in petrol and set alight. With a wild battle cry she spins the chainsaw in a wide arc and hacks the bird's head from its body.

I try to scramble away, but end up slipping on my own blood and falling back onto the deck. I want to celebrate the Crow's demise with Sue, but I just lie there with blood squirting rhythmically from my hand. I think about the Yakuza and how they sacrifice fingers as penance to their bosses. I think about kids who have accidents with farm equipment. I think about voluntary finger amputation for body modification. Having your pinkie removed by a flying demon is either so much more stupid or entirely cooler than any of those things. I'm still trying to decide which when I pass out.

When I wake up, Rafe is holding my good hand and patting my head with a damp cloth. He looks at me disapprovingly, as if I were a naughty kid who had run into the road to fetch a ball and been hit by a car.

'Stowaway,' I say.

He gives me a smile.

Ronin opens the door to the cabin. 'Time to go, sparky,' he says. He looks at me sympathetically, but we both know we're too far into this. The options are fairly simple at this point: either we're going to pull this off, or we're going to die spectacularly.

15

ASSAULT WITH INTENT TO DO
GRIEVOUS BODILY HARM

The *Salt Dragon* lists hard to one side as the currents of the Maelstrom claw at her hull, desperately trying to drag us into the dark green-grey spiral of water that spits huge crests of foam up into the air.

On the bridge, Severance has braced herself against the control panel, her lean, wiry biceps bulging as she struggles to keep the wheel steady. 'Radar's down,' she says, nodding at the screen.

We beat off the bird attack, but I know it's only the beginning. There had only been a few birds and one of those had retreated. Three of Sue's crew had died and we had squandered at least a dozen of the Molotovs with wild throws.

I look down at the bandaged stump where my pinkie used to be. I have a morbid fascination with my missing digit. I keep on looking down every couple of seconds and wiggling my fingers. I wonder if I will develop a phantom pinkie.

Rafe is standing next to me on the bridge and peering at the Maelstrom with fascination.

'Stowaways are bad luck,' one of the sailors mutters.

'Too late to turn back,' Sue says. 'We'll just have to deal with it.'

Now whatever happens I'll have Rafe with me. Weirdly that makes me feel better.

'Shiver me clitoris, that's an evil vessel,' Severance says. We look out at the dark ship that rises out of the sea in front of us. I catch a glimpse of the iron cross that protrudes from its deck like a tower.

The *Salt Dragon*'s engines whine with strain, but Severance is an expert pilot and she guides the boat past the Maelstrom like she's dancing the tango. We accelerate and the *Dragon* cuts a path toward the port side of the warship. No guns greet us and we can only hope that their radar is suffering from the same kind of malfunction as ours.

'This is it,' I say to Ronin.

'Yep,' he says. 'Try not to fucking shoot me this time.'

The sailors fire motorised grappling hooks over the side of the warship with practised ease. Somehow I don't think this is the first time they've boarded a ship. A weathered sailor with dark hair that reaches to his waist takes off his shirt, straps an assault rifle to his back and puts a knife between his teeth. He clips himself to the line and pulls himself slowly to the top.

After a couple of seconds a uniformed body sails over the edge and disappears into the dark water.

We clip in and hang suspended, leaving two sailors to pilot the *Salt Dragon*. I try to make Rafe stay behind but it's no use. He clips himself to a line and won't budge. The lines sway in the wind and salty spray from the ocean stings my skin as we're hoisted to the top.

The deck is slick with the blood of the dead sentry. The long-haired sailor is crouched with his assault rifle braced against his chest. Gredok and the dwarves follow the sailor around to the other side of the deck. The idea is that they'll clear the deck of sentries while we go below.

The rest of us make our way across the open deck. The iron cross comes into view and I see that there is definitely something on it. A bird, to be precise. The leader of the Murder is impaled on the cross, his wings stretched across and held in place with bolts. The head hangs loosely from the body and blood stains the deck below him.

'The betrayer can't help but betray,' Ronin whispers.

'That's our door,' Sue says, pointing into the shadows with one of her pistols.

'Eyes of a hawk,' Ronin says.

'And the body of a tiger, bounty hunter,' the captain says, unsheathing her other pistol and cocking the hammer.

'Oh, I remember,' Ronin says.

We descend a flight of stairs and reach a long, windowless corridor. Doorways open up to both the left and right. I look at the schematic that Kyle downloaded onto my phone. 'We go to the end and take a left,' I say. We're about to continue along the corridor when a member of the crew scrambles out of one of the doorways, almost running into Ronin. Without missing a beat the bounty hunter smashes the butt of Warchild into his sternum.

The guy drops groaning and Ronin brings the shotgun down on the back of his head twice in quick succession.

'I would have gone for the temple rather than the sternum,' Sue says matter-of-factly.

'Always were a backseat fighter,' Ronin growls.

Rafe walks alongside as if we're in the mall, his shaggy red hair bopping up and down to some inaudible melody. He's unarmed except for a single Molotov, which he carries in his hand like a soft drink.

My forehead begins to itch as we progress down the long corridor. The grey metallic walls have begun to shimmer and they feel like they're closing in on me. I rub my forehead with the back of my hand. Just keep it together, Zevcenko. No more fucking visions, ᴏᴋ?

Ronin turns a corner and gunfire ricochets down the corridor. He reappears and slams himself flat against the wall. 'Three of them,' Ronin says, ducking back. 'Heavily armed.' Another burst of gunfire sprays across the passage.

Severance holsters her guns, leans against the wall and lights a cigar. 'They're wasting ammo,' she says. 'Wait for the reload.' Another burst of gunfire. Sue takes a drag and blows a smoke ring. Another burst. Sue looks at her nails. As the next burst finishes ripping down the corridor she draws her guns, strides into the corridor and empties both of them. She steps back, takes the cigar out of her mouth and blows smoke in Ronin's face.

Ronin rolls his eyes at me as we round the corner. The three dead sentries look up at us with blank eyes. They were guarding a line of cells with heavy metal doors. Severance digs through one of the corpse's pockets and comes up with a ring of keys dangling from her finger.

She opens a door and steps inside with both her guns levelled. Rafe follows her and I follow him. Over his shoulder I see that the prisoner is not Pat. It's Esmé, sitting on the bed cross-legged. She's still wearing that stupid polo neck, but is also holding two chunky handguns. I'd prepared myself to face all manner of monstrosities. Four-headed snake beast? Yawn. Death-dealing flying scorpion? So last season. But seeing my former sweetheart sitting there and calmly pointing two guns at me stops me dead. You know those stupid and annoying people who use 'literally' incorrectly? I'm not one of those people. I literally don't know what to say.

'Baxter,' she says with a smile. 'So nice to see you.' It's the look in her eyes that causes me to take evasive action. I grab Rafe's collar and pull him backwards, slamming both of us back against the wall as she brings the guns up to fire. Sue reacts like a cat, dropping down, launching herself forward and knocking Esmé's arms to the side just as she pulls the triggers.

The gunshots are incredibly loud in such a confined space. They ring in my ears as Sue whips her own pistols up and pushes them into Esmé's throat.

'Don't kill her!' I scream. Sue gives me a quick look and then, instead of pulling the trigger, slams the handle of her pistol into Esmé's nose. She drops onto the bed unconscious.

'Explain,' Sue says to me, taking another drag of her cigar.

'That's my girlfriend,' I say.

'It both is and it isn't, sugar,' Katinka says, shouldering her Uzi. 'Look.'

I turn to see Esmé pulling herself up into a seated position. The neck of her polo neck has slipped down and I can see the thick, distended body of an Anansi jutting from just above her shoulders.

'She's …' I say.

'A zombie,' Tone says. 'We're going to have to force that little parasite to let go of her. If we try and cut it off, it'll kill her.'

Esmé gives us a cruel smile. 'Over her dead body,' she says. She leaps off the bed and rakes her fingers across Sue's face. Sue gives a shout of pain and falls back. Esmé makes a grab for one of her guns, but Tone sends a shrill blast of sound that knocks her against the wall. He keeps the sound going through some kind of circular breathing.

Ronin steps forward and pushes his elbow against her throat and Tone stops the sound with a gasp.

Ronin spins Esmé around and shoves her face against the wall. She's writhing and kicking.

'Baxter,' she whimpers. 'Help me!'

Sue, Rafe and Katinka help Ronin to hold her as he pulls his mojo bag from beneath his coat, empties the contents onto the bed and begins to sift through the herbs, bones and trinkets.

'Anansi are like weeds,' he says. 'We need to pull it out at the roots.' He finds a small bottle of powder and opens it, holding it under Esmé's nose.

'Like the smell of that, eh?' Ronin says.

'Don't,' Esmé says. 'Please don't.'

'Oh, OK,' Ronin says. 'Since you asked so nicely.' He upends the bottle over the spider's body and then strikes a flame with his lighter and puts it to the powder. It ignites with an iridescent green flame and Esmé begins to writhe and scream.

The green flame engulfs the Anansi's body, causing a black, sulphuric smoke to pour from it. Ronin puts an arm across his mouth and everybody quickly follows suit. Ronin pulls the knife from his boot with his other hand and jams it between Esmé's neck and the Anansi and begins to work it back and forth. Esmé stops screaming and a thin wail comes from the thing itself. Ronin pushes the knife upward and the arachnid releases its hold on Esmé's neck and jumps to the floor, trailing long, spiky tendrils behind it.

Katinka reacts the quickest, jumping forward and jamming her red stiletto heel through the thing's body like a dagger. It lets out a piercing squeal and then stops moving. Katinka removes her heel and wrinkles her nose in disgust. 'And you said assaulting a ship in high heels was impractical,' she says to Tone.

I run over to Esmé. She looks up at me with wild eyes. There are several large purple puncture wounds in her neck and her nose is still bleeding from where Sue hit her. I wrap my arms around her. She smells sulphuric, but her body fits into mine perfectly. 'It's OK,' I whisper into her ear. 'You're OK.'

'What happened?' she mumbles, clutching me. 'The last thing I remember was being in my room.'

'Lots happened,' I say. 'You're safe now.'

'OK, lovebirds, we have to get out of here,' Ronin says, peering out into the corridor. 'I'm pretty sure Mirth isn't just going to let us waltz through his ship.'

'Who's Mirth?' Esmé says and looks at me.

'I'll tell you later,' I whisper. 'Just don't let go of me.'

We walk down the corridor and try the next cell. Pat is in there, dirty and bruised, but her blue eyes are shining.

'Jackson,' she says with a smile as Ronin helps her to her feet, 'you came to get me.'

'Someone had to,' he says, giving her a hug. 'You ready to go?'

'Mirth,' she says bitterly.

'Always fun, isn't he?' Ronin says. 'Let's go kill him.'

We turn back into the corridor and gunfire thuds into the walls around us. We run further down the corridor. I consult the schematic. 'This way,' I shout, pointing to a door to our left.

The ship's kitchen is deserted. Either the kitchen staff fled when they heard gunfire or proper nutrition wasn't high on Mirth's priorities. We're edging our way through the stainless-steel galley when the door on the other side swings open.

Two canine-like Gogs snuffle through the doors. They have grey scaly reptilian skin and thick matted manes of black hair. Corded muscles ripple in their necks as they fix their pink eyes on us and bare twin rows of vicious teeth. Nice lizard doggies.

Sue and Ronin open fire at the same time, sending a barrage of bullets thumping into them. One jumps snarling onto the stainless-steel countertop, sending pots skittering across the floor.

Rafe regards the dog with a look of mild amusement on his face. I grab his arm and hold onto it, just in case he tries to walk across and pet it. The dog stalks across the countertop toward us.

I grab Rafe and Esmé and pull them out of the door as Katinka swoops up to the ceiling. I've just found the real Esmé and there's no way I'm going to let her get eaten by a canine lizard.

Rafe looks at me with a smile. 'Don't do anything stupid,' I say. 'Seriously, Rafe, just stay here. We'll wait until they deal with those things. Just this once be smart.' He gives me a serious look and nods. 'Good,' I say. With amazing agility he wrenches his arm from my grasp and trots off down the corridor. 'Rafe!' I shout. Swearing, I put my arm protectively around Esmé and follow him.

He is walking through the corridors calmly but quickly, looking around as if he is a tourist late to meet his tour bus. We round a corner and watch as Rafe ambles toward a wooden door. He stops at it, turns to look at me with the knowing-eye, and then opens it and steps inside.

'I don't know if we should go in there,' Esmé says, holding my arm.

'We shouldn't,' I say with a sigh. 'But we have to.'

Mirth is sitting drinking tea at a breakfast table. His grey hair is pulled back in a ponytail with a red satin scrunchie and he's wearing a T-shirt that says 'Information Wants To Be Free'. The cabin is large and stately with high book-filled shelves and an aquarium filled with colourful fish. One of the walls is made of thick glass and looks out onto the Maelstrom.

'Baxter!' he says. 'Right on time.' He motions to an empty chair at the table. 'Please, have a seat.'

'Baxter,' Esmé says. I touch her arm. Rafe stands next to her and grabs her hand. He smiles idiotically at me.

'Asshole,' I whisper.

I walk over to the table and sit down. Mirth pours me a cup of tea. The orangey scent of Earl Grey wafts up from the cup.

'And how are the delusions coming along?' he says warmly.

'I keep having these violent thoughts about cutting you up into little pieces,' I say.

'Classic projection,' he says. 'I think it has to do with your mother. Anyway, it's lovely to see you again. Family is so important, don't you think?'

I watch his face. He's unlike anybody I've ever had to manipulate, cajole, extort or persuade. I can see the mind behind his eyes whirring like a thousand microprocessors crunching numbers, facts, probabilities and contingencies. I feel like Kasparov facing Deep Blue. He's already played me more than I could possibly imagine. My whole life has been a setup, carefully planned and executed so that I could become exactly what he wanted.

He hands me the tea. I take a sip. 'I'd like to ask some questions,' I say.

He nods. 'I think that's fair. What would you like to know? I'd love to impart some great-great-grandfatherly wisdom.'

'Esmé's kidnapping,' I say. 'Why did you do that? Why not just approach me and offer me money or power?'

He sighs and shrugs. 'It was my only choice. The Octopus exoskeleton has the potential for time travel and, unlike the Mantis, requires a very simple method to operate it. Blood, you see, is the key.'

'The Mountain Killer,' I say.

He puts his hand to his heart. 'Guilty as charged. Blood allowed me to use the power of the Octopus to set up a situation where someone capable of piloting the Mantis exoskeleton would eventually be produced. I needed to know for sure that your gift was awakened. When you began to show signs of attachment to the girl I decided to use that as a test. One you passed with flying colours, I might add.'

'So what now?' I say.

'You work for me,' he says. 'Think of it as an internship. You operate the Mantis and I'll help you to develop your gift. I know you're interested in power. With my help you can build the biggest corporation the world has ever seen.'

I want to say that I don't think about the power. I want to say that my good side is developed to the point where I laugh at the offer. Where I tell Mirth that no amount of money or power could tempt me.

'OK,' I say.

He looks at me curiously. 'I expected some sort of struggle. Some sort of declaration of nobility.'

'Listen,' I say, leaning forward on the table, 'you created me. You purposefully activated the side of me that gives a shit. You manipulated me into caring so that I would end up the way you wanted me.'

'Yes...'

'You've done what you've needed to do,' I say, 'and so have I. I don't need to keep this farce up any more.' I turn to look at Esmé. 'You were right,' I say. 'Even if it wasn't really you speaking. I'm not a good person. I deal porn and I manipulate people. People say that's abnormal, they say that teenagers shouldn't be like that. I say that's bullshit. Why feed us this crap about the world being a noble and heroic place when it's just not? The world is an ugly, brutal, uncaring place. And the only way you get ahead is to be even more ugly, brutal and uncaring than it.'

Mirth giggles. 'Quite right,' he says.

'I want to see these vehicles,' I say. 'I want to see what you've fucked my life up for.'

He leads me into a room that holds two sculptures made from burnished brass, copper and glass, every inch carved with strange glyphs and demonic doodles. One is an Octopus, large and sprawling, its tentacles thick golden chains, eyes made from amber holding ancient trapped insects. Its large body is like a heavy copper bell and there's a thick, viscous aura around it, the air seeming to twist and curl as if it wants to get away from this monstrosity.

'A vehicle and a prison,' Mirth says, stroking it with the back of his hand. 'A remarkable piece of magic. I was impressed by your little speech, but you'll understand if I take certain precautions.'

He climbs onto one of the tentacles and steps behind the face of the Octopus and into an indentation big enough to fit a person. He slides into place and through the amber I can see him positioning himself as if in a cockpit. 'Should you attempt to interfere with my plans, I'll kill your brother and girlfriend for the trouble.'

'Your manipulation of my life was masterful,' I say. 'I want to learn from you, not oppose you.'

'That would be more than I could have ever hoped for. Now please,' he says, gesturing to the other vehicle, 'you won't believe how long I've waited for this.'

The Mantis looms up above me like an insectile mech warrior. Its body is long and slender and its claws hang in the air like serrated blades. Close up I can feel a hum in my solar plexus, like you can feel the bass from a seriously pimped-out car stereo.

I climb onto its hind leg, step into its carved-out centre and slide into a person-shaped hollow in the middle. It's surprisingly comfortable and I can feel the warmth of the metal against my skin. Inside, the whole thing seems to hum. There are levers and pulleys inside, but I look for the controller. The mouse. The joystick. Nothing. I pull a lever. One of the legs of the Mantis moves. If the control system is at all logical, then the other lever must move the other leg. I pull it. The other leg moves.

'Comfortable?' Mirth calls. 'Then please activate it.'

'How?' I say.

'That's why you're here,' he says impatiently. 'To tap into the power of a trapped god.'

Sure thing. The power of the Mantis God coming right up. I could probably work out the control system given enough time, but tapping into a god trapped inside? There's probably not an FAQ or a Wiki for that. I try to slow down my breathing. I look across at Rafe. He smiles and looks back at me with the knowing-eye. It burns into me and I feel my forehead open like a sunflower opening to the sun. Everything splits into little fractals.

'Holy mother of God,' I whisper as the world shudders and tears in half. I'm on the floating disc again, but the Singer of Souls is nowhere to be seen. Instead Rafe sits cross-legged on the disc and looks up at me.

'Rafe?' I say. 'What's going on?'

'I knew that I was a Siener lonngggg before you did, you know?' he says with a smile. His voice here is rich, deep and melodious, nothing like the mumbles and grunts he usually communicates with. 'But you were always such an asshole. You never picked up the hints I was giving you.'

'I …' I say. 'You're talking. In full sentences.'

He shrugs. 'It's easy here. Not so easy when I'm stuck in my body. We're Sieners and that's part of why you've always hated me. You knew that something impossibly strong held us together and you didn't want to be linked to me in any way.'

'I never hated you,' I say.

Rafe laughs. 'Shut up, Baxter,' he says. 'For once I get to talk. I usually just watch you strutting around like an arrogant little rooster, creating your little schemes, playing your little games and generally thinking that you're the cleverest thing on the goddamn planet.' I try to talk but he holds up a hand. 'I said shut up. First of all I want to say screw you for burying Mr Bobble in the garden when I was eight. That was a major dick move.'

Mr Bobble was Rafe's favourite fluffy toy. He was a little rabbit with one eye and a bow tie. I buried him in the garden to punish Rafe for telling on me. It left him traumatised for months.

'Second,' he continues, 'stop calling me retard. I don't talk a lot, but I understand what you're saying.' He waves his hand and the disc disappears and suddenly we're floating above Table Mountain. 'My sight is a lot deeper than yours,' he says. 'I can create whole worlds inside my head, so excuse me if I don't spend a lot of time spouting mundane bullshit like you do.' He clicks his fingers and we're back on the disc.

'I've been really bad to you, haven't I?' I say.

'You're not the only one. You know that time Karyn Dorman suddenly dumped you?'

'Yeah …' I say.

'I sent her an email from you saying you thought her mom was hot.'

'Asshole!' I say.

'I learnt from the best. I know you're not going to do what this lunatic wants you to do,' Rafe says. 'So what's your plan?'

'Unleash a trapped god, I guess,' I say.

'I can help you,' Rafe says and holds out his hands. I take them and the disc begins to spin. Slowly at first and then faster, like we're on a cosmic merry-go-round. I feel the force from the spinning drilling into me.

Then I see them. Radiant sigils invisible to the naked eye are etched onto the frame of the Mantis. They form a kind of control panel on the inner metal. I reach out my mind and touch one of them. It hums with a deep, subsonic bass. My brain rattles against my skull with the resonance. I touch another one. It's a higher frequency, but it harmonises perfectly with the bass. It's an invisible, space–time Casio keyboard. So I do what everybody without any musical talent does when they sit down in front of a keyboard. I play 'Chopsticks'.

Reaching out my mind, I search for the subsonic tones that will make up the simple melody. They rumble and hum internally. The Mantis begins to shift. It moves like it's doing t'ai chi, coiling and rolling through the ether, space and time rushing off its body like water.

'Perfect,' Mirth says from within the Octopus exoskeleton. I reach out my mind wildly to the sigils, like mashing your fingers around on a game controller to try and make your character shoot a fireball. The Mantis lurches like a drunken roller skater, but I manage to keep it under control. So far it's not much of a superweapon.

'Stop,' Mirth says. He activates the Octopus and it stands up on its tentacles. With my mind I make the Mantis move toward the Octopus and send a fiery charge of energy at it. Mantis weapons capabilities activated. But the Octopus deflects the blast and rears up, slamming me against the wall with its tentacles. 'I warned you,' Mirth says. I look at the sigils on the Mantis. Controlling fire is great, but where are the missiles? Where's the photon cannon? A tentacle snakes out and I'm thrown against the wall again. I'm trying to get up when I'm lifted into the air. The Octopus wraps the Mantis in its tentacles, snaking them through the cockpit. One wraps around my mouth and nose and stops me from breathing.

'A small part of me hoped that we would actually work together,' Mirth says. After a few seconds my lungs begin to explode. I suddenly feel calm. I look at the luminescent sigils and I understand. I understand how the Mantis works. I focus my mind and then let it go. The Mantis and I blink out of existence and take the Octopus with us.

APOCALYPSE NOW NOW

We're in the Cape Town CBD. I stand up between the familiar buildings framed against Table Mountain. I see the three tampon-shaped towers looming above Vredehoek. Next to me the yellow-and-grey trains clatter in and out of the station. Things are almost the same. Almost. The one small difference, which I don't notice at first but which very quickly becomes glaringly obvious, is the logo. The red Octogram logo appears on everything. Billboards on the sides of buildings sport the logo. Octogram pennants outside shops flutter in the wind.

'You could have chosen anywhere in space and time and you chose a dimension where my plans have already succeeded,' Mirth says. The Octopus slides toward me, its metallic tentacles rattling against the tarmac. 'It says something about your deep-seated desires.'

Alternate-reality Capetonians are crowding around us and peering at the exoskeletons quizzically. They probably think it's some kind of art installation. A bus with a large advertisement plastered on the side drives past me. 'I don't think this is quite the reality you're thinking of,' I say. I use the Mantis limb to point to the ad on the bus. Mirth turns to see my stern bespectacled face staring back at him. 'Don't be a non-playing character,' it says. 'Help your Supreme Leader to help you.'

Mirth turns back to me. 'You?!'

'I'm sure I gave you good severance pay and a gold watch for your service,' I say.

'Perhaps you are more dangerous than I initially assumed,' Mirth replies.

I smile. 'A lot of people make that mistake.'

The Octopus shudders with energy and begins to grow. Its tentacles spill forward onto the tarmac and crush a group of curious onlookers. Suddenly aware that this might not be the work of some avant-garde art collective, the rest of the alternate-reality folk begin screaming and running.

The Octopus continues to grow, its metallic body glowing hot with energy. 'You can still bow before me,' Mirth says, his voice amplified and echoing down the city streets. 'Or run.'

I do neither. I have control of the exoskeleton. All the power I've ever wanted is right here in these sigils. I see how easily it must have been to become Supreme Leader. With this kind of power this whole world, maybe all worlds, could be my Sprawl. I reach out my mind and touch the necessary sigils. The Mantis begins to lurch, shift and gain in size. I grow until I stand facing the Octopus. Gargantuan Time-travelling Octopus versus Giant Inter-dimensional Mantis. Fight!

Mirth lunges forward but I sidestep and drive a giant Mantis leg through one of his tentacles, pinning it to the tarmac below. He lashes out again, wrapping another tentacle around a train and swinging it through the air like a grey-and-yellow whip. The driver's carriage hits the Mantis in its oblong head and sends me sprawling backwards into a building. Glass from a hundred windows shatters and I find myself staring into an open-plan office where people look up from their cubicles in disbelief.

I resist the urge to apologise and force the Mantis to lurch around as Mirth brings the Octopus rearing up to hit me with the bulk of the huge metal body. I'm flung sideways and land heavily on a delivery truck, crushing it. I try not to think of the person who might have been inside it.

I bring the Mantis back to its feet and quickly instigate evasive manoeuvres as the Octopus begins launching cars at me with its many limbs. I dodge a luxury sedan and crash through the streets, hiding behind a large investment-bank building. I'm breathing heavily and the hum of the Mantis shudders through my body. Despite the obvious power of the Mantis, I'm clearly no match for Mirth in a street fight.

So I do what I'm best at; I evade. I quickly cross between buildings and pass behind the Octopus, dodging as tentacles shoot out toward me. I try not to think about the death toll as my giant Mantis legs crush vehicles beneath me as I run.

As I crunch my way over cars and trucks, I realise the fatal flaw in my plan. I'm controlling the Mantis with my mind and my mind is getting tired. My temples begin to throb with the strain of it. I begin to slow down and I have to force myself to concentrate to keep it going.

Mirth is gaining behind me. With my mind I uproot several minibus taxis and send them sailing toward him. He bats them out of the way with a contemptuous flick of a tentacle. The effort of launching cars has tired me even further, but I continue to keep the Mantis stumbling forward.

Mirth comes within reaching distance and grabs one of the Mantis's legs and with a jerk sends me sailing into the air. I spin through the evening sky and crash through the faux-Renaissance vaulted roof of a nearby mall. I wince as I see two chubby shoppers with ice creams crushed beneath me.

I push my exhausted mind to pick the Mantis up and erupt out of the ruins of the mall as Mirth looms above me. I manage to push past his tentacles and drive a metallic leg into the cockpit where he sits. He twists and the leg misses, but I manage to pin two of his tentacles down and make the Mantis rear up, ready to drive its legs through Mirth's brain.

That's when I'm hit by the missiles. The natives of this alternate Cape Town have obviously tired of the two behemoths wrecking their city and have retaliated by sending several attack helicopters at us. I'm thrown backwards as the missiles slam into the Mantis.

The helicopters surround us and machine-gun fire chatters, sending bullets thumping too close to where I sit. Missiles thud into Mirth and he responds by grabbing two choppers and piledriving them into the earth. He whips a tentacle around his head, destroying another two helicopters in midair. The remaining two execute a wide evasive arc and retreat toward the mountain.

The Octopus, its head scorched by missile blasts, grabs the Mantis by the head and slams me into the earth. The force of the shock is titanic and I lose focus completely. Mirth picks me up like a pro wrestler and throws the metallic body of the Mantis across several Northern Suburbs neighbourhoods.

Black spots swarm across my vision like excited amoebae. My neck feels numb and I struggle to move it. It isn't broken, but I wonder how close it came. I battle to concentrate my mind but know if I don't I'm going to be dead in seconds. I push the Mantis to its feet and get caught in several layers of razor wire. I look around. I'm being thrown through the outer wall of the nuclear power station at Koeberg.

As I turn around I'm again hit by a tentacle, which sends me slamming into the power station. The Octopus blocks out the setting sun in front of me. I lie there in the Mantis exoskeleton and close my eyes. I've done all I can. I've been swallowed by

Cape Town's supernatural underworld, digested and excreted. I've given it my best and it just wasn't enough. I stop struggling. I let my mind drop from the controls of the Mantis. It's been great, but after sixteen years I've come to the point where it's time to say sayonara to this mortal coil. I let go completely. And then I see.

I see what I can do. I reach out my mind to the reactor next to me and with a single thought I ignite it. At the same time I focus every inch of concentration left available to me to create a bubble of force around me. The reactor ignites and an immense blast wave spreads around me. I'm thrown about in a tsunami of fire – swept along on a radioactive wave that rips through the city.

Trees, cars, houses and people cease to exist around me. The wave flings me across the city and sends me sprawling against the mountain. Struggling to keep the bubble of force around me, I bring the Mantis to its feet and climb to the top. I stand on the flat surface of Table Mountain and look down.

The city is aflame. Buildings collapse into themselves. The water of the bay is alight, which sends massive plumes of steam into the air. It's the South African Armageddon, Apocalypse Now Now. And I caused it.

Mirth is lurching his way toward me. The metal of the Octopus is bent and twisted and most of his tentacles have been scorched into stumps. He comes closer and my mind is too tired to stop him. He reaches out his one remaining tentacle and pulls me to him. We stand locked in a deadly embrace on top of Table Mountain. I look at the pathetic, burnt Octopus and marshal the last of my strength. I draw the Mantis's forelegs back and then arc them forward like pincers. They slice through the cockpit and pin Mirth to the seat, his arms splayed like some exotic moth being mounted by an entomologist.

Frothy pink blood erupts from his mouth with a pathetic little gurgle.

I make the Mantis bend down in front of him. 'Game over,' I say.

'You almost believed me,' he wheezes through a mouthful of blood. 'Give me that at least.'

'If you're expecting some kind of grudging respect for the complex beauty of your plan, then you can forget it, you pathetic, ponytailed freak,' I say.

That seems to hurt him more than the spike of ancient metal I've jackhammered through his ribcage. His face sags and he struggles for breath.

'I created you,' he says. 'I changed the course of history to create you. Think of that. I could have done anything and I created you.'

'How touching,' I say, 'a Luke-I-am-your-great-great-grand-father moment.'

'We are family,' he says, his breath coming in shorter and shorter gasps. 'You can't change that.'

'No,' I say. 'But I can watch you die with a smile on my face.'

'That's my boy,' he chokes out and then begins to convulse.

I watch until the last spasmodic jerk racks his body and he lies still.

Fire laps at the edges of my protective bubble as I stand looking over this decimated version of Cape Town. 'I'm sorry,' I say and then feel stupid. Somehow I don't think these people need my platitudes after I have brought nuclear Armageddon upon them. I focus my mind again and try to remember what I had done to jump dimensions. Closing my eyes, I create an image of the Dark Lady in my mind. I need to make sure I get my dimension, not just one similar to it, so I focus on the one thing I care enough about in my version of reality. I focus on my version of Esmé.

The jump back is easier than I thought it would be. Like stepping through a beaded curtain. I see Rafe and Esmé on the deck of the warship. Esmé turns to me and I smile. It's her. It's my

Esmé. She runs toward me, but I shake my head and she stops. There's something I have to do first.

CrowBax: You've got to admit it, this Mantis is a seriously pimping ride.

SienerBax: You know we can't keep it, right?

CrowBax: Maybe we could keep it in the garage and take it out on weekends, like a vintage Porsche?

SienerBax: I hope that's a joke.

CrowBax: Even I can see that idea, however awesome, wouldn't work.

SienerBax: Do you know what this means? We're actually agreeing on things.

CrowBax: If you start crying I'm going to give us a brain haemorrhage.

Think of smoking dark-chocolate-flavoured heroin cigarettes while inhaling pure sunshine through your pores and having sex with the entire world screaming your name in adoration and worship. Think of having that for eternity. That's what having complete control of the Mantis is like. And then think of walking away from that. Impossible! Unthinkable! But that's what I do. It's not because I'm a good person. It's precisely because I'm *not* a good person that I do it. If I keep the Mantis I won't use it for good. Oh sure, maybe at first I'll try to do good things. I'll try for universal peace and all that, but pretty quickly my Crow side will kick in and I'll start being power hungry and evil. A universe with Baxter Zevcenko as the Supreme Leader? Nobody wants that, least of all me.

I dig my mind into the exoskeleton and unravel it. Particles begin to unwind as I reverse the magic African metallurgists created thousands of years ago. I see windows to other worlds close and it saddens me. It would have been cool to see some of those versions of reality without bringing a nuclear winter down onto them. I step out of the Mantis and watch as it crumbles into dust.

'Baxter,' Esmé says. She pulls me to her and kisses me on the lips. It's not the honey-sunshine-heroin power of the Mantis. But it's pretty close.

LET IT BURN

Kyle and I are sitting on the roof of one of Westridge's prefab classrooms when Anwar is stabbed. We watch him walk haughtily across the Sprawl without any of his enforcers. That's Anwar's way. He wants to show everyone that he's not afraid of anything. Which doesn't stop a group of the Form from surrounding him and sticking a knife into his belly.

He collapses, swearing at his assailants, and then rolls into a ball on the tar.

'We need to get this on video,' Kyle says, searching his pockets for his phone as Anwar rolls onto his back clutching at his stomach. It's two hours after school has ended and there is nobody else around except us.

'We could sell it,' I say.

'Denton will pay a lot for this,' Kyle agrees, finding his phone and aiming it at Anwar. 'But we might make more from ads if we put it on YouTube.'

'You know we have to help him?'

Kyle turns to look at me. 'I think you've lost the entrepreneurial spirit, Bax,' he says and flicks his camera closed with a sigh.

'I know,' I say.

We climb down onto the tarmac and walk over to where Anwar is lying in a pool of blood on the tar.

'Come to gloat, Zevcenko?' he croaks.

'Actually, we thought we might help,' I say.

Anwar tries to laugh and then grimaces from the pain. 'If you think I'm going to give you the porn back, you're an idiot,' he says.

'We don't want it,' I say.

'We don't?' Kyle asks.

I shake my head. 'The Spider is done with the porn business.'

Kyle takes out his phone again and points it at Anwar. 'Snuff films, Bax, please tell me we're moving on to snuff films.'

I push Kyle's phone down. 'Nope.'

Anwar manages a contemptuous smile. 'Your little girlfriend has made you soft, Zevcenko.' I stick out my foot and jab my hard school shoe into the knife wound. He breathes in sharply and closes his eyes.

'Maybe,' I say. 'But don't fucking push me.'

We call an ambulance and put pressure on the wound with a school jersey while we wait for it to arrive. Anwar stoically refuses to look at us. I think of leaving him to die more than once.

When the ambulance finally arrives the paramedics usher us away and then strap Anwar down and lift him into the back. 'I suppose you want me to thank you,' he says from behind the oxygen mask.

'Your happy smiling face is all the thanks I need,' I say. He manages to lift a hand and give me the middle finger as the medics close the ambulance doors.

'You know what this means?' I say as the ambulance pulls away.

'That we're in serious shit,' Kyle says. 'This is what we've been working to stop. They're going to question everyone. *Everyone.* There's no way people are not going to squeal. Shit, the cops are going to get involved. Bax, what the hell are we going to do?'

'We're not going to do anything,' I say.

'What?!' Kyle looks like I've just punched him in the stomach.

'I can't do this any more,' I say.

'Bax,' he says, 'think logically. I know it's been a lot to deal with but we can't just –'

'No,' I say. '*We're* not going to do anything. I'm going to do it. I'll confess to it. All of it.'

'You're not making any sense,' Kyle says, his eyes wide and teary. 'You want to be some kind of martyr? What will that achieve?'

'I don't know,' I say, looking at him. 'Maybe it'll make me feel better about the shit I've done. Maybe it'll stop you guys from having totally fucked-up lives. Maybe I'll feel like the kind of guy that Esmé deserves and not some fucking science-fictional, time-travel-spawned, half- Crow bastard child. Shit, maybe it'll make me feel that Tomas's death wasn't totally and utterly meaningless.'

'Yeah and maybe it'll do absolutely none of those things,' Kyle says sullenly.

'You're right,' I say. 'But where I'm at at the moment, I have to give it a try. You've always been there for me and I'm asking one last thing from you. Let it burn.'

'You remember that time when we were little kids and you convinced me to eat a cockroach?' he says.

'Yeah,' I say with a laugh.

'This is worse than that. But, Bax, I trust you. I always have. And if this is what you need to do then I'm with you all the way. No matter what a dumbshit, Darwin-award-winning, Kardashian-level, Ben Affleck-in-*Gigli*, written-in-Comic-Sans-font idea this is.'

I smile. 'Thanks, man, that means a lot.'

* * *

The rest of the week is chaos. Lockers are searched. DVDs, hard drives and cellphones filled with porn are found. Kids squeal like little pigs and the Spider is immediately implicated. All of us are called into the headmaster's office, but I request a private emergency meeting with the Bearded One.

He ushers me into his office, his face red and grave. 'This err umm is very serious, Baxter,' he says. I nod. I know what kind of trouble I'm in. But it's time for one last manipulation.

'I umm ahhh never expected this from you,' he says. 'Do you have anything to say for yourself?'

'Yes,' I say. 'First of all, I'm not apologising. I merely provided a product for which there was a demand.'

'I've seen some of your product,' the Bearded One says. 'It is disgusting.'

I shrug. 'One man's art is another man's moral panic.'

The Bearded One slams his hand down on the table. I've never seen him this angry. Which is exactly where I want him. 'You are going to tell me everything about you and your accomplices' little business,' he says. He raises a finger to point at me. 'I'm warning you, Zevcenko.'

I smile. Compared to Mirth and the giant Crows, bearded headmasters are pretty low on the list of things to be afraid of. 'No,' I say, 'I'm not. It's me and only me. Everybody else that has participated is merely a pawn in my game.'

'Everybody involved needs to face the consequences,' he says.

I lean back in the chair. 'Think about it,' I say. 'Either the press will report that Westridge is running rampant with knifemen and porn syndicates. Or that one rogue pupil is responsible for it all.'

'You'll take responsibility for everything? Even the stabbing?' he says suspiciously.

I shrug. 'I have a motive. Anwar was a threat to my business.'

He rubs his beard thoughtfully. 'You realise that your

punishment will be far more severe if you insist on maintaining that you're the only one responsible.' I nod. 'Normally I wouldn't do something like this,' he says. 'But we have to think of the future of Westridge.'

Weapons chemists, headmasters; they're all the same. Once you isolate their core motivations, you're halfway there.

I'm expelled with criminal charges pending. I burst out laughing when my lawyer suggests that I might be able to plead temporary insanity. I make a call to Tone and he says he may be able to get me off the attempted-murder charge if I agree to enrolling in a school sponsored by MK6. I tell him I'll think about it.

My parents are predictably appalled. I'm subjected to several emotionally draining episodes where they beg me to tell them what they did wrong when I was a child. I'm unable to give them satisfactory answers. They're horrified by my missing finger and begin to believe I've become involved in some kind of self-mutilation cult. They make an appointment for me with a psychiatrist. I promise myself that this time I'll lie about everything.

In the days that follow, I seriously begin to regret my noble gesture. In my rush to prove to myself that I'm not inherently evil I may have gotten carried away. Being tried for attempted murder and distributing pornography to minors is no way to be repaid for saving the world. But like I said, the world is unfair. Those kids with dial-up Internet minds are going to become lawyers, politicians and doctors, and mediocrity will continue to rule the day. Perhaps being Supreme Leader wouldn't have been so bad after all. Is it too late to change my mind?

But at least I have Esmé. That Saturday night, five days after Anwar was stabbed, she climbs up my drainpipe and slips into my room.

'Thought it was the least I could do after you came to rescue me,' she says as she flops down onto my bed and lights a cigarette.

We lie back and stare up at the ceiling together.

'I thought you'd dumped me,' I say after a short silence.

'If I dump you, I'll tell you about it,' she says. 'And include a spreadsheet list of all the things you've done wrong.'

I laugh.

'Can't believe you thought I'd date a guy with a mullet,' she says.

'Yeah, I don't know what I was thinking,' I say.

'It's weird to think that I was a zombie,' she says. 'I mean, I didn't really feel anything. No emotions, no nothing.'

'I know the feeling,' I say with a laugh.

'You're not a zombie, Bax,' she says. 'You never were.'

'I meant what I said back on the ship,' I say. 'The world is totally screwed. I may have saved it, but nobody is going to thank me or reward me for that. I thought I'd feel some sense of satisfaction that I'd done the right thing. But I don't really. Being a hero is pretty damn stupid.'

'You came to get me,' she says, looking into my eyes. 'Bax, that means a lot.' She pushes me down on the bed and straddles me. 'You're a knight in shining armour,' she whispers into my ear.

'Not even close,' I murmur as she slides down my body.

Grandpa Zev's funeral is at an old cemetery in Woodstock filled with rows of ancient, crumbling gravestones. Esmé comes with me. She wears a black dress and black sneakers and looks beautiful.

Grandpa Zev wasn't religious so we have a humanist celebrant who seems somewhat at a loss as to what to say. Apparently without all the prayers and psalms there's not a whole lot you can say about a death except that it happens and that it sucks.

The family takes turns to say a few awkward words about how

great he was. My dad talks about going to rugby games with him when he was young. My mom reads something really New Agey about entering the light after a period of darkness. Uncle Rog prays for his father's soul, which is nice in a twisted sort of way. I feel like I have to say something and I know exactly what I want to say.

'My grandfather believed that there were giant crows out to get him,' I start. There's a sharp intake of breath from the family. Uncle Rog glowers at me. 'But so what? There are people who believe much crazier things than he did.' I give Uncle Rog a look.

'Grandpa Zev taught me that sometimes things don't work out the way you want them to and that instead of whining you've just got to suck it up and carry on. He taught me that if you love something, you have to fight for it.' I reach into my jacket pocket and pull out a hipflask. 'To Grandpa Zev and to the death of giant Crows,' I say and pour some gin onto his grave. 'Bye, Grandpa,' I whisper.

Esmé and I are walking back to the car when a blonde, middle-aged woman with a pug face intercepts us. She introduces herself as the head of Shady Pines, Grandpa Zev's retirememt home.

'I'm very sorry about your grandfather,' she says in a drawling, nasal voice.

'Thanks,' I say.

'Of all the things that were said, I think he would have appreciated yours the most. He really was a very stubborn man,' she says, twirling her finger in the string of pearls around her neck. 'Very stubborn. Which is why I need to give you this.' She hands me an old, leather-bound book and the photo of Klara, my great-grandmother. 'It is our policy to give all personal effects to the deceased's children. But he insisted that I give these to you myself. He said he'd come back to haunt me if I didn't.' She lets out a high-pitched, tinkling laugh. 'And I kinda believe the old bastard would be stubborn enough to do it.'

'Thank you,' I say.

Esmé and I walk up the small hill behind the cemetery and sit beneath an old, gnarled oak tree.

'Read it,' she says softly to me. I open the leather-bound book to the first page. It is written in Afrikaans, but someone has lovingly translated each page into English with a soft pencil.

The Diary of Ester van Rensburg

Klara is born! A more beautiful and precious daughter I cannot imagine. It is hard to believe that such innocence could come from such a monster, but perhaps that is the way of life. I have resolved never to tell her about her father. I shall say that he was a sailor and that he drowned at sea. It is better that way.

Living with Luamita's family has been wonderful. Her father is named Tomas, as are all the males in their family, and he is a strong and gentle man. He tells the most beautiful stories about the history of the Obambo. Their scriptures say that they are destined to almost die out, but that their race will once again bloom like shining flowers on the face of the Earth. I hope it is so. They are too beautiful to disappear.

Sadly they cannot hide me forever. Luamita has helped me to find passage on a ship bound for Poland. I am terrified of leaving. This land is the only one I have ever known and I feel I will be leaving my father and all my ancestors behind. But for the sake of Klara, I must. I cannot risk having that evil man find us.

I think a lot about what has happened. Has it all been real? I think for the sake of my own sanity I must put it from my mind. I must live for Klara now. Oh, Klara. What will you become? I hope your life takes a different path to mine. I hope that you live a long and happy life. I hope that you will make my father proud.

I close the book and rub the dust from the picture of my

grandfather's mother. Klara. In the picture she is about my age, young and as beautiful as her mother. From what I know of her she did exactly what her mother wanted of her. She lived a long and happy life. I'm glad for that.

Rafe comes traipsing up the hill with a stupid grin on his face. 'I'll give you two some time together,' Esmé says and walks down through the cemetery, her fingers splayed and brushing over the tops of the gravestones.

Rafe sits down under the tree next to me.

'I'm sorry about Mr Bobble,' I say.

He looks at me and shrugs.

'Thanks for helping me,' I say.

'ok,' he mumbles. He scribbles something furiously on a piece of paper and hands it to me. 'I want your ps3,' it says.

'Screw you,' I say and punch him on his shoulder and then pull him into an awkward hug. I think it's the first time I've ever willingly hugged my brother and the experience is actually not that bad.

I phone Tone and tell him that I agree. I have a month's break and then I'm going to be attending Hexpoort, a reformatory school that is actually a front for an mk6 training academy. It means I'm not going to go to jail, but also that the rest of my schooling is going to be in the hands of sangomas. If I'm forced to play Quidditch, I swear, someone is going to get shot.

This arrangement mollifies my parents, but it's still weeks before I'm allowed to leave the house without supervision. My first excursion is to the beach. I trudge down the stairs to Clifton Second Beach, my flip-flops slapping the concrete in an irregular rhythm.

I push my sunglasses down onto my nose as I reach the soft

white sand and scan the area, finding a familiar figure standing at the water's edge. He's wearing his army boots and trench coat with silk cartoon boxers and no shirt underneath.

'All right, sparky?' he asks.

I nod. 'You?'

He opens his trench coat to show me the empty scabbard.

'You'll find another gun, Ronin.'

'It won't be the same,' he sniffs and lifts his hipflask to his lips. 'I'm seeing more of Sue though,' he says. 'We're trying to work things out.' I think of Ronin and Sue together and wonder how much of 'working things out' involves knife fighting and full-contact kickboxing.

'Maybe she'll give you Warchild back,' I say brightly.

'Yeah and maybe she'll give me her heart and lungs too,' he says with a snort.

He hands me the hipflask and I take a sip of the burning liquid.

'I was expelled from school,' I say.

He nods. 'I heard. But, hey, I don't have a high-school education.'

'Yeah, and look how you ended up,' I say.

'True,' he says with a grin.

'Tone got me into Hexpoort,' I say.

He whistles through his teeth. 'My old alma mater,' he says. 'You're going to be getting some pretty gnarly education, sparky.'

'Awesome,' I say with a sigh. I miss my life already. Zikhona and the Inhalant Kid are trying their best to fit back into normal school life. It's difficult. The Spider gave power and authority. Now they have to get people to like them. Kyle is managing OK, although I think he's a little depressed. He still thinks I made a big mistake and that we could have dodged the bullet. But he's coming to terms with it slowly. I miss them and I miss dealing porn. It wasn't so much the money as the sweaty, eager faces clamouring for the next hit. I know it wasn't exactly noble. But it was fun and I was good at it. Sometimes it seems like that should be enough.

'You'll find your way, sparky,' Ronin says. 'We all do eventually. And after you're done, you can work with me. We could be like Batman and Robin.'

'You want me to dress up in tights, old man?' I say.

'Dress however you want,' he says with a grin. 'Just remember that I'm the one in charge. I'm serious, think about it. Fighting supernatural crime and saving Cape Town from beasties, demons and freaks.'

'Sounds all right,' I say.

'All right?' Ronin asks, fixing me with his blowtorch eyes. 'It's fucking life affirming is what it is.'

And you know what? Maybe he's right. Hear that in your third eye.

ACKNOWLEDGEMENTS

Writing a book is hard. Here are the people that deserve thanks for making the journey that much easier. Thank you.

To Lauren Beukes for being my friend, all-round writing Miyagi and the only mentor that's ever mattered. Thank you for everything.

To my agent John Berlyne for all the help and sage advice. Your input has been invaluable.

To Sarah Lotz for all the enthusiasm, encouragement and feedback.

To Joey Hi-Fi for the truly magnificent covers.

To Nechama Brodie, Matt du Plessis and Sam Wilson for being my first readers.

To Jack Fogg at Century for really getting it and for being so supportive.

To my own high-school Spider for chasing the Mantis with me.

To Deni and Carlin for being my favourite inter-dimensional wizards.

To both my grandfathers for all the stories.

To my beautiful wife Georgia for being the best muse I could ever ask for and to my talented step-daughter Chloé for all the fun and laughter.

Finally to my parents, Pru and Ian, for always being there for me and for recognising that not all those who wander are lost. Thank you.

ABOUT THE AUTHOR

Charlie Human is a graduate of the University of Cape Town's creative writing programme and has contributed short pieces to print and online publications. He works in online media, is married and lives in Cape Town. Follow him on Twitter @charliehuman.

KILL BAXTER
CHARLIE HUMAN

The brilliant follow-up to the critically acclaimed *Apocalypse Now Now*.

The world has been massively unappreciative of sixteen-year-old Baxter Zevcenko. His bloodline may be a combination of ancient Boer mystic and giant shape-shifting crow, and he may have won an inter-dimensional battle and saved the world, but does anyone care? No.

Instead he's packed off to Hexpoort, a magical training school that's part reformatory, part military school, and just like Hogwarts (except with sex, drugs, and better internet access). The problem is that Baxter sucks at magic. He's also desperately attempting to control his new ability to dreamwalk, all the while being singled out by the school's resident bully, who just so happens to be the Chosen One.

But when the school comes under attack, Baxter needs to forget all that and step into action. The only way is joining forces with his favourite recovering alcoholic of a supernatural bounty hunter, Ronin, to try and save the world from the apocalypse. Again.

For more fantastic fiction, author events, exclusive
excerpts, competitions, limited editions and more

VISIT OUR WEBSITE
titanbooks.com

LIKE US ON FACEBOOK
facebook.com/titanbooks

FOLLOW US ON TWITTER
@TitanBooks

EMAIL US
readerfeedback@titanemail.com